A

What can I say that hasn't been said before?

How can I say it differently to make you want to interview me?

The answer is, I can't. I'm still the same brilliant writer that gave the world *Flipside* and *The Onion Girl* and now here comes yet another magnificent offering that should make you sit up and say, "Hey, this girl has got something!"

But it won't.

'Cause, you see, I'm normal. I don't have a drug problem, a social problem, a drink problem, and sadly I haven't made it in another medium before I took up writing (though I can act, I've just never had the inclination to do it professionally) so there really is nothing we can talk about.

Oh, don't get me wrong, I can talk. I'm a great story-teller and most of the stuff I do talk about is about me and my childhood and my adolescence. Like the way we (my sister and I) used to slide down the stairs in a cardboard box, or the way we invented millions of games.

Tortures, for instance, was a stunning example of my bossiness transferred into imagination.

I was the Sergeant Major. My brother and sisters were the slaves. No matter what I said, they had to do eg. learn verses by heart from Christmas cards, describe pictures I showed them, bow whenever I entered a room. At the end of a 'day' – a day was anything from ten to thirty minutes – they got tortured. This involved me sitting on their backs while they lay spread-eagled beneath me. I had to tickle them while they counted from one o'clock to twelve o'clock. If they'd failed in any of their duties during the day, extra o'clocks were added.

There's also the shameful story about an aborted attempt to enter the Eurovision song contest. (We were twelve.)

Or the endless plays I wrote and the endless secret societies I set up and the endless stream of no-hoper fellas I attracted.

Millions of stories.

And somehow, through all this I did write my first few books – the gang books which thankfully have never seen the light of day.

And now, twenty-odd years on, even though I'm a mother of two, teach speech and drama, direct the odd play (some might say, very odd play) and freelance for the *Herald*, I still love to write stories.

And though I'm blessed with being normal and thus not obvious interview material, I do believe that the world will always love good books and great storytellers.

Is this L♥ve?

Also by Tina Reilly

Flipside
The Onion Girl

Is this Love?

TINA REILLY

POOLBEG

Published 2002
Poolbeg Press Ltd.
123 Grange Hill, Baldoyle,
Dublin 13, Ireland
Email: poolbeg@poolbeg.com
www.poolbeg.com

13 5 7 9 10 8 6 4 2

A catalogue record for this book is available from the British Library.

ISBN 1 84223 094 8

Cover designed by DW Design, London
Typeset by Patricia Hope in Palatino 10/13.5
Printed by
Omnia Books Ltd, Glasgow

Acknowledgements

Thanks to everyone I've thanked before.

With the additions of:

All me Ma's friends who buy my books. All their families who read them especially Rory McCann who just reads them so's he won't have to look at Westham losing all the time!!

My Ma's work colleagues who also bought my books. Thanks a million!!

All the bookshops who had gorgeous displays of *The Onion Girl* in their windows. Special thanks to Ursala, Maynooth Bookshop, who's been brilliant to me.

Also, special mention to Rebecca, Joseph and Siobhan. And to as yet an unnamed new person coming into the world who will be included next time.

And all the cool people I've met who also publish books. Sarah Webb and Larry O'Loughlinn being just two.

A big thanks to Poolbeg for all the work they've done – Paula, Suzanne and the rest, and especially to Gaye my editor who's been such a laugh and a pleasure to know.

And as always, to my family, my Mam and Dad and most especially to Colm, Conor and Caoimhe – three of the best!

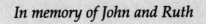

In memory of John and Ruth

Prologue

Dad's funeral

I guess it should have been a sad day. I feel awful saying this, but it wasn't; it gave me the biggest laugh of the year. Probably the biggest laugh of my life. Dad would literally have died again if he'd seen what happened the day of his funeral. As it was, he was probably whizzing around in his coffin, making himself dizzy.

Oh God. I felt so sorry for Mammy in the graveyard. Poor Daddy dead, Mammy and me crying and Maggie having a good look around to see who'd turned up.

That's the way Maggie is, she never cries over things. She's strong, just gets on with life. Anyhow, there we were, the three of us in the graveyard all holding onto each other, the rain coming down in buckets and everybody muttering their responses to the priest's prayers. And then . . .

And then, a huge gust of wind from out of nowhere

blows the feckin' priest right in on top of the coffin. Oh God, it was a bit of a shock. The thump of him as he landed on top of Dad. For a few seconds everybody was stunned. And the priest was mortified and he tried to clamber out of the hole but he's only a small guy so two lads, Dick, who's Pam's fella and Jason, who was my fella at the time, go to haul him out and . . .

Poor Dick fell in on top of the priest. He was furious. I could see it in his face. I knew he'd think it was just another bad day mixing with my family. I felt sick and sort of responsible. I wanted to try and get him out but others were doing it. And besides, poor Maggie was shaking so much I had to stay with her.

I never laughed so much in my life. The state of pompous auld Dick covered in muck. His suit'd never recover. The only one I felt sorry for was Mam. She was white.

Mam wouldn't talk about it after. I wouldn't blame her. It was the worst, most humiliating experience of all our lives.

Chapter One

My finger shook as I rang my mother's front-door bell.

This was the second nerve-wracking thing I'd done that day.

The first had been stealing away while John was at work. The minute he'd climbed into his battered Fiesta and driven out of sight, I'd grabbed my suitcase, shoved a pile of CDs into a carrier bag and lastly dialled a taxi. I left a note for John, telling him not to bother coming after me, that I was leaving and that was that. It was something along those lines. I can't really remember.

The taxi came, I jumped in and three hours later I was in Dublin airport getting off the plane from London.

And now, now I was home. Or what had once been home. It didn't feel like that any more. But it looked exactly the same as I remembered. White walls, white windows, white door. Dad had always loved white. Mam obviously still wanted the house to look the same as when he'd been alive.

3

The only difference was the door bell. Instead of buzzing, it now jangled.

The minute I had the bell rung, a horrible feeling that I'd just made a huge mistake washed over me. It wasn't as if I'd really thought the whole thing out. In fact, leaving John had just been instinct.

A good instinct, some inner voice said.

But maybe I shouldn't have come home?

Maybe I should have just left him.

But I'd have to come home at some stage.

But why now and why –

Little chirpy footsteps tap-tapped up the wooden floorway inside the house. The door opened a fraction and my mother peered out. At least I was pretty certain it was my mother. She'd really glammed herself up since the last time I'd been home. Short wavy hair, even if she had let it go grey, and some nice clothes. Well, nice for her age group if you know what I mean. A blouse and skirt sort of thing.

"Hi, Mam, guess who?" I forced the habitual smile onto my face. If I smiled, the chances of being asked in were higher.

"Maggie!" The door was flung open and my mother stood beaming up at me. "What a surprise! You didn't tell us you were coming."

"Aw, it was a spur-of-the-moment thing." Then, and I don't know what made me say it, I added, "I've left John."

She laughed uproariously and made ushering motions with her hands.

4

"I really have, " I insisted, stepping into the hall, "*and* I've taken his favourite CDs." I held up the plastic bag. Why I'd taken the CDs was beyond me. I think it was to hurt him or something. "And hopefully," I added, "I'll never have to set eyes on the prick again."

More loud laughter, this time threaded with a note of uncertainty. Then, "Don't use that word, Maggie. It's not a nice way to describe somebody."

She was exactly the same. In a way it was comforting but somehow depressing.

I knew, the minute I felt that way, that I was home.

Mammy rang. I was in the middle of breastfeeding Shauna while changing David's nappy when the phone rang. At first I was just going to leave it, I mean the person would surely ring back, but then I thought, sure, why not answer the thing. I mean, phone calls in our house are so rare that getting one is a novelty in itself. Of course, if the call was for me, I knew it would either be Mammy or Dick. Anyone different usually rings for Dick and now that he has his mobile no one ever rings the house any more.

So anyhow, Shauna hanging from my breast and David hanging from my leg, a new nappy half-on and half-off him, I shuffled out into the hall.

"Hello?" I said putting on my good voice. Dick says it's important to create a good first impression, even if it is only over the phone.

"Pamela, it's you, is it?"

It was Mammy. "Of course it is," I said. "Who else would be here? D'you think I've a housekeeper now?"

5

Mammy laughed. She likes a good joke. "You'll never guess what," *she said, and her voice was all excited.* "Go on, guess."

I'm not much good at guessing games, but by the tone of her voice I supposed that Mr Parker had asked her out or something. I don't know what's got into Mammy. Daddy dies and he's not dead six years when she starts seeing Mr Parker. They go on walks and she cooks him his tea and that kind of thing. It's a bit much.

"I can't guess," I said, trying not to sound pleased for her. It'd only encourage her. "You tell me."

"Maggie's only after arriving home!"

"Maggie? Our Maggie?"

"The very one. Seems she wants to work over here now. Tired of the restaurant trade in London, she says. Good news, isn't it?"

I suppose it was good news. But I didn't feel too happy about it. I mean, I know she's my sister and everything but I prefer her at a distance. "Great," I said. Then, "What about her fella, the guy she was living with?"

Mammy took a deep breath. "She wasn't living with him. Don't be so crude, Pamela." *Pause.* "OK, they were seeing each other and they lived in the same house, but that's all." *She stressed the 'all' before proclaiming,* "Maggie isn't that sort of girl."

I said nothing, just wondered what she meant by 'that sort of girl'.

"Anyhow, she says she's left him, but I think she was joking. A fine fellow like that, she'd want to be mad."

"So where is he?" I pressed. I was feeling annoyed. The

*mention of Maggie and her fine fellow always made me feel
like that.*

"Mam-mmmy!" David began to wail.

"Is that David I hear?" Mammy's voice began to coo. She
loves David.

"Say hello to Nanny, David," I held the phone out to him.

David shook his head and sucked his thumb.

"David?" I tried to be stern.

His face crinkled up and huge tears gathered in his eyes.
His lower lip began to tremble.

"It's OK, honey. Don't talk if you don't want to."

"You spoil him, Pamela. You'd want Dick to sort him out."

"Oh Mammy!"

"The child won't talk to anyone."

"He will when he's ready."

"Mmm," she sniffed. Then, "So that's all my news. Great,
isn't it?"

"Yeah."

David started to piddle on the carpet. Dick'd kill him if he
found out. "Listen, Mammy, I have to go."

"I'll see you all on Sunday then, will I?"

"Sure."

She rang off. I sat for ages staring at the phone. Even the
fact that Shauna started screaming didn't bother me.

Mags was back.

Wow.

Mam had just placed in front of me the biggest dinner
I'd seen since I'd left home five years ago, when the
phone rang.

"I'll get it," she stood up from the table and motioned for me to sit back down. "It's probably for me, probably Mr Parker wanting to see if I'm free to go out tomorrow."

The way she said 'Mr Parker' was loaded. "And who's he?" I asked, knowing she was only dying to tell me.

"Ohh," she gave a girlie giggle and flapped her hand at me. "Tell you when I come back."

I grinned at her retreating back. As soon as she was out of the kitchen, I threw some ham over to the cat. The smell of it was making me feel sick. The cat, a massive marmalade Bag-puss lookalike, peered at the meat and then sniffed at it. Very delicately, he began to nibble.

"Will you eat it a bit quicker, " I hissed. I could hear Mam returning. There was nothing for it, I made a dash across the kitchen, retrieved the meat and put it back on my plate. The cat hissed at me.

"It's for you." Mam, looking slightly worried, poked her head in the door. She dropped her voice. "Sounds like John."

"I don't want to talk to him." I began to mush the spuds into the plate.

"What?"

"Just tell him I'm not in."

"Maggie," Mam stood looking down on me, "I can't do that. I've already said that you're here. All the poor chap wants is a word. That's what he said. All I want is a word, Mrs Scanlon." She paused. Took a breath. "He sounds a bit upset."

John. Upset? I couldn't look at Mam as I said, "So?"

"Fierce upset."

"I still don't want to talk to him," I muttered.

"Oh, now, Maggie, come on. Give the lad a chance."

I knew she wouldn't let it drop. That she'd nag me into talking to him even if he had to hang on the phone all night. Which, come to think of it, wasn't a bad idea. It'd serve him right if he'd a huge phone bill and, knowing John, he wouldn't be able to pay it.

"I don't know if you've really left him and I hope you haven't, but the least you could do is talk to him."

"Look, I've left him and that's all there is to it."

Mam winced. Then tried to smile. "Maggie, please – " I didn't want her to ignore the problem. "I *have* left him, Mam, and I'm not going back."

She gave a tight smile. "A tiff. That's all. Go talk to him."

That was the brilliant thing about my mother. If I'd been responsible for Armageddon, she'd find some way of making it all nice and pleasant again. Probably tell me it was laid down in the book of Revelations and couldn't be helped. And then we'd all sit down to 'a nice cup of tea'.

"It's more than a tiff," I snapped, standing up and shoving my dinner away from me.

She started humming and flicking through the paper.

Stomping into the hall and closing the kitchen door so she couldn't earwig I picked up the phone. "Yes?" I snapped out.

"Well, well," John's voice made me catch my breath, "and how's the traveller?"

He didn't sound upset. Not sure if this pleased me or not, I snapped, "All the better for being a few hundred miles away from you."

John laughed. But I knew it wasn't a real laugh. "Aw, you're only saying that." He paused. "I'm thinking of becoming a psychic, you know."

"Really? Well, why doesn't *that* surprise me?"

"It shouldn't surprise you." I could picture him at the other end of the line, blue eyes crinkled, mouth turned up in a huge grin. "After all, how did I know where you were? All I had was a rather badly spelt, hastily scribbled note to go on." Laboriously, trying to make out he couldn't read my writing, he read out, "John, pissed off with your effing – and that's spelt wrongly, by the way – with your effing attitude, can't take it any more. Bye." He stopped. "And from this note, I concluded that my Mags had gone home to good auld Mother in Ireland. Now, tell me, is that not *bloody* brilliant?"

"Wonderful."

"So, what's the story? Have you dumped me?"

"Yes, John." I confirmed. "You may consider yourself dumped."

There was a silence from the other end. I thought maybe he'd hung up. Just as I was about to say his name, his voice came back on line. Very slowly, as if he was talking to a moron, he said, "Now, Mags, I'm going to ask you that question again. Consider carefully before you answer. You have a fifty-fifty chance of saying the wrong thing. Hint, your last answer was most definitely not the one to give."

Despite myself I smiled.

"The right answer," he did a sort of happy buzzer noise, "guarantees you a lifetime of devotion and love and the other answer," he made a sound like a fart, "just makes you into a hard, bitter auld spinster. Now," he took a breath, "am I dumped?"

"Yes," I said slowly. I wasn't a hard bitter old spinster. And I didn't need his love or his devotion. "You are dumped."

The farting noise.

Silence.

Then, "Why?"

I knew he'd ask that. John was a real 'why' person. He needed a reason for everything. "It doesn't matter why," I snapped. "It's the end result that counts."

"Aw, Maggie, come *on* – did I do something. Is it Rat? What?"

"It's what."

"Jesus."

I did a big weary sigh. "John, we were going nowhere; there's nowhere for us to go. Let's just leave it at that."

"No. That's crap. You wouldn't marry me. D'you remember I asked you and – "

"You always remember the stupid things."

He paused. I think I'd hurt him. Obviously deciding that I hadn't meant to, he continued, "So marry me if you want us to go somewhere."

11

I knew he'd say that. I *knew* he would. "John," I spoke as if I was speaking to a six-year-old, "the only place I want us to go is our separate ways – right?"

He gave a bit of a laugh. That was John all over. As far as he was concerned, I'd never say anything horrible and *mean* it. After a few more seconds of inane chortling, he asked, "So – right, we're going our separate ways. Agreed."

I have to say I was a bit taken aback at that. I thought I'd have to do a bit more wrangling.

"Uh – huh."

"Well, then, how about giving me back my CDs?"

"*Your* CDs? They're mine. I bought them."

"For me," he challenged.

I shrugged. "Yeah . . . well . . ."

"Honestly, Mags, I need them. There really isn't a lot of call for CD-less DJs out there."

"There isn't a lot of call for you anyhow."

"Ouch."

Silence.

"Well?" he said.

He sounded pathetic. "Piss off, John." I hung up.

"That's not a nice way to speak to anybody." My mother, arms folded, looked at me accusingly from the kitchen doorway. "What sort of a way is that for a girl to talk? Nothing gets solved by using obscenities."

I wanted to tell her that I didn't want anything to be solved, but there was no point in having an argument the first night back. There was no point in explaining anything to my mother – I didn't think she'd understand. Or that she'd even want to understand.

12

Is this Love?

I don't know if I understood really.

"So who's Mr Parker?" I managed a semi-smile. "Some sort of sex-god or what?"

"Maggie!" A shriek followed by a giggle. "You're an awful girl."

Yeah. I guess she had a point.

I am an awful girl.

Dick came home for tea tonight. Normally he has his dinner out as I'm not much of a cook but tonight he arrived home.

I was lucky. The kids were clean and the house had just been hoovered before he arrived.

"Hi," I smiled at him. He looked lovely in his suit and tie. "I've some chips on. D'you want some?"

"Really Pam," he muttered, "our children need something more nourishing inside them than chips and . . ." he looked under the grill, "sausages."

"Oh, it's just tonight," I said. "A sort of a treat."

Dick really cares about what the kids eat. He's brilliant like that.

"Treat?" he scoffed. "When was dinner ever meant to be a treat?"

Of course he was right, but it was too late. I'd already promised David and Dick junior that they could have chips. And anyhow, they were made.

"Sorry," I mumbled.

Dick ruffled my hair. "Forget it." He turned to the kids. "So, who's going to bring Daddy's coat upstairs for him."

"Mammy is," Dick junior chirped.

He's five and as bright as a button.

13

Dick laughed. "Attaboy." He pretended to box with him before saying, "Mammy's a bit busy so maybe you can do it for me?"

Without hesitation, Dick junior took his coat from him and began to make his way upstairs.

It's brilliant the way Dick can make him do things. He won't listen to a word I say.

But then again, I was never much good with children.

Chapter Two

I'd been living in London just over two weeks when I met John. I was in a club with a few girls from work, desperately trying, through imbibing loads of booze, to shake off the guilt of leaving my mother all alone in a big rattly house in Dublin. Dad had been dead a year and Mam was still wearing black and singing his praises. To be frank, I was beginning to feel seriously pissed off and depressed. So I applied for a job in London, not really expecting to get it.

I'm in the restaurant trade. This job was to manage a 'well established city-centre restaurant'.

Anyhow, to everyone's total amazement, including my own, I got offered the job.

Two weeks later, I'm on a plane heading for a big adventure in a big city.

Only I was guilt-ridden. And the night I met John, guilt was seeping out of every pore on my underdressed body.

I was standing at the bar, trying desperately to keep my skirt below my buttocks and swirling the remains of my fifth Bud about in my glass. Everyone I had come with was up dancing or getting high on 'E'.

I preferred the booze. And anyway, I wasn't into socialising with people from work, especially people I was meant to be in charge of. So, I thought, spending the night up at the bar was the ideal way to keep my distance from them.

I'm not the sort of girl lads queue to chat up. Only John did. Chat me up, I mean. Maybe it was the skirt or lack thereof.

He sauntered over to the bar and stood beside me. A few seconds later, he bent down to my level, peered into my face and grinned.

Totally invading my space.

I recoiled as any normal person would.

"Good." He took out a notebook and pen, and then, tongue shoved out the side of his mouth, he made a big deal of writing something down. After a few seconds he smiled again at me and began pocketing his notebook in his shirt pocket.

"Sorry, what did you just write there?" I asked. I had to speak quite slowly as my speech was a bit slurred. I wasn't legless though.

I don't get legless.

"Oh, nothing," he waved down the barman. "Guinness and . . ." he looked questioningly at me.

"Bud," I said.

The barman nodded and moved away.

"Thanks," I muttered.

"No problem." He grinned. "I've been watching you." He nodded sagely, before pronouncing, "You're very interesting."

"Sorry?"

"Oh, don't be. It's fine to be interesting."

"No, I meant . . ." I wondered if I was dreaming. This whole thing had a sort of surreal quality about it.

"I'm doing some research into body language. I hope to publish a book on it." He looked me up and down. "You've great body language."

"Have I?" I would have preferred if he'd told me I'd a great body, but still, take what you can get, that's my motto.

Before he could answer, our drinks arrived and he paid the barman. "Keep the change," he grinned.

The barman sneered. "Ten pence. That's generous of ya, mate."

"Don't mention it."

I smiled slightly at the horrible look the barman gave him. There was no way he'd be served again that night.

"Cheers," John lifted his pint and clinked it off mine.

"Yeah, cheers."

We both took a few gulps in silence, before he said, "My guess is – and this is only a guess – right?" As I nodded, he continued, "I guess you're feeling very lonely. It's the way you're sort of hunched up and defensive."

"Am I?" I was beginning to notice how good-

17

looking this guy was. Tall, brown-haired with the bluest, crinkliest eyes I'd ever seen. His dress sense didn't look very clubbish though. Combats with a T-shirt and baggy V-necked jumper. His black Docs weren't even polished. Still, he had a nice smile.

"Absolutely, you are." He gave me a demonstration of 'hunched-up-and-defensive'. "And what's more," he continued, "I'd say you're only in London about," he screwed up his face, "a week or so?"

"Two weeks." I tried not to sound pathetic about it. "And I suppose you're right, I am sort of lonely, but it's no big deal. I like being lonely." I hoped he'd get the hint and leave.

He didn't. He did a stupid-looking bow and said, "There you are now, Dr Jung at your service." He pronounced 'Jung' wrongly. I was about to slag him over it when a delighted smile danced across his face. *"You're beginning to open up!"* he practically yelled all over the place.

"Whoa! Get it while ya can mate!" some loser beside us leered.

John laughed while I rolled my eyes.

"Naw," he shook his head. "I mean, she's responding to me."

"Christ, no hands. You're some operator all right."

John ignored him. "See," he indicated my body from top to toe, "your arms are more relaxed. You're smiling." Pause. "It's obvious you like me."

"Oh *please*!" Drunk as I was, I wasn't falling for that crap.

"Your voice says one thing but your body another."
He jabbed his finger. "You can't lie to me . . . Maggie."

It took a second to register that he knew my name.
"What – how . . ."

"They told me all about you." He thumbed in the
direction of my workmates and grinned. "Welcome to
London."

"So you're not . . ."

"No."

He held out his hand, I took it in mine and we
shook. "John Delaney."

"Maggie Scanlon."

"You've gorgeous legs, Maggie Scanlon."

"Stop!"

"Naw, honest, good legs say a lot about a person.
Some women, right, you'd see better legs dangling
from a nest, now yours . . ."

He stopped as I gave a splutter of laughter.

"What?"

His look of bemusement made me laugh harder.

It was the first time I'd laughed since I'd arrived.

I liked this guy.

Dick.

I remember the first time I saw him.

I actually think that the first time I saw him I fell in love.

*I'd just been given promotion in work. I was now
officially head programmer in Atlas Computer Software. To
be honest, I don't know how I got promotion. I mean, I was
good at my job and everything but I wasn't exactly dynamic.*

And so, it had been tactfully put to me by one of the managers that I could benefit from a course in people management. In getting things done without doing everything myself.

So I'd been sent along to a session. Five sessions actually. Every Wednesday.

The first week I'd been shaking. I was convinced that everyone would see just how bad I was.

There were ten of us on the course. Five women and five men. All older than me.

And Dick had walked in.

I knew there was a God. If this man was going to be spending every Wednesday teaching me how to manage my staff, I was perfectly content to let him. He was tall, over six foot, dark, sallow-skinned and he had the brownest eyes. Big pools that you could drown in. He wore a suit – a grey one. I sat up straighter in my chair. I took my pen from my mouth.

"Hi," Dick grinned at us.

"Hi," we chorused back.

"I'm your course leader for the next five weeks."

"Goody," some old lady said.

We laughed. Dick smiled briefly.

"By the end of the five sessions you'll all be able to run smooth efficient offices."

Forget about thanking God, I thought. This guy had to be God if he could make that happen.

Dick asked us our names and what we did.

"I'm Pamela Scanlon and I'm head computer programmer with Atlas Software."

People gawked. I flushed.

Is this Love?

"So you've an important job, Pamela?"

"Ohhh," I flapped my hand around. "Mmmm."

"And what are you here for, Pamela?"

Oh flip. "Well," I licked my lips, "I'm not very good at ordering people about. I end up doing everything myself."

A bit of a discussion ensued. Apparently I had used the wrong word. "Ordering is wrong," Dick said. He leaned towards us, "If you're nice to people, if you treat them well in the beginning, they'll do anything for you."

"But I am nice," I said, trying to stick up for myself.

"You'll see what I mean," Dick grinned.

And boy, did I see what he meant.

Not then, but later.

In that moment though, I knew that whatever he meant, I would do it.

Chapter Three

Maggie Scanlon, that's me. Totally ordinary. Twenty-nine, average height. Unfortunately above average build – a Marilyn Monroe type figure would be a nice way to describe it. I've got brown hair, blue eyes and no man. Well, not since I ditched John. I've done my Leaving Cert and I got enough points to go to college. I don't even know what the course was called. I just did it 'cause I couldn't get a job. Then I got work in McDonalds, ditched college – much to the horror of my Dad – and eventually, after working in a few Dublin restaurants, I ended up in London managing a nice restaurant there. But I already told you about that.

Let's see, any more? Oh yeah, I've a mother, still alive. A father, stone dead. Sounds a bit harsh, doesn't it, but hey, you know, that's life. And, oh yeah, I've a sister. The brains in the family, Pamela. She'd older than me by two years. And thinner than me by about two stone.

C'est la vie.

Is this Love?

Oh, God. Here I am rabbiting on and I haven't even told you who I am. Well, not properly anyway. Dick'd go mad. He'd say that no one would even listen to someone they don't know properly and that complete strangers discussing their problems in public are embarrassing in the extreme. Not that I have problems – well, not really. The major one at the moment is Shauna. She's eight weeks and still not sleeping through the night. Dick has moved into the spare room. I don't blame him. It's hard to get up for work every morning when you're awake at least three times during the night. It's easier for me – it's not as if I really do anything during the day.

Ooops! There I go again, rabbiting on. OK, here goes. I'm Pamela Scanlon and I'm thirty-one. Yep. The big three-one. It's horrible being that age. But at least I'm married. Mam always says that women should be married by at least thirty. 'Any marriage is better than none,' she says. And she's right. We all need a partner in life. My poor sister Maggie has only a year left to find somebody and, frankly, there isn't much hope. She left her boyfriend a few days ago. Just upped and left. Still, what do you expect? He probably threw her out. She was living with him. 'Putting the carrot before the stick,' my mother says about people who live with each other before marriage. Of course, she won't admit that her precious Maggie could do something like that. Oh no.

Oops! That sounds a bit like jealousy, doesn't it? But I'm not. Jealous, I mean. For one thing, I'm thinner than Maggie and for another, I'm heaps cleverer. I used to be a top programmer with a top firm. I was earning huge money. But then, I got married . . .

I don't regret leaving work. Not for a minute. I have three kids and I love the bones of them. There's Dick junior, who's five. He's just started school and he's great. He can read and everything. Then there's David who's two. He's quiet. And then there's Shauna. My little girl.

I'm married about six years, I got married about a month after Daddy died. It kind of spoilt the day a bit but Dick says that these things happen. I suppose he's right. I still see Mammy though. We all call up every Sunday to see her. Dick sometimes goes, if he's not too busy. Mammy and I talk about Daddy and the laughs we all used to have. But lately she doesn't talk about him so much.

Anyhow, that's me. That's my life.

I'm just an ordinary Joe.

Chapter Four

Dressed in my good suit, the one I wore to practically every important occasion in my life, I stood outside *Louis' Bistro* and listened to the sound of my heart hitting my boots. Sorry, shoes.

Compared to the restaurant I'd managed in London, *Louis' Bistro* was a tip. In fact, compared to any restaurant, anywhere on the planet, *Louis' Bistro* was a tip.

A real chew-up and spew-up.

First off, it was more like a café than a bistro. The entrance was totally out of character with the rest of the place. Big, heavy, over-ornate door painted yellow. The letters LB intertwined to make the handle. Pushing open the door would have tested the strength of Hercules and then, once inside, it was dark. Not seductively so, just inconveniently so. I was afraid I'd trip over something – a rat maybe – as I made my way to the top of the room.

A woman in a blue and white stripy apron looked up as I came in. A butcher's apron I noted with disbelief. "What can I get ya?" she asked. She looked me up and down. "Nice suit."

"Thanks." Despite the fact that there was no way I wanted to work here, my heart had begun to hammer at the thought of the interview. "I, eh, don't want anything. I'm here for interview."

"Oh." Her jaw dropped. "Eh, hang on. I'll just get Louis."

"Fine."

"Take a seat."

"Thanks."

"LOUIS!" She bellowed at the top of her voice, making me jump. "GIRL'S HERE ABOUT THE JOB!"

"TELL HER TO HANG ON!"

The woman turned to me and smiled. "He says to hang on."

"I heard." I managed a weak smile.

"Yeah, suppose you did. Our Louis is terrible loud." She indicated a cup. "Want a cuppa while you're waiting?"

Hastily I studied the tea machine. It looked clean enough. "Yeah, OK, thanks." I watched while she poured.

"Milk?"

"Yeah."

"Here you are." She brought the cup over to me and lowered herself into the seat opposite. Taking a packet of fags from her apron, she lit up. "Want one?"

"No. Thanks."

"So, what's the story?" she asked. "You pretty stuck

for a job or what?" She exhaled a long stream of smoke into my face.

"No." I knew the minute I'd said it, I'd done so too quickly. Of *course* I was desperate for work and despite the booming economy, managerial jobs were hard to come by. But *Louis' Bistro* was most definitely not what I'd been looking for.

"Oh yeah," the woman said patronisingly, "'*course* you're not." She waved her arm about. "Bloody hard work running a classy place like this."

I didn't know whether she was being serious or sarcastic.

"I mean, Louis is a dead bleeding loss as a manager. He owns the place but can he run it?" She waited for me to reply, but I just smiled.

"Not – a – hope," she answered. "The guy couldn't even run a chip shop in Cambodia never mind anything else." She shook her head. "A dead bleeding loss."

I took a cautious sip of my tea and tried to smile in a non-encouraging way. There was no way I wanted Louis to hear his employee and his interviewee discussing his shortcomings. I mean, I wanted to be *offered* the job, just to bolster my ego.

"SEND HER UP!" The loud voice again.

The woman smiled. "There you go. Orders from above." She pointed to a sad-looking brown door. "Go through there, luv, up the stairs – mind the third one, it's sort of rotting a bit – and it's the first door on your right."

It was the only door on my right. I straightened my

jacket and skirt and ran my fingers through my hair before knocking.

"COME IN."

Head high, I entered. I kept repeating those confidence-boosting words as I made my way across the room. *I don't want this poxy job. I don't want this poxy job.*

"Sit."

I sat. *I don't want this poxy job. I don't want this poxy job.*

The room was in a shambles. I don't know why I was surprised; it just reflected the state of the rest of the place. Louis sat behind a huge desk, papers strewn about everywhere. It was unfortunate that the desk was so huge because it only emphasised the fact that Louis wasn't. Small shoulders, emaciated neck and a tiny face with little pointy features. He reminded me of a gnome.

"Hello, Margaret," he smiled at me. "Great you could come."

"Yes." I folded my hands in my lap so I wouldn't fidget.

"I've read your, your . . ." he indicated my CV, "your stuff and it's great. Very impressive."

"Thanks."

He sat back in his chair and I was afraid it'd swallow him. Two huge wings on either side seemed to embrace his scrawny body. "Sooooo," he said slowly, "let me give you a run-down of the job and then I'll ask you a few questions and you can ask me a few questions – all right?"

"Sure."

"Like some tea before we start?"

"No, thanks. I've just . . ."

"JOSIE – TWO TEAS. PRONTO!"

I jumped. Small man. Big voice. Freud would have a field day on that one.

"Shouting works better than an intercom," Louis was saying. He sounded proud of himself as he added, "It's cheaper too."

"Right – I must remember that one." I meant it as a joke.

"Ohhh yes. You're never too old to learn. That's what my father used to say."

"Really."

"Really," he confirmed. He picked up a biro from the desk and began tapping it off his teeth. "Now, where were we?"

"You were going to tell me about this place."

"Right." He frowned slightly. "Well, it's been in my family for years. My father had it and he's left it to me." He made a face. "I've a lot of other projects in the pipeline – big projects, you know, and I haven't had as much time as I'd like to run this place. So I figured I could do with a manager," he indicated me, "or a manageress."

"I see." The place needed more than a manager; it needed a miracle.

"It's a grand place, should be a doddle to run. We've regular customers; the food is just ordinary plain stuff, none of your fancy curries or foreign slop. Just chips and burgers."

"Chips and burgers, " I said. "Nothing foreign about that." I don't know why I said it, I think he was getting on my nerves a little. I hated men that made out things were easier than they were. This place wouldn't be a doddle . . .

"And," he said, totally missing my sarcasm, "anybody'd *love* to work here. My father was very lucky with staff. We all pull together and muck in. One big happy family."

"Here's yer teas." Josie burst into the room, a cup of tea in each hand. Banging them onto the table where their contents slopped out, she snarled at Louis. "And don't be telling me to get things 'pronto'. I'm not your fucking slave!" She thumbed in the direction of the bistro. "*And* I had a customer."

"One of our regulars, eh, Josie," Louis said jovially, winking at her.

"Yeah, a regular asshole," Josie snapped.

Louis gave a laugh, obviously pretending it was just a happy banter between him and his employee. "Thanks for the tea."

She muttered something about incompetent pricks as she left.

"That's Josie," Louis said amicably. "Rough and ready. Good worker though." He waited until she was gone downstairs before saying, "So, that's it. The hours you'd work can be sorted out. Obviously there'd be some late nights and stuff. And early mornings." He winked. "Hope you're not too much of a party animal."

"No." I didn't even smile. There was no way I was working here.

"So any questions?"

"No." I was feeling pissed off with disappointment. So much for managing 'a large city centre restaurant'.

"Oh." He had the grace to look taken aback.

"To be honest," I threw caution to the wind, "your advertisement in the paper was a bit misleading. This *isn't* a large city centre restaurant."

"No," he agreed, "but it could be."

"But it's *not*," I said. I sought for what else the job advert had stated, "And who's your international clientele?"

"The Bosnians," he replied. "They love this place. They come when they get thrown out of their B&B's."

"Great."

"Isn't it?" he said. "Piles of them about now. They buy their tea and just sit around for the afternoon. Not a bit of trouble out of them."

Unbelievable.

"So how about it?"

"Sorry?"

"The manager's job?"

"Pardon?"

"I'm offering you the job." Louis beamed at me. "Welcome aboard."

Gobsmacked, I stared at him. "But . . ."

"I mean with your experience it'd be a doddle."

"It wouldn't be a doddle." My voice took on a hard edge. "And I don't want it."

31

He looked genuinely bewildered. "You don't want it?" Pause. "But why?"

"I don't like being conned into applying for a job and then finding out the job isn't what it was meant to be."

"Sorry, I've, eh, I've lost you."

"The job isn't what I was expecting." I forced my voice to be polite. Standing up, I indicated my teacup. "Thanks for the tea."

"So, what are you saying. That you *really* don't want to work here."

"Yes."

"Forget about the early mornings." He waved his hand expansively about. "Don't do them."

"Sorry?"

"And the late nights, forget about them. I'll get Romano to sort it."

"Romano?"

"Homeless Bosnian, he works for me. He's very obliging." He smiled. "One big happy family."

"Look, I'm not – "

"Free rein. You can do what you want in the place."

"No, honest – "

Louis lifted himself from his chair. All five foot nothing of him toddled around the table. I could see the dandruff in his hair. Looking up at me, he sighed and said, "Look, I'll be straight with you. We're pretty desperate here. We need someone badly."

It took a lot for him to admit that. I almost felt sorry for him. "Look," I said, more gently now, "I'm used to big places. I wouldn't be any good here."

"Oh, now," he flapped his hand. "Such a lack of confidence. You'd be *fantastic* here. I know you would. And I'd be here to help if it got too much."

"No, honest – "

"Think about it." He cut me short. "I'll ring you in a couple of days. Now remember, you can make the place your own – free rein. No lates, no earlies, hell, you needn't work at all if you don't want." He gave a weak laugh. "I'll contact you later in the week."

He virtually pushed me out of the office before slamming the door.

Dazed, I walked out of the café and into the street. There was no way I was going back to that dingy joint.

No way.

"How'd the interview go?" Mam asked the minute I came in the door.

"Don't ask!" I flung my jacket across the banisters in the hall and stomped into the kitchen.

"Oh, don't be leaving your clothes all over the place," Mam fussed as she picked up my jacket and trotted behind me into the kitchen. She placed the jacket neatly on the back of a chair. "Now, how about a nice cup of tea?"

"If I see another cup of tea, I'll scream."

"Oh now, there's no point in taking it out on me just because you didn't get the job. That never solved anything. Anyhow, what's meant to be, will be. Put your trust in God and he'll come – "

"I did get the poxy job."

"Oh." Speechless for a millisecond, she stared at me. "Well, isn't that nice? Great stuff. Oh, that's . . ."

"Mam, did you not listen? It's a *poxy* job."

"Well, it's your own fault then, applying for . . ." she didn't want to say 'poxy', ". . . for jobs that aren't nice. Why didn't you apply for a nice manager's job, one that you could *do*? Still, maybe it's for the best. Maybe you'll like it when. . ."

"I'm not taking the job." I gritted my teeth. "Can we just drop the subject?"

"Fine." She held up her hands and laughed. "I can't do right for doing wrong. I don't know. You apply for a job; you get the job; you don't want the job." She moved away from me out into the hall, muttering to herself and laughing. "Young *people*, they're as *contrary*."

To top a totally rotten day, John rang again. Once more, he managed it just as I was sitting down to dinner. Once more Mam thought it was the mysterious Mr Parker and once more I went through the 'I refuse to talk to the bastard' routine until Mam ended up looking so pained and martyr-like that I just took the call to get away from her.

It was a real déjà-vu scenario.

"John?"

"Aw, how's it going, head?"

His usual crappy Dublin accent. I made my voice ultra-polite. "Very well since you ask. I got a job offer today."

I could tell by his silence, he was a bit stunned at

that. "What as?" he asked, unable to keep the curiosity from his voice. Then, "Naw, naw, hang on, don't tell me. I'm working on this psychic routine." He made a weird noise as I rolled my eyes. "I got it! You've got a job with the hottest crooks in Dublin. You rob CDs! Am I right? Huh?"

I refused to be drawn. "John, do you have to be so childish?"

"So you're staying over there, are you?"

He sounded hurt. "That's the plan," I said.

There was a second's silence before he muttered, "Well, if that's the case you'd better tell me where in Christ you put the tin-opener or I'll bloody starve."

"Sorry?"

"The tin-opener. I'm making beans for my dinner and I can't find the tin-opener."

"And you rang me to ask that?"

"Well, unless there's someone else who knows where it is." He gave a bit of a laugh. "And much as you seem to be going through some weird breakdown, I'd hardly think you'd want me to starve."

If there was one thing John could do it was make me mad. The only thing he and my dad had in common. "Open your fucking eyes and look for it," I screamed as I slammed down the phone. "AAAGGHHH!"

"Margaret!" Like yesterday, my mother stood at the kitchen door. "How can you expect a man to respect you when you carry on like a street girl!"

"I don't want his respect!" I shouted.

"Oh dear," Mam shook her head. "And to think I

thought you were grown-up. Getting all upset over a row. I don't know. Come on in and finish your dinner."

"Give it to that big fat cat that keeps hissing at me," I shouted. I couldn't control myself. Wrenching open the front door, I walked out.

I'd be fine when I got some time to cool down and I knew Mam wouldn't want to rock the boat by mentioning the row again.

Mam was right though. I hadn't grown-up, not really. My life was still in as big a mess as it always had been. Only now things were worse than ever.

Chapter Five

"Pamela, where the hell is my pale blue shirt?"

Honestly, Dick is hopeless in the house. He never knows where anything is. "Try the wardrobe," *I shouted up to him. He's like a big baby. I'd managed to get myself and the three kids dressed and he was still fumbling around trying to dress himself. I don't know how he manages on work mornings.*

"I've already tried the wardrobe. What the hell do you think I am – stupid?"

Rolling my eyes, I put Shauna into her bouncer and made my way upstairs.

Dick had every shirt in the wardrobe pulled out and scattered over the bed and the floor. He was standing in the middle of the mess with a furious scowl on his face. "I've looked everywhere," *he snapped.*

I wanted to tell him that if he'd looked everywhere, he'd have found it, but when Dick is in bad form, you don't joke with him.

Normally though, he's good at taking a joke.

"Let's have a look," I smiled. I got down on my knees and began to go through the pile of shirts on the floor.

Dick stood, arms folded, watching. He didn't say a word.

I went through the mauve shirts, just in case I'd mistakenly hung it up with them, but it wasn't there. It wasn't with his dark shirts or with the white ones. My heart started to thump. I hoped to God I'd washed it. Mentally I began to try and figure out when he'd last worn it. It'd been ages ago. At least two weeks. Dick didn't like his shirts being in the washbasket for too long. And who could blame him? Things get smelly in washbaskets. I knew I'd have washed it. It had to be there.

My searching began to get more frantic. "It has to be here, Dick," I said cheerily. I didn't want to annoy him. For the first time in weeks, he was home on a Sunday and it would be just typical of me to spoil it.

"It should be there," he said, "but it's not."

His voice was calm, measured. I hated when he talked like that.

And then, I saw it. The relief I felt almost made me feel sick. For a second, I couldn't even reach out for the shirt. I had to steady myself. Then, slowly, trying not to show how pleased I was that I'd found it, I said, "Look, here it is." I pulled it from under the deeper blue shirt. "I must have hung the two on the one hanger."

"And now it's all creased," he pouted. "I can't wear it." He reached for a wine sweatshirt. "I'll put this on instead." Pulling it over his head, he stalked into the bathroom.

Is this Love?

I picked up his shirts and replaced them in the wardrobe, putting the sky-blue one on the bed so I'd remember to iron it later.

Shauna had begun screaming from the kitchen.

Motherhood, huh?

I brought the three kids to Mass in the car. It's no joke trying to hold a baby and keep a five-year-old and a two-year-old under control, especially when the five-year-old keeps pretending to snore and, after that, shouting out at the top of his voice that Mass is boring.

And I couldn't slap him. I wanted to but I couldn't.

"Mammy, when can we go home?" he yelled out just as Communion was starting.

"Soon," I whispered back.

"Mammy, you're whispering. I can't hear you!" He yanked Shauna's arm. "Mammeeee! Listen to me!"

Shauna began to wail and I held her up to me and cuddled her. I think Dick had really hurt her arm. There was no way she was going to stop crying.

I suppose it was no harm to leave Mass early. Just this one Sunday. Anyhow, we were all expected over to Mammy's for dinner, so it'd be nice to get there early and have a chat beforehand.

"Come on so," I said and Dick's face lit up. "And do you know who'll be there today?" I whispered as we made our way from the church.

"Mr Nosy Parker?" he said, giggling.

He really is the most beautiful child when he's in good humour.

39

"No," I said, catching David's hand and pulling him along. "Your Auntie Maggie – home from London."

More's the pity, I wanted to add, but didn't.

We went to Mammy's in Dick's BMW. He drove. I wouldn't have the confidence to drive a car like that. My limit is the little Ka. Dick says women are useless drivers and I have to say I agree with him. They've no sense of direction and are always stalling at traffic lights. Dick says they should be banned from the roads. I'm pretty sure he's joking about that bit. I mean, if he really thought women were so terrible, he'd hardly let me drive his three kids about, now would he?

The last time I'd seen Maggie was last Christmas. She'd come over from London bearing gifts and trying to charm everybody. She'd brought John along with her. She'd been going out with him for a good few years, but Christmas was the first real formal introduction to the family. Mammy had been delighted, convinced Maggie was going to settle down at last. I must say, I'd liked John. He'd been nice, really friendly and he seemed to be mad about Maggie. If she got up, his eyes followed her, he laughed at her jokes and once, she'd even told him to make tea for everyone and he had. He was a nice guy. Dick hadn't liked him much; he'd said that he was too showy. He'd said that any fella that made a fool out of himself to impress people had no self-respect. And maybe he was right. After all, John was off the scene now.

We arrived about half an hour early. Dick spent ages locking up the car before he'd let us out.

"I want to see Auntie Maggie," Dick junior kept whingeing from the back seat.

"Shut up, you," Dick snapped. "When I lock the car, we can all get out."

"Be quiet, angel," I said. "Daddy's trying to concentrate."

"But I want to seee . . ."

"If you don't shut up," Dick snapped, "I'll shut you up!"

Instant silence except for David. He began to whimper. He's still not used to Dick when he shouts.

"Shut that kid up!" Dick glared at me.

"David, honey . . ."

"OK, all out," Dick had finally mastered the crooklock on the steering wheel. Opening his door, he went and let the two lads out from the back seat. Grabbing their hands he pulled them out of the car and ordered them to stand still. I got out and opened the other back door. Stooping in, I pulled Shauna from her baby seat. She looked gorgeous, all long lashes and pink cheeks. As she snuggled her little body into mine, I kissed the top of her head. She had the innocent smell of new babies. For a second, my throat hurt, as if there was a lump in it. I suppose it was just because she was so beautiful. I hugged her harder to me.

"Come on," Dick said impatiently. "Are you going to stand there all day?"

Dick junior laughed. "Don't stand there all day, Mammy. You'd get cold!"

"I would, wouldn't I?" I smiled down at him. Slamming

the door, I turned to face Dick. "Right, let's go," I said.

He smiled down at me and tweaked my hair. "Another Sunday to endure your mother's cooking."

"Absolutely!"

And we both laughed.

Chapter Six

"Wasn't that nice?" Mam said as she began the big clear up. "My two girls together for Sunday dinner."

I smiled, not wanting to spoil her little happy family fantasy.

"And isn't Dick junior an *absolute* divil?"

He was an absolute brat as far as I was concerned. He'd bounded in, ignored my mother, smirked at me and, locating the cat cowering under the table, he'd encouraged it out before giving it an unmerciful boot up the backside.

I wasn't too mad on Malcolm – the cat – myself, but I wouldn't have kicked him. "That's not nice," I'd said. "The cat has done nothing to you."

"Piss off!"

I looked to Pam for support, but she mustn't have heard him – she was too busy dragging David into the house while balancing her new baby in her arms. Dick was no help; he just strode past me into the sitting-room. Plonking himself in a chair he located the remote control and put on Eurosport.

Pam pushed David towards Mam. He's the shyest kid going. According to Mam he comes up every Sunday and won't move from the chair he's put sitting in. He hardly talks either. "David," Pam said in her meek little voice, "give Nanny a Teletubby special."

"Big hug," David opened his arms wide and began to squeeze Mam around the neck really hard.

"Honestly, Pamela," Dick spoke, managing to tear his eyes away from the telly, "will you stop encouraging the child to make a fool of himself. It's a hug, nothing more, nothing less. Teletubby special," he mocked, winking over at me.

I smiled back, not really wanting to. Only doing it out of politeness. I'm not mad into Dick though Mam loves him.

Dick junior now had Malcolm by the tail. The cat yowled and tried to escape.

"Leave the cat alone," I said. I tried to say it nicely.

"Nope." Big brown eyes gazed up at me. He yanked the cat again.

"Dick, leave the bloody cat alone!"

Dick's sharp voice made us all wince. Dick junior dropped the tail as if it had stung him. "Sorry," he muttered. He slouched off into a corner and scowled at everyone. But at least he was quiet.

David clung to Pam's leg as she came into the room. When she sat down, he wrapped himself around both her legs. How she puts up with it I don't know. I'd be claustrophobic if I'd a kid like that. Still, that's Pam all over. She puts up with things.

"Cup of tea anyone?" Mam asked brightly, smiling around at her assembled family.

"Coffee," Dick said without even looking up at her.

"Anyone else?"

"I'll have a Bud," Dick junior spoke up from his corner.

"Oh, Dick junior!" Pam put her hand to her mouth and looked at her husband.

I giggled. "Bottled or draught?"

"Don't encourage him," Pam flapped her hand at me. "Honestly, what would people think? I mean it's not as if Dick or I ..."

"Oh will you leave it, Pamela. The kid's only having a joke."

Pam flushed and began to concentrate on the baby, tickling her under the chin and cooing at her.

Dick once again turned his attention to the box.

Mam bustled out of the room, laughing softly to herself and calling Dick junior a 'caution'.

Was it me or what – but if some guy, especially my husband, had talked to me like that I'd have strung him up. Still, maybe I was overreacting. I was a bit sensitive like that or so I'd always been told. Pam didn't seem too offended, so maybe Dick hadn't meant it the way it sounded.

Pam was still clucking over the baby.

"And how's my new niece?" I asked, smiling. "Let's have a look at her."

45

Pam looked up at me. "You were invited to the christening." She sounded hostile. "But you never came."

"Mmmm," I shrugged, not able to meet her eye. "Something came up. I sent a present though."

"Yeah, we got it."

Almost tripping over David, who was still clinging to Pam's leg, I plonked myself down beside my sister. "So can I see her?" I asked.

"Sure." Gently she placed the warm body in my arms. "Mind her head now."

Shauna must have known the difference between her Mammy and me because she squirmed a bit and then opened huge dark blue eyes. The way she gazed at me, silent and steady, unnerved me a bit. I couldn't talk for a second or two. Instead, I took my eyes away from hers and studied Pam. She was thinner than ever – you'd never think she had had a baby. Her face looked tired.

"Up all night with her, are you?" I asked, trying to sound sympathetic but not really having a clue.

"Not *all* night."

Her tone hurt me. Sort of snappish.

"Most of it though, huh, Pammy?" That was Dick.

She shrugged. "You get used to it."

"Not me, I wouldn't." Dick made a face. "The screaming of her. I sleep in the spare room now."

"Get lost!" I laughed. "That's awful! I thought the whole idea was that you both pull together to get over the horrible first few weeks."

46

"Oh, I don't mind," Pam said hastily. "Dick has to be up early for work."

"*And* it's the mother's job."

I laughed, then saw that Dick hadn't been joking. The smile died on my face. "But . . . come on . . ." I looked from one to the other. Dick was scowling and Pam had a smile that was too bright. Sort of like wearing the wrong-coloured lipstick. There was something here I didn't quite get. Time to shut up, Mag, I thought. I mean, what did I know?

"So where's Johnny?" Dick snapped out.

"Pardon?" The change of subject startled me. *And* the nasty way Dick had asked the question. I bristled.

"The guy you brought over last time," he smirked. "Where is he?"

"Yes, Mammy says you've left him, Maggie."

They regarded me like two vultures. I shrugged, trying not to let them get to me. "It's true. I've dumped him, time to move on."

"To what though?" Dick arched his eyebrows. "I thought you'd got it made in London. Your mother's always telling Pammy here how well you're doing."

"Yeah, well, sometimes you get bored with being a big hot-shot success." I grinned and seized my opportunity. "Not that you'd know much about that Dick, huh?" Yeah, I know it was a bit nasty, so I tried to grin, to make it seem as if it was just a joke.

His eyes crinkled slightly, trying to smile. Pam stiffened beside me. Maybe I shouldn't have said that? Maybe I'd got it wrong again, maybe they were just interested in my life. "So anyhow," I breezed, standing up and smiling, "I'll just take this little lamb for a walk and show her the sights of Grandma Scanlon's house."

Deafening silence.

I couldn't get out fast enough.

I showed Shauna all over the house, talking to her all the time. When I reached my bedroom, I brought her over to the window and began telling her the stories of everyone who lived on our street. "See, there's where Mrs Doyle lives," I pointed to a green house across the road. "Only we didn't call her Mrs Doyle. Oh no," I did a big exaggerated shake of my head, "we called her," I lowered my voice for dramatic effect, "the *dragon*. And she *was* a dragon. She complained about *everything* we did. And when she went out and had a few jars, we'd call her the dragon with the flagon." Shauna made a sort of cooing sound. Encouraged, I continued, "And when she drove in her car we'd say," I put on a high-pitched voice, "Oh look, there's the *dragon's wagon*."

Shauna smiled. All gummy and charming.

My heart lurched.

She'd smiled at *me*. At me who didn't deserve it.

I had to sit down on the bed. The baby, sensing something had changed, started to whimper. "Ssshhh," I bounced her up and down, trying to see her through the funny mist on my eyes.

"It's no wonder she's crying when you tell her those horrible stories!" Pam had the gift of earwigging and being silent about it, just like my mother. Crossing the room, she removed her daughter from my arms.

"She was fine," I protested. "It's just – "

"Mammy says dinner is ready and to please come down." Pam turned on her heel and left the room.

God, who'd rattled her cage?

They were all sitting around the table when I returned. All except Pam. She was feeding the baby.

"I've made your favourite, Dick." Mam placed a huge lasagne on the table and beamed at him. "And I've made it extra large so you can take some home and re-heat it tomorrow."

"Aw, that's fabulous, Doreen." Dick rubbed his hands and picking up a knife began to hack into it. "There's no one can make lasagne quite like you."

Mam giggled and pooh-pooed. "Pam is a great cook, always was. I'm sure she looks after you well enough."

"Aw, well enough, I suppose." He turned and winked at Pam.

Pam's face lit up. It was like a switch turned on behind her eyes.

It sort of shocked me to discover that she really, actually loves the prick. I guess I knew it but I'd never seen her express it so nakedly before. It made me feel guilty for sniping at him. I suppose he *does* have to get up early for work and he has got *quite* a good job. Not as good as what Pam's had been, but pretty close. I vowed I'd make a determined effort to get on with him, especially as we'd be seeing a lot more of each other now that I was back home. And besides all that, I wanted to be on good terms with Pam. It hurt me to think that we'd once been quite close, not mega-lovey-dovey or anything, but we used to talk to each other and in the past few years she'd grown away from me.

And me from her too, I guess.

I wanted to change that.

I had to.

I needed a friend.

One dinner never solved anything. In fact, Mam monopolised the conversation at the table. I couldn't get a word in edgeways – it was almost as if she didn't want me to talk.

"So, Dick," she leaned towards him, "how was work this week? Pam said you were working all hours!"

"Oh yes," Dick picked up his wine glass and took a swig. "All hours. I've a big deal to close, have to massage a few egos." He winked at Mam. "Power lunches, power dinners. You know how it is."

"Oh, I do. I do."

I almost choked on my own wine. What the hell would my mother know about business? The nearest she'd ever come to a power lunch would be eating high-fibre bread.

"I landed a biggie last week. The big noises were V impressed."

V? V impressed? Where did this guy get off?

I forgot my resolution of being nice. I was right, I'd

always been right, the guy was a – for lack of a better work – prick. "That's V good, Dick. V good indeed. In fact it's V excellent, if you ask me."

"Well, no one *is* asking you, are they, dear?" Mam smiled at me. It was her way of telling me to shut it.

"No, but I'm just expressing – "

"Well, don't, there's a good girl. In fact, just run outside and see if the apple tart is heated, will you?"

Dick smirked at me as I stood up from the table. He had Mam in his pocket right enough. He was the son she'd never had, the replacement husband.

"And what happens if the tart is V hot?" I asked.

"Maggie – "

"It'd probably burn your V big mouth, wouldn't it?" said Dick.

Mam clapped and laughed. "Oh, very good, Dick, very good!"

"Don't you mean V good?" he said.

I left them laughing at their pathetic humour.

The apple tart was burned to a cinder. Mam had a habit of doing things like that. She always wanted things done pronto. A throwback to living with Dad, I guess. Pam and I had christened the switches on our cooker the fast-forwards. Put on the beans and fast forward. Turn on the oven and fast forward.

We were the first people in Ireland to actually live with an incinerator. It was called Mother.

Maybe I'm being cruel again.

I was just having a dekko in the press to see if maybe

51

we'd another apple tart when Pam arrived in. The first I heard was when she closed the kitchen door.

"Aw, hi, Pam, it's too late. The apple tart had committed tartacide in the oven."

She didn't even smile. Instead, she studied me with her weary-looking face and said quietly, "Listen Maggie, I'm just telling you to leave Dick alone."

"Aw, Pam. It's just," I bit my lip, so I wouldn't laugh, "he's so sexy. I can't help myself."

"You know what I mean," she said, flushing. "He's sensitive. He doesn't like being joked about."

"Mmm." I located a tart on the top shelf and, pulling over a chair, I stood on it. My fingers brushed off the tart and I stretched harder.

"Why did you come home anyhow?"

I froze. This wasn't the time or place. And the way Pam sounded, I don't think she was even going to give me a sympathetic hearing. "Another day, huh?"

I wanted her to name a day. But she didn't. With a slow, sort of triumphant smile, she said, "So it wasn't just about dumping John?"

"Nope." I had the tart in my hands and was peeling off its wrapper. It was four weeks out of date but I didn't think anyone would notice. I'd just make sure I wouldn't have any and enjoy the scene as Dick stuffed himself stupid.

"So?"

"Look, Pam, can we leave it for now?"

She shrugged.

"I'm sorry about Dick. I was only having a bit of fun.

He takes himself too seriously." Tart in the oven, dial on.

Pam stood, hopping from foot to foot, before blurting out, "Well, well . . . you take *nothing* seriously. You never have and I'm the one that's always paid for it."

"Sorry?"

She took a deep breath and blinked rapidly. "I'm going back inside. I've had enough of this."

"Pam?"

But she was gone, scurrying away like some little bunny rabbit. Sometimes I got the feeling that Pam didn't much like me.

But, nah, she is my sister after all.

The rest of the dinner went off fine. Dick did eat most of the apple tart and now I'm consumed with guilt in case he dies or something.

They left about seven; Dick junior had to be up for school in the morning.

Mam got a phone call at eight. The mysterious Mr Parker. She was like a kid giggling away over the line to him.

I felt a bit jealous of her actually.

Mad, isn't it?

Chapter Seven

I didn't sleep with John the first night. As my mother would say, I'm not *that* sort of girl. But I did arrange to meet him for a quick coffee the following day.

I was in bits before he turned up. You know the way drink always makes you think people are gorgeous and then when you meet them in sobriety they never live up to the witty, handsome charming person of the night before? That's if you can remember the night before.

Well, I could. Sort of.

I'd given John my work number and I'd told him my age. Twenty-four. He was twenty-five. He'd wanted to know my favourite colour so I'd told him blue. He'd said 'snap', that his favourite colour was a light to medium blue. That was it, he announced; we were totally compatible.

At the time I'd found his logic dazzling and seriously funny.

After I'd agreed to meet him, he'd left. Just said he had to go and left.

That hadn't impressed me much but at least it showed he wasn't going to get too serious with me.

I arrived at the café before him. I wondered if I should leave and keep a watch on the place just in case I was about to be stood up. But no, that was the sort of thing my mother would have advised.

And where had it got her? All alone, mourning a fantasy.

So, walking into the small café, I sat down and ordered a cappuccino. Then I browsed through the rest of the coffee menu with great interest.

"You'll scare him off." I could almost hear her. *"Arriving first – he'll think you're desperate."*

"But I am desperate, Mother."

"Aye, desperate stupid."

It was a recurring conversation in my life.

"I like a girl who's on time."

I looked up and there he was, hands in pockets, grinning at me. He looked good. Almost as nice as I'd remembered. The only fault was, and this was a biggie, he had his denim shirt tucked *into* his jeans.

"So, Maggie," he pulled up a chair and sat down opposite, leaning towards me, elbows on the table, his chin cupped in his hands, "how are *you* since last night?"

"Oh, fine."

That was it. Nothing else would come. I shouldn't have agreed to this. It was going to be difficult, having a conversation with a virtual stranger.

He nodded, studying me with his crinkly blue eyes. "You don't look as lonely today." A slow grin. "Body language definitely opening up."

Whenever I'm uncomfortable, I either joke or throw out some incredibly sarcastic remark. I liked John.

"It's the coffee. Always does that to me."

"I'll have to ply you with loads of coffee so."

More flip comments called for.

"Mmm." I pretended to consider. "It sometimes makes me violent."

"I reckon I could put up with that."

"Nah, you couldn't – you wouldn't like me when I'm angry."

"If you go all green and your chest expands and your clothes rip, I'd say I'd like you *very* much."

"Stop." I *actually* giggled.

I despise girls that giggle at fellas but I couldn't help it. The night before I'd giggled because I was merry, now I'd no excuse.

His smile grew bigger. And, despite myself, mine did too.

He pulled back then. His eyes never left my face though. I squirmed a bit. I hate being looked at. "Where exactly are you from, Maggie Scanlon?"

His accent was sort of posh English. I'd always considered it a poncy-sounding accent, but coming from this six-footer it was sexy. Pure oestrogen heaven.

I could smell his aftershave. "Lindub." Ooops. "Dublin. It's eh . . ."

"Ireland? Yeah, I know it." He grinned, put on a

dreadful Dublin accent and said, "Hey, how's it going, head?"

Again I giggled, though it wasn't very funny. I tried to pull myself together. In a real Dublin accent, I replied, "Great, head. An' yourself?"

"Couldn't be better."

The slow serious way he said it made all the warning bells go off in my head. I didn't mind having a laugh, but I wasn't about to have some guy I barely knew trying to get all heavy on me.

"Well, it *could*." I narrowed my eyes. "You *could* do a course on improving your chat-up lines for one."

"Ouch. Thank you *very* much." He made a big deal of looking offended.

Not hurt. Offended.

I'd have to try harder.

The waitress arrived over and he ordered a coffee. Turning back to me, he said, "My chat-up couldn't have been too bad. I chatted you up and . . ." he did a sort of flourishy thing with his hand, ". . . here you are."

"Yeah, but that's me. I always feel sorry for guys like you."

"The desperate blokes that chat up the girls that no one else wants?"

"Hey, that's – "

"And not only do we chat them up, we *also* bring them out. Show them a good time."

"Well, you're failing miserably on that score. I'm bored stupid."

He laughed, teeth sparkling in a handsome face.

He *laughed*. He wasn't supposed to laugh.

My heart lurched.

"So let me bring you out, say Saturday?" His voice turned serious. "A movie or something?"

What did he want from me? I wondered. I wasn't about to embark on a relationship with anyone. Still, I thought, the pictures couldn't hurt. Shrugging, I said carelessly, "Forget about the something, the movies will be fine."

"Great. Saturday it is then." He sounded delighted. Glancing at his watch, he said, "I'd better go. They're laying people off in our place so I have to be on my best behaviour." He stood up and winked, "I'll ring you at your work during the week, OK?"

"Fine."

I thought he was about to say something else. He looked at me, opened his mouth, paused and just said again, "Saturday, OK?"

I nodded. "Yep."

I watched him leave. He was nice, I decided. Well, he was *all right*.

But it was impossible to judge someone on a quick conversation. And there was still the shirt tucked into jeans factor to consider.

I'd wait and see how Saturday went.

Dick was brilliant. Really great. He could make us laugh and at the same time show us what he was talking about. We discussed body language. Apparently mine was uptight and defensive. He showed me how to look relaxed. He told us that when we crossed our arms it was a clear message to someone that you didn't want your space invaded. When you wagged your foot in company it meant you were bored. It was all very fascinating.

And he made it so interesting.

He asked what we looked for in good staff.

And then what we looked for in a partner.

And how they were the same.

"Pamela," he said, "what would you look for in staff?"

I hated when he picked on me. "Well," I bit my lip, "eh, ability to do the job, someone reliable, mmmm, loyalty — "

"And in a partner?"

I frowned, "Much the same, I suppose."

He nodded. "Even though you're the boss, the whole thing is still a partnership. Everyone should really work together."

Everyone in the room nodded.

By session five we'd all learnt that a bit of charm goes a long long way. Ask for things in the right way, respect people but don't let them walk on you, be generous and then when the time came to be hard, people would still love you.

They would, he assured us. All you had to do was flatter them.

One woman, she was the one that just when we were all about to go would ask a question, spoke up. Isn't there always someone like that? Anyhow, she put up her hand, "Dick," she said. (She'd a really posh accent.) "Something is bothering me about all this. I mean, you're really telling us to be insincere with the staff. Telling them they're great when they're not."

"That's not what I'm saying." Dick sounded impatient. He

didn't like being challenged. I mean, who would when it was all so obvious? "What I mean is that it's more important to point out the good they've done than focus on the bad. Start off with that and then you can tackle the other stuff later when they're so, I dunno, enthralled by you that they'll do anything."

"Mmm." She didn't look convinced.

"Is that it?" Dick looked around.

And wouldn't you know it, someone else asked a question. "Are you telling us, Dick, that we've to sort of change to be in charge."

"Yep. If it's not in you to be the boss, just assume confidence and go for it." He looked at us.

I looked back at him. God, he was gorgeous.

"I mean," he continued, "let's be honest. We're all different people when we're at home to when we're at work, yeah?"

Most people agreed with that one.

"So it's just another step to being a boss. A mask you wear, I suppose. Like when you were in school and you thought your teacher was a bitch and it turned out she wasn't."

"That never happened to me," the posh woman sniffed.

We laughed, though I got the impression Dick didn't think it was funny.

At the end of the last session, we all went to the pub for a drink to say goodbye to one another. I'm not a pubby person but I went because Dick asked me if I'd be going down. And when I nodded he said he'd see me later.

I mean, he'd singled me out.

"So," the posh woman asked when we were all seated, "what did you make of that?"

A bit of shrugging.

"It was good," I said. "I learned loads."

The other nine looked at me. "Really?" some guy said. "I dunno, it all sounded a bit crap to me. I mean, I'll try it but I don't think it'll work."

Most of the others thought the same. I couldn't believe it. I thought he'd been great. Still everyone is entitled to their opinions, I suppose.

At about eleven Dick arrived in. There were only four of us left. "Hi," he came over to us and sat down. "Only the hardened few left then?"

"Yeah."

"Drink, Dick?" The guy who'd been doing most of the giving out asked.

"Great, yeah. A mineral water."

"What?"

"I don't drink," Dick said shortly.

I liked Dick more and more.

"Glad to see you're still here," he said in an undertone to me.

"Oh, right." I went pink with pleasure. I didn't think he'd noticed me at all during the five weeks. I'd kept my head down, admired him from a distance and didn't waste time by asking questions.

Dick's water was put in front of him. "Cheers," he lifted it to his lips.

People started to talk again. I'm awful sorry about this, but I'm useless at names. Dick had told us a trick for remembering them but I hadn't yet put it into practice. Anyhow, when the others were chatting among themselves, Dick turned to me.

"So, how'd you find it?" he asked. "The course."

"Great, really helpful."

"You should ring and let me know how you get on."

I didn't know if it was an invitation he tossed out to everyone, so I just nodded.

"Or maybe," he said, "I'll ring you."

"To see how I get on?" I asked. This guy took his job very seriously. No wonder he was so good.

"Maybe. Or maybe just to ask you out."

No way. This was a set-up. "Yeah, right."

"Or maybe I could save myself a phone call and just ask you now. How about it?"

"Me? Go out with you?"

He nodded.

I wanted to ask why. I mean, I'm not ugly but I wasn't gorgeous. Dick could have dated a supermodel. And he was so lovely and interesting and confident. And I wasn't. Still, he must have liked me a bit, so I nodded. "Well, OK, that would be nice."

He leaned over and whispered, "I liked you. You didn't waste my time with stupid questions." He made a face over at the posh woman and I giggled.

I liked that he liked me. I liked that a lot.

"Saturday, eight o'clock?"

"Fine." I gave him my address and for the rest of the night we talked and talked. About what, I don't know. Most of the stuff I talked with Dick about I can't remember now.

And before he left, he gave me a grin that almost sent me into meltdown.

Chapter Eight

Dick was sick. I could hear him in the bathroom throwing up. I think the first time he got sick was around three o'clock. I was feeding Shauna when I heard a groan from the spare room. I decided to ignore it. Then I heard it again and the sound of Dick's feet pounding across the floor into the en suite.

More groans.

Then vomiting.

Sorry to be so graphic.

For a few minutes afterwards there was silence. I hoped he wouldn't get sick again. "Please God, don't let him be sick again." I kissed the top of Shauna's head and closed my eyes.

He got sick again.

"For fuck's sake . . ." I heard him yell. Then a wrenching open of the spare-bedroom door and more footsteps until he stood in all his pyjama-striped glory in front of me. Of course I felt awful for him. I don't mean to have a jokey tone, but men are such babies when they're sick.

He looked really mad. His hair was standing on end and his eyebrows came together in a scowl.

"That is the last time I am ever going to your mother's for dinner," he shouted. "The fucking last time!"

Shauna stiffened in my arms. I heard Dick junior calling "Mammy!" from his room.

Lowering my voice, I said mildly, in a nice way, "You offered to come, Dick. You didn't have to."

"Don't play word games with me."

"Oh, Dick, I'm not. You know . . ."

"Her and her bloody lasagne. I'm going downstairs to throw it out right now." He pounded out of the room.

I heard him slamming about downstairs, looking for it.

"It's in the fridge," I called.

Dick junior peered around the door. His beautiful big eyes looked all scared. "Mammy, can I come in with you?"

"No, Dick, it's best if you stay in your own room. You know Daddy . . ."

"ARE YOU OUT OF YOUR BED AGAIN!" Dick, lasagne in hand, glared at Dick junior.

"Oh, Dick, he's only going to the toilet."

"Well, what's he doing in our fucking room then?"

"Just saying hello to Mammy and baby Shauna." Dick junior's voice quivered but he managed to look his dad in the face.

Dick didn't get a chance to say any more. He turned and fled and we heard him getting sick again.

Dick junior smirked. Then he turned and stuck his tongue out at me. And finally he trotted back into his own room.

I was glad he was happy again. He sometimes gets nightmares and it takes ages to calm him down.

Shauna had finished feeding and her eyes had closed. Gently I put her back into her basket. She was really improving. She only woke to feed at night now and when she'd had her fill, off to sleep she'd go. I looked at her for a few seconds before going to see how Dick was.

"Dick, are you —"

He pushed past me on his way out of the bathroom.

I watched him go into his room and heard him turn out the light.

Great, I thought, that's OK. I can go to bed.

"Oh, by the way," I heard him call, "you better clean up the bathroom. I'll want to use it in the morning."

I have to admit, I felt a little bit annoyed at that. I mean, sick and all as he was, surely he could flush the toilet. Gritting my teeth, saying nothing because Dick was sick after all, I entered the bathroom.

It took me a second to realise what had happened.

He'd obviously fallen while holding my mother's lasagne because bits of it were smeared all over the floor and the walls.

It was going to be some job to get it out of the carpet.

Still, these things happen. I remember the time Dick junior had painted next-door's dog with the emulsion we were keeping for the kitchen. Now that had been a toughie.

This'd be nothing by comparison.

Chapter Nine

The 'bleep' of the alarm clock woke me. Just as I reached out to switch it off, a wave of nausea hit and I was forced to lie very still. When it passed, I turned the alarm off and cursed the pressure of my life for making me feel like that.

All the tension – leaving John and trying to rebuild my life whilst looking for gainful employment – was not doing me any good.

I needed to relax a little.

And I would when I found a suitable job.

Desperation had set in big-time. I'd been to quite a number of interviews in the past few days, mostly for jobs for which I wasn't qualified.

I'd *even* gone for one on an assembly line. The interview panel had found my story of wanting a change of direction in my career hard to swallow.

"Why would a manageress of a successful restaurant in London want a job building computer parts?" a real smart-assed little prick had asked, smirking. He was about twenty, with a major ego and major acne. He wore a Copeland suit with about as much panache as an over-ripe tomato. In fact, Copeland would have sued if he had seen him.

Yep, he got on my nerves.

"You know what?" I'd said. "I don't know." I stood up. "Coming to this interview and being asked totally irrelevant questions by someone who's only twenty minutes off his mother's breast has just put me off working here."

That shook them.

I didn't get the job though.

I told my mother I hadn't bothered going to the interview. She would have died of shame if I'd told her the truth.

And now, I had to face another interview, this time for a catering assistant. And not only was I under pressure, so was my good suit. In fact, my good suit was looking just a little bit like a not-so-good suit. At this stage I was like one of those cheapo dolls that had only one set of clothes. It badly needed to be cleaned, only I hadn't much money and there was no way I was spending my meagre savings on dry-cleaning.

There was nothing else for it, I'd have to ring John and ask him to sell my car. I didn't want to ask any favours from him, but things were beginning to look increasingly dire on the job front. And on the home front. And on just about every other front as well.

Aw, to hell with it, I decided suddenly. I'll give

myself a break and go for more interviews when I get the suit fixed up.

Yawing widely and very pleased with my decision, I got out of bed and went downstairs to grab a cup of tea. The plan was to take it back to my room and have a lie-on.

I heard Mam laughing loudly in the kitchen. Then I heard another deeper voice. Thinking she was listening to something funny on the radio and would be in great humour, I walked in. There was a man, *a man*, sitting at the kitchen table with a mug of tea in front of him. A big slab of cream cake stood like a monument on his side plate.

Now, my mother very seldom has visitors. She's very private, has no friends that I can name and here she was, entertaining *a man*. And a fine big fat man at that.

"Maggie," Mam said, blushing, "this is Mr Parker that I've told you about."

"Maggie," Mr Parker nodded. Mashed-up cake peered at me from his mouth as he spoke. "Pleased to meet you." Bits of cake escaped to fly all over the table.

I couldn't quite see what Mam saw in him.

"Hello," I nodded and smiled.

"Are you not going for an interview today?" Mam asked.

Trust her to remember.

"Eh, well, I decided to give it a miss." I shrugged. "Nothing to wear." I poured myself a cup of tea. "I'm just going back to the *leaba*." I nodded goodbye to Mr P and began a hasty retreat from the kitchen.

"And what's wrong with your interview suit?"

Halted at the door. "It's scruffy."

"Oh." Mam paused. "Sure, I've loads of clothes, wear something of mine. There's a nice beige two-piece that'd fit you."

Honestly.

"Eh, mmm, beige just isn't me, Mam, I'm afraid."

"Well, Maggie, you or not, you'd want to get yourself a job."

It was the nearest thing to a lecture she'd ever given me. I was stunned. "I will, don't worry."

She frowned. If Mr Parker hadn't been there, I'm sure she would have shown me the 'lovely' beige two-piece. And maybe even forced me, in her nice way, to try it on. But she didn't.

"You're putting on weight," she said then. "That's what being out of a job does to you."

"Sloth," Mr Parker nodded. "One of the seven deadly sins."

So was gluttony, but I kept my mouth shut. Instead, I smiled brightly and said, "That's why they're called the deadly sins, 'cause they're deadly!" Ignoring Mam's 'I'm going to smile even though I'm mortified' expression, I left.

Back to bed with a nice cuppa in my hands.

Heaven.

I must have been more tired than I thought because I slept like a log. All through the morning and into most of lunchtime. I was about to embark on a dream about

John – something horrible and nasty, I bet – when I was saved by a hammering on the door.

Mam's voice, all excited, came from the other side. "Maggie, there's a phone call for you." She poked her head in and gave a cheesy, knowing smile.

"If it's John – I'm gone out with a big lump of over-sexed testosterone."

A pause whilst she digested what all that meant. Then she laughed. "Talking in riddles again – honestly," she shook her head, "I don't know *why* you just can't say what you mean."

"If I did that you'd have me out on my ear for using bad language. But," I gave a dramatic sigh, "if you insist. If it's John, tell him to f – "

"It's not John," she interrupted hastily. "It's a *man*." Big stress on the 'man.' My mother loved when men rang me. It was a sign that I was a normal heterosexual female. "*And* he wants to talk to you."

"About?"

"Oh, Maggie!" She gave me a hopeless look. "Now, I didn't go into details. That's his business."

"What does he sound like?" I asked suspiciously. I was afraid it was John, putting on an accent. He was under the impression that he was a brilliant mimic. Nobody seemed to have the heart to disillusion him.

"He sounded like a man," Mam said, puzzled. "You know, deep voice, full of authority."

"Definitely not a man," I muttered, flinging off the bedclothes and shoving my feet into my enormous *Winnie the Pooh* slippers. "Men are just full of bull-shit."

She ignored me. My cynical comments failed to agitate her any more. I was seriously losing my touch. It was called 'too long living with a moron'. I'd become soft.

She followed me downstairs, almost getting into my clothes. I swear, if I'd halted at all, she would have tripped over me and sent us both flying to our deaths. "Now remember," she whispered, just in case the male caller could hear. "Be *nice*."

I wasn't too sure what nice was. Her version and my version were poles apart.

She stood beside me as I picked up the phone. I stared hard at her and she smiled pleasantly back. So I stared some more. Eventually, she got the message and began slowly backing toward the kitchen. I waited until the door was closed before I said, cautiously, "Hello?"

"Margaret Scanlon?"

It wasn't John. I knew the voice but it took a few seconds before I could place it. "Eh, Louis, is it?"

"I knew you were the girl for us. Good manager, good memory!"

I wanted to kill myself.

"So, have you considered my, and I have to say this, very generous offer?"

Very generous, yeah, right.

"I have."

"And?" Hope sang in his voice.

"Well, I've a few other options to consider. I'll get back to you."

"Well, as I said, you don't need to do early mornings or late nights. Well, maybe the odd late night here and there because Romano, that's the homeless Bosnian I was telling you about, well, he can't do *really* late nights. *And* you'll have free rein, if you want to make a change," he paused, serious voice, "I'll be behind you all the way."

That thought was seriously scary.

"I mean," he gave a very forced laugh, "short of tearing the place down, you can do what you like."

I knew I was scraping the very bottom of the barrel when I said, "You've certainly tempted me." And he had. It was the only managerial job on offer. It was the only thing I'd be able to do. The only thing I *could* do.

"So?"

I wanted to die. "I'll give it a go."

"Great." He switched back to business mode, as if he wasn't all that bothered one way or the other. "So can you start soon?"

"Next week," I muttered. I needed time to get my head around the fact that I'd sunk this low. Oh, how the mighty have fallen. John would have cracked up laughing. But he'd never know.

"No sooner?"

"Nope." My answer sounded rude, so I modified it. "I'll just have to ring up the other places and tell them I'm not taking their jobs."

"And that'll take the best part of a week?" He gave a laugh.

"Yes, it will," I lied scathingly.

"Oh, oh right, OK." Then, "So, we'll see you next Monday, bright and early."

"I thought that I didn't have to do earlies?"

"Well – "

"You'll see me Monday," I decided to give him a break. There was no point in pushing my luck. "It'll be before opening time. I'd like to meet the rest of your staff, if that's OK?"

"Fine," he said. "No problem. They'll be dying to meet you."

I couldn't wait.

That's sarcasm by the way.

Mam poked her head out the kitchen door when I'd finished. "You got a job," she clapped her hands and looked delighted. "And in a lovely French restaurant and all."

"French?" Bewildered, I looked at her.

"Louis?" she said. "Isn't that what you called him?"

"So the French have a monopoly on that name, do they?"

"Sorry?"

"It's an Irish café, if you must know." I glowered at her.

"Great. You'll be working for the home economy, supporting your own."

"Please, Mam!" Wearily, I began to tramp back upstairs. I just had to bury myself under the covers and hope I'd suffocate.

"Well done!"

I knew she was beaming from ear to ear.

It was confirmed when a little round of applause followed. Then, "I'll bring you up a lovely lunch to celebrate!"

Mmm, that sort of cheered me up a bit.

Chapter Ten

Dick finally went back to work today. He was ill for three days and to be honest, it was a bit of a strain having him home. It wasn't his fault that we found it a strain, not at all. I mean, the last thing a sick person needs is three noisy kids around the place.

Dick just wasn't able for them.

Even when David was playing quietly with his blocks, Dick complained that it disturbed him. He let out a yell and, of course, that sent David into hysterics.

It took ages to calm the poor child down.

And by this time Dick was pacing the floor of his bedroom like a mad thing.

Honestly, it was like a comedy show.

It's something to laugh over in the future.

Anyway, the patient went back to work today. He's lost weight and he's very pale, but he said he couldn't stand being around the house any more. That's Dick, a real workaholic. I'll worry all day about him until he comes home.

At lunchtime, because Dick hadn't been in contact, I rang him. Just to make sure he was feeling all right.

Rose, his latest secretary, said that he was in a meeting and couldn't be disturbed. I explained who I was and asked her to please put me through, but she said that there was no way. "It's very important," I said.

In the end, whingeing a bit, she finally did.

I mean, I know if I didn't ring Dick, he'd get all offended and say that I didn't care about him. Then he probably wouldn't talk for a few days, so it was important that I talk to him.

"Hi, Dick, it's me," I said, when he answered.

"And?" he sounded annoyed.

"Just calling to make sure you're all right."

"Jesus!" He slammed down the phone.

I suppose he got embarrassed. I suppose I should have looked at things from his point of view. It's like when you're a kid and your Mammy kisses you in front of everyone – you want her to do it but it's embarrassing.

Still, at least he knew I was thinking of him. Dick's very insecure; he needs reassurance all the time. He normally rings me at least twice a day from work, just to make sure I'm still at home. If I'm out, he sulks. I think this whole insecurity thing comes from having a really critical mother. Whatever Dick does, it's just not good enough for Mrs Maguire. Of course, Dick doesn't see that. He thinks the sun shines out of her. Still, she's his mother, I suppose he's going to think like that.

I've told Mammy all about how badly Mrs Maguire treats Dick and so she makes a big fuss of him. And I know Dick loves it even if he does give out about her at times. Everyone needs someone to fuss over them.

Mammy rang today as well. Full of news about Maggie. Apparently she's got a job. As a manager in a restaurant. "About time too," I said to Mammy. "I mean," I said, "she has to start paying her way. She can't sponge off you."

"Oh," Mammy said, "none of my children ever have to think they're sponging off me. Home is where you go when you can't go anywhere else."

"But she can," I pointed out, in a reasonable voice. "She can go back to London. Back to John."

"Oh no," Mammy said. "Something funny has happened there, mark my words. But you know Maggie, she plays her cards close to her chest. Doesn't give too much away."

If you ask me the only funny thing that happened to Maggie was that she ever managed to land a fella in the first place. But I didn't say that. God, no.

"And," Mammy dipped her voice, "I've high hopes for her in this new job. The owner, Louis is his name – isn't that a lovely name? – he's V impressed with her. He's letting her run the whole place whatever way she pleases. She could get herself well in there."

"Mmm."

"Trapping her boss, that's the way to do it. I mean, John was only a . . . what was he now?"

"DJ or something?"

"Something," Mammy sniffed. "Something not worth remembering, that's for sure. Anyhow, that's the news. So," she asked, "how's the patient? Is he better yet, the poor lamb?"

And I had to fill her in all about Dick.

She gave me some great advice on what to cook for him, food that wouldn't upset his stomach. She's great like that.

And then she was gone.

After that, I washed and ironed. It was a great day for getting the clothes dry. Breezy and fresh.

Dick junior came home from school with a note for me to go and meet his teacher. I'm looking forward to that. Dick's so clever. Takes after his dad.

And me too, I suppose.

I used to be clever.

Chapter Eleven

Ali, my hastily acquired London flatmate, was agog. "You're a fast worka," she said in her cockney accent as she gazed at me from behind a giant pizza.

Sharing a flat with her was a serious mistake. She'd a fetish for all things junk. And I'd a fetish for eating like a pig if someone else was doing it. It dispelled the guilt of doing it on my own. Sort of like exams in school. It didn't matter if you didn't study once your friends didn't either.

"It's just the pictures," I said, feeling a bit annoyed with her comment. "It's not as if I'm going to jump into bed with him or anything." I deliberately put on my old jacket. The one that didn't quite match my navy denims. I didn't want him to think I'd made any sort of an effort.

"Wear your odda jacket – it's nicer, innit?"

"Yes."

"Oh." Ali rolled her eyes, probably convinced that I

was just another odd Irish person. She took an enormous bite of her pizza and held out a slice for me.

Oh, why did she have to do that?

I took it from her and bit into it.

"I took all the onions orf," Ali said. She lifted her slice high in the air. "Cheers."

"Cheers."

I told Dick to beep his horn when he arrived outside my house and I'd run out and meet him.

There was no way I was having him call to the door.

It's not that I'm ashamed of my family or anything, don't get me wrong. It's just, well, firstly, Daddy isn't the most sociable man. Mammy says he's shy. Every time Maggie or me bring a fella home, Daddy turns up the television or puts on music so that it's impossible to think, let alone talk.

And Mammy. Well, she's a romantic. She'd ask about a million questions, including how many kids we were planning and what sort of a dress I'd be wearing. It's not that she means to embarrass, it's just that she loves weddings and romance and stuff.

And Maggie. Well, Maggie's out on her own. Sometimes she's fine, a great laugh and other times . . . well, she's totally antisocial. She's at her worst if she's just after getting into trouble with Daddy. It's like when she gets in trouble she takes it out on me.

Anyhow, I'm wandering off the subject. Dick arrived on the dot of eight. He beeped the horn and without waiting to say 'goodbye' to any of them I flew out the door.

Dick had a big silver shiny Alfa. He was obviously very proud of it as the paintwork sparkled and even the spokes between the wheels were clean.

So I said as I got in, "Wow, your car is gorgeous!"

His eyes lit up and he patted the dash affectionately. "Yeah, she is, isn't she? Twenty-four valve, fuel-injected engine."

I have to confess that I wouldn't know one end of a car from the other. I drove my car and basically left everything else to the mechanic and the AA. Still, I managed to give a very convincing low whistle as I said, "I'm impressed."

"CD player, air conditioning, heated windows."

"It's lovely." And it was. There wasn't a stray bit of paper anywhere in it. In fact the car looked as if it was straight out of the showrooms. "All I have is a six-year-old Nissan."

"Aw well, I'd say it's big enough for you."

"Yeah, it is." I sat deeper into the seat. "But I could get used to this."

He grinned. "And I could get used to having you here."

We stared at each other. I was the first to drop my eyes. I think I was afraid of giving too much away.

"You look great."

"Thanks."

"Belt up," Dick fired the engine and the car took off.

John had a car. An old Fiesta. He tooted its horn when he arrived outside the apartment block.

Ali, not making any attempt at discretion, almost fell out the window trying to get a gawk at him. "I can't see 'im." She turned to me and glared, as if it was my fault that he hadn't got out of the car. "You'll 'aveta bring 'im up later on."

"I don't have to do anything," I smirked.

"Well, if you don't, it's the last time I'll share my pizza wiv ya!"

I hoped it would be. Maybe then I could shed a few stone. "Byeee!" I slammed the door on her.

"Oy!" she yelled, opening it up. "I'll want to be 'earing all about the end of that film!" With a cackle of laughter she was gone.

Dated comments or what?

John had the radio in his car turned up so loud that when I knocked on his window, he didn't hear me. He was strumming along to some kind of a guitar solo and had his eyes closed. He looked seriously disturbed. I stood on the path, waiting patiently for a break in the music before I knocked again. This time, his eyes flew open and he gave me a sheepish smile. Reaching across he popped open the door. "Hello," he shouted above the roar of music that had started up again. "You're looking great!" He tapped a button on a very sophisticated radio and there was instant silence.

I sat in beside him, once again feeling awkward because I didn't know what to say. "Nice radio," I muttered unconvincingly.

His eyes lit up and he turned from me to it. "Isn't it?"

"Yeah."

"It's a state-of-the-art radio/cassette system," he said. "I installed it myself."

"Great."

"I'm an electrician by day and a DJ by night."

As if I wanted to know. I felt the old familiar irritation build. The fact that this fella liked me seemed to induce it. I plastered a smile on my face and tried to clamp it down.

"I need this little baby," he indicated the stereo, "to hear all the new sounds. I get a lot of demo tapes sent in to me so it's good to listen to them while I'm on the road and, when I get into the studio, I play the best ones."

"So what station are you with?" It sounded quite glamorous actually. Me, Maggie Scanlon, seeing a DJ. Not that I was seeing him but -

"HTBS FM."

Should I know it? "Oh, right."

"Never heard of it, have you?" He looked amused. "It's actually a local station. It's good – " he frowned then grinned and in a real Irish accent finished, "crackle."

"Sorry?"

"Fun?"

"Good *craic*," I corrected managing to inject a note of hostility into my voice.

"Right." He rolled his eyes and smiled at me, totally missing the fact that I was glowering at him. "I'm always getting that one wrong." Then, starting his car, he said, "I've got a great film booked. One to make you feel right at home."

He chatted all the way to the cinema. I hardly had to

say a word, which was just as well. For the first time in my life, I was stuck for something to say to a guy. I don't know what it was. Usually my glowerings and caustic put-downs had fellas running madly in the opposite direction. But John had just smiled.

Still it was early days.

He brought me to a restaurant on the Green. A really fancy place. Before I had a chance to get out of the car, he was around the other side and opening the door for me. Mammy would have been really impressed. He put his hand on the small of my back as he escorted me into the restaurant.

"Ah, Mr Maguire," the head waiter rushed forward, "I have your table over here."

"Thanks."

"Do you came here a lot?" I whispered.

"Now and again."

The waiter pulled my chair out for me and I sat down. Dick handed me a menu. "Or would you prefer if I order," he asked. "I know all the dishes here."

I hesitated. I was a picky eater. I mean, to bring me for a meal is really a waste. It's my stomach; it seems to be allergic or something to most foods. If I eat a lot, it goes into acid overload.

Dick quirked his eyebrows. "Well? What do you want?"

I think he was trying to impress me. And I was touched. To hell with my stomach, I thought – if he wants to get me a nice dinner, I'll let him. "OK, great."

"The beef is on, that's really good here." He smiled at me across the table.

Beef was the one meat I didn't eat, but still, his smile made me go all wobbly.

"Great." *I smiled back at him. It was like I couldn't stop smiling.*

He clicked his fingers. People looked up. I was a bit mortified. I didn't think clicking fingers was something that people really actually did. No one came. Dick clicked again.

A waiter, pen poised, appeared at our table. "About time," *Dick muttered.*

I gazed out the window. I mean, I didn't want the waiter thinking I endorsed that comment. Dick gave our order and the waiter left.

"Sometimes they can be slow here," *Dick said.* "But they'll always knock a few pounds off if the service isn't up to scratch."

"Oh, right."

He reached across the table and took my hand in his. He began to trace small circles on the palm of my hand with his fingers. Small shivers travelled up my whole body.

"You look beautiful," *he said.*

"Oh, thanks."

"Your hair," *he cocked his head to one side,* "it's a shame to have it up on your head like that. You should wear it down." *He nodded at me.* "Definitely down," *he said.*

I'd spent money getting my hair piled onto my head. I felt a little offended, but I'm sure he didn't mean it.

"It's so glossy and shiny when it's down."

I went pink with the compliment. "I'll wear it down the next time," *I said.*

"The next time? So you'll come out with me again?"

I giggled.

Our starters arrived. Some kind of vol-au-vent pastry concoction. There was a sauce in it. I'm not into sauces, mainly because most of them contain garlic and, garlic and me, we're old enemies. So I broke the vol-au-vent up and scattered it all over my plate and ate a bit of mushroom.

Dinner came. Two plates with loads of beef, loads of sauce and loads of side vegetables.

I ate some potato.

I declined dessert.

Dick looked at me in amusement. "You don't eat much, do you?"

"I survive."

Over dinner he asked me all about myself. "Well . . . I, eh, work in computers as you know."

He nodded, studying me with dark brown eyes.

"I like it a lot."

"And how's being the boss going?"

I was afraid he'd ask. It was still a bit shaky. I was now doing all the work only I was giving people in the office credit for it. "Oh, fine. Early days."

"I lied on the course, you know," he said, his gorgeous eyes sparkling.

"What?"

He studied me. "Well, not everyone is cut out to be in charge – some people don't have that killer instinct." He grinned at me. "I'd say you could be one of them."

I didn't know if it was a compliment or not. I suppose it wouldn't be nice to have a killer instinct. I gave a hesitant smile and fiddled a bit with my napkin. "No, I guess I'm not like that, but, you know, I'm doing OK."

"I'm sure you are," he said and I got the feeling that he was making a joke, so I laughed.

He laughed too and changed the subject. "So, how many in your family?" he asked, leaning toward me and making me feel as if I was the most interesting person in the world. "I want to know all about you, Pamela."

And I told him about Maggie and of how she had got a job in McDonald's and how she was now in a real restaurant. And I told him about Mammy. And I told him a bit about Daddy. "He doesn't work any more. He's sick a lot. It makes him a bit moody but sure, we all understand."

Dick nodded in sympathy. "I hope he'll be OK."

He did the clicking of the fingers routine again when he looked for the bill. I went to the loo while he sorted it out. When I came out he was in deep discussion with the head waiter. I stood at the door waiting for him.

He caught up with me. "I'll have to bring you out more often," he chuckled. "They didn't charge me for your meal. I told them you ate next to nothing."

"Oh, Dick!"

"That's showing them who's boss." He tweaked my cheek. It hurt a bit. "You'd do well to remember how to do that."

And he laughed.

And I thought to myself that this was a man in complete control.

The film was great. A comedy set in Ireland. John and I

laughed in all the same places, groaned in the same places and both of us even clapped at one point. We came out of the cinema, him holding a huge carton of popcorn and both of us eating from it.

"That was good," John grinned at me. "Tell you what, I'm never visiting Ireland. You all seem to be desperately stupid over there."

"Get lost," I belted him and he began to choke on some of the popcorn.

At first I thought he was messing and then, when he began to go purple and indicate his throat, I knew it was for real. Dropping my bag on the ground and giving a squeal I began to bang him furiously on the back. He made loads of horrific noises as he tried to hack his guts up.

A few passers-by stopped for a gawk.

They began whispering among themselves and only that I was so worried about John I would have told them to get lost.

"You'd want to do a hemlock remover on him," some woman remarked eventually. "You know, put your arms around him and sort've push the stuff out."

Murmured agreement from the rest of the spectators.

John gasped as the final bit of popcorn dislodged itself from his throat. "She can put her arms around me anytime," he said weakly.

People laughed and began to move on.

"Jesus," I said shakily. "I'm sorry about that. Are you all right?"

I felt sick.

John nodded, still a bit red-faced. "Yep." He smiled suddenly and my heart unexpectedly flipped about a bit. "Thanks for saving my life," he said earnestly. "You know what that means, don't you?"

"No." I couldn't think straight.

"It means," John said, "that I have to follow you about forever. I'm your slave now until I can return the favour."

I gave a weak laugh. "Great," I said. "Sounds good. Does it mean that you can buy me drinks and stuff?"

"Anything your heart desires."

"Fine. Let's go get a drink in. I need one after that."

As if it was the most normal thing in the world, he caught his hand in mine and together we walked to the nearest pub.

It felt weird.

"Now, where were we before I nearly died?" he asked. "Oh yeah, I was wondering how come you're all so stupid over in Paddy-land."

This time, I was too afraid to give him the belt he deserved.

"So . . . well?" Maggie was still awake when I came in at five minutes to one. She crept into my room in her nightdress and settled herself on the bed. "What's the story?"

"Daddy will kill you if he sees you," I whispered. "You know the mood he's in at the moment."

"He's always in a bloody mood," Maggie giggled softly. "He's hormonal."

"Stop."

Maggie was terrible. She said the most awful things sometimes. But she was funny and she could make me laugh.

"Go on," she pressed again. "What happened with Dick?"

"Nothing much."

"Sure." She rolled her eyes.

I couldn't help the dreamy look on my face. Unwrapping my scarf from around my neck, I hugged it to me. The smell of his aftershave was on it. He'd leaned across and kissed me and he'd left a lovely smell on my clothes.

"Of course," Maggie giggled, "Mam thinks you'll be heading off to choose the wedding dress next week. And Dad says there is no way he's giving you away to a fella called Dick."

I giggled. "Did he really say that?"

"Mmm," Maggie shrugged. "Sort of. He wasn't as diplomatic with his words."

"Well, I had a great time." I sat beside Maggie and began to pull my pyjamas out from behind my pillow. "We got on fine. He's funny. Sometimes he gets quiet, doesn't say much. But, that's OK, isn't it?"

"I like them quiet," Maggie said. "In fact, I've my mind made up that I'm going to marry a deaf mute."

"Maggie!"

"I am."

She didn't sound as if she was joking. She looked sad for a second before breaking into a smile. "So, go on. Tell me. I want to know everything."

I wasn't going to tell her everything.

"Did he kiss you?"

I savoured the memory of it. A hard rough kiss, full of passion. Then he'd let me go. He hadn't looked at me, just turned on the engine of his car and said, "I'll see you again."

Again!!

The word was like magic.

"He did and I'm seeing him again."

"Great. Brilliant." Maggie hugged herself. "Only one thing. Don't go and get married too soon. I don't want to be left on my own here with the gruesome twosome."

I didn't even smile. My sister could say the most hurtful things about Mammy and Daddy sometimes. I think she thought it was cool.

"'Night, Maggie." I snuggled into bed.

She took it as her hint to leave. "'Night."

When she left I closed my eyes and relived the whole night again.

I was so happy. I don't think I'd ever felt like that before. Pure in-love happiness.

I ended up slightly tipsy and John, who was being really sensible, was stone-cold sober as we pulled up outside my apartment block.

"I enjoyed tonight," he said.

"Me too."

"D'you want to do it again sometime?"

"Maybe."

Now that the night was over and the possibility of seeing him again was more than a possibility, I was beginning to panic. I liked him. A lot. But still. . .

"John," I said haltingly, "I'm not looking for a major

serious relationship." I looked past him, out the car window. I was afraid he'd dump me if he thought I wasn't interested in a big-romance type thing.

"Aw shit," John thumped his forehead, making me jerk around and look at him. His face was twisted up in anguish. "And here was me going to propose to you and all the time you're just out for cheap laughs." More face-twisting. "I feel so *used*." He did a big tortured sigh.

"Stop," I giggled. "You're making a laugh out of me."

"I wouldn't do that." He gave me an amused glance. "Listen," he took my hands in his and I loved the warm feeling that filled me up, "I only want to see you again. Nothing heavy, right?"

"Right."

"So, would you be on for going out again?"

It scared me the relief I felt when he asked that question. Attempting nonchalance, I muttered, "Call me during the week."

"Right."

A sort of a silence. I don't think he knew what to do. I certainly wasn't inviting him up for a coffee. It wasn't because of Ali, I just didn't want to give him the wrong idea. Or maybe, my mind whispered evilly, the *right* idea.

"So, I'll see you." I picked my bag from the floor.

"You will." His eyes studied me, top to toe. "Can't wait."

What a sad life he has, I thought. "Bye."

He leaned over to kiss me and I let him just brush his lips off mine. The shock of it frightened the life out of me. I'd been kissed before, don't get me wrong, but it wasn't the softness of his lips, it was something else. Something I didn't want to think about. "I better go." In half a second flat, I was out of the car and opening the front door to the apartment building.

Why hadn't I let him go when I had the chance?

Things would only get too messy now.

That's what I told myself. But inside, somewhere deep, part of me was having a party.

Chapter Twelve

Monday. The first day of my 'illustrious' new job. My stomach felt like a rollercoaster as I braved the bus journey into the city centre.

I hadn't thought that I was nervous, but obviously I must have been because I'd got sick that morning and I felt sick again now.

John would have called it 'The Jelly Belly Syndrome'. The first time he'd ever mentioned it to me, I'd thrown a huff, thinking that he was talking about my weight. But no, he'd explained, sounding totally animated, the stomach or bowel – I'm not sure which – has its own set of nerves which are connected to the brain. That's why people got butterflies in their tummies and suffered from irritable bowel syndrome.

Stuff like that fascinated John. He'd read it out on his show. He'd take calls from listeners and have some geeky expert giving his opinion on the whole matter.

Then, he'd play a track with a title like *Bellyache* or something.

I was *so* glad I'd left him.

I still hadn't rung him to ask him to sell my car. Sitting on the overcrowded bus, I vowed to do it that night. At least then I could afford to buy a second-hand car and drive to work in comfort.

Another alarming stomach lurch. Picking up my bag, I staggered up the bus and asked the driver to let me off.

"Can't. Not an official stop." He didn't take his eyes from the road. Which on reflection was a good thing, I suppose.

"But I'm about to . . ." Heave. Another heave. "Puke."

Brakes on. Everybody thrown forward. Doors open. And I escape to vomit blissfully onto the path.

I tried not to look, as people, first wondering what the matter was, turned away once the contents of my stomach splattered themselves all over the pavement. Trying to regain some dignity, I straightened my back and, without looking around, strode purposefully on.

I ignored my shaking legs and sweaty forehead.

Instead I focused on the day to come. The staff of the bistro wouldn't know what had hit them.

Maggie Scanlon was coming to take control.

I'd asked Louis to get together all the staff that worked in the bistro so that I could meet them and have a chat with them before opening time. I'd prepared a nice speech, a sort of a 'I-might-be-the-boss-but-we're-all-on-the-same-team' type thing.

The usual crap everybody spouts but never means.

Louis had been very enthusiastic about the idea. Thought it sounded 'very managerial'.

He met me at the door as I was doing my best to push it in. Holding it ajar, he announced to the darkened interior, "This is Margaret Scanlon, everybody, your new boss."

A few mutters and grunts came from the darkness.

Louis beamed at me. "They can't wait to meet you," he whispered. He walked before me up the room. His skinny bum wiggled in a pair of navy pressed trousers; they looked as if they'd been bought from the schoolboy section of Dunnes. His black hair was slicked back with so much oil, he could have fried chips for the week in it.

Three people waited at the top of the room. *Three.* Somehow, I was expecting masses.

There was Josie, huge and well proportioned in her stripy butcher's apron. She had her arms folded and a pissed-off look on her face. A fag was dangling from her lips. Next to her was a lanky though quite handsome youth. He was Romanian or Bosnian, I guessed. Aged about twenty, he was dressed in jeans and a tee-shirt. The shirt read, *Taste it. It's nice.* A big arrow pointed in the general direction of his fly. And lastly, there was a girl, also about twenty, though she could have been younger. Dressed in a tight black skirt and even tighter black top, she had blackened eyes and spiky white hair. Her mouth moved up and down and sideways as she chewed a pink-coloured piece of gum. She neither looked impressed nor disinterested.

"This is Josie," Louis pointed to Josie.

"Hello, Josie, we've met." I tried to sound friendly yet efficient.

"Yeah, we have." Josie gave a not too unfriendly smile. "And I've met your suit as well."

The smile stiffened on my face. Mmm, I thought, Josie might be a problem.

"And this," Louis said hastily, before any more unpleasantries could be exchanged, "is Romano."

"Hello." My voice was more efficient than friendly this time.

Romano beamed widely. "Hello," he nodded. Then again, more vigorously, "Hello, hello, hello." I thought his head would fall off with the next rally of nods. "Hello, hello, hell – "

He was stopped mid-sentence with a puck in the ribs from the girl.

"Shu' up. You sound like a moron."

Romano stopped. His beaming smile grew wider and he clenched and unclenched his fists while standing to attention. The look of naked fear sort of marred his smile.

I turned to the girl.

"And this is our youngest member of staff," Louis said jovially. He nudged the girl, who inched away. She made a point of rubbing her arm where Louis had brushed off it. Louis gave a hollow laugh. "This, Margaret, is Lucy Linda."

"It's *Lucinda*. Jaysus!" Lucinda raised her eyes upwards and gave an extra hard chew of gum.

"Hello, Lucinda Jaysus." I held out my hand.

"No, I think she just meant – "

"How's it going," Lucinda said, a reluctant smile crossing her face. She gave me a sideways look and a half-hearted handshake.

"And that's it," Louis said, smiling at me, "our little company of slaves. Only," he pointed to the girl, "it's Lucinda, not Lucinda Jaysus."

I ignored him. It seemed to be the thing to do. Instead, I took a deep breath and began my little introductory speech. "Well, as you all know, I'm Margaret Scanlon. I've come to manage this bistro and hopefully get it on its feet again. Louis," I turned to Louis, who nodded and moved closer to me, "has agreed that I can basically have free rein to make whatever changes I like in order to achieve this." Romano had his hand up. "Yes?" I said, delighted that someone was showing an interest.

"I, eh, how you say, don't, eh . . ." He paused and looked at the two ladies.

"Don't what, Romano?" I asked nicely.

"Understand," Lucinda said.

"Speak English," Josie said.

Both of them began to cackle.

I really *hoped* they were joking.

"His English is a bit rusty," Louis whispered to me. "But he's a good worker."

"And what exactly does he do?" I asked. Maybe he cleaned or something.

"He serves the customers."

"Sorry?"

"So are they!" Lucinda shrieked.

Josie and her fell about the place laughing. Romano looked on, bewildered.

"How does he do that if he can't speak English?"

"Like this," Lucinda did a demo of someone serving. More riotous laughter.

Louis joined in.

I didn't think these people were taking me seriously. I didn't manage a London restaurant for five years for nothing. "I like a joke just the same as anyone," my voice had the deep freeze tone that terrified John. "But there is a time and a place. I'm here to run this place and run it I will. The first thing," I pointed to Josie, "from now on, there will be no smoking in the restaurant."

Josie looked askance at me. "Pardon?" Her voice now terrified *me*.

"Put out the fag." I held my ground. "You can smoke outside, not in here."

She looked to Louis for support. Confident that he would back me, I looked to him as well. Somehow, he'd managed to distance himself from us and was busy examining the tables.

"Louis, did you hear this?" Josie asked. "She's after telling me to put out me fag."

"Mmm."

"Louis!"

Louis jumped. "She's the manager," he mumbled.

Josie spat out some expletive or other and then locked eyes with me. We did some hard eye-to-eye combat before she turned her back and stomped off. I was gratified to see her dump the fag down the sink.

"And as well as making this place a smoke-free zone," I continued, looking pointedly at the semi-naked Lucinda, "there will also be a uniform."

"Pardon?" That was Louis.

"So," I did my best to smile at them all, despite the fact that Josie was giving me the two-fingers underneath the counter and Lucinda was glowering at me and Romano had his hand up again to ask what the hell I was talking about. "I'm sure we'll all get along great." Turning from them, I smiled at Louis, "So, Louis, let's discuss uniforms."

I ignored Lucinda's "I'm not dressing like a prat," as I followed Louis up to his office.

In honour of me, Louis must have had his office cleaned. Instead of stacks of paper scattered everywhere, they were now placed in a massive mountain in the centre of his desk. It wasn't possible to see him from behind them. Both of us moved our chairs along the desk.

"What was that you were saying about a uniform?" Louis asked. He ran his hand through his hair. "Is it not a bit . . . well . . ." he gave a nervous laugh, "a bit *drastic*?"

I was determined to do this job properly. Just because he owned the place there was no reason for me to fear him. At least I'd inherited one good thing from the years of growing up in our house. The ability to be unintimidateable. That, plus the fact that I knew what I was talking about and he didn't, made me say, in an 'oh-so-casual way', "Oh, so you'd prefer a woman in a dirty butcher's apron, a guy in jeans with a crude slogan on his tee-shirt and a half-dressed kid running the place – would you?"

"The last bit sounds good," Louis gave a weak smile.

Everything about this guy was weak. I picked up my bag as if I was going to leave.

"No! No! Hang on." His panicky voice almost made me smile. "Don't be mad. Of course you're in charge." He shook his head. "Poor Romano. Lucy Linda bought that tee-shirt for him. I don't think he has a clue what it says. But, you know, he wears it because it was a present."

"Bully for him."

I know I sounded hard. Well, I guess, I *am* hard. At least that's what everyone says. Louis flinched. Then, shrugging, he muttered, "Uniforms are a good idea."

"Good." I allowed myself to smile at him. "I'll go today and see what's on offer. I'll price things and see what you think."

"I'll have to buy them?" Horror-struck he gazed at me.

"Well, you don't expect the staff to, do you? Sure, they'd never wear them then."

He didn't say anything.

101

"Look, Louis," I put on my sincere voice, "I'm here to do a job and I'll do it but you have to trust me."

"Mmm."

"Good." Standing up, I said, "I've a list of shops here. I'll head out this morning and investigate. You're welcome to come with me."

Sighing, he stood up. "I suppose I'd better." He rubbed his hands together and emitted another weak laugh. "I know you women, spend, spend, spend. Huh, you'll probably deck my staff out in, oh . . ." he waved his hand about, "Eves Saint Laurence or something."

I grinned. "Yeah. Right."

The two of us smiled at each other.

Maybe it wouldn't be a totally horrible job after all.

Oh, every crumb will do when you're down to your last loaf of bread, the voice in my head slagged.

It sounded exactly like John taking off my mother.

Chapter Thirteen

Mammy minded the children for me this afternoon. I had to drive over to her, drop them off and then drive back to see Dick's teacher. It would have been handier if I could have just dropped the kids in to a neighbour, but all our neighbours are a bit stand-offish. Or maybe it's me. I'm not very good with people. Dick says that I always appear awkward when talking to strangers and I do. I spend all my time wondering how to keep a conversation going and then after sweating through a few opening sentences, I worry how to end it.

And I say the stupidest things.

Once, when one of the neighbours, Monica Byrne, from the house beside ours, told me her mother had died, I was so nervous I told her that it was great. Then I tried to cover it up by saying that it was better than seeing her poor mother suffering and Monica snapped my head off by saying that her mother hadn't been suffering. She'd been run over by a truck.

She hasn't really spoken to me since.

And I don't blame her.

I'd hate it if someone told me it was great that my mother was dead.

Anyway, I dropped the kids over to Mammy's, had a cuppa and left when Mr Parker called. Him and Mammy are bringing the kids to the park for the afternoon. How Mr Parker will manage to walk around a park is anybody's guess. The man is huge. And he annoys me. And it takes a lot to annoy me. But when I get annoyed I really do. I can't even talk to the man without sounding hostile.

Anyway, I got home and had a shower, put on my best suit and some make-up. It's only right to create a good impression, even if it is only your son's teacher. Plus, I'd never been to a parent-teacher meeting before and I didn't know what to expect.

I arrived at the school fifteen minutes early, so I sat in the car listening to the radio. Joe Duffy was on talking about teenage pregnancies. He was interviewing some young girl who'd had a baby at fifteen. I turned over, the story depressed me and, to be honest, I was out for the afternoon, on my own for the first time in months and the last thing I wanted to be hearing about was babies and kids having babies. I'm in my thirties and I find it hard enough to manage. What chance has a fifteen-year-old got? I turned to Today FM because there was a song playing that I liked. I just sat in the car, listening to the music and I could feel, literally feel, my body seeping into the seat.

It ended up that I was five minutes late for the appointment.

That's me. Even if I've got it right it'll go wrong.

Dick's teacher didn't seem to have anyone else with her as

I approached the classroom. She had her head down and she seemed to be writing. Miss Ryan, that's her name. She's young and pretty. I gave a tap on the door and she looked up. When she beckoned, I walked in.

"I'm sorry I'm a bit late. I actually arrived early and sat in the car and almost fell asleep. I'm sorry, I really am."

"That's no problem, Mrs Maguire."

"Pamela, please."

"Pamela." *She indicated a seat.* "Please, won't you sit down?"

I sat, knees together, clutching my bag." Relax, *I mentally told myself. I smiled and put my bag on the floor.* "So how's he getting on?" *I asked. I couldn't wait to find out. Dick was almost three months in school now and every night he'd come home with words to learn and read. I loved the way he could do it.* "He loves his reading."

Miss Ryan gave a brief smile. "I'm glad to hear that," *she said.*

"Yes. He likes school generally, really. Especially the reading." *I stopped. I sounded like a prat. As usual.*

I didn't want this girl to think that Dick's mother let him down. I sought for a question to ask that sounded reasonable. "So . . . eh, how's he doing in other subjects?"

Miss Ryan put her pen down on the desk and leaning toward me, she said softly, "Mrs Maguire, eh, Pamela, I called you in today to discuss Dick's behaviour."

"Oh." *Her tone made me uneasy. Dick's behaviour?* "What about it?"

"He seems to be having a lot of problems adjusting to school."

"Problems?"

"I'm afraid so."

I felt as if she'd hit me. "But he likes school," I said faintly. "I know he does."

"Well, he doesn't give us that impression." She said the words gently as if she knew how stunned I was. "He's unsettled, he won't sit still and he bullies some of the other children."

Now that was a lie. "What do you mean by that?" I asked. I straightened up in my seat. How dare she say that my Dick was a bully.

"He hits and punches the other boys."

For a second I didn't know what to say. Then it dawned on me. "Sure, they probably pick on him. How do you know it's Dick?"

"Because, Pamela, it's always Dick that's involved in every fight. And even in class, he pushes the other children out of his way – he seems to demand constant attention."

"He's just boisterous."

She ignored me. Instead she leaned her elbows on the desk and said earnestly, "It's up to you to have a word with him about it. Nothing too heavy. Just ask him if he always does what the teacher says or something like that. Explain to him that I'm his Mammy when he's in school."

"I'm sure he doesn't mean it." I wanted to tell her I was sure she was mistaken, but I couldn't.

"Well, have a word with him and we'll take it from there."

Take what from where? There was nothing to be done. My son was just into a bit of rough-and-tumble. That was all. Honestly, the big fuss over nothing.

"Thanks for coming in, Pamela. Hope I didn't put you out."

I'd been called in specially. I didn't want to think about it. "Well, as a matter of fact," I said haughtily, "I am a bit busy. I've got to rush."

"Bye now."

I didn't want to reply, but I had to. "Bye." I bolted out the door and the minute I got into the car, I burst into tears. Don't ask me why. I think I just felt hurt for poor little Dick junior. His dark head bent over his words, reading with his pudgy little finger and all that bitch of a teacher could say was that he was a bully.

There was no way it was true.

No way.

I called Mammy and asked her if she could keep the kids for tea. She was delighted. I told her how to make up a formula bottle for Shauna if she needed it. Then I asked her how the other kids were.

"Oh Pamela," she gushed, "we had a great time in the park. David fed the swans and as for Dick, well, he's a howl."

"Why?" I smiled. I was gazing at my red puffy eyes in the mirror and wondering why on earth I'd let myself get so upset. "What'd he do?"

"He kept holding out the bread for the swans and then he wouldn't give it to them. One bird got awful angry, puffed up its wings and everything." She stopped and chuckled, "And do you know what your son said?"

"What?"

Mammy put on a passable five-year-old's voice. "Well, if

107

you're going to have that attitude, you can do without your bread."

We both laughed. It was like a coil of tension unravelling within me.

"So," Mammy asked, "what did his teacher have to say about him?" Before I could answer, she said, "I suppose she said that he's brilliant?"

"Something like that," I lied.

"Oh, I knew it. He's a clever little boy."

There came a yowl in the background and then a man's voice, Mr Parker's I suppose, said, "Doreen, that young lad is pulling Malcolm's tail. You'd want to stop him."

Mammy laughed. "He has the poor cat persecuted. I'd better go and sort him out. Now you go and have a nice day for yourself, Pamela. Don't worry about us."

The phone clicked off.

I sat for a while, then I went upstairs, soaked my eyes in cool water and, after the puffiness and redness had gone, I changed into my jeans and sweatshirt. Taking my credit card, I decided to indulge in a little shopping for the kids. I hadn't bought new stuff for them in a long time.

Before I knew it or was even aware of it, I'd gone over the limit on my credit card. I'd bought piles of new clothes for the three of them. I'd even bought myself a few new things. Dick likes me to look nice especially when he drags me along to business dinners and things. I hate those functions but Dick says networking is very important. He says it builds up his contacts and keeps him in touch.

I'd bought myself a blue and white suit in a shop in The

Westbury Mall. Then of course I had to get shoes and a bag to match it. It was hard finding the exact shade of blue but in the end after hours of walking I eventually did. And on the way, I saw another suit that I liked so I bought it as well. I mean, when would I have another opportunity to shop on my own?

I don't know how much I spent. That's the beauty of credit. You never know until the bill comes.

At about four, I decided to go in for a cup of coffee in Arnott's. I hadn't been inside the place in ages and I hardly recognised it. I bought coffee and a cake. It was quite difficult to manage the piles of shopping and carry a tray to the table at the same time, but a man helped me.

"There you are." He put the tray down and winked at me.

"Thank you," I said gratefully.

He nodded and went back to sit with his wife or maybe it was his girlfriend. They smiled at each other and he leaned over and gave her a kiss. Nothing major, just a quick peck on the cheek.

I had to tear my eyes away from them.

And suddenly, for some reason, I couldn't eat the cake or drink the coffee. So I just sat there, watching people, letting the coffee grow cold.

Chapter Fourteen

Pamela was leaving when I arrived in from work. Apparently Mam had been minding her kids all day while she went shopping. That sister of mine has a great life.

"You've a great life," I commented jokingly as I walked past her. "Dumping the sprogs on Mam and high-tailing it into town."

"Not compared to some people," she snapped back. "Dumping jobs *and* boyfriends and high-tailing it back so Mammy can take care of you."

Ouch! Obviously Pamela wasn't in the mood for jokes.

"Don't be silly, Pamela," Mam laughed. "Sure my children and grandchildren are always welcome here." She tickled Shauna under the chin and the baby smiled.

"Yeah." Pamela's mouth went thin and straight.

"So what'd you buy?" I asked. "I hope you remembered my birthday."

"Will you go away outa that," Mam rolled her eyes

and gave me a puck on the arm. "Your birthday's not for another," she did a quick calculation, "nine months."

"It still has to be remembered," I said.

Pamela didn't even crack a smile. I swear, the day she smiles at me, her face'll throw a rave.

The sound of a car squealing made us jump.

"*Pamela!*" Mam squealed, "Look, Dick's gone out onto the road."

Pamela gave a shriek, which set the baby howling. Then she clattered down the path, baby dangling from her arm in pursuit of Dick junior. Mam waddled after her.

I stood at the door for a second or two, just to make sure Dick junior was all right. Then, kicking off my shoes and leaving them lying in the hallway, I walked into the kitchen. Mr Parker was there, eating a huge fry-up. Well, I assume it had been huge, there was only a piece of a sausage left on his plate. I'm sure if it could have, the sausage would have begged for mercy as, jowls wobbling, fork poised, salivating at the mouth, Mr P went in for the kill.

"Hello, Mr P," I said. I walked past him and put the kettle on.

"It's Geoffrey," he snapped. "If you're going to call me Mr P, I'd rather you just stuck with Geoffrey." He said it through a mouthful of sausage.

"Well, Geoffrey it is then," I smiled. "Want a cuppa, Geoffrey?"

The offer of a beverage seemed to soften his attitude. "Yes, thanks."

The front door slammed just as the kettle boiled and Mam bustled into the kitchen. "Honestly, that child is a terror. He almost got himself killed that time. He ran straight out in front of a car."

"He's all right though?"

"Oh, as right as rain!"

"And when was rain ever right?" Geoffrey Parker said. "I hate the rain."

Both of us looked at him.

"Ruins your day, doesn't it?"

A gobsmacked silence ensued. One of the unwritten rules in our house had always been never to criticise the family. Where it had come from, I don't know. It was just one of those instinctual things you learn as you grow up. Sensing an opportunity to stir it, I asked innocently as I poured him his tea, "Are you trying to say that Dick ruined your day?"

"Of course he's not!" Mam sounded outraged at the very suggestion. "We'd a great day together. I think Dick really took to you." She offered Geoffrey a biscuit.

He took about five. Not that I was counting or anything, that'd be just plain rude, wouldn't it? He didn't bother replying to Mam, just started munching away.

"And now, Maggie," Mam bustled toward the oven, "how'd your day go?" She removed a fry and placed it in front of me. "I didn't know if you would be eating in the *restaurant*," she stressed 'restaurant' and looked at Geoffrey. "She's managing a *restaurant*, you know."

"Yes, I do believe you told me." He sounded irritated. Looking at me, he muttered, "Congratulations."

I didn't bother enlightening him as to the kip my 'restaurant' was. "Ta."

"So, did you?" Mam asked. "Eat?"

The greasy fry was cooking on my plate. "Eh, yeah, I did," I lied. The fried egg had turned a browny colour. "I'm full, thanks."

"I'll eat it so," Geoffrey said. His biceps wobbled as he reached across and took the plate from under me. He stuffed the last biscuit into his mouth along with a whole rasher.

Interesting combination.

Ginger snaps and rashers.

Maybe Josie would try it out at the 'restaurant'.

The thought of it made me feel sick. "I, eh, have to make a phone call," I said. As Mam looked questioningly at me, I added pointedly, "It's private."

To my surprise, John hadn't changed our answering-machine message since I'd left. It was a ritual he had. Every few weeks he'd put another, supposedly hilarious message for any callers unfortunate enough to ring. He'd done or tried to do Arnold Schwarzenegger's "I'll be back" routine. He'd done the 'we'll answer as soon as penetration has occurred' complete with orgasmic sounds in the background. OK, I'll admit, I'd found that funny but only because he'd used his own voice. He'd done Chris De Burgh singing a version of *Missing You* and he'd done a version of Boyzone's

Coming Home Now only he'd called his *Coming Home Soon*. But the message that had been on the phone when I left almost a month ago was still there. "Hi," John said, "this is Saddam Hussein." That part was in case the caller didn't know who he was doing, which nobody did because let's face it, nobody *ever* did. "You have reached 666, the underground bunker in deepest Iraq. We're all out now, making the mother and father and brother and sister of nuclear weapons, so don't dare leave a message or they will trace it. Don't even leave a number. Thanks for calling though." A silence, then a loud explosion. Then John aka Saddam, "Shit, who put the red wire in there. AAAAGGGHHH!"

The bleep went.

"John, it's Maggie. 'Bout time you changed your pathetic – "

"Mags. Hi."

"Oh, so you were there after all."

"I was. Well, I *am* here. No past tense about it."

He sounded strange.

"Couldn't keep away – huh?" he said

"Oh, absolutely." My voice dripped in sarcasm. "That's why I'm here and you're there."

"So, why'd you ring? Gonna beg me to let you come back? It won't work, you know. I can't be treated like this."

"Then you'll be relieved to know that I only rang to ask you to sell my car for me."

Silence.

"John?"

"I heard you." He paused. Then in a lonely kind of a voice he said, "Mags, what's gone wrong? Can't we talk it over?"

I hated when he sounded like that. It annoyed me. "There's nothing to say. All I want is for you to sell my car. You can bin everything else."

"Just tell me what to do, Mags. I'll do it."

"Good. Sell my car."

"Mags – "

"Bye, John."

"Please, Mags, come on!"

I gave a sigh, trying to convey how bored his begging was making me. "Just sell my car, John. Will you do it or do I have to do it myself?"

"Naw, I'll do it but – "

"Fine. Bye."

Yep. I know. I'm hard. I have to be.

I put the phone down.

Behind me I heard the kitchen door softly clicking closed.

My mother had never learned the meaning of privacy.

I didn't want to go back into the kitchen and have to answer her questions. Instead, I sat on the stairs, chin cupped in my hands, wondering, not for the first time what the hell I was doing.

I sat there for ages.

And then I went to bed.

Chapter Fifteen

Dick found my new clothes tonight. I'd hidden them in the back of the wardrobe about a week ago in the hope that I could casually bring them out in time.

"What are these?" He held up my navy suit and bag.

"Oh, just a few bits and pieces I picked up in the sales." I was pulling my jumper over my head, getting ready for bed. I didn't want to look at Dick's face.

"And when did you go shopping?"

"Last week, when Mammy took the kids." I slid my skirt off and quickly pulled my nightdress over my head. I sat on the bed, my heart thumping.

"You left our children with your mother while you went shopping?"

"Uh-huh." Picking up a hairbrush I began to do my hair. It kept my mind occupied. "You know the kids, they can be a bit of a handful. Dick keeps pulling the emergency switch on the escalators and the security men go mad." I laughed to show Dick that I thought it was no big deal. "And poor

*Shauna wouldn't be able for a day in town. It's too cold for
her."*

*"Well, you shouldn't have gone then." He tossed my new
suit on the bed and glared at me. "Anyhow, I don't like our
children being around at your mother's too much."*

"She takes good care of them and, anyway, they like her."

"Kids like anyone who lets them do what they want."

*I said nothing, just climbed into bed and pulled the duvet
over me. He had a point, I suppose. Mammy lets the kids
away with murder – if she had them all the time, she'd have
them ruined. But she didn't have them that much.*

*I felt Dick getting into bed on the other side. Now that
Shauna was sleeping the night, he'd rejoined me. I hoped and
prayed he'd leave me alone. It had been a stressful day and all
I wanted to do was get some sleep. There'd been another note
from Dick junior's teacher. I'd found it in his bag when I'd
taken out his lunch box. It had just said that Dick was still
disturbing the other children and for me to have a word with
him. I had to sign the note to show I'd read it. I didn't know
what to do. I was afraid to tell Dick about it, he'd go off the
deep end altogether. Or maybe he wouldn't. It all depended on
his mood.*

"So why'd you hide the suit?" Dick asked.

*My heart thumped. "I didn't," I lied. "It must have fallen
down by accident."*

*"What? Fallen down and made its way right to the back?
That's some suit you bought."*

*His tone was jokey. I loved him when he sounded like that.
"Maybe that's why I got it cheap," I replied. "It's got powers
of mobility."*

"Well, as long as it's mobility extends to me being able to tear it off you whenever I want."

"You never know your luck."

He rolled over into the middle of the bed and reached out for me. He ran his hand up and down my arm. "I'm glad you bought it," he whispered. "You'll be able to wear it to the dinner next week. Bet you'll look great."

I tried to smile. Oh God, not another torturous dinner. Dick wrapped his arms around me and kissed me.

I tried to respond but all I could think about was the horror of sitting down to dinner with Dick's contacts.

"What's wrong?" He withdrew sulkily.

"Nothing." I tried to get near him again. Dick was very sensitive about having his advances rejected.

"You've gone all frigid on me."

"No, Dick, that's not true. Come here." I patted the place beside me in the bed but he looked at me darkly.

"Don't patronise me. I know when I'm not bloody wanted."

"Shush, don't wake the kids, Dick."

"The kids, the kids. That's all you ever – "

Shauna began to cry.

"Jesus Christ." Pulling the duvet around him he jumped out of bed. "You might as well see to her now. I'm going into the spare room."

I don't know whether I was glad or sad to see him go. I knew one thing though. I'd be sorry in the morning.

The whole house was woken up this morning. Dick was in a towering rage. I knew it was only because he hadn't got what *he'd wanted last night but he made out it was because he couldn't find his black tie.*

"Where's my black tie?" he thundered, slamming open my bedroom door. "I can't find it anywhere!"

Shauna, ever the light sleeper, began to howl.

"Jesus, does that kid ever shut up!"

I reached over to Shauna's Moses basket and plucked her out. Holding her against me as tears squeezed from her eyes, I tried to say calmly, "You upset her, Dick. She was asleep and you woke her."

"Well, you've upset me. Where the fuck have you put my black tie?" He strode over to the bed and glowered down on us. Shauna was nuzzling, looking for my breast. I knew if I started to feed her, Dick'd get even more enraged. Sighing, I got out of bed and padded over to the wardrobe. "All your ties are in here. I always put them there."

The door creaked open and Dick junior peered around.

"Get back to bed, you!" Dick shouted.

He hesitated, looking wide-eyed at us.

"I'll be in in a minute, honey," I said.

"Not if you don't find my tie you won't." Then, "BED!" Dick junior fled.

"Here," I reached in and pulled a black tie from the tie rack. "Is this what you want?"

"No. I have a lighter black one."

He didn't and both of us knew it. "Well, Dick, that's the only one there." Shauna had calmed down, her body snuggled into mine. I tried to keep my voice low so that she wouldn't start to get frightened again.

"I have another one."

119

He was like a big baby, standing there, arms folded with his black shirt open to his waist. Dark tousled hair fell across his forehead. "I'll look for it later," I said, holding out the tie to him. "Use this for now."

"Jesus!" He yanked it out of my hand and bad-temperedly began to button up his shirt.

"Here, let me." I put Shauna on the bed and began to do his shirt up for him. Then I took the tie from his hands and tied it for him. He scowled all the time.

He looked lovely. Black suited him. He reminded me of what Heathcliff might have looked like in Wuthering Heights.

"Mammy!" It was Dick junior. "Can I come in now?"

I looked questioningly at Dick. He shrugged and stomped from the room. "Yes, honey, come on."

Dick junior arrived in. He bounced onto the bed and gave me and Shauna a hug. I knew I'd have to get up and make Dick his breakfast soon so I didn't want to get too comfortable.

For a second, a flash of what my favourite fantasy used to be shot through my mind. Me, Dick and faceless kids all snuggled up in bed together on rainy Sunday mornings, eating toast and joking with one another.

Too much naiveté and too many episodes of The Waltons.

But, even though I knew it wasn't a realistic thing to want, I felt sad.

Lately, I'd been feeling like that a lot.

It must be postnatal blues.

He'd sat through breakfast, eating without saying anything. I hated when he was like that. At least when he gave out you knew where you stood, but silence could mean anything. The kids knew it too. Dick ate his cornflakes up without a pause and David, the lamb, sat up straight in his chair instead of slouching like he normally does. Slouching drives Dick insane.

Shauna sat and smiled around at everyone from her bouncer.

But no one dared to respond to her gurgles and coos.

Still, I do have sympathy for Dick. He is under a lot of pressure at work and not being able to find things in the morning does just add to things. I'll have to persuade him to take a break later in the year. Meantime, I made a mental note to ask him what he wanted to wear and lay it all out for him every night. That way neither he nor the kids need get upset.

It was a bit of a relief when he left for work though.

I dressed Dick junior for school and made his lunch up for him. David was playing with his blocks and Shauna had fallen back asleep. As I was brushing Dick's hair I said idly, "Dick, d'you remember what I said to you last week about always doing what the teacher says in school?"

I felt him tense.

"Well? Do you remember?"

"Yeah." He pulled away from me and started banging the toes of his shoes on the carpet.

"Don't do that. Dick, you'll ruin your shoes."

"I won't."

"You will."

"Won't."

"Will."

He stuck his tongue out and ran off.

Kids, huh?

Chapter Sixteen

Josie picked up the frilled green apron of her new uniform with an expression normally reserved for handling someone else's dirty knickers. "This is poxy lookin'. There is no way I am getting into this."

"Well, Josie, now," Louis licked his lips and looked nervously in my direction, "Margaret says it'll look more professional. Give the place an air of, you know, professionalism."

"I'll give *her* professionalism. Professionalism, me arse. How does a frilly green apron and a white smock make you cook better chips? Huh? You tell me that, Louis Devine."

"Well, now, that's not exactly . . ."

"It makes *you* look more professional, Josie," I said icily.

"As in?" she spat.

"As in the fact that you now look as if you're working in a restaurant and not a butcher's shop."

"Nobody objected to what I wore before." Another glance at Louis. "Did they?"

"Well . . . no, but – "

"There you are." She pushed her uniform away. "If it's not broke then don't fix it." She placed her hands on the counter and smirked at me.

I could hear Lucinda catch her breath. She hadn't put on her uniform either. I think she was waiting to see what would happen with Josie. It was make-or-break time. I took a deep breath and slowly pushed Josie's uniform back at her. "It's important you wear it, Josie, for the sake of the restaurant."

Lucinda blew a big bubble with her gum.

Romano, the only one to have donned his uniform, calmly poured himself a coffee. I don't think he had a clue what was going on or, as in this case, not going on. He began to hum.

Louis said placatingly, "Yes, yes, for the sake of the restaurant, Josie."

Lucinda snapped, "Romano, will you shut the fuck up. You're annoying me."

Josie said, "The restaurant, me arse."

Romano looked at Lucinda and said, "Hello."

I said, "Josie, you're a valuable member of staff – "

"Oh, a very valuable member," Louis chimed in.

I gritted my teeth and continued, "And it would be a shame if you didn't co-operate. We'd hate to lose you."

"What do you mean, lose me?" Josie.

"What do you mean, lose her?" Louis and Lucinda.

"Shut up, yous. I can ask me own questions!" Josie

glared at them and then at me. "I've been here twenty years. There is no way you can fire me."

I folded my arms and shrugged. I don't know what sort of a deal she had with Louis but then again, she probably didn't either. But I knew he'd told me I could have free rein and though I hated to fire people, Josie wouldn't really be a loss. Chips was about all she cooked. Sometimes she did burgers and maybe the odd sausage and rasher.

Not exactly a menu to tempt the palate.

The silence stretched on as Josie made her decision. Lucinda fled into the loo to change and Romano gave himself another coffee refill.

"First no smoking and now this!" Josie yanked her uniform from the counter and stomped into the loo. "Bloody mad. As if a uniform is going to make people come in here. The poor Bosnian regulars will run back out again. Huh, the last thing they want to see is a frigging uniform!" The toilet door was slammed shut behind her.

"Well done," Louis made exaggerated mopping motions to his brow. "Tough call."

I ignored him.

Now that the drama was over, I felt a sense of anti-climax. I hated to admit it, but I'd have loved a fight. I was angrier than I realised and I don't think it was just at Josie.

I walked past Louis and got myself a coffee. Sitting down, I stared out the window and if I'd been on my own I would have screamed.

It was my first full day working in the restaurant. I'd

been there a week and a half and so far I'd spent most of my time searching for reasonably priced uniforms. I'd popped in and out but it was my first day to observe just how everything worked and what our busy times were.

Breakfast was quiet enough despite the fact that *Louis' Bistro* did a good-sized breakfast. Sausages, rashers, pudding, egg and beans all for under two quid. I couldn't understand where all the customers were.

"Is there another place around here that does breakfast?" I asked Louis.

"Naw," he shook his head, unconcerned. "I just think most people don't eat breakfast any more."

The man was a moron.

"I think we need to advertise the fact that breakfast in here is so reasonable," I said. "You know, run up some posters for the front window, hand out flyers, that sort of thing."

"Mmm." He looked uncomfortable. "Won't that cost money?"

"Oh no," I shook my head. "There's like *loads* of people willing to do it for free out there. Just ask. Ask and it shall be given unto you."

"Very droll."

I shrugged. "It'll not cost much and anyhow, you need to speculate to accumulate."

"Yeah," he said glumly. "No pain no gain."

"That's the spirit."

"I was never one for pain really."

I walked off and left him. He'd come round. He had to.

There was a customer at the counter. A well-dressed fella, about my age. He had *The Irish Times* under his arm so I knew he definitely wasn't one of the regulars.

"Yes?" Romano smiled at him.

"A breakfast please and a cappuccino."

Cappuccino?

"Sit," Romano said with another smile. "One minute."

I intervened. "Sorry, we don't actually do cappuccino."

The fella looked confused. "Oh. Well, I had one yesterday."

"You did? Here?"

"Yes. That lady there got it for me."

Josie pretended not to notice him pointing at her. She continued frying her sausages.

"Oh, right." I shrugged. "Sorry, I must be mistaken. I'm the new manager here." I held out my hand, "Margaret Scanlon."

"Patrick Doyle."

"Well, sit down, Patrick. We'll have your breakfast in a minute."

I watched him go to a seat by the window and open up his paper. Josie continued with her frying. "He wants a breakfast and a cappuccino, Josie."

"Mmm, I heard."

"I wouldn't mind a cappuccino either."

Deafening silence. "Well?"

Lucinda, who was manning the till began to shake. She put her head down and kept on shaking.

"Is there something funny, Lucinda?" I barked. This job was getting worse by the day.

"I think . . ." Lucinda spluttered, "I think . . . that maybe . . . the cappuccino machine might be out of action." More giggles.

"Sorry? What exactly is going on here?"

"Excuse me," Josie elbowed me out of her way as she shoved the fry-up at Romano. "Here, for the young fella by the window."

"Hello?"

"For him." Josie talked louder as if that would somehow make Romano understand. "Over there." She did a big gesture.

Romano nodded and scurried across the room.

"He wants a cappuccino, Josie."

"And I'm gettin' it." She gave me a look that would have floored Mike Tyson.

Lucinda exploded.

Josie took out a sachet and a cup. She then proceeded into the back room and there came the sound of gurgling and splurting and sizzling. Out she arrived with a frothy cup of coffee which she handed to Romano.

I couldn't say anything. Slightly dazed I walked into the back room. It was filled with boxes of supplies and a kettle of boiled water. "Josie," I called.

In she came with a mutinous face on her.

"What is going on?"

"Well, Louis thought it was a good idea."

"What was?"

"The cappuccino machine."

"*What* cappuccino machine?"

"Well, I make the sounds of it. No one knows the

difference, well, hardly anyone. We just use the packet stuff and we charge a fortune for it."

"You're joking."

"No." She had the grace to look uncomfortable. Defensively, she added, "Well, Louis thought it was great. He pays me extra."

I didn't bother arguing. "From lunchtime today, the cappuccino machine is broken, all right." I turned on my heel and walked out of the room.

I know he owned the place but Louis was in for it. I was going to throttle all his money-saving ideas out of him.

He saved cold sausages and reused them. The same with rashers. He bought yesterday's bread from the shops at 'real cut-down rates'. He 'recycled' tea-bags. He paid Josie and Romano extra for cleaning up at night and serving food at the same time.

"That's not easy," he justified himself. "Not just anyone can clean *and* cook."

"That's because nobody should." My fight was going to happen. My blood was boiling. "It's like saying not just anybody can stand for twenty minutes in nuclear radiation. It's totally stupid to do it anyhow."

"Aw, well, you have your opinion and I have mine."

"This whole place could get shut down in the morning if you don't clean up your act."

"Oh, don't be overreacting. We've survived all that stuff."

"Louis, if you don't start taking me seriously, I will

leave." He made to say something and I said firmly, "I mean it. Your staff are uncooperative."

"Didn't they put on their uniforms?"

"Wonderful."

"And isn't Josie going to stop doing her cappuccino machine?"

I bit my lip.

"Though why she should, I don't know."

I ploughed on. "I want money to advertise breakfast *plus* I want to employ a real cleaner."

"Mmm."

"I also want Josie to learn how to cook a few more dishes."

"The words old dog and new tricks come to mind."

"The words spice of life and variety come to my mind."

He looked puzzled. "And what would that mean?"

"I want you to tell Josie that she's going to have to cook an alternative dish every day along with her chips. Just one other dish. Surely she can cook something else?"

Louis bristled. "Of course she can. She *is* or was a chef."

"Good."

"Only you can tell her." Louis put his minuscule head down and pretended to be studying the paper. "You are the manager."

I suppose he had a point.

I was knackered as I left work that evening. The day had been a complete disaster. Josie, though, had agreed to cook extra meals. Surprised by her co-operation, I'd said nicely, "You can decide. Just give me the order for whatever foods you need."

"Fine."

Then her and Lucinda had started whispering. I knew it was about me. I think they thought I was a bitch. Still, that's the way the boss is meant to be.

They hadn't liked it in London. They were hardly likely to be different here.

But *I* was different. The way they whispered hurt me. In London I hadn't cared. Maybe it was because in London I'd had John to come home to and things hadn't seemed so bad with him around . . .

I pushed him out of my head.

To top the night off properly, I fell asleep on the bus and missed my stop. The driver woke me up at the terminus and I had to walk about a mile home.

Mam made the comment that walking would do me good. I was getting plump, she said.

Ignoring her I stomped upstairs.

It wasn't like my mother to criticise. I wondered if she was trying to drop subtle prying hints. But that wasn't my mother's style.

She believed that ignorance was bliss.

And I was doing my best to believe it too.

Chapter Seventeen

John's parents were dead. He had one brother and no sisters. His brother's name was Rat and he was a smack-head. Not a real one though, John assured me, Rat was just going through a difficult time. "But he's there, Mags," John said earnestly, during one of his more serious moments, "and he'll always be there and I have to look out for him. D'you mind?"

"No." And I didn't. It made me feel . . . I dunno . . . sort of safe or something.

"It's just," John said, "the last girl I went out with couldn't handle it. I mean at first she was great but then, well, things started to get to her."

I didn't want to hear about other girls. "She must've been a selfish bitch," I smirked. "I'm not like that. I'm dead nice."

"She was dead gorgeous though."

I hit him for that.

And after he'd laughed, I'd asked, "Was she?"

"What?"

"Was she gorgeous?"

"Yeah."

"Oh." Bastard, I thought,

"Not as gorgeous as you though." He wrapped his arm around me and planted a kiss on my cheek. "You're cutiful."

"Huh?"

"Cute and beautiful."

And I fell in love with him right at that moment.

And I pushed all the panicky, sick feelings away, as far back into my head as they would go.

Dick was a private person. It was something of a shock to discover that. I mean, he was so chatty and funny and everyone in my work thought he was gorgeous. In fact, I think they were wondering how I managed to get him but they never said that, of course.

I'm going on again, amn't I?

Like I said, Dick was a very private person. He didn't seem to like me asking questions about his family.

Well, as he eventually told me, he had no family. Just a mother.

She lived in Cork. "When I moved out of home, she moved down to Cork," he said.

"Oh."

He shrugged. "She's great."

"And your dad?"

Another shrug. "I dunno. He's gone now. I think he's dead. But my mother's great. She worked hard, days and nights, to make money for us. She sent me to college, the lot."

"She sounds wonderful."

"She is."

"And," I snuggled up to him, we were in his car, "have you had any other girlfriends?"

I felt him tense beside me. "What have you heard?"

"Nothing or I wouldn't be asking."

He relaxed, ever so slightly. "Why d'you want to know? I mean does it matter?"

"Well, I've told you about mine."

"Yeah, your complete lack of them."

His tone made me flinch. But he couldn't have said it to hurt me, Dick wasn't like that. "Only because I didn't want them," I gave a bit of a laugh. "I only go for the ones I want."

"How nice." He shrugged me off and started up the car. "Listen, we'd better be getting back."

I was so hurt by his shrugging me off that I forgot about the girlfriend question and the fact that he'd never bothered answering.

The fact that John's parents were dead cheered me up greatly. Let's face it, it meant that I wouldn't have to impress them. I just knew that if they'd been alive they wouldn't have been too thrilled with me – I was probably the sort of girl they'd warned John about.

And then when he'd told me about his brother being a druggie, I'd had a fleeting moment of pity.

Then I'd been thrilled.

No brother to impress. Unfortunately, though, I

would probably still have to meet him. And I knew he'd hate me. Most people did.

So far I'd managed to avoid meeting John's friends or anyone close to him. I told John that I wasn't into meeting loads of people, which I wasn't, but the real truth was that I knew they'd all see me for what I was.

A total fraud.

I don't know how I'd managed to con John into thinking that I was a 'cutiful' cuddly funny woman but I knew for sure there'd be no conning his friends. They'd see me for the ugly, fat cow I really was.

And I don't have low self-esteem. I'm just a realist. I call a spade a spade. Always have done, more's the pity.

I met one of Dick's ex-girlfriends by accident.

We were in town. Dick loved shopping. Well, he loved going shopping with me. He was a rare breed, a man who would come into all the boutiques, wait while I tried on clothes and actually offer his opinion.

Girls giggled at him as he'd study me critically. "Naw, it makes your hips look big," he'd say. "We'll go somewhere else."

And we would. We used to spend Saturdays traipsing town. Dick had good taste. Most of the stuff I bought when he was with me looked great on me. And if he wasn't there and I bought something, he'd have a fit. "I dunno what you did for clothes before I came along," he teased. And I didn't either.

I don't know how he fancied me in the things I used to wear.

Anyhow, we were in town. I was up at the desk buying a

pair of trousers and Dick was standing behind me. He was caressing my shoulder ever so softly as I counted out some cash. And then, suddenly he wasn't caressing any more. His nails were digging into my shoulder blades.

"Ouch!" I turned and shrugged him off. Only he wasn't even looking at me. He was staring at a girl behind me in the queue.

A small skinny girl with shoulder-length brown hair. And she was staring back at him and her eyes were wide and her face was white. She held a cerise pink top in her hands and she looked as if she was frozen. I mean, her hands sort of held the top at arm's length and that was it.

"Come on." Dick came out of his trance. "Let's go."

"But I haven't paid – "

"I said, let's go." He grabbed me by the arm and started pulling me to the shop door.

The girl with the pink top bowed her head and someone, a woman, put her arm around her shoulder. Then the someone began to march towards us and Dick began pulling me harder. I dropped the trousers and let him yank me out onto the street. But he hadn't been fast enough. Pink-top's friend arrived out after us. "What are you at, Dick Maguire?" she yelled. "Trying to follow her now, are you? Well, she's well out of it!"

I thought Dick would walk away. Or maybe I hoped he would. But he didn't. He advanced on the girl. His face was twisted up in a sneer and I was frightened.

"Follow her?" he sneered. "I wouldn't follow that tramp into Paradise!"

"Well, just as well because you'll never get into Paradise the way you treated her."

"Gimme a break. She was a slut! A bloody slut!"

135

"How dare you! How – "

I had to stop this – people were looking. I grabbed Dick by the elbow. "Dick, come on, please!"

"Stay out of it, Pamela!"

The girl turned to me. "Are you with him?" she asked in disbelief.

"Yes. Yes I am." I made my voice strong.

"Well, you'd do well to – "

"Let's go, Pamela." Dick cut the woman short. He seized my arm and dragged me off down the street.

The woman yelled something after us but I didn't catch it.

When we'd gone about halfway down the street, Dick let me go and his whole body seemed to slump.

"Dick, what was all that about?" I dreaded asking because I knew he didn't like talking about himself, but I mean, I had to ask. Any normal person would have to ask.

"Remember you wanted to know about my ex?" Dick said. His voice was low, barely audible. His eyes were down and he seemed very upset. "Well, the girl in the shop, that was her. Nicole."

"Oh." We'd stopped walking. I put my hand out and clasped his. "D'you want to tell me about it?"

Slowly he nodded. "Not here though. Let's head back to my place."

And although I knew what he was going to tell me wasn't going to be pleasant, my heart soared. He was bringing me back to his apartment. I'd never been there before. It was another step in our relationship.

I met Rat by accident.

John and I had gone to John's house as John had offered to cook dinner. Rat was in the kitchen when we got there.

"I thought you were going out," John said to him.

Rat, who was sitting at the table lifted his head to look up. He fixed me with his gaze and asked, without looking in John's direction, "Who the fuck is that?"

"That's Maggie," John said. He didn't elaborate. "I thought you were going out."

"Yeah, so you said." Rat stood up. He looked like a rat, all long skinny limbs. Dark greasy hair was caught up in a ponytail and it hung down his back. He wore a black tee-shirt and I could see needle marks marching up the lengths of his arms. The sight shocked me so much that I gasped. From what John had said, I thought he was only a casual user.

"Hello, Maggie," Rat slithered towards me. He grinned and held out his hand. "Welcome."

"Hi," I stammered, trying to smile. I held out my hand and he took it.

And he squeezed.

"I suppose John's told you all about me?"

I looked to John for support and he answered, "Yeah, yeah, I have. Now will you bugger off while I – "

"It must be serious so," Rat still had hold of my hand. "John only tells his deep dark shames to the serious ones."

"You're not a deep dark shame," John strode towards us. "Now will you let Maggie's – "

"Has he told you I killed my parents?" Rat asked. He stared at me with dark sunken eyes.

137

"Eh, no. No, he hasn't." I badly wanted him to let go my hand. I didn't like being touched. Not by strangers. My heart began to speed up.

"Oh, so there's still some brotherly loyalty left then, is there?" Rat dropped my hand and turned to John. "Good on you, bruv."

John said nothing. He just gazed hopelessly at him.

"I'm heading out now. Make you happy, does it?"

"Yeah."

The two brothers glared at each other.

"Well," Rat was the first to drop his gaze, "I'm all for making you happy. You know that."

He pushed past me, knocking me sideways.

The front door slammed and he was gone.

"Eh, that, that was my brother," John said. "Sorry about that."

He turned away and began to put on the dinner.

Dick's apartment was beautiful, like something out of a magazine. Chrome and black. See-through coffee-tables. All the fridge magnets arranged in neat rows.

"This place is beautiful," I said as I stood in his little hallway. Attempting to cheer him up, I gave him a puck and joked, "Did you plan to have me here anyway? Did you just have it cleaned?"

He looked genuinely puzzled. "No."

"So how long have you lived here?" I asked, following him down the hallway. It couldn't have been too long; the place still looked new.

"Ever since I left home. Five years now." He looked

around, jangled his keys, "It needs to be done up. The paint isn't as bright as it used to be."

"Will you get a grip," I wrapped my arms around him. "Our house at home is like a tip compared to this place."

He didn't even smile. Instead he shrugged me off and said lightly, "Well, I like stuff to look good. I mean, what's the point otherwise?"

"Oh, yeah, me too." I followed him out into his kitchen. This time though I didn't say anything. I didn't want him to think I wasn't used to places looking nice. Our house was nice only not as nice as this. His kitchen was like, well, it was like a hospital I suppose. In the nicest possible way. It was white and bright and clean.

"Tea?" Dick asked, shoving on the kettle.

"Fine." I watched him making the tea. He took things down from the press and when he'd used them he put them back up in the press. I liked that.

Order.

"Nicole never appreciated this place," he said as he carried our cups into the living-room. "She hated my taste. She hated everything about me."

My heart literally ached at the hurt in his voice. "Well, I think it's lovely."

He grinned gratefully at me. "You're brilliant, Pam, you know that?"

And I knew that whatever he was going to tell me, I'd understand.

John was mostly silent as we ate the meal he'd prepared. He talked a bit about his radio show the following night, apologised for the state of the kitchen and the rest of the house and that was it.

Tense atmosphere.

I, normally being the expert on creating tense atmospheres, hadn't a clue how to disperse one. After a mad search as to what to say, I muttered lamely, "Your brother doesn't look much like you."

John's head shot up. He looked sharply at me and said, "Thanks – I think."

"No, I didn't mean that he was . . . or that you were . . ." Gulp. "What did he mean when he said he killed your parents?" The question shot out of my mouth. It seemed to hit John around the face and then it bounced off the walls where it died a death.

"Shit." I looked down at my half-eaten dinner. "Sorry."

"Don't be."

"No, it was awful rude of me. I didn't mean . . ."

"My mom and dad died in a car smash. Rat was driving."

"Oh."

"He was drunk at the time." John spoke to his plate. "He's been a mess since it happened. That's why, he's, you know, dabbling in drugs and stuff."

I didn't know what to say. It didn't seem right to tell John that Rat looked as if he was *wallowing* in drugs and stuff, never mind –

"I'm sorry you had to meet him like that, Mags, and I know, right, that you said you could deal with him and I *have* been holding off introducing him to you in case it would put you off, but, well . . . look," he leaned towards me and said sombrely, "I'd understand if you didn't want anything more to do with me. We're sort of a package in a way, me and him. Just until he stops doing the drugs though," he finished hastily. "Once he stops, that'll be it. I'll be on my own."

"What?" Confused, I looked at him.

"I'd understand if you, you know, didn't want to see me any more."

He was afraid I'd dump him. Me?

He'd been afraid of me meeting *his* family!

And it looked like, the way he was talking, that I didn't have to impress anyone. John was the one trying to impress. I wanted to laugh with relief. Laugh until I ached.

Laugh until I got sick.

"I'm fine with that," I said as calmly as I could. "Honestly."

And with those words it was like the tension seeped out of the room. John sat still for a second, before saying slowly, "You're brilliant, Mags. Really."

Guilt hit me.

"I don't deserve you," he said then.

If I'd been the great person he thought I was, I would have put him straight. I would have said, "Nope, it's the other way round." But I didn't. I just smiled and let him think what he wanted.

It was nice that way.

We were sitting in the dining-room. Two mugs of tea were on the glass coffee-table. Dick had his arm around my shoulder and he was running his hands through my hair as he spoke.

"I met Nicole about two years ago," he said. "She was nice girl, funny and witty. I started seeing her and things were going great."

I kept the smile on my face. I mean, it's the last thing you want to hear, isn't it? That your boyfriend had a good time with his ex?

"Anyhow, she got promotion in work," Dick said, "and then things started falling apart. She was never at home when I rang, she worked late all the time. And to make things worse, she was working with this guy who was literally mad for her."

"And what happened?"

Dick shrugged. "We started fighting. She accused me of trying to wreck her career. According to her I was hassling her. Me?" Dick laughed bitterly. "Of course I was bloody hassling her, every time I rang there was no answer from her place. So I had to keep ringing, didn't I?"

I nodded. What a horrible way to treat someone, I thought.

"Anyhow, she told me she wanted to end it and . . ." he gulped, looked ashamed. "Well, I grabbed her hard and sort of shook her and begged her not to leave. I think I frightened her a bit but bloody hell, what was I supposed to do? And then, well, she left. And I just know she started seeing that fella in her office. I just know it."

"That was awful."

"Yeah, if she had just been straight with me I wouldn't have hit her."

"Hit her?"

*He stiffened and looked down at me. I know I looked
shocked. "Well, not hit," he said, "just the shaking, you
know. I mean, Pamela, I was in bits. I loved her like mad."*

I hated that he'd loved her.

*"I mean, I'd never have done that only for I loved her, you
know."*

I did know.

"And now?" I asked. I was afraid I'd cry.

*"And now what?" He studied me. A hint of a grin about
the corners of his mouth. The first smile he'd given since the
afternoon. He pulled me to him, rested his head on mine.
"And now I've got you," he whispered. "I don't need her."*

And he kissed me.

And I knew he loved me too.

My happy feeling didn't last too long. John wanted to
know all about my family. "Go on," he said, "I've told
you all about mine. Even about Rat, the skeleton in the
cupboard."

"There's a whole graveyard of skeletons in our
cupboard," I said. I was slightly tipsy otherwise I'd
never have said anything.

I think he thought it was a joke. He laughed.

"And I haven't been as lucky as you," I said. "Only
my dad is dead."

That wiped the smile from his face.

"Ooops, sorry," I said. That was the drink talking. I
wasn't a bit sorry. "You probably loved your parents."

"Yeah, I did."

"Well, good for you."

"And you don't?"

We were in his sitting-room, a horrible affair with scratchy orange chairs and bare boards. John had said that with Rat being the way he was, Rat'd hock anything to buy a fix so John literally had to lock all his good stuff in his room. There was nothing nice in the house at all. We were both on the couch and he had his arm around my shoulder. I was looking away from him. It made talking easier.

Well, in my opinion anyhow.

"Sorry – I don't what?"

"Love your parents?"

"Parent," I stressed. "One down, one to go." Before he had a chance to say how cruel I was, I shrugged, "Aw, I suppose I do love my mother. It's just, you know, she's irritating. Sort of old-fashioned. Thinks having a man is the ultimate achievement."

"Sounds like a sensible person to me."

"She thinks my sister Pam has it made." The bitterness in my voice surprised me. "Pam's married to a guy who makes good money, they live in a fab house and now they have the ultimate accessory as far as my mam is concerned."

"What – a pool or something?"

"A *child*, dear boy," I said. "A real live baby."

John laughed. "A little sprog to puke all over the fab house."

"And keep them awake all night bawling his cute little head off."

"And to grow up and become a pain-in-the-ass teenager."

"Smoking, drinking, breaking his mother's heart."

"Ugh!" We both said together and laughed.

"Lucky them," John ruffled my hair.

"And what's more," I continued, "he's a *junior*. Dick *junior* they called him. My mam thinks that's really posh."

John gave another laugh and then kissed the top of my head. He did that a lot, kiss me for no reason. It'd been hard to get used to, being so physically close to someone, but I liked it.

Sort of.

"And what other funny things does your mother think?" he asked, amused.

"That's it," I shrugged. I'd said too much already. Before I knew it he'd be asking me all sorts of stuff and I wasn't ready to tell him. I'd never be ready to tell him. Wriggling out from under his arm, I glanced down at my watch. "Better go," I said. "It's late and I'm in early in the morning."

"Stay," he said.

It was only one word, but the way he said it sent shivers down my spine.

"Go on," he caught my hand. He turned it over and kissed the palm, keeping his gaze on my face, "We could have some fun. And Rat won't be back."

I wanted to. But at the same time . . . it was too much. Too soon. "Maybe next time." I pulled my hand from his grasp and jumped up from the sofa. "Now where did I leave my bag?"

"You didn't have one."

"Oh, yeah, right." I wondered if I'd brought a coat. I couldn't remember.

"I'll go and get the car keys, will I?" John asked.

"Well, unless you're thinking of walking me the ten miles home."

"Naw," he shook his head, "I was hoping to use up my energy in other ways."

That I ignored.

"So," John swayed from foot to foot. "Car keys."

"Car keys," I confirmed.

He drove me back to the flat and just as I was getting out of the car, he caught my hand and asked, "Maggie, are you sure about the whole Rat thing?"

"Yep."

"'Cause, well, the invitation tonight, for you to stay, I didn't make it casually. I'm crazy about you." He let my hand go. "Just so you know."

I hadn't replied. As usual when I was happy, I was scared. But I did dance all the way inside. Just to experience what being happy was all about.

Then I clamped it down.

Feeling happy never lasted.

Chapter Eighteen

"Oh, I can't. I'm so sorry. I just can't. I'm going out with Mr Parker tonight. But sure . . ." pause, "maybe Maggie will do it!"

Her triumphant voice carried up the stairs. It carried into my bedroom and caused me to sit bolt upright. Deeply suspicious, I crept from the bedroom. Maybe Maggie would do *what*?

"Maybe I'll do what?" I asked. I tried to sound non-encouraging.

"Oh, there you are!" Mam spoke as if I'd just materialised from outer space. "Come on down here and talk to your sister." She turned back to the phone. "Honestly, Pamela, it's the perfect solution. No, no, I'm sure she won't mind."

"Won't mind what?" I stood beside my mother now, barefoot and freezing. A vicious breeze was blowing in under the front door and it made me shiver.

"Here," Mam thrust the phone at me. "Pamela wants a word."

I sat down on the stairs, holding the receiver to my ear.

"Next week you'll be complaining of a cold," Mam muttered, looking at me disapprovingly. She removed her cardigan, the ones that people her age wear, beige and thin with fancy stitching. Putting it around my shoulders, she said, "I don't know! You've a perfectly good dressing-gown upstairs and you won't wear it. I don't know."

I rolled my eyes.

"And don't be rolling your eyes. I don't know." She began to shuffle back into the kitchen. "I'll make you some breakfast, will I?"

No matter what I said, she'd make the breakfast anyway. I turned my attention back to the phone. "Hello? Pam?"

"Hello, Maggie."

Pamela sounded as if she was talking to a business associate or something.

"So what's the story? What's this thing Mam is convinced I can do for you?" I didn't wait for her to reply. Big-mouthed, I ploughed on, "I absolutely refuse to lend you any of my clothes. No way. You'll only stretch them. And I don't care if you want to seduce Dick in my little black – "

"Will you baby-sit for me?"

The question was fired down the phone. Pamela didn't waste time on jokey small talk, that was for sure.

"Try not to laugh too hard, Pam," I said dryly. When that remark was met with a titter followed by a deafening silence, I asked, "When do you want me to baby-sit?"

"Tonight."

"Tonight? Jesus, you don't believe in giving a person much notice, do you?"

"I forgot," she snapped.

I'm telling you, she had a bad way of looking for favours.

Feeling slightly miffed, I said, "I'm working today," and added, "and some of tonight."

She gasped. "Oh." Then, her voice sounding slightly shaky, she said, "Oh," again.

The meek little voice made me feel a bit guilty. "But . . ."

"Yes?" Breathless. Hopeful.

It might be nice to leave work early, I thought. Things weren't exactly going smoothly in the bistro and I'd a feeling that today was going to cause more ruffled feathers. "Well, what time are you talking about needing me?" I asked.

"From around eight." Now Pamela sounded as if she was going to cry. "Can you do it, Maggie?" And with some reluctance, she added, "Please?"

I thought for a while. Technically I was in work until nine, but I supposed at a push I could leave at seven. Louis couldn't make too much of a disaster of things in two hours. "Yeah," I nodded, "I should be able to. Tell you what, I'll leave work early and go straight to your place. That should get me there on time."

"Fine. Fine. Thanks."

She sounded embarrassingly grateful. I squirmed a bit.

"So what's the story? You going out or what?"

"Yes. Yes, we are."

Silence.

Pamela was *definitely* not into small talk. "So will I stay the night or what?" I asked.

"No." Snapped out. Then, "No, Dick'll drive you back to Mam's."

It was nice to know I wasn't wanted. I didn't know if I felt hurt or relieved. "Fine. See you then."

"Sure." Then, "Thanks, Maggie. Thanks a lot."

The way she said it was strange. I was just about to ask her what was up when she put the phone down.

"Isn't Pam a bit weird?" I said as I arrived back down from my room and into the kitchen. I had donned my new pair of black trousers and a new white silk shirt.

Mam had made a pot of coffee and, shoving a mug of the foul-smelling stuff under my nose, she said sharply, "That's not a nice way to talk about your sister."

I pushed the coffee away from me so that the steam rose in the opposite direction from my nostrils. A plate of toast was shoved at me then. "Eat up," Mam commanded.

She took up a position on the other side of the table and watched me with narrowed eyes.

I sat very still.

She sat very still.

"How can I eat when you're watching me?" I said then. "I hate when people do that."

"Ohh, you're very touchy this morning altogether," she said. "First you give out about your sister and now you give out about me." Up she lifted herself. "I don't know."

"Well, Pam *is* weird," I lifted a piece of toast up to my lips and the smell of the melted butter nearly made me gag. Just as she glared at me for that remark, I shoved a bite-sized piece into my mouth and began to chew. It went all soggy and squishy. I chewed and chewed, afraid of my life to swallow it. In the end, after about five minutes of solid munching, I steeled myself and let it slide down.

Not as bad as I'd thought. I shoved another piece into my mouth. "She's really narky with me," I said, deciding to continue with the 'Pam' conversation. "I – "

"And 'cause she's narky with you, that makes her weird, does it?"

"Well, no, but – "

"Well then."

Subject closed.

Mam began to potter about doing Mammy things. Totally useless things that she had always done, wiping down the draining-board and then putting a wet glass on it and then wiping it again. Rubbing the kitchen counters. Picking up bits of crumbs off the floor.

Suddenly, I felt sick.

The coffee was beginning to smell again. The toast

was too buttery. Holding my hand to my mouth, I stumbled from the kitchen and vomited into the toilet.

I sat on the floor of the little bathroom – the one under the stairs and right beside the kitchen – and waited for her to come in to me. For her to ask me if I was all right.

But she didn't.

I slowly got to my feet and, wiping my face with a face cloth, I straightened my shoulders and prepared to face her in the kitchen.

Only she wasn't there.

She'd turned the radio on and she was out the back hanging out the washing.

In the rain.

Nothing ever changed in our house.

I left the kitchen and, going up to my room, I grabbed my coat, my purse and the invoice for the posters I'd to collect on the way into work.

I knew she'd come back inside when I'd left.

I didn't want her to catch pneumonia so I exited as soon as I could.

"Aw, hello, hello!" Louis' robust voice always got on my nerves in the morning. It was so determinedly cheerful and upbeat, despite the fact that his restaurant was most likely going to fall to bits about him.

I struggled in the door, arms full of flyers and colourful posters. "I had to get a taxi in," I panted. "The flyers and stuff would have got wet otherwise." I nodded toward the door, "You'd better go and settle up with him."

That took the smile off the scabby fecker's face. "It's saving money you're supposed to be," he muttered, shaking his head and grabbing a few quid from the till.

I dumped the posters down on the counter and looked around. Two customers. The *Irish Times* guy and a foreigner. The former had the full breakfast while the other guy just nursed a cup of coffee between his hands.

"What are *they*?" Josie nodded toward the posters, her eyes narrowed in deep suspicion. Behind her, sausages and rashers sizzled.

Lucinda wiggled her way over to us. She'd developed a new walk in recent days. Sort of a snake-like effort. "Dat's the way de models walk," she'd said. "I seen dem on *The Late Late Fashion Show*."

"And are you surprised?" Josie scoffed. "The amount they eat they're probably all constipated."

Lucinda had given her the two fingers as Josie cackled loudly.

But Romano couldn't take his eyes off her. I don't know whether he found the walk sexy or just scary.

Lucinda began unrolling the posters. "Looks cool," she said. Reading loudly from the poster, she said, "Great value breakfast. Two sausages, two bacon, beans, mushrooms, egg and hash browns. Toast and tea. All for two ninety-nine." She gave a low whistle. "Wow, sounds like a great place. Where it is?"

"Where is what?" I began to open the flyers.

"The place dat serves all dat food."

"It's here!" I gawped at her. "They're posters for the windows."

"Oh."

"But we don't serve mushrooms and hash browns." Josie's voice was low.

"We do now." I looked at her. "From tomorrow."

"Aw, here, I'm employed to cook a breakfast. A *real* breakfast. Normal people don't eat that sort of crap first thing in the morning." She turned to Lucinda and Romano. "Do yous eat mushrooms and hash browns?"

"Pu-ky!" Lucinda said loudly.

Our two customers looked up at her.

"Will you keep your voice down," I snapped. "At least try and act like a professional."

"And you?" Josie turned to Romano. "Do you eat mushrooms and hash browns?"

"Sorry?"

"Yeah, you would be if you did," Josie nodded vigorously.

"I eat them," Louis chirped up. None of us had seen him come back in. He stood behind Romano and all we could hear was his voice. "I love mushrooms."

"You *are* a fucking mushroom," Josie sneered. "Best kept in the dark and fed full of shit."

"Well, thank you!" Louis attempted to draw himself up to his full five foot. "Thank you very much."

"No problem." Josie folded her arms. Then, turning to me, she stated, "I am *not* cooking mushrooms and hash browns."

I stared at her and sighed inwardly. Why did she have to try and mess me up at every turn?

"You are," I said.

"I'm not."

"You are."

"Sorry, excuse me. I'd like to order another tea if I may?"

The *Irish Times* guy. I tried to remember his name. Patrick, I think it was.

"Of course, Patrick, we'll have it down to you in a minute." I smiled at Lucinda. "Lucinda, would you mind?"

"'Course not," she beamed up at Patrick and wiggled her way behind the counter.

"Good memory," Patrick was smiling at me now.

"Thanks." I turned back to the flyers.

He nodded at the posters. "Mushrooms, I love them."

"Well," I couldn't help the jubilant tone in my voice as I replied, "from tomorrow you'll be able to order them."

"Lovely." He winked at me and walked back to his seat.

I turned to Josie and smirked. I know it wasn't nice but I couldn't help it.

"You planted him there to say that," she spat.

There was just no winning with that woman.

The afternoon was even worse. I needed bodies to hand out flyers.

"Not in my job description," Josie said.

Neither was drinking tea and eating the breakfast leftovers, but I didn't say that. Anyhow, I wasn't expecting her to do it. We needed her there to cook.

"Lucinda," I handed her a bundle, "will you go down to Grafton Street and hand those out?"

"Aw, Jaysus!" She looked with dismay at the thousand or so I'd given her. "How'll I get rid of dem *all*?"

"You will," I assured her. I took the liberty of handing her her coat. "Now get going."

Muttering, she put it on. "Who'll serve the customers?"

The place was deserted at the time.

"I will," Louis said.

He was really getting to me. He'd taken to hanging around downstairs for most of the day, drinking coffee and smiling at me every time I went past his table. I wondered where his big projects were, the ones he'd told me he was working on. "Well, actually, Louis," I said, trying for once in my life to be tactful, "I was hoping you'd do some distributing yourself." I proffered him another bundle, not as thick as Lucinda's.

"What?" His mouth dropped open. "Me?"

"Yes." I said it as if it was the most natural thing in the world.

"But I own the place!"

"Exactly."

Behind us, Josie began to snigger.

"I can't do that!"

"Too difficult for you, is it?" Josie called.

He made a face and said nothing.

"I do it." Romano spoke up.

"There, there now," Louis smiled, pleased. "Romano's the man for the job."

I was surprised that Romano even understood what was going on.

"He's going to serve the customers," I gritted my teeth. I had to have Louis out of my hair, at least for the afternoon.

"I'll serve them." Louis turned back to his coffee. "No problems there."

I knew I wasn't going to shift him. "Fine," I said. Then, "By the way, I'll be leaving early tonight. More business. You'll be here won't you?"

"Sure."

Resignedly, I handed the leaflets to Romano.

He bounded out the door with Lucinda. She lent him her hat against the rain. Together they walked off toward Grafton Street.

I decided to join Josie and Louis in a cup of tea.

I only hoped the flyers worked, because with zilch customers there'd soon be no restaurant to manage.

Chapter Nineteen

Maggie was late. It was five past eight and there was no sign of her.

Dick was edgy. He paced the room in his good suit muttering to himself about how unreliable my family were. "Honestly, Pamela," he scolded, "what possessed you to ask Maggie? You know what she's like."

I was sitting on the sofa, trying to watch the television, but my stomach was tied up in such knots, I couldn't concentrate. What if Maggie didn't show? What if she'd forgotten?

"I mean, when did you ask her?" Dick stood over me, blocking my view of the telly.

"Last week," I lied. Oh God, Oh God, I prayed, please let her turn up. I looked at a point on Dick's leg somewhere. If I looked at his face and he saw how shaky I was, he'd be sure to know I was lying.

"Last week!" Dick shoved his hands into his pockets and began to rock back and forth on his heels. "Last week!" His *voice sounded as if he'd laugh. "And tell me, darling," he said the 'darling' really sarcastically, "I suppose you didn't give her a ring to remind her?"*

"I did. I rang her this morning."

That took the wind out of his sails.

"Well, she could try and be fucking on time then," he snarled.

He began his restless pacing and I resumed pretending to look at the television. At least the kids had the sense to stay quiet. Dick junior was up in his room having a play on his Nintendo before bed and David was lying in his cot. Sometimes David scares me; he's so quiet and it's like he's not even in the house. He lies in his cot for hours on end just staring hard at the walls or the ceiling or whatever. He hardly talks either, just says 'Mammy' and 'big hug'. He hasn't learnt to say 'Daddy' yet and I think that's why Dick is so impatient with him. Imagine, a big fella like Dick being so sensitive. Shauna was in her pram having a sleep before her last feed. I'd expressed some milk . . . ooops, sorry. That's what happens when you've kids, well, it happens to me anyhow, I talk about them all the time and bore everyone within ten yards. Well, that's what Dick says. He thinks I'm always on about the kids.

Anyhow, I couldn't take Dick's pacing any more. I got up from the sofa and glanced out the window.

"What the fuck are you doing now?"

He was really getting annoyed. Dick hates to be late, especially when he's going to work-things.

I hate being early.

"I'm just seeing if Maggie's on her way."

"And looking out the window is supposed to hurry her up, is it? Supposed to make her magically appear?"

"Oh, Dick, don't . . ."

"Why the fuck did you ask your family?"

I felt like telling him that it was because his ould bat of a mother would never oblige us in a million years, but . . . well . . . I didn't. Those kind of remarks cause trouble in our house. Instead I sat back down and began to examine my nail-polish.

"I don't know why you're looking at that," he snapped. "I mean, it's not as if we'll be – "

He was stopped short by the sound of the bell.

My heart lurched. Standing up, I raced into the hall praying that it was Maggie.

I wrenched open the door and almost collapsed with relief when I saw her outside.

"Hi," she smiled at me. I couldn't say anything. I just opened the door wider to allow her to come in. Standing in the hall she began to pull off her anorak. "The traffic was awful out of town. I think there'd been a crash or something."

Dick gave her a swift smile and pushed past her. "Hello, Maggie. Come on, Pamela."

"Nice to see you too," Maggie snorted.

"He's under pressure," I said. I grabbed my coat from the coatstand and, shoving my arms into it, I began to gabble all about the expressed milk in the fridge for Shauna. Then I gave her instructions on how to manage the two boys.

"Come on, Pamela!" Dick began to blast his horn.

Shauna woke up.

Is this Love?

"Oh no!"

Maggie gave me a shove. "Go on before he self-destructs."

I was tempted to laugh but it was my husband she was sneering at. Instead I smiled awkwardly, "Thanks."

"No probs. Enjoy yourself."

All I wanted to do was run and hide where Dick wouldn't find me. Instead I took a deep breath and made my way to the car.

When I worked with the computer firm, I'd been able to manage business dinners without getting all stressed out. I mean, I was never the life and soul of the party, but I didn't have to be. All I had to do was turn up and eat and smile a bit at the clients.

But now, now I was hopeless. Maybe it was because the clients were Dick's and he seemed to know everyone in the place and I felt I had to live up to his image. I mean, Dick was great, just great. He talked and laughed and people responded to him. And then he introduced me and people seemed to wait expectantly for me to say something dazzlingly brilliant and I'd mutter a shaky 'how do you do?' and smile an even shakier smile and I'd feel Dick getting all tensed up beside me and I'd want to vomit.

Tonight was going to be another night like that, I could feel it.

The place was fairly packed. We'd been given seats beside Dick's boss, Justin and his wife Marie. "Great," Dick muttered sarcastically out of the side of his mouth. "That's all we need, two dry shites like Justin and Marie."

I said nothing, just followed Dick as he sauntered toward the table, a big insincere smile on his face.

"Hi, Justin, how's things?" Dick pulled out a chair for me beside Marie and he sat down beside his boss. "Hello, Marie," he nodded to her, "you're looking great."

"Thank you," Marie smiled at him and turned to me. "And how are you, Pamela? How's the baby?"

I glanced at Dick out of the corner of my eye. I wondered how much I should say. He didn't like me going on and on about the children. "Fine," I muttered.

Marie seemed to be wanting me to say more so I said 'fine' again.

"Right."

Marie turned to the woman beside her and began to talk to her.

As usual, I was left in the cold. Maybe I should have elaborated? But she'd have been bored. I stared around at everyone and plastered a smile on my face. I had to pretend I was having a great time for Dick's sake. There were two other couples at the table that I didn't know. Clients of the firm I supposed. All the women, except me, were wearing dresses. The suit, which I'd thought was lovely, now looked boring against the colour of the others' clothes. In fact it looked downright dowdy and middle-aged. Even my sensible shoes looked just that, sensible.

No wonder Dick was embarrassed by me. I wanted to crawl under the table and die.

Instead I knocked back the wine that the waiter had poured.

Dick was deep in discussion with Justin and another man. All were laughing and I turned in their direction to make it seem as if I was involved in the conversation.

Is this Love?

"Dick here," Justin slapped Dick on the back, "now there's a man who knows how to get results."

I smiled to myself.

"D'you know, he got four new contracts for us last week alone?"

"Worth over a million," Dick confirmed.

The third man, bald, fiftyish, with an enormous belly, looked impressed. "A million, very good."

"Well, we are the best. We cover everything from . . ."

Blah, blah, blah. I'd heard it thousands of times before. A new client looking for someone to maintain and insure his offices. Obviously an important guy because Justin and Dick were almost salivating at the mouth.

There was blonde girl hanging from his arm, barely out of her teens. "Roger," she simpered, "what's . . ." she studied the menu and read haltingly, "cauliflower aw gratton?"

"Cauliflower au gratin," Roger said, smiling down on her, "it just means cauliflower with cheese poured over it."

The three men laughed indulgently as the blonde smiled.

"Hi," she proffered a neat hand, "I'm Janice."

"Justin," Justin shook her hand.

"Dick," Dick gave her a huge smile and my heart almost stopped, but I knew he was only doing it for the sake of business.

"And?" Janice looked at me.

"That's Pamela," Dick said shortly.

"Hello," I said, glad to have someone to talk to.

"Are you Dick's wife?" Janice asked.

"Yes. Yes, I am." I was conscious of Dick's eyes on me. I hoped I wouldn't say anything stupid.

"How nice," Janice smiled. "I'd love to be married." She looked pointedly at Roger who made a face.

"Well, once you meet the right man, it's great."

It was the wrong thing to say. Dick kept the smile on his face, but I could see the shadow behind his eyes. I reddened. I began to gulp nervously.

Janice giggled. "How nice! Roger won't marry me." She gave the rotund Roger a dig and said, "Did you hear what Pamela just said, did you, Roger?"

Roger turned back to her. "What did Pamela say?" he asked her the way you'd talk to a child.

Beside me Dick began to breathe heavily.

"Go on, Pamela, tell him." Janice wrapped her arm around his and snuggled into him. "I want him to hear it. He's terrified of commitment, you see."

Her high-pitched, excited voice drew the attention of everyone around the table. Now they all looked at me to see what I'd said.

"Go on," Janice coaxed.

Tension was coming off Dick in waves. And I knew why. I'd just said something really stupid again.

I steeled myself and stumbled out, "I said that marriage is nice once you meet the right man."

"Awww," all the women went.

The men laughed and began to joke with Dick who I must say took it all very well.

My dinner was wasted. I couldn't eat a single bite of it.

After the dinner it was even worse. Time to mingle. Dick was great at it. Usually I just followed him around trying to be nice.

"Stay there," he hissed at me as I made a move to rise. "God knows what other stupid things you'll say to embarrass me."

"I was only trying – "

But he didn't listen. He left me and, drink in hand and a smile on his face, he approached a man, held out his hand and in a booming voice said, "Hello, Maurice."

They were soon in deep conversation.

I was lucky really because after about five minutes Janice came and sat beside me. "Isn't this dead boring?" she asked. "When Roger asked me to come, well, I thought it was going to be a real blast, you know, but Jesus!" Her eye swept the room. "Such a lot of boring auld egos." Then a tipsy giggle, "Ooops, I didn't mean your husband, of course – I mean, he's quite dishy, really."

"Thanks."

"And the food! God! I asked the waiter for some chips and, imagine, they don't do them." More eye-rolling. "What sort of a kip doesn't do chips, I ask you?"

"A kip where you pay about two hundred quid for your meal, that's where," I smiled.

Her jaw dropped so suddenly I wouldn't have been surprised if she'd dislocated it. "Two hundred quid!" She shrieked it all over the room. A few people looked in our direction and I cringed. "Two hundred frigging quid! Oh," she jumped up and waved her bum and arms around, pulled down her cerise pink dress and said, "Wait till I tell Roger."

"Oh, no – " I made a grab to pull her down but she was off, tottering over to Roger across the room.

Roger had just engaged Dick in conversation.

I jumped from the table and raced into the loo before Dick could see me.

The bit that I had eaten came spewing up.

Why was I so stupid? So thick? Letting Dick down at every opportunity?

The drive home was a nightmare. As it always is. Every time I go to one of these functions I'm determined not to fuck up. Sorry about the language. But I always do. I seem to be pre-programmed that way.

Dick came over to the table at around twelve and told me that we were going. He said it with a smile on his face and for a second I fooled myself that he wasn't furious. He helped me on with my coat and put his palm at the small of my back as he steered me from the room. Waving and smiling to everyone, we left.

He opened the door of the car for me and I sat in and smiled up at him.

A nervous smile.

Slam! The door was banged hard and he stalked over to his side of the car and slam! he sat in beside me.

"Thanks for making me look like a fucking fool yet again, Pamela!"

"Oh, Dick, I'm sorry," I attempted to put my hand on his arm but he shrugged me off.

"You're pathetic," he snarled and switching on the engine he let the car roar.

It was best to say nothing. Let him calm down.

He jumped out of the car when we got home and unlocking the front door he stormed upstairs.

"Hiya, folks," Maggie, rubbing her eyes and looking even more exhausted than I felt, came out of the front room. "Good night?"

"Great," I smiled brightly.

"Tea?" Maggie asked. She waved her arm in the direction of the kitchen. "I've put cups and stuff out for you."

"No, no, it's fine." All I wanted to do was go to bed and try and forget about the night plus I really didn't want to have to make conversation with Maggie. Isn't it funny – she's my sister and I didn't know what to say to her. "How were the kids?"

"Oh, fine. Dick was a bit of a handful – the minute you left he was jumping in and out of bed. David was great and Shauna . . ." her voice trailed off and for one horrible moment I was afraid Shauna had been sick or something.

"What?"

Maggie shook her head as if she was clearing it and she gave a slight shrug, "Well, she's lovely, isn't she? So small and smiley and, and everything."

I felt a rush of tenderness for Maggie. I even managed a smile. Nothing was ever that bad. OK, I'd ruined the night but it wasn't the end of the world – I had my kids, didn't I? "She is lovely," I agreed.

"Anyhow," Maggie broke the mood, "I'd better be going." She put on her coat and said, "Is my chauffeur ready?"

"Hang on. I'll see." I climbed up the stairs and into our

167

room. Dick was lying, fully clothed, on the bed. His fists were clenched and when he heard me come in, he turned his head in my direction. "What?" he spat.

"Eh, Maggie needs a lift home."

"And?"

I couldn't ask him. "Well, I was going to take her. Will you keep an ear out for the kids?"

He didn't answer, just turned his back to me and sighed heavily.

I walked outside the room and pondered the situation. I was pretty sure he'd mind the kids but at the same time I wondered if I was in a fit state to drive. As the night had worn on I'd drunk more and more in an attempt to relax. Maybe I was over the limit and Dick would freak if I got stopped by the police.

"He's, eh, after falling asleep," I explained softly to Maggie as I descended the stairs. I gave a rueful smile. "And, well, I think I'm over the limit. Tell you what, I'll call you a taxi."

Maggie didn't seem to mind. She's like that, just takes things as they come. "Fine. I'll stick on the kettle while we wait for it to arrive."

It was the most awkward cup of tea I've ever had. I didn't particularly want to talk about the night and, when I did, Maggie didn't seem to be listening. It was as if she was thinking of other things while I talked.

Just before the taxi came, in the middle of my description of Janice, she said suddenly, "Pam, there's something I'd like to tell you."

"Oh?"

"Yeah." She stopped, stared into her mug, swirled her coffee about and eventually placed her cup on the table. "It's hard to say, but I hope you'll understand."

She was going to say something about Dick. I knew she was. Well, there was no way she was going to criticise him. She didn't know him like I did.

"You're the only person I can think of — "

A car horn blasted in the street outside. Jumping up, I ran to the window and said, "Maggie, it's your taxi. Quick, get your stuff or he'll keep up that racket and wake the baby."

I had her out the door in seconds.

"Any chance we could meet up sometime?" she asked on her way out.

Yeah, I felt like saying, a big fat chance. I mean, what had we in common? What free time did I have to go gallivanting out with her? "Thanks for baby-sitting," I said. "I owe you one."

"I'll give you a ring," she said as she ran down the driveway.

"Great."

Closing the door, I fell against it and closed my eyes.

Bed. Dick rigid, his back to me. In a way I was glad, at least I could get some sleep. Climbing in, I pulled the covers over me.

"Get out," he said. "Get out. Do you honestly think I want you beside me after you made a holy show of both of us tonight."

I was too stunned to say anything.

"Go into the spare room."

"Aw, Dick, come on. I mean – "

"I'll wake you if Shauna wakes." His voice had gone louder.

I knew what he was saying. If I didn't do what he said, he'd shout and have all the kids awake. Fighting back tears, I slowly got out of bed. "I didn't mean – "

"'Night." He pulled the covers around himself and turned away from me.

Chapter Twenty

"Eh, eh, Margaret," Lucinda edged up to me, "we're, eh, heading off now, is that all right?"

"Better be," I heard Josie mutter under her breath.

It was after eleven and the place had closed.

"Everything put in the dishwasher?"

"Uh-huh."

"Tables wiped?"

"Yeah." Lucinda looked up at the ceiling, obviously trying to give me the hint that everything was done and not to keep asking the same questions night after night.

"Our arses are wiped too," Josie added in a mock-helpful tone. "You can check if you want."

I ignored her. "Fridge closed? Presses closed?"

"Mmm."

I nodded at her. "Fine so, off you go."

"Thanks." She turned to Josie, "We can go now."

"Bloody great. Yippee," Josie muttered.

I felt like throttling her. Unexpectedly my eyes filled

up. Lately I'd been doing that a lot, getting to the verge of crying without actually blubbering. Maybe it was because I felt so knackered most of the time. And Josie would knacker anyone.

Even Our Lord.

On speed.

"Oh, by the way," I said, turning away, just in case my eyes watered some more, "Louis told me to tell you that you both did a great job with the crowd at breakfast this morning. He says well done."

"Oh," Lucinda sounded pleased. "Thanks."

"I suppose he'll show his appreciation by giving us extra money?"

"Not a chance, Josie," I retorted, glad to burst her bubble. Ignoring her foul mutterings, I turned to Lucinda, "You obviously handed the flyers out to the right people."

"Oh yeah." She smiled and, to my alarm, began to walk towards me. I didn't like engaging in conversation with staff. Especially volatile staff. "I made sure to hand dem to de best-looking fellas and Romano handed dem to de best-looking girls. We had a great day." In her enthusiasm, she perched herself on my desk. "I *even* got a fella to ring me."

"Oh, right. That's great."

"Nobody liked the mushrooms this morning though," Josie said ponderously. "Plates of them came back."

"Naw, they didn't," Lucinda said, sounding puzzled, "Anyone I served ate dem."

"And how many people did you serve?" Josie asked her. "Not too many. Too busy chatting up all the fellas, so you were."

"I was not. Dat is a bleedin' lie!"

"Yeah. Yeah. Right."

"It is so!"

I watched dispassionately as they went for one another. I wished they'd leave. I figured that if I stood up they'd take the hint and go. And if that didn't work, I'd find some crazy job for them to do. That'd be sure to move them. As I rose from the chair, I had the weirdest sensation. It was like the world sort of shifted inside my head. Everything began to spin. I clutched the edge of the desk for support and I must have gasped because immediately the bickering ceased.

"Are you all right?" Lucinda peered into my face. Her voice suggested that if I wasn't all right, she was going to do a runner.

"Yeah, yeah, I'm fine." Gently, I lowered myself back into the seat. I massaged my forehead. "I'm just a bit tired."

"You look pale," Josie said gruffly. "D'you want a cup of tea or something?"

More eye-filling. I couldn't even answer. I just shook my head.

"Maybe something stronger," Lucinda said. "Me and Josie are heading down to the pub – d'you want to come with us and get a whiskey or something?"

I wish they'd shut up. "No. No thanks. You two get going before closing time." I turned back to the papers I'd been studying.

"I'll go and get you a sweet cup of tea," Josie said. Her voice had lost its sharp edge. "You sit there and hang on."

"No. No, I'm fine. Honestly. Just, just go." I waved my hand towards the door.

They hesitated, then moved off.

"Bye," they said.

It was the first time they'd ever bothered saying goodbye to me. "See yous," I said back in a small voice.

The door closed behind them and I turned back to the accounts.

The way they'd sounded so nice made me feel sort of weepy.

I bit hard down on my lip. What was I like? An eejit.

My head was fuzzy. I couldn't concentrate. Maybe, I thought, I should get myself a cuppa and it'd help me stay awake so that I could balance the books. Gingerly, I stood up and gave my head a little shake. It seemed fine now. Pushing the dizzy spell to the back of my mind, I switched on the kettle and prepared to work for another while.

It was after twelve when I got in. I'd taken to coming home quite late to avoid speaking to Mam. Oh, don't get me wrong. It wasn't that I minded talking to *her*, it was the other way around. She seemed to always find excuses to leave the room whenever I entered. Either the cat needed to be fed or she had a phone call to make or she had emergency dusting to do.

I wanted to spare her all the lies.

I knew, somewhere in the back of my mind that I'd have to have it out with her at some stage, but I didn't know how. So we just smiled at each other and tiptoed pleasantly around each other and discussed the weather and the soaps and Mr Parker.

However – big surprise – she was waiting up for me that night when I arrived home.

"Maggie, I'm in here," she cooed.

Momentarily surprised and immediately suspicious I opened the living-room door. She was in a chair, her feet curled up under her. She waved at a white registered envelope sitting on the table. "That came for you today," she said. "It's from *London*." Big stress on the 'London.'

She pretended not to look as I tore it open.

Inside was a cheque for five hundred quid.

Five hundred quid!

Who, I wondered, could possibly be sending me money?

A slip of paper fluttered onto the carpet. Bending down, I picked it up. I immediately recognised John's handwriting. *Sale of car* was all he'd written.

"Sale of car," I read out in disbelief. Then, "Sale of car!" I gawked at the cheque. Five hundred measly quid. Five hundred for a three-year-old Nissan Micra. There had to be a mistake.

"I have to ring John," I said.

Mam beamed. "Is it from him?" she asked. "I thought it was. Has he asked you to come back?"

"Asked me back?" I almost laughed into her face.

"Asked me back? The fecker has only sold my car for five hundred quid. Jesus, I'll kill him. I'm going to ring him now!"

Her face crumpled up. It was like seeing the air being sucked from a paper bag. "Oh, oh, I see." She stood up and, averting her eyes from me, she muttered, "Well, you can't ring him now. It's too late. He'll be in bed."

"Exactly!" I did an about-turn and marched into the hall. I picked up the phone and began to punch the pad furiously. Every time I hit a number, I said 'prick!'. Mam pushed past me on her way up the stairs. There was no 'goodnight', no giving out to me for my language.

The silent way she left me alone in the hall dampened my anger. But it soon increased again when I heard Saddam's voice on the answering machine. The message was cut short by John. I think he'd got a fright by the late call because he sounded alarmed as he said, "Sorry? Sorry? Who's this? This is John."

"And this is Maggie."

"Maggie. My Maggie?"

"I'm not your Maggie."

"Oh, yeah, right. So what do you want? Are you all right?"

"Well, I will be when I get the rest of the money for my car."

"Oh, that." There was a hint of satisfaction in his voice. "Well, would it not be better to discuss it at a more *normal* hour of the day?"

"What would you know about normal?"

He ignored me. Instead, he teased, "Or can't you

sleep without me? Is this the way you cure your insomnia, by phoning people in the dead of night?"

"Talking to you would cure my insomnia pretty quick," I said back.

"Ouch!" Then, "So, what's the problem? Not happy with your pay-off?"

"Not happy would be an understatement."

"Really." More smug satisfaction.

"Yes, really. That was a good car."

"It was a great car."

My grip tightened on the receiver, I think I was trying to imagine it was John's neck. "So how come you sold it for only five hundred?"

"I didn't. Five hundred was what *you* got. The balance was my commission."

"What? What did you say?" Was it so late that I was becoming confused?

"My commission." His voice was serious. "I mean, you never asked me what it was going to be. I decided that ninety per cent was fair enough."

"Sorry?"

"My seller's fee was ninety per cent of the sale price. Four thousand five hundred pounds."

"You *are* joking."

"Fortunately for me, I'm not. I'll buy a lot of CDs with that."

I have to say, I was stuck for words. I couldn't believe that John was actually going to screw me out of four and a half grand. It just wasn't him. "You're being – being childish," I snapped.

He laughed. *Actually* laughed. It wasn't a nice laugh, more bitter than anything. "And you're not?" His voice, which up until now had been friendly enough suddenly had hostility seeping into it. "You live with me for what . . . three years. And you disappear one morning and leave me with a poxy note! I'm bloody tearing my hair out ringing people wondering where you've got to. In the end it was Rat, *Rat* who suggested you might have gone home. You won't talk to me, won't discuss things with me. And that's not childish! Gimme a break!"

Again, I was a bit taken aback. John just wasn't the 'outburst' type. "Well," I managed at last, "you said you guessed where I'd gone yourself. And you didn't seem too upset when you phoned me."

"Upset? Of course I was bloody upset! Who the hell wouldn't be? My girlfriend dumps me after three years and – "

"John, I just want my money."

"Well, Mags, if you want your money, come and get it."

"I'm not going over there."

"Fine." Then he gulped. His voice shaking slightly, he said, "Come home and talk to me – come on."

I hated when he got emotional. Not that he did too often. He's not a 'new man' or anything as horrible as that. "This is home," I said. "Now just send me the money and stop messing about."

All I could hear was the hum of the line before he said firmly, "When you grow up I will."

The nerve! The bloody nerve! "It's my money."

"It's my commission."

"You prick."

"You know where I am if you want me," he said. "Night, Maggie."

Beep. Beep. Beep.

Chapter Twenty-one

For four days Dick sat at the breakfast table and glowered at me and at the kids. Dick junior came in for a lot of flak as he just wasn't able to sit still. He kept messing with his cornflakes and mooching up and down and kicking his legs off the table.

"Sit still!" Dick shouted at him the first morning after the horrible business dinner.

Dick junior looked at him and sat still. Unfortunately, he had a spoon in his mouth at the time and he didn't take it out. So he sat, rigid as a statue, with a big spoon sticking out of his gob.

"Take that spoon out of your mouth!"

"I can't," Dick junior said, the spoon bobbing up and down. "I'll have to move then."

His defiance was admirable. I was about to exchange an indulgent smile with Dick when, with a furious roar, Dick lunged across the table and wrenched the spoon from Dick junior's mouth. The sound of it being pulled made me wince.

Dick yelped in pain and tears welled up in his eyes. He looked across to me, his little hand holding his mouth.

"You have to do what Daddy says," I explained gently.

It's important that parents present a united front to their children. Mammy always says that and I agree with her.

"That'll teach you not to be so bloody smart in future," Dick said, throwing the spoon down. "Now eat your flakes and if there's one left – even one – Mammy will tell me and you'll be in trouble when I get home." He marched out of the kitchen and slammed the door.

Dick junior glared at me and with a furious face he began to spoon the flakes into his mouth. He did it at high speed, making a mess everywhere.

For four days that week it was the same. By the end of the four days Dick junior sat still on his chair whenever Dick was in the room. David sat up straight in his high chair and even Shauna made less noise than normal.

Dick had a way of making kids obey him that I couldn't master.

But through all those four days, Dick never spoke a word to me. It was as if I didn't exist. I made him his breakfast and his dinner. Three out of the four nights he worked late and by the time he got home his dinner was ruined. I ended up making him something else while he sat and read the paper.

I really must've wrecked things for him, I thought. For him to stay so angry at me I really must have messed up in style. He wouldn't even let me in the bed. I slept in the spare room for three nights. The third night had been particularly bad. I cried for about an hour into the pillow. I knew things

181

were my fault and I knew I was a bigmouth but I just couldn't cope with the feelings I was having. Things were piling up and up. I deserved to feel bad, I knew I did, but it was the unloved feeling that did it. The way I cooked and cleaned and ironed and washed and for it not to make a difference to him.

He must really hate me, I thought, for him to treat me like this.

On the fourth day, Dick arrived home from work at the normal time. I'd taken to getting the kids their dinner at around four so that Dick wouldn't be bothered by them jumping up and down at the table. Plus, that way he couldn't give out about what I fed them.

I was sitting on the sofa, curled up reading a computer magazine, when I heard his car arrive. I'd spent the afternoon cleaning the place from top to bottom and catching up on all the ironing so that it would look nice for him coming home. It was a last-ditch attempt to make amends for the stupid way I'd behaved at the dinner.

The sound of him unlocking the door made my heart pound. Dick junior looked up from Cartoon Network *to say, "Daddy's coming in."*

He said it every night because the words drove David crazy. The child would literally hurl himself across the floor and crouch beside the playpen. Dick junior thought it was a great laugh. Anyway, David curled up beside his pen while Dick continued watching the telly. Shauna was sleeping quietly in her pram.

Things couldn't be better for Dick coming in.

I got up from the sofa and, slipping my feet into my slippers, I padded out into the kitchen.

"Something smells nice," Dick said as he poked his head around the door. He gave me a smile and was gone. "Just going to take my jacket off," he called and I heard him going up the stairs.

He was talking again. Waves of sheer relief washed over me. I even had to sit down to get myself together.

I'd made him a lasagne and some garlic bread. There were chips too if he wanted them. Flicking on the deep-fat fryer, I took two plates from the press and put them in the oven to heat.

A few minutes later, Dick arrived back downstairs. His jacket was off and he'd undone the top button of his shirt. He looked so gorgeous, especially with the big grin on his face. My heart turned to butter.

"Sit down and I'll get you your dinner," I said. I didn't smile though, just in case he thought that I took it for granted that I was forgiven.

"What is it?" he asked. He came behind me and gave me a squeeze, resting his chin on the top of my head.

"Your favourite," I said, snuggling into him. "Lasagne."

"Great." He kissed the top of my head and moved away. "Well, it's great if it's not your mother's lasagne."

"It's mine," I laughed gently. Suddenly the fact that I'd cried myself to sleep the night before seemed stupid. That was me, a total overreactor. I felt light and happy again. I loved this man. Taking his plate out of the oven, I cut a large piece of lasagne for him. "Chips?"

"Yeah, please."

A pile of chips and two slices of garlic bread were added to the plate.

"Thanks, Pamela." *Another fabulous grin.*

I got my own dinner and sat down opposite him. "Oh, you're eating tonight," *he remarked.* "You didn't eat much the last few days." *He stared to crunch on a piece of bread.* "I was beginning to think you were sick or something."

"Oh no," *I shrugged.* "Just, you know, just upset about, well, about the dinner."

"Forget it," *he said.* "I have."

"Yes, well . . ."

"You're just not cut out for big business, Pamela. You say too much. You have to play things close to your chest."

"I know."

"You don't."

It was a joke and we both laughed.

That was one of the reasons I loved Dick. He never expected too much from me.

There was a nice silence broken only by the sounds of cutlery scraping plates. The muffled squeaks and squeals of cartoons came from the telly room.

"Much nicer than your mother's," *Dick said indicating the lasagne with his knife.*

"Thanks."

"Oh, by the way, talking about mothers. My mother is coming to stay for a while."

He dropped the remark as casually as one would talk about the weather. Only weather conversation wouldn't have totally nuked my world. "Pardon?" *Horror-struck, I gazed at him.*

"You heard me, Pamela," he said, irritated. "My mother is coming to stay for a while."

"But why? I mean, how do you know?"

"Because her flat is being redecorated by the corporation and she has nowhere else to go, so I told her she could come to us."

"But . . . but I thought your mother hates coming here."

"No, she doesn't. Why should she hate it?" He carefully put his knife and fork on the table and studied me. "She's my mother and you will welcome her into this house."

"But she doesn't like me!" I wanted to cry.

"Oh, for Christ's sake, will you ever grow up? Anyway, I'm her son; I can't turn my back on her. And if you were any sort of a wife you'd understand. But then, you let me down all the time anyhow, don't you?"

Inside, David began to whinge. He always does at raised voices.

"Shut up!" Dick yelled.

His whinging grew louder.

"Christ!" Dick stood up from the table, pushing his chair back with the force. "Wait until I get my hands – "

"When is she arriving?" I asked hastily.

"Saturday." He was still standing but the fact that I'd asked about our impending visit from the dark side seemed to calm him down. "She's coming on the lunchtime bus. I have to pick her up in Abbey Street."

"Well, I'd better make up the spare bed then, hadn't I?"

"Looks like it."

Sitting back down, he resumed eating.

I pushed my plate away and wondered if life could get any worse.

Chapter Twenty-two

It happened very gradually, so slowly that I didn't even notice it was happening until it was all over. Sort of like the way sunshine creeps in through a room in the morning, very softly at first and suddenly, before you realise it, you're sort of blinded so much you can't even look at it any more.

Well, that's the way it was with me. The happiness seeped into me over a period of months. I woke up one morning, stretched and pulling on a dressing-gown, made a beeline for the shower.

· And I hummed.

And I realised that I didn't mind going to work, didn't mind that I wasn't liked. Didn't mind that Ali kept nicking my food from the fridge. Didn't mind anything in fact.

It was like a bubble I was in. Warm and safe and secure.

Is this Love?

For the first time ever, I liked my life.

I never really knew what true happiness was until I met Dick. Oh, sure, I'd been a happy child. Mammy and Daddy were great, but with Dick, it was like I was living in some kind of golden glow, all warm and safe. And I knew that if Daddy ever got too cross with me, I had Dick.

I had Dick to cuddle me and tell me that I didn't need anyone else. He kept saying that all we needed was each other.

I felt really sorry for Maggie at that time. She didn't have anyone, except a loser called Jason that she just used for double dates.

Her life was empty so I was extra nice to her.

It's easy to be nice to people when you're happy.

Chapter Twenty-three

The driver pulled up halfway between the two bus stops.

"Excuse me. Excuse me." Shoving people aside in my haste to exit, I flashed the driver a fleeting smile before charging down the steps and vomiting onto the path.

"See you tomorrow mornin', luv!" the driver called as he pulled away.

I gave a weak wave and ignored the sympathetic stares of the other passengers.

Seeing Maggie Scanlon vomiting onto the pavement had become a regular occurrence in the lives of those who caught the 7.30 bus from Dundrum to the city centre. The driver always pulled up in the same spot to let me off. It was at that stage that the bus would have become so crowded and overheated that I'd always feel bad. The state of my health was a topic of conversation for whoever sat beside me on the morning run though

I have to say that not many people fought over the seat.

Anyway, after getting sick I sat down on a nearby wall to recover before beginning the fifteen-minute walk to the bistro. I needed that rest because on arrival at the bistro, the smell of sausages and rashers frying would inevitably bring on another bout of nausea.

And if that didn't, dealing with Louis and Co would.

My job and life were the pits.

He caught up with me just as I was rounding the corner towards the bistro. I hardly noticed as he fell into step beside me. "Hello there," he said cheerily.

"Oh, hi," I replied. I wasn't into making conversation in the mornings, especially when I'd just got sick, but this guy was one of the bistro's regular customers. He'd even recommended our breakfasts to everyone in his work, so I couldn't afford to be rude. "How's things?"

"Just got good this minute."

"Really? How so?" I was planning on the least contentious way of approaching Josie about the menus. She'd had over a month to vary the dinner menu and so far all she'd managed to produce were chips, curry chips, garlic chips, crinkly chips, oven chips and . . . well, you get the idea. And on one spectacular day when she'd been bitching about me to Lucinda, she'd managed incinerated chips. I was only barely listening to Patrick as he warbled on about how meeting me had cheered up his morning.

Meeting me?

"Sorry?" The alarm system in my head jangled a bit too late.

"D'you fancy going out somewhere?"

"What?" Slightly confused I stared at him. "What did you say?"

"I'm asking you out. I think I'd like to get to know you."

Any guy that ate breakfast day after day in Louis' Bistro was not the sort of guy I wanted to encourage. "Eh, sorry," I mumbled. "I've got a boyfriend."

"Oh right." He didn't seem too worried. "Aw, well, maybe you'll split up with him. If you do, let me know." He smiled and pushed open the door of the bistro. Holding it so that I could pass through, he said, "I'll be waiting."

The smell of the fry hit me like a brick wall as I entered. Unable to reply to Patrick, I shot up the room and into the ladies'. Pushing open the door of a cubicle, I hadn't time to lock it before retching violently. The smell in the toilet made me sicker again and I heaved and heaved. Sweat broke out on my forehead and I wished that I was at home in bed with nice warm blankets wrapped around me.

"Are you all right?"

The shock of hearing Josie's voice caused me to bash my head against the cistern. She must have been there all along. Belatedly, I tried to shut the door with my foot. "Fine," I said swiftly, depressing the handle on the toilet. "Just a bit queasy."

"So I noticed." Josie eyed me as I came out.

I turned on the tap and began to soap my hands.

They got the best wash ever as I concentrated on them in order not to have to meet Josie's eye.

Eventually, after a few minutes' silence, with the hot tap scalding the fingers off me and Josie standing like Darth Vadar watching me, I snapped out, "Haven't you work to do? There's a crowd outside."

Still nothing.

"You'll pay for the sausages if they burn. I'll take it out of your wages."

"Are you up the pole?"

I shook my hands dry. Shake. Shake. Shake. Now, hand dryer.

She followed me over. Mouth almost to my ear. "Up the pole? Preggers?"

Depress the switch and rub hands under the stream of air. That's what I did. Hygiene is very important in the restaurant business. Or V important as Dry Shite Dick would say. I smiled to myself.

A hand on my shoulder. "What I mean is, like, are you having a baby?"

A baby.

A baby.

I froze.

"Well?" Josie again. Only she didn't sound like Josie.

The heater switched off. My hands were nice and dry. I had customers to see to. Work to be done. I shook off Josie's hand. "Come on. Let's get to work."

"If you have a bug, you should go home."

Oh, she'd love that, so she would. "I haven't a bug," I replied. I felt better now. In control again.

"So you're having a baby."

The plainly spoken words made me gulp. *I was having a baby.* I hadn't dared admit it to myself for the last three months since I'd found out. Instead, I'd coped by leaving John and wiping it from my mind. Pretended that it wasn't happening. And it *was* happening. And Josie had noticed.

To my horror, tears welled up in my eyes. Only this time they began to spill over onto my face. In front of *Josie* of all people. And I wasn't crying, just 'tearing' if there's such a word. Big, huge, silent tears. I hadn't cried really in years. I can't remember the last time I did cry in fact. Furiously I tried to wipe the tears away but more kept coming. They were like acne. "I don't know what's the matter," I said, as I took a tissue Josie proffered. "Don't mind me. Just get to work."

"Your emotions go bleedin' haywire when you're going to drop," Josie said. "Bleeding haywire."

"Really?" I asked, momentarily forgetting myself.

"Oh yeah, I remember when I was going to have my eldest, he's twenty-nine now, I cried at everything. If I saw a baby crying, I cried. If I saw one laughing, I cried. If I saw someone taking a piss, for God's sake, I'd bleeding cry."

"That'd make me puke," I sniffed.

Josie laughed. "So how far gone are you?" She rested her large bulk against a sink and folded her arms, obviously under the impression that we were going to have a nice chat. Before I'd a chance to answer, she said, "About four months or so – right?"

I shrugged. "I dunno. I'm not sure. Look maybe you should – "

"You don't bleeding know? You don't know?" Her jaw dropped and I was shown a mouth full of tea-stained teeth. "Have you not been to the hospital?"

"Nope."

"Well, Jaysus, you have to go to a doctor. What are you planning – d'you want to have it in the middle of frying a few hash browns?"

"Oh Josie!" Impatiently, I waved her away. She was trying to take control of my pregnancy. It was none of her business. "Let's just get to work, all right!"

"The Coombe. I had all mine there. They're lovely in there, so they are. You should ring up the Coombe and make a first appointment." Then she nodded knowingly, "Jaysus, no wonder you went mental with me smoking – sure you wouldn't want to be in a smoky place and you having a kid."

"Who's having a kid?" Lucinda had come in. I wondered who was serving.

"Her." Josie pointed to me. To my horror, she put a big arm around my shoulder, "Sure no wonder you were such a narky ould cow – pregnancy does funny things to your hormones."

Lucinda gawked at me. "Is it true. Are you having a kid?"

This was awful. I wished there was somewhere I could crawl into. I had visions of the whole of Dublin knowing my business.

"And she doesn't know when it's due – imagine."

"Who's it for?"

"I think it's time we went to work." It was funny, I couldn't get the conviction into my voice. There was something about people knowing things about me that made it hard for me to control them. "The place must be filling up."

"It's mental," Lucinda confirmed. "Dat's why I came in here in de first place." She looked curiously at me. "Now that you say it," she said, "you do look preggers."

I wanted to point out that I hadn't said *anything*.

"The Coombe," Josie said, before she followed Lucinda out. "Ring them up."

"Eh, Josie," I stopped her, "eh, can you tell Lucinda to keep it to herself. And you too." I gulped, hating asking this woman for a favour. "I'd appreciate it if you didn't tell anyone."

"Aw, Louis won't care. Jaysus, he thinks the sun shines outa your arse."

"Yeah, well, still . . ."

"Fine. Fine." With a slam of the door she was gone.

I slumped against the sink, drained. It wasn't Louis I was worried about. It was telling my mother. I'd put it off too long. I felt sick all over again as I realised that I'd have to do it before the week was out.

I generally took my lunch-break around twelve, before the lunchtime rush. Normally I nipped out and bought a cake and a mineral water. Being pregnant had turned me off tea and coffee though the taste for tea was slowly coming back.

Arriving back into the restaurant with my purchases, I felt quite pleased to see a few customers in. Half of them were foreign and they were drinking their coffees but the others all had plates of chips and eggs in front of them. I made a mental note to tackle Josie on the chips issue.

"Drinking water?" Josie beamed approval at me. "That's good."

I gave her a weak smile back.

"Exercise is very important too. For the muscles here." She pointed between her legs. "I forget what they're called."

"I wouldn't mind helping you exercise those muscles, darlin'," a leery ould fella said, looking up at us with an egg-stained mouth.

"You fuck off, you," Josie spat.

Normally I'd have given her an earful on being civil to the customers but that day I really couldn't have cared less. I was planning to do what she suggested and ring up the Coombe. I'd left things too long. For some reason I was nervous about it.

The ould fella was just telling Josie that fucking off was exactly what he was planning to do as I left.

Up in Louis' office, I dumped my lunch on the table and picking up the Yellow Pages, I scanned the hospital pages. My finger shook as I dialled the number. I think that by booking myself an appointment, I was finally accepting the fact that this awful thing had happened to me.

"Coombe Hospital."

"Eh, I'd like to make an appointment – "

"Hold."

Click. "Appointments."

"Eh, I'd like to make an appointment."

"For?"

"Eh, pregnancy."

"First?"

"Yes."

"How many weeks are you?"

"I don't know. Maybe about four months."

"Four months?" She sounded surprised. "OK, well, seeing as you're quite far along, how about next week? Next Thursday at two?"

"Fine." I wrote it in my diary. The girl gave me all the details and hung up.

Next Thursday at two.

Without even realising I was doing it, I put my hand on my stomach. It wasn't a maternal type gesture, it was more . . . I dunno . . . more fear than anything.

Yep, I was terrified.

Chapter Twenty-four

Dick was hyper. He buzzed around the house, checking that it was clean and tidy. He wiped the fridge down; he wiped the front of the dishwasher; he even dusted the shelves in the dining-room. I was mortified when he showed me the dust on his cloth.

"Don't you ever clean anything, Pamela?" he asked. And then, without waiting for an answer, he was off again, hoovering, polishing, shining things up.

He hid David's blocks. Taking them from him, he said, "I'm putting these up until my mother leaves. She's frail. She might trip over them and hurt herself."

"Blocks," David said. He stood up and attempted to reach them. "Mammy?"

"Come outside and I'll give you a lollipop," I held my hand out to him and led him into the kitchen. Getting the jar down from the press, I took one out, removed the wrapper and gave it to him. He toddled back inside, the blocks momentarily forgotten. Of course, the minute Dick junior

saw the lollipop he wanted one too. Out he bounded, his face eager and hopeful. He grabbed it off me and went back inside. I think the sight of his daddy doing housework had him mesmerised. He couldn't stop staring at him.

I started cleaning out the presses. Mrs Maguire is very particular about press hygiene. I'd just managed to clean out the food press when a roar from the other room made me jump. David started to squeal and my heart leapt into my mouth.

"Is he all right?" I was afraid to go in just in case something horrible had happened.

Dick appeared, dragging David by the hand. "Stay in here," he shouted into David's face. "Jesus, Pamela, what are you like, giving him a lollipop! He's after rubbing it on the sofa. Now the sofa is all sticky! Jesus!" He gave David a shove and the child fell. I rushed to pick David up and cuddle him, but he wouldn't let me. He lay on the floor all curled up, sucking his thumb. Instead, I stroked his hair and said, trying to keep my voice calm so it wouldn't upset either Dick or David, "The sofa is leather. It can be wiped down. I'll do it myself."

"That's all very well. What if I hadn't noticed and my mother had sat in something sticky and ruined her clothes?"

I said nothing, just wished David had put superglue on the sofa to keep Mrs Maguire glued into position. Visions of her starving away in our dining-room, unable to make it into the kitchen to eat, kept me entertained as I got a cloth and wiped down the sofa.

At twelve thirty, Dick announced that he had to go and pick her up. She wasn't due to arrive in Abbey Street until *two, but I said nothing. Maybe when he was gone, I could get down the blocks and let David have a little play before they came back. He was still lying on the kitchen floor refusing to get up.*

"Can I go with you, Daddy?" Dick junior asked.

"Only if you promise to be a good boy and kiss your granny when she arrives."

Dick junior considered this. "No. No, I'll stay with Mammy."

Of course, that made Dick haul him out into the car with threats of what would happen to him if he didn't give Mrs Maguire a kiss.

More trouble was on the way.

At three, I heard the sound of a car pulling up. David was having a nap in his cot and I was breastfeeding Shauna in the kitchen. I'd managed to get her onto a bottle at lunchtime but the afternoon feeds were still a bit of a battleground with me giving into her every time. She really was the most determined little scrap. Her little finger was curled around mine and her big blue eyes gazed steadily up into mine as she sucked.

The front door opened and Dick junior stomped into the hall.

"Room!" Dick yelled and then there came the sound of Dick junior stomping upstairs. I grinned to myself, though I probably shouldn't have. Dick junior had sense. I hated kissing the ould battle-axe myself.

"I've two cases, Dick," Mrs Maguire's voice resonated around the house. "Put them in my room, will you."

"Fine, Mother. You go on in and Pam will make you a nice cup of tea."

"God knows I could do with one. That bus is really terrible but sure when you're my age and you've no one to offer to drive you anywhere you're forced to depend on the bus. Go easy with that case, Dick. I don't want anything broken or ruined."

Broken or ruined? How long was the woman planning on staying? Surely she wasn't going to set up house in our spare room. Panic-stricken, I watched through the frosted glass of the kitchen door as she made her way toward the kitchen.

In she came. All five foot eight inches of her. Dick's mother was built like a Sherman tank. All chest and hefty forearms. I know I sound awful by saying that, but it's true. She walked with her boobs stuck out and her big red shiny face moving in all directions like a rooster or a hen or something.

"Hello, Mrs Maguire," I gave a nervous smile. I couldn't tell her she was welcome. I just couldn't.

She took one look at me and reddened. "Is that where you do," she paused, inclined her head, "that."

"Pardon?"

"Feeding."

"Well, yes. Or if David and Dick are up I'll do it in whatever room they're playing in so that I can keep an eye on them."

"You do it in front of your sons."

It was more an accusation than a question so I didn't bother to say anything.

"No wonder men grow up with no respect for women's bodies. In my day men barely knew women had bosoms. And now, my God, they see their own mothers displaying them."

I gritted my teeth. How could she make something so natural and loving sound so disgusting? But that was her all over.

We sat in the kitchen in a stony silence, her staring ahead at the back door and me concentrating on Shauna. Dick arrived in, all smiles, banging his hands off one another. He took one look at us and I saw his face harden.

Stalking over to the kettle he asked his mother if she wanted a cuppa.

"If it's not too much trouble."

"Of course not." He filled up and looked at me. "How much longer will you be at that?"

He was only carrying on like that because he knew his mother disapproved. I tried not to look hurt as I answered, "About another five minutes."

"Move inside, Pamela, will you? The kitchen's very open. Maybe one of the neighbours will see you."

"If not, her own sons will," Mrs Maguire sniffed.

Not wanting to annoy Dick because he seemed so happy to have his mother in the house, I got up off the chair and moved into the front room. I wondered if he'd bring me a cuppa, but he must have forgotten.

The sound of him chatting to his mother pounded into my brain as I sat with my daughter in the front room.

Maybe I was just tired, but a tidal wave of sadness washed over me.

And then Shauna pulled away from me and smiled.

I kissed her cheek and knew that whatever way I felt, it was all worth it.

Babies were great.

Chapter Twenty-five

Mam was putting down the phone when I came into the hall. She was tut-tutting to herself and didn't seem to notice me as I crept up behind her. Well, she couldn't have noticed me because if she had she would have scurried as fast as she could to some other part of the house. At least that's what she'd been doing lately. It was almost as if she didn't want to look at me.

Just like old times.

"Mam," I ventured shakily, "can we talk? I've eh, something to tell you." My palms became greasy with sweat. I don't know why I was so uptight. I mean, I was a twenty-nine-year-old woman for God's sake. It wasn't as if I was a teenager.

She jumped as if I'd just electrocuted her. "What? What?" Big open eyes. Wide mouth. "Pardon?"

This wasn't the way it was meant to be. Initially I'd planned on telling Pam first. For some strange reason I'd thought that once I was home for good, Pam and I would become friends just the way we used to be. I'd had visions of telling Pam and of her giving me a lecture and then being all supportive when I told my mother. But Pam was even more unapproachable than Mam. It was like she was behind a big sign saying 'Do Not Touch'. My mam on the other hand was behind a big sign saying 'Do Not Rock the Boat'.

"I need to talk to you, Mam."

"Oh, can't it wait?" Mam sounded impatient. She pointed to the phone. "That was Pamela on to me. Mrs Maguire is staying with them and apparently she's driving Pam mad. And you know your sister, it takes a lot to annoy her." Mam started to walk towards the kitchen. "But I mean, she's made her bed, she has to lie in it."

"Mam, about lying in beds . . ."

"I told her that Mrs Maguire is Dick's mother and as such she deserves her respect." She began to bustle about the kitchen, taking out pots and pans and making lots of noise. "I mean, we can't all just do what we feel like, can we?"

"No. Mam, if you'll just let me – "

"I mean, just say Pamela gets fed up. She can't just walk out on Dick, can she?" She flicked on the radio and noise flooded the room.

"No."

"Exactly. Being committed to someone takes a lot of work." Bang. Bang. Bang. "A lot of work."

Crash!

The cat yowled in fright and began to hiss at me.

Me.

"Mam, will you sit and listen to me!" I sounded harder than I meant to but it was ridiculous. It was as if she didn't want me to talk.

As if she didn't want me to talk.

The revelation seemed to burst into my head and I took my gaze away from the hissing cat and focused it on my mother. She was there, holding the lid of the saucepan in her hand, staring at me. Spring sunlight fell onto the back of her head, making the shadows on her face appear deeper. And harder.

And I *knew* that she already knew.

And I knew that she didn't want me to say it out loud.

Because like every other time in the past, if I kept quiet, it could all be ignored.

Only this time it couldn't.

This time there would be no denying of the facts.

"I'm pregnant, Mam," I said.

I saw the way she fought to get herself under control. The way her grip tightened on the saucepan lid and the way her face went pale. Then she said, "Do you like salmon? I've forgotten whether you eat it or not. I got some yesterday at a really good price so I hope that you – "

"Mam, did you hear what I said? I said – "

"Maggie, I asked you a question. Do you want salmon or not?"

"Eh, yeah," I said slowly. "Yeah. OK. Fine."

"Good. Dinner will be in an hour." She turned away and left me staring at her back.

Is this Love?

It was strange, now that I'd told her, I felt more alone than ever.

Maggie is pregnant, can you believe it? I couldn't. She rang me tonight to let me know. "Just thought I'd let you know," she said as if she was giving me the date of a show or something.

I didn't know what to say. I mean, I was floored.

"I don't know what to say," I said. I mean was it a case of congratulations? Or consolations?

"What does Mammy think?"

Maggie gave a bit of a laugh. "I dunno. She won't talk about it."

"Oh, don't be silly, Maggie. Of course she will."

Another laugh from Maggie. I mean – really – laughing? It was no laughing matter, as Dick said later. "You know the way Mam is," Maggie had the cheek to say then. "She doesn't like to look under too many rocks."

"Look under rocks?"

"You know, see all the creepy crawly horrible things."

"That's not very nice to say about Mammy."

"Yeah, well," Maggie sounded a bit pissed-off, "she's driving me mad."

"Well, maybe she's a bit shocked. I mean, what do you want her to do, throw a party?"

Maggie said nothing to that and I felt a bit ashamed of myself. Trying to be nice, I asked, "So when's it due?"

"Dunno. Five months' time maybe."

"So it'll be a September baby?"

"Suppose."

"And, well, is it . . ."

"It's John's."

So that's why she came home, I thought. He doesn't want to know about it. "Well, you'd want to make sure he pays his share then, Maggie. It's no joke bringing up a baby on your own."

And then she said, and I must say, I was floored again, she said, "He doesn't know about it and that's the way I want it."

"He doesn't know?"

"Nope."

"Well, you'll have to tell him."

"I don't have to do anything."

That's Maggie all over. Stubborn. It was better not to push a point with her. "No, of course you don't," *I said. So I asked her how she felt.*

"Sick."

"No, how do you feel about the baby."

"Sick."

I wanted to say something to make her feel better, I really did, but I couldn't. I wasn't close to her and I didn't know what she wanted to hear. I wanted to tell her just to accept it, that it always makes things easier if you accept them as inevitable. Instead, what popped out of my mouth was "Well, you've made your bed . . ."

The line went dead.

Pam was even worse than Mam. It was like she was gloating or something.

Still, I don't know why I was surprised.

They'd always let me down in the past. Why should now be any different?

Chapter Twenty-six

"So, you heading off to the hospital now?" Josie asked me on Thursday afternoon.

Honestly, the woman had an inbuilt radar detection system. I must have looked surprised because she added, "I heard you telling Louis you were taking a couple of hours off this afternoon."

"Yes," I gave a curt nod, though I knew I was blushing. "I rang the Coombe and they told me to come in today."

Lucinda and Romano had stopped work to listen. Lucinda swayed over. As well as walking funny, she'd taken to wearing massive high heels as well. The girl was going to be crippled before she was twenty. "Is dis your first visit?" she asked.

I debated whether or not I should answer her. My life was not public property, especially as I was the manager. Instead I gave a bit of a shrug and made as if I was leaving.

"Well, if it is," Lucinda said, "you won't be back here before, oh, six at least."

"At least," Josie confirmed.

Romano nodded vigorously too.

"I won't be waiting *four* hours to see a doctor," I gave a bit of a smile. "This is Ireland, you know."

"Well, whenever I had me first visit, I was *always* waitin' bleeding ages," Josie said. "I swear, if I'd been left hangin' around any longer I woulda dropped there and then."

Things change in twenty-odd years, Josie, I felt like saying.

Lucinda nodded. "Yeah, and when I'd Leonardo, I was waiting ages too."

Double-take. "What?"

"I know," Lucinda grinned sheepishly and rolled her eyes. "It's not a name I would've gone fer meself only fer seein' yer man, Leonardo, in *The Titanic*. God, he's flipping beautiful."

"That's not . . ." I shook my head. "D'you have a baby?"

"Aw yeah, he's two now."

I know it was rude, but I gawked at her. "But, but what age are you?" The question was out before I could take it back. The girl would probably tell me to mind my own business – I know I would have.

"Nineteen."

"And, like, who minds him when you're at work?" Another question that just popped out. She'd definitely tell me to mind my own business now, but it didn't seem to bother her.

Tossing her head, she answered, "Me ma, but like, I get her to come over to my gaff. There's no way I'd have Leonardo in her house. No way."

"Her dad's a tosser," Josie said. "Drinks like a fish."

"Drinks like a bleeding *whale*," Lucinda confirmed, nodding. "No way is Leonardo going to see that."

"Oh right." I was finding it hard to take in. Lucinda a *mother*. She was only a baby herself. I began to wonder how she fed her child when, in the bistro, she had major problems doling out sausages and chips. How did she manage when it was younger? Where was its dad . . .

"So, how 'bout you," Josie asked. She poured herself a cuppa and looked at me expectantly.

"Oh . . . well, nothing to tell." I indicated my watch. "I better not be late."

"You've ages," Lucinda said. "Come on. Spill the beans. Have you got a fella or what?"

I felt trapped with all their eyes on me. "Well . . ." I managed a smile.

"Yes?" Even Romano seemed interested.

It was a real *quid-pro-quo* or whatever it was in that film *The Silence of the Lambs*. No wonder Lucinda had told me all about herself. She just wanted to find out about me.

I was about to snap out that they should all go back to work when Lucinda said, "Sorry, dat was just me being nosey. Forget it."

"I had a fella," I admitted. "He's, he's gone now."

Horrible sympathetic looks were thrown at me.

"Isn't that always the way?" Josie said. "Men are bastards."

"Bastard," Romano nodded vigorously. It was the clearest thing he'd said in English all day.

"No," I don't know why I was bothering, except for the fact that I didn't want their pity, "*I* left *him*."

"*Sure*."

"Absolutely."

"Don't worry. You'll get over it."

Now they were being condescending. Life was too short.

"I better go."

"Have you got your sample with you?" Josie yelled as I closed the door.

That's it, I fumed. I was *really* going to roast *her* over her lack of a dinner menu.

I'd do it as soon as soon as I got back.

Names, addresses, father's name.

"Eh, well, I don't want it on the form," I snapped.

I found the whole hospital thing mortifying. Talk about delving into someone's life! I was asked if I had Aids, my blood was taken. And eventually I was told to head down to the doctor. Armed with a set of directions, I got lost. So I had to ask someone, and that someone turned out to be a chatty person who wanted to know all about my pregnancy.

I think she found my lack of enthusiasm a bit disturbing, so I embellished my story a bit. I told her I'd been very sick and was told not to have any children because my other three, Dick, David and Shauna were difficult births. Eventually she let me go after wishing me all the luck in the world. "I'll say a prayer for you," she promised.

"Maybe a million decades of the rosary might just swing it," I chortled.

She thought I was *so* brave to be like that.

Her directions were good though. I found the clinic no problem but couldn't believe the size of the queue in to see the doctor. Queues put me in bad humour. This one was a whole room full of women, holding charts and looking fat and placid.

"Is this the queue to see Dr McCarthy?" I asked.

The girl nearest the door nodded. "Check in with reception first though," she advised.

So I did. And then I sat down and began to wait.

And wait.

And wait.

Some clever women had brought books to read.

Some stupid ones had brought their husbands. They sat like spare parts, whispering away to each other. Huh, I could imagine John in this scenario, holding my hand, cracking jokes, thrilled at his manhood. I pushed the image of him looking thrilled from my head. Huh, he wouldn't be too thrilled when he received the solicitor's letter for the money for my car. Of course, it wasn't a *real* solicitor's letter, just one I'd designed up on the ancient computer in Louis' office, but it looked good. Hopefully it would fool the toerag into paying up.

"Next." The doctor poked his head out the door.

At last. I jumped up, grabbed my chart and followed him into his office.

It was a tiny room with a desk and two chairs. Some bits of equipment stood in the far corner of the room as did a trolley.

"So, Margaret," the doctor began to flick through my chart, "how's things? This is your first visit?"

"Yes." I sounded defensive.

"And you think you're about four months gone?"

"Uh-huh."

"When was your last period?"

I shrugged. Sometime around Christmas. When I'd bought John . . . I shook my head to get rid of him. "Maybe last January."

"But you're not sure?"

It wasn't a thing I'd ever been sure of. I'd found it a complete waste of time monitoring my cycle. If it came, it came. If it didn't, brilliant. It had proved to be the one thing in my life that I'd never been able to control or predict so I didn't bother with it.

"Climb up on the couch," the doctor said, "and we'll find out a bit more about the little fella."

The little fella. Typical.

"We call all babies fellas in here," he said. Then, "Saves us giving the sex away. A lot of people don't like to know."

"Oh."

"D'you need a hand getting up?"

"No." I wasn't a waddling fat penguin yet. Well, cancel the fat bit. I was *always* fat. Up I got and lay down. I wondered uneasily what he was planning on doing. I hate being touched by strangers.

"Lift up your shirt there," he said, lathering his hands in what looked like a jelly substance. "I'm just going to spread this on you."

Not able to look him in the eye I did as I was bid. Staring hard at the ceiling, I found myself holding my breath as he smoothed the cold mixture over my stomach.

He pulled over a small machine and flicked it on. "Now, junior," he spoke to my stomach, "prepare yourself for the camera."

And then he put a bit of a roundy thing that was attached to the machine onto my stomach. He began to press it down gently until he said softly, "Bingo."

I was still staring ceiling-wise.

"Take a look at the screen," he said.

So I did.

A green screen with shadows. Among the shadows was a small ball twisting and turning about. "Say hello to your mammy," the doctor cooed.

Did this guy sound idiotic or what?

"See there," he indicated the screen where a little light was flickering on and off.

"Yeah."

"That's its little heart."

From nowhere a rush of emotion welled up in me. This tiny thing actually had a heart. beating away, keeping it alive.

"And hands," the doctor said. A series of green dots appeared on the screen, I wanted to ask what they were but I couldn't take my eyes off the flickering light.

"I'm taking a few measurements to see the size of the baby," the doctor said. "It'll give us a better idea of when it's due."

"Oh right." Quiet suddenly, looking at the beating heart, my head had begun to numb up. That thing on the screen was inside me, growing and living. And it didn't feel real. It was too weird. I was Maggie Scanlon. I couldn't look after a baby. I just couldn't . . .

"Don't tense up," the doctor said, still taking his measurements. "I won't be much longer."

Eventually he was finished and he flicked the machine off. The absence of the picture and electrical hum allowed feeling to flood back into me. My feet tingled, my hands ached with the tense way I'd been holding them and my head filled with noise and lights and colours.

And, to my horror, I got sick all over the floor.

They let me go two hours later after I kept reassuring them that it was just a morning sickness carried into the late afternoon type thing. I left, armed with leaflets and one nurse had even written out some nice bland foods that I should be able to keep down. They told me to take it easy and rest.

Rest.

Fat chance of that.

I had to go flat-hunting.

There was no way I could live with my mother now. I don't know why I'd even come back to stay with her.

Well, yes, I did.

214

There wasn't anyone else in the whole world I could go to.

No close friends, no even semi-good friends. Just some lukewarm family who didn't want to know.

Fuck them.

Chapter Twenty-seven

Saturday was my salvation day. Mrs Maguire wanted to go into the city to do some shopping. I had offered to take her but she pulled a face and asked how on earth could she go and shop in comfort with three kids hanging out of her in the city? How could she sit easy in the matchbox of a car I drove? Then, turning to Dick, she ordered him to drive her and before he'd a chance to say anything, she added, "I'll need you to carry my bags as well."

Dick whitened. He hates to be made do things. Pointing at me, he said, "Aw, let Pam go. She loves shopping. I'll mind the kids."

That was a first. Dick never minds the kids. He hasn't the patience.

"Oh fine," Mrs Maguire sniffed, "fob me off on your wife. Huh, it's a great day when a son won't even bring his mother shopping. Oh, a great day." She folded her arms and glared at him. "I don't know what I reared."

I waited for Dick to give some snappy retort, to tell her she

was out of line. But of course he didn't. I mean, it was his
mother after all.

"Don't be like that, Mam," he said trying his best to
sound jovial. Giving her the sort of smile I'd use on Dick
junior to get him to eat his broccoli, he said in a placatory
way, "If it means so much to you, of course I'll drive you."

"Huh, I wouldn't want to put you out."

"But you won't," Dick said. He reached out and patted
her arm. "In fact, I'll even treat you to lunch, how's that?"

She shrugged and said nothing.

Dick kept his smile glued to his face though I could see the
hurt in his eyes.

My heart ached for him but another part of me, the
horrible part, was eating itself alive with jealousy. Why
didn't he ever drive me into town? Why didn't we ever have
lunch out? But I suppose, she was his mother and she was old
and so maybe that's why he did it. He felt sorry for her and,
well, I wouldn't want him feeling sorry for me. No way,
that'd be awful. And the positive thing was that at least I'd
have the auld battle-axe out of my face for Saturday.

It was like school holidays when Mrs Maguire and Dick
drove off on Saturday morning. Dick junior made me laugh
when he punched the air and began to jump about singing
"Olé, Olé, Olé!"

"Stop," I said between giggles. "That's not nice."

He stuck his tongue out. "Neither is Nana. I hate her."

"Dick!" Now I really had to sound firm. If his father
heard that, there'd be murder.

"I hate Daddy," David said. At least that's what it

sounded like. I couldn't be sure. I mean, David hardly ever speaks and when he does, it's all sort of babbly. Shocked, I turned to look at him. He stared back at me out of crystal blue eyes and then turned away and toddled off.

"David hates Daddy," Dick junior began to dance about chortling and laughing.

"Dick, stop it!" I had to shout over his chant. "He didn't say that. He said he hates, he hates, well, Paddy."

"Paddy?" Doubtfully, he looked at me.

"Yeah, the guy that was in a programme he was watching one morning last week. He kept stealing the Tellytubbies' washing."

"Oh." Dick looked disappointed.

"So that's who he meant."

"Oh."

I felt relieved as he too wandered off.

The three kids dressed and washed and fed, I bundled them into the car and headed for Mammy's. I decided to visit as I hadn't heard from her since the night I'd rung to moan about Mrs Maguire. I'd thought for sure that she would have rung to talk about the 'Maggie' situation but she hadn't.

"Where are we going?" Dick asked as I strapped him in.

"Nana Scanlon's."

"Borr-ing!"

Everything was boring to Dick nowadays. Ignoring him, I strapped David in and when I was sure they were secure, I started the car.

"What did he steal?" Dick asked.

"What?" I was busy trying to reverse out of the driveway.

"*The Paddy man.*"

"*Oh, him – ummm, socks and shoes and things.*"

"*The Tellytubbies don't wear socks.*"

"*Well, they did in this episode.*"

"*What sort of socks? Yellow ones?*"

"*Yeah, yellow.*" Out of the driveway and ready to go. I put the car into first.

"*All of them?*"

"*All of them what?*"

"*Wear yellow socks?*"

"*All of who wear what?*"

"*Do all of the Tellytubbies wear yellow socks?*"

"*I don't know!*"

"*But you said that the Paddy man stole . . .*"

Somehow, I knew that despite my earlier optimism this was going to be a very trying day.

Mammy opened the door without a word. She nodded to me and walked back into the kitchen. I ushered David and Dick into the front room, switched on the telly for them and then, carrying Shauna in her car chair, I went in to talk to Mammy. She was sitting at the kitchen table, a big pot of coffee in front of her. "Want one?" she indicated the pot.

"Yes, OK." I put Shauna beside me as I slid into a seat.

For a brief second, Mammy's face softened as she smiled at the baby. "Lovely little thing," she murmured before turning to the press and getting me down a cup.

I waited until she'd poured the coffee and put some biscuits on the table before venturing, "I heard about Maggie."

219

"*Pamela, if you don't mind I'd prefer not to talk about it.*"
"*Oh.*"

Silence as I spooned some sugar into the coffee and stirred it. I wondered what else there was to talk about. "*So where is Maggie?*" *I asked at last.*

Mammy shrugged. "*Out looking for a flat, I think. At least that's what she said.*"

"*A flat?*"

Mammy wouldn't meet my eyes.

"*What do you mean, a flat?*"

"*A flat. Somewhere to live.*"

"*But, but . . .*" *I floundered for something to say without talking about 'it', if you know what I mean. In the end, the best I could do was,* "*But you can't let her leave. Not now!*"

"*She's a big girl. She's lived in London without my help. She can do what she likes.*"

"*But mammy, she's pregnant!*"

"*Stop it!*" *Mammy put her hands up to her head as if to ward off the words.* "*I've said I don't want to talk about it! Isn't it enough that I've to listen to her getting sick every morning and look at her flaunting herself in front of me without you coming here reminding me.*"

Shauna began to whimper at the loud words. I put my foot to her chair and began to rock her gently. As calmly as I could, I said, "*Mammy, I didn't come here to remind you. I just came to see how you were.*"

"*Well, I'm terrible. Just terrible.*" *Mammy got up and began to pace around the kitchen, wringing her hands and shaking her head.* "*I just can't even bear to think about it. I just can't. It sickens me, so it does.*"

"Yes, Mammy, I know it's awful and everything – "

"Awful – huh," she threw back her head. "It's worse than awful!"

"But, Mammy, it's not the worst thing that could happen." Actually, I'd thought it was terrible until just now. "I mean," I sought for something worse, "she could have got rid of it."

Mammy said nothing.

"And like, didn't she come home, and didn't she tell you? It'd be worse if she tried to keep it a secret from you."

"Really? How?"

I gulped at the harsh way she asked the question. Gabbling slightly, I said, ""Well, if it was Shauna, I think I'd want her to be able to come to me. And Maggie must feel she can come to you and, well, it's a sign that you've been a good mother to her."

"A good mother?"

"Yes."

"Oh." Her voice sounded quietly amazed as she repeated softly, "A good mother." She turned to me. "Do you think I'm a good mother?"

"Oh Mammy, of course I do."

"Really? Do you?"

I don't know why she was so intense about it. "Of course I do."

She smiled, almost to herself. "I'm glad about that." Then, minus the smile, she asked, "So you think I should try and get Maggie to stay on here?"

"Well, I don't know." I bit my lip. "I suppose it would be safer for her, you know, until she has the, you know, baby." I said baby sort of soft so it wouldn't annoy her. "And then she could look for somewhere."

"But, that means," more agitated pacing, "I'd have to tell Geoffrey and what will he think of me having a pregnant daughter and the neighbours . . ." she gave a shudder. Turning to me, she said, "I suppose Mrs Maguire knows."

I nodded. Though it hadn't been me that told her – Dick had said it at the dinner table. I'd wanted to kill him. Mrs Maguire had never been too fond of Maggie, disliking her even more than me, if that were possible.

Mammy moaned a bit. "Oh God, how will I look her in the face?"

"That's not your problem, Mammy – it's Maggie's and she'll cope."

"And Mrs Doyle . . ."

I said nothing. Mrs Doyle, the dragon, was a bitch. The less said the better.

"And the priest."

"It's a little baby, Mammy, not the Antichrist."

The comment made Mammy laugh a little and I smiled too. It was nice this. Being there for Mammy, making decisions. It'd been a long time since I'd done that. A long time since my opinion counted for much.

"And what does Dick think?"

The comment irritated me, I don't know why. "Mammy, just worry about what you think and what you're going to say to Maggie."

Mammy nodded. "Yes. Yes, I suppose so." Then her bottom lip trembled and she blurted out, "Oh God, it's awful, isn't it?"

I got up from the chair and put my arm around her shoulder to cuddle her. She clung onto me and it felt good..

"I mean, she'll never get a man now, not with a baby."

"Well, maybe . . ."

"At least you did things the right way around, Pamela. You got a good man and got married and now, look, you've lovely children. And Maggie . . ." She didn't say anything for a few seconds. Instead she pulled my head down to her and rubbed her cheek against mine. "I'm so lucky to have you, Pamela. You're sensible and good and, oh, I never have to worry about you."

She said some more stuff but I didn't hear it.

The fact that my mother didn't worry about me made me feel sort of hopeless. Drowning.

I don't know why.

Hey, guess what? I arrived home this evening – legs tired, back aching – after dumping a massive deposit on a crummy-looking flat and Mam says to me that I shouldn't go.

Totally weird or what?

In I came, dumped my coat at the end of the stairs, just the way Mam hates it and in I go to the kitchen. Mr P and Mam are sitting at the table. Mr P gazes sorrowfully up at me. "Hello, Maggie," he says in a very ponderous voice.

"Geoffrey," I say back to him. I made my voice bright and cheerful so that he wouldn't think that I'd anything to be sorry about.

Mam, of course, said nothing. Each week her communication with me lessens.

"I'll leave you to it," Mr P said to Mam. He struggled to get his massive bulk up from the table. "Bye now."

We both watched him leave. Mam scurried out after him when she heard him opening the front door. "Are we going out later on tonight?" I heard her ask. She sounded anxious.

If things had been normal I would have slagged her off about chasing men, but I suppose I was in no position to talk.

He muttered something. It must have been a 'yes' because she came smiling back into the kitchen. Of course, when she saw me, she reddened and turned away.

"Dinner won't be long."

"I won't be here for dinner," I said. A spur-of-the-moment comment, one I'm sure I was going to regret, but another meal in silence was not what I wanted. "I'll be moving my stuff to my new flat."

She stiffened and looked a bit shocked. I was glad. At least she had some sort of emotions hidden underneath her indifferent exterior. For the first time in days, she looked me in the face. "But, you don't want to be leaving just yet," she said. "Stay and have something to eat."

"No." I turned to leave.

"Look, Maggie," I heard her take a huge whoosh of air into her mouth, "you're, you're welcome to stay here, you know. You don't have to go."

That was a laugh. I didn't have to go! "I don't have to go?" I turned around to her and she let her gaze drop. "Mam, you can't even bear to be in the same room as me. You won't talk to me. In fact, you'd prefer if I had never come back, wouldn't you?" I gave a sort of a laugh.

Mam said nothing. Her shoulders slumped.

"Wouldn't you?" I barked out, surprising myself by shouting.

Her body jerked, startled, but I couldn't bring myself to apologise. I'd been determined to remain cheerful, but anger at the way she kept treating me was pushing its way up. "Well?" I demanded.

To my complete amazement, she shook her head. In a small voice, she whispered, "No. I'm glad, well, glad that you felt you could come to me."

Glad I could come to her. There was no one else for Christ's sake.

"I am your mother after all."

Yeah, I felt like saying, some mother.

"And, well, I've been thinking and I want you to stay."

"What?" I was like a balloon deflating. All the fight in me had nowhere to go. The beginnings of a headache came marching up on me all of a sudden.

"Please stay, Maggie." Now, she looked at me. The glisten of what seemed to be tears were in her eyes. "I, well, I just panicked when I found out and, you know me, I can't cope with bad news," She laughed a bit.

I didn't laugh back. It wasn't funny that she couldn't cope.

The smile dying on her face, she said softly, "Won't you stay? It's the least I can do."

And it was. She was right. And home was nicer than the flat I'd been going to rent. "Will you talk to me if I stay?" I asked. I sounded like a stupid kid. I hated myself for the question.

"Yes, yes, I will."

I shrugged. Attempted nonchalance. "OK so, I'll stay. I'll be happy to."

She attempted to reach out to me but I involuntarily pulled back. Turning away quickly, she said, "And dinner will be in an hour."

I watched her begin to organise the spuds and the carrots and I wanted to ask her why she'd changed her mind. I wanted to tell her how grateful I was. But, as she said herself, it was the least she could do.

The very least, I wanted to say.

But didn't.

Chapter Twenty-eight

A few months into the so-far-chaste relationship with John, I began to get itchy feet. The happy feelings ebbed away. Edginess and irritability came in their place. I couldn't look at John without saying something horrible to him. Week one started off with me telling him that he'd terrible fashion sense. I spent the whole evening moaning on about the fact that the shirt he wore was about a decade too late and his jeans could do with being replaced.

"But you liked these last week," he grinned.

Even his grin got on my nerves.

Week two began when I told him I thought his radio show was terrible. "You play crap music."

"You've just got crap taste in music." He yanked my hair and planted a kiss on my lips. I didn't talk to him for the rest of the night.

Week three I didn't bother turning up to meet him after his work.

That's that, I thought, only feeling a little guilty.

I bought a giant bar of chocolate back to the flat and polished it off in front of a foaming-at-the-mouth Ali.

Then she wouldn't talk to me for the rest of the night.

John caught up with me the following day. He walked into the restaurant Sunday afternoon, just as I was leaving on my half-day. And boy, did I need a half-day. Suzi, spelt with an 'i', the owner of Dylan's, had given me a right ear-bashing. Apparently some of the staff had complained about my attitude. God, I felt like saying, can't they take a bit of criticism without running to Mammy. But I didn't, I held my tongue and fumed inside. I smiled and nodded and gave her the two fingers behind my back.

And I vowed to come down even harder on the little rats that had complained about me.

Unfortunately, I had a tendency to do that, take it out on everyone else when things weren't going right for me, and what with it all being over with John, I felt justified in terrorising my staff.

Anyway, I couldn't be too nice to them or they'd start taking advantage of me, the way people always do in the end.

Anyhow, as I was leaving, John was entering.

"Ah," he gave a bit of a smile, but I don't think he was really smiling, "the elusive Maggie Scanlon."

"John," I gave him a curt nod and attempted to push past.

He followed me out onto the street and strode along beside me.

"I wanted to see you," he said. "I just had to ask if you enjoyed your trip in an extra-terrestrial craft last night?"

Typical John. Trying to sound funny or say obscure things just to make me ask him what he was talking about. Imagine, I thought dispassionately, I used to find him amusing.

"John, I haven't – "

"Well, it's the only explanation I can come up with. I mean, you vanished off the face of the earth last night for sure."

"Right. Funny." I walked faster. Hugging my arms around myself, I tried my best to ignore him.

"So what happened? I waited for ages for you to show."

Was the guy a moron? I mean, three weeks of constant nagging and being stood up and here he still was, like a stupid dog or something. I'd never liked dogs and now I knew why. I kept those thoughts in my head as I walked on, ignoring him.

"I *would* like an explanation as to why you left me standing in the middle of Oxford Street like a thick last night." He sound angry. "Jesus, you don't show up; you don't ring to cancel. I'm stuck waiting for you in the middle of the street like a moron and you can't even give me an explanation?"

His voice was rising. People were looking. "I didn't want to go out with you," I snapped, hoping to hurt him so much he'd leave me alone. "Satisfied?"

I did hurt him, I could see it in his face. Faster and faster I walked, blanking out the look from my mind.

Back he was beside me again.

"And you couldn't fucking ring to let me know?" He was mad. I felt a sort of triumph in it. "I waited for two fucking hours in the rain for you. I'm going out of my mind worried. I leave messages on your machine and you don't reply. And all because you didn't want to show?"

He was standing in front of me, blocking my path. But I'd stopped walking anyhow. "You were worried about me?" I asked, for the first time looking at him.

"Forget it. Jesus." He shook his head and made to leave.

"I didn't think," I said hastily, reaching out to stop him from going, "I didn't think you'd worry. I'm . . .," this was hard, "I'm sorry."

"Sorry?" A hard laugh. "Forget it." He shoved his hands into his jacket, put his head down and slouched away from me. I turned to watch him leave. I should have been delighted. This was what I wanted. This was what I'd been aiming for the past three weeks. This was how any relationship of mine had ever ended.

Only I didn't feel so good this time. There was no smug pat on the back.

I supposed I just realised that I wouldn't be so happy any more, that the glow would definitely be gone.

It'd be gone.

But maybe that was a good thing. People pull you in and then fuck you up.

But still . . . there'd be no one to worry about me.

"John!" I called out, surprising myself. He stopped but didn't turn towards me. "John, please, let me explain." I hated myself for being so weak, for needing him. I didn't smile as he turned and walked back up the street.

He wasn't smiling either. "Yeah?"

"I can't talk here," I gulped. "Maybe back in the flat?"

"Come to my place. Rat's away for the day." He took out his car keys and said, "OK?"

In silence we walked back to his car.

I needed the space to try and work out what I was going to say to him.

I mean, it was only polite and normal to give an explanation when you didn't want to see someone any more – right?

It was awkward sitting next to John in his rattly old car as he sped through the streets on his way back to the house. I couldn't think of a single thing to say to him and I don't think he knew what to say to me either. Pulling up outside his house, he strode up the driveway and waited for me to join him at the door. Opening up, he let me in first.

"Go on into the kitchen," he said, his voice not quite so hard as it had been. He began to wrestle with the lock, trying to get his key out. "I'll be with you in a sec."

I was sitting on a chair when he came in. "Tea?" he asked, putting on the kettle.

I nodded, watching him moving around the place, getting cups down, rinsing out the teapot, getting milk from the fridge. I felt sick and sad and hopeless as I realised it would be my last time in this horrible house. Only now, after a few visits, I didn't think the house was so kippy – mainly, I suppose, because it was where John lived.

"There's no biscuits," John said apologetically as he placed my mug in front of me. "Rat found all my money and spent it on a hit." He sat down opposite me and smiled glumly. "I'd a bloody awful row with him this morning over it. Must be the day for it – huh?"

"Must be," I gave a weak smile back.

"Still, he's going clear now. He told me so."

"Good." I didn't want to talk about Rat.

"Is it Rat? Is that the problem?"

"No," I shook my head. "No, it's not him." I wish it had been.

"Sure?"

I nodded. I couldn't speak. I mean, John was such a decent guy. I didn't deserve him. And sooner or later he'd realise that.

"So, what is? Don't you fancy me any more?"

I felt cold. I wrapped my hands around the mug and hoped that they'd warm up. I studied the table, hard, as I sought for the right words to explain. Words that wouldn't hurt him or me. "I do fancy you," I muttered. "It's just . . . well . . . I think it's probably better if we don't see each other any more."

"Why?"

I'd never been asked to explain before. I'd never wanted to. "'Cause, well, I mean, sooner or later this will end. Us. We'll end and so what's the point of it all?"

He didn't speak for a second and when he did, he sounded totally confused, "I don't get you. What are you saying?"

I took a deep breath. I couldn't make him understand; he wasn't me; he wouldn't think the same way I would. "I'm saying that I don't want to get any more serious because there's no point. You'll – "

"No point – why? You think it'll be over or something?"

"Yeah." I looked up – he was staring at me.

"But why do you think that?"

I shrugged. "Just a hunch."

"But, but, I thought you were happy. I thought we were happy."

I gulped. I should never have come. But I didn't want him to think I was a complete bitch who stood fellas up. I wanted him to think well of me. "Yeah. We were, but, you know, maybe we won't always be. Maybe – "

"That's crap!" John surprised me with his vehemence. "Jesus, what are you at? Just say you don't like me any more and spare me the bullshit. Or say it's Rat or something." He came towards me. I shrunk back against the chair, wondering if he was going to lash out. "Just tell me the truth, Maggie," he said, sounding pissed-off. "I'm a grown man. I can take it."

He didn't grab me. He didn't shake me. He just looked hard at me.

I didn't know what to make of that. "I am telling you the truth," I muttered.

I think he believed me because he stepped back and seemed to peer into my face. He said slowly, "You don't want to see me any more in case the whole thing crashes in a few months?"

"Yeah." Not in case, I felt like adding. It will *definitely* crash.

"You want guarantees?"

I shrugged. "There are no guarantees."

"I know." John knelt down so his face was on a level with mine. "So why don't you just grab all the good stuff while you can, Maggie?"

I pulled back from him. "No. No. That's not the way it works."

"It is for me."

I stood up. He stood up. Hugging my coat around me, I said softly, "Well, you're lucky then. I've no intention of getting all upset when it's over. I can do without the grief."

"But it *mightn't* be over," John said.

I blocked that out. I walked past him. "I'll get the tube back."

"Maggie, for Christ's sake, this is madness."

I couldn't let myself look at him. I walked to the door, put my hand on the latch and was about to open it when he blurted out, "I love you, you know."

Some guys would do anything, say anything to keep you where they want you. And I didn't want love.

Not ever.

Out I went into the day.

I didn't cry about it being over. I never cry. Well, I'd never cried in years.

Instead I ate.

And ate.

And ate.

It was like I was trying to fill a hole inside. A hole where all the warm stuff had been.

In a week I put on over seven pounds.

And working in a restaurant and living with a bulimic flatmate didn't help.

Ali kept arriving back to the flat with armloads of chocolate. Despite the fact that most of it was reject stuff that she got free in work – she worked in a chocolate factory – we spent our evenings eating it.

She had attempted to ask me about John at the start, but after a series of short, sharp monosyllabic answers from me, she'd seen sense and shut-up.

However, the second John-less Saturday night she must have plucked up courage again. Or maybe she was just getting a bit pissed-off with me swiping all her goodies. Anyhow, she eyed me and said, "I thought you cared about your weight."

"I do," I nodded. "I care a *lot* about it. I care about it so much, I just want to keep getting more and more of it." There was something about eating loads of chocolate that made you feel as if you were drunk.

Ali giggled. "I must remember that one. That's a

good one." Down went a chunky bar in one swallow. "But seriously," she continued. "I – "

"I don't like serious," I said. I was cross-legged on the floor, debating whether or not to eat my third Crunchie. "It often means things are going to get, well, serious."

"If you and John were still together, would you still be in 'ere with me?"

"We're not together," I snapped. I didn't want to talk about John. I was missing him more than I'd thought. Wanting to hurt Ali for bringing the subject up, I said caustically, "And though I like you, Ali, as dates go, you're probably a minus ten."

She wasn't offended. "So ring 'im. Ask 'im out. I mean eating is all very well, but as you know, you can only do so much with a Crunchie." She winked broadly and began to cackle at her own joke.

I didn't like her advising me on John. To spite her, I unwrapped a Crunchie and shoved it into my mouth.

Ali convulsed with laughter. "Not the same at all, is it?" she chortled.

The girl really had the foulest cesspit of a mind.

When she'd finished her one-woman appreciation of her joke, she switched back to her serious mode. Cocking her head to one side, she remarked, "I mean, the guy seemed dead keen on ya and you liked 'im."

"Mmm." I pretended I couldn't say anything as my mouth was too full.

"Eating for pleasure is one thing but eating for consolation – now that's bad."

Is this Love?

A classic case of the pot calling the kettle black. This was the girl who never went out, preferring instead to stay in and eat. But I kept my silence. There was no point in adding her to my list of people who weren't talking to me.

It had been a rotten week. It started off with Mam ringing me and asking when I was going to pay her a visit. So I told her that I'd be over for Easter. "But your daddy's birthday is next week. Pamela and I are going to have a little celebration and visit the grave."

"Well, enjoy it. Give a blow on a party-horn for me."

That hadn't gone down well; she'd acted hurt and disappointed in me. And then hung up.

After that, one of the waitresses had spilled some coffee on the restaurant carpet and because of John and Mam, I'd blown a gasket. And that had led to the rest of the waitresses ignoring me when I spoke to them. The nerve of them. The bloody nerve. I'd told them very politely that I was hired to run a restaurant not to win popularity contests and if they didn't like it they could lump it. That shook them.

And the rest of the week had been a case of similar incidents. The waitresses only talked to me if it was absolutely necessary, which suited me fine.

Agony Aunt Ali interrupted my thoughts by again shoving her oar in. "I mean," she continued, "imagine if you *never* get back with him. Think how *huge* you'll be then." She indicated herself. "Two years ago a fella I was mad about dumped me and look at me now."

Of course, it was a joke but I did look at her and a

horrifying thought that it might indeed be me began to squirm its way to the top of my consciousness. "You look fine," I said weakly.

"Oh, well, in that case, no need to worry," Ali handed me a Club Milk. "Eat up."

So I did.

About ten o'clock the same night, just after I'd had a shower, done the rosters for work and retired to bed with two Crunchies and a cup of cocoa, Ali came and tapped on my door. "There's someone outside to see you," she said, coming into the room. Her eyes were all shiny and excited.

My mind raced as to who it could be. I knew no one in London really. The girls from work certainly wouldn't call around to see me. I'd only gone out with them once, the time I'd met John.

John!

For some reason, hopeful feelings rushed through me. "Is it . . ." I couldn't say it in case I was wrong and then I'd feel a right fool.

"It's John!" Ali hugged her arms around herself. In a loud whisper, she confided, "I think he's come to try and make it up. Come on!" She held her hand out to me and I balked.

Hurt flashed across her face. "Come on," she said again, though this time slightly more warily. "He's out 'ere. He won't wait forever, ya know."

I was in my PJ's. The faded cotton ones I'd had for years. I wondered if I should change. Into clothes I mean, not into a seductive nightdress. Not that I had any of those.

"Out in a sec," I said.

Ali stood there. "He won't wait a sec," she whispered. "I'm telling you, he's dying a death out there."

Making a big deal of looking fed-up, I grabbed my dressing-gown from the bed and pulled it around me. I yawned widely as I made my way out to the kitchen.

John stood with his hands shoved into the pockets of his black jeans, the ones I'd told him looked really good on him. His shirt was untucked and he wore a black biker's jacket that I hadn't seen before. He looked nice, if a bit uneasy.

"Oh, sorry," he muttered. "I hope I didn't wake you."

"Doesn't matter," I said casually.

"She'd only just gone to bed a few minutes ago," Ali said.

I glared at her, but she turned away and plonked herself on the sofa.

John gave us both a tentative smile.

I didn't bother to smile back. I wasn't falling for any tricks.

"This is great," Ali cooed. She sat in the chair and looked from John to me. "Betta than the frigging movies."

John gave me a desperate look.

I gave Ali one.

Ali smiled brightly at the two of us. "Well, get a move on. I ain't got all night to sit 'ere, ya know."

"Can I talk to you?" John asked. He lifted his eyes from his shiny Docs to glance at me.

I shrugged. "If you want."

"Somewhere . . ." his eyes flicked over to Ali, "else?"

I wondered what he wanted to say. Maybe he wanted his tapes back, the ones he'd bought for me. That was the likely explanation. "There's only my room," I said. "Unless you want me to change and we can go to a pub or something?"

"Aw, 'ere," Ali said crossly. "That's no good. I ain't got no money."

"That is good," John cracked a smile. "In fact, it's very good."

Despite myself I laughed.

Ali gave us a snotty look and flicked on the telly. "Like a power-cut in the middle of a film or the last frigging page missing from a book," she grumbled.

"So?" I asked John, who was half-smiling at Ali. "What's it to be?"

His smile faltered at my brisk tone. Shrugging, he muttered, "I don't mind. Your room if you want. I don't want to go dragging you out into the cold."

"Fine." I pulled my dressing-gown tighter around me and said, "Come on then." I was glad it was my room. By bringing him in there, at least he knew I'd no designs on him. I mean, if I had, the last place I would have gone would have been my room.

He followed me in.

Removing a bundle of unironed clothes from my bedside chair I told him to sit down, then I dumped my clothes and myself onto my bed.

We looked at each other and I nodded to him. "Well?"

"It's about that guarantee you were after," he began.

"I wasn't after a guarantee," I snapped.

"Yeah. Right." He closed his eyes and clasped his hands together and for the first time I saw how hard it had been for him to come here.

But I couldn't apologise. It would have been like giving a part of myself away or something. Instead I said, "Go on." But I said it softly, in what for me was a gentle voice.

John stared at the palms of his hands. Then he turned them over and stared at the backs of his hands. "I miss you, Maggie," he said, to his hands. "And, well, about what you said, about not seeing me any more 'cause you think it's not worth it – "

"I said it wasn't worth it in the long run," I clarified.

He was still gawking at his hands. "Whatever," he shrugged. "Well, I guess I can see what you mean. Like I can't guarantee that we'll always stay together; no one can ever do that."

I said nothing. There was nothing to say. I began to stare at him staring at his hands.

"But I can guarantee you one thing," John muttered. "And like, I'm laying all my cards on the table here. Nothing ventured, nothing gained, right?"

"Yeah." I gave a weak smile. What was he on about? Had he borrowed some of his brother's hash stash?

"I can guarantee you that no one will care for you as much as I do," he said quietly. He looked at me. "I mean that. I really mean that, Maggie."

And he did. I could see it in his eyes. His openness

shamed me. I opened my mouth to speak and nothing came out. Just as well.

"And like, you saved my life and I'm bound to you forever until I repay the debt." A crooked, embarrassed smile. "I haven't done that yet."

But he had. He'd saved me from eating until I exploded. But I didn't say that.

"So?" he asked.

"So? What?" My heart was hammering very fast. I felt sick.

"I want you back."

It wasn't good enough. I couldn't . . .

"I need you back, Mags."

He needed me. No one had ever said that to me before.

I felt all watery and liquid inside and then it went. Instead, I shrugged and making an attempt to sound reluctant said, "OK, you can hang around until you save my life and then you have to fuck off."

"Put like a lady."

Neither of us knew what to do then. So we grinned awkwardly at each other until he said, "Come here." He held out his hand and I took it. He pulled me onto his lap and pushing back my hair from my face, he said, "You're beautiful, Maggie Scanlon."

Then he kissed me.

And I kissed him back and for the first time in my life I *felt* beautiful.

And for the first time in my life I felt ready to take a chance with a fella I cared for.

I mean, he'd come after me.

He *needed* me.

I was the one in control.

A few months into the relationship with Dick, I'd plucked up the nerve to invite him in for tea after we'd come back from the cinema. I'd warned him about Mammy being all romantic over things and Daddy being gruff because he wasn't feeling well.

But the night I brought him in hadn't been the ideal night to pick. Daddy was worried about Maggie. She was meant to come in at one and she hadn't arrived. He was pacing about the room like a tiger in a cage.

"She's late," he muttered. "I told her to be in no later than one o'clock."

Mammy and I smiled uneasily and I glanced at Dick who was sitting on our sofa, a cup of coffee in his hands. At first things had gone very well Dick had told mammy all about his job and how he had just landed a big job as a PR rep with a multinational firm. Mammy had been great. She cooed in all the right places and acted as if she knew what Dick was talking about. I knew Daddy had been impressed too. But Daddy's quiet. He doesn't say much. In fact, he hadn't said anything at all to Dick. Except once. He'd said that PR probably stood for Perverted Rotter.

Of course it was a joke and we all laughed.

Well, Dick stiffened a bit and then laughed.

Daddy had gone behind his paper again.

But now, now things were getting a bit edgy. Daddy was getting a bit annoyed and Dick didn't seem to be showing any signs of leaving.

"Please leave now, Dick," I willed. "Please."

But Dick didn't. Taking another bun from the plate, he told Mammy that she was a lovely cook. Mammy beamed with pleasure and giggled like a schoolgirl.

In the middle of the room, Daddy stopped his pacing. He banged his fist into the palm of his hand. "I'll kill that girl when she comes in," he said in his quiet, low voice.

Mammy started off chatting again while I tried to stop my hands from shaking as I poured Dick yet another cup of tea.

At one twenty, Dick laid down his cup and said that he had to go. Mammy jumped up and ran into the kitchen to pack a doggy bag of buns for him. "Won't be a sec."

Dick rolled his eyes to heaven and shot me a pained look. "Thanks, Mrs Scanlon," he said.

"Oh, call me Doreen," she shouted from the kitchen.

"Right so, Doreen it is," Dick shouted back. He turned to Daddy. "Bye, Mr Scanlon. See you again."

"Not if I see you first." Daddy muttered.

Dick gave an uneasy laugh while I tittered. "Come on, Dick. I'll see you to the door."

Daddy looked at his watch. "One twenty-five," he said slowly. "She's twenty-five minutes late now."

I grabbed Dick's hand and led him gently into the hall.

In the hall, Dick shook my hand off. "What is your dad's problem?" he asked, quite loudly.

I smiled. I reached out and touched him. "He's fine. There's no problem. It's just Maggie. She's late in."

"I don't think it was just Maggie. He was quite rude to me. And all you could do was laugh."

"He was only joking." I tried to look into Dick's face, but he averted it. "Come on, Dick. You hardly think he meant it. I mean, what person would say things like that and be serious?"

He didn't answer, he drew his eyebrows together and his mouth turned down sulkily at the corners. "I don't find him a bit funny."

I wanted to kiss the hurt look from his face, I wanted to wrap my arms around him and win him back to me. But, well, I was in our hall, wasn't I? And Mammy was scurrying out of the kitchen with an enormous bag of half-baked black buns.

"There you are," she placed the bag in Dick's hands. "You might as well have the lot of them. My girls don't eat buns at all." She patted him on the arm. "I enjoyed meeting you."

"Thanks." Dick gave her his lovely smile.

"Hopefully we'll see a lot more of you?"

The question made us both blush.

"Hopefully," Dick replied. His voice was sort of clipped though Mammy didn't notice it.

"Good." She patted him on his sleeve. "Bye now." And in she went to Daddy.

"That bitch is half an hour late now!" Daddy's voice, sounding quite loud, came at us as Mammy closed the door.

"What am I going to do with these?" Dick whispered furiously, holding up the bun bag. "It was bad enough having to eat the few I did." He sounded really annoyed. "Why didn't you tell her not to bother, Pamela?"

"But I thought – "

"No, you didn't think. I mean, if you'd thought I

wouldn't be going home feeling insulted and sick." He turned
and opened the door. *"I'll see you next week."*

"Oh, Dick don't leave –   *"* I was stopped by the sight of
Maggie strolling up the driveway. She had a fag in her hand
and was puffing peacefully on it.

"Oh, oh, here's trouble." Dick actually gave Maggie a
smile as she came towards us.

"Hiya, folks," Maggie blew a long stream of smoke in our
direction. Dropping the fag onto the path, she quenched it
with her foot. *"Good night?"*

"You are in such trouble with Daddy," I hissed at her.
"He's really going to kill you."

"Oh, I'm so scared." Maggie threw her eyes heavenwards
and pushed by us. Turning to Dick, who was beaming
broadly at her, she said, *"Ignore the sounds of skin and hair
flying and of shit hitting the fan generally, all right?"*

"Maggie!"

Dick actually laughed. *"I'll try,"* he said.

"Is that you, Maggie?" The fury in Daddy's voice was
enough to burn down the door. *"Get in here!"*

"Now there's an invite I can't refuse."

Dick gave another laugh and I forced a smile on my face.

"Don't look so worried, Pam. I'm not dead yet!" Maggie
made slashing motions with her finger across her throat as
she opened the sitting-room door.

"And what time do you call this?" Daddy shouted.

Muffled voices as the door was closed. I wanted Dick to go
now before things got really bad. Maggie and Daddy didn't
get on at all. Mammy said that they were too alike or
something.

Dick and I faced each other and I tried to ignore the yelling coming from inside. It was hard and I felt so embarrassed.

"Your family are mad," Dick remarked. He sounded amused. "But I like your sister. She's gas."

Huh, if I said I liked someone, he'd go mad and here he was . . . "You can have her if you like," I said.

"I might just do that." He studied me for a second and repeated, "I might just do that."

I couldn't help it. Tears formed big pools in my eyes. I blinked but he'd noticed. A sort of smile touched the corner of his lips. He reached out and touched me. "Then again, I might not. I like skinny girls."

It was as if he'd lifted me from despair to euphoria. "See you next week?"

"Mmm."

I wanted him to reach over and kiss me, but he didn't. "I'll be seeing you," was all he said as he walked to his car.

As he drove off, I felt a burning anger at Maggie. If she had only come home on time, none of this would have happened. I mean, I thought, what man wants to kiss his girlfriend when there's a huge row going on?

I hoped Daddy gave her what she deserved.

After Dick left, I went to bed. There didn't seem much point in staying up, the fighting could go on all night. I tried to blot out the sounds of yelling by shoving a pillow over my head but it didn't do any good.

Why did Maggie go out of her way to cause trouble? Why couldn't she see that by toeing the line and doing what

Daddy wanted, which wasn't excessive, she could avoid most of the messes she seemed to create.

I began to recite maths tables to myself to try and get some sleep. It had always worked when I was a child, but lately it didn't seem to be doing much good.

There was a crash from downstairs. The television was highered.

And then, quite suddenly, there was silence.

Thank God.

A few seconds later I heard a door being opened downstairs and footsteps coming up. Slow footsteps. The murmur of voices started up again. Mammy and Daddy talking to each other.

I heard Maggie go into her room and close the door.

Now at last, I thought, I can get some sleep.

I think I did sleep for a while. I can't be sure. But when I woke, the clock was flashing two thirty. A noise had woken me. I strained my ears to try and hear it again. It seemed to be coming from Maggie's room. Very quietly, I slipped out of bed and padded to the door. Yes, definitely, there was a strange sound from the room next door. I had to go as softly as I could. Daddy would freak if he thought I was creeping into Maggie's room late at night.

Outside her door, the sound was louder, though still muffled. Gently I tapped, "Maggie, Maggie, are you all right?"

Silence.

"Maggie?"

Still there was no answer so I pushed open her door. Light fell from the street light outside the window onto her bed. Maggie always slept with the curtains pulled back. I could see her curled up underneath the covers. "Go away." *Her voice was muffled by the bedding.*

"Are you all right?"

She didn't answer. Instead her body began to shake. Despite the fact that I was still angry at her for ruining my night, I couldn't help it. In a flash, I was across the room and sitting on her bed. "Come here."

Gently she eased the covers down and in the dim light, though she had her back to me, I could see the glint of tears on her face. "Oh, Mags," *I put out my hand and ran it down her arm,* "don't."

She pulled away from my touch. "Just leave me, Pam. I'm fine." *Like a kid, she balled up her fist and rubbed at her face, making her tears streak in funny directions.* "Go on. Just go."

"Sure you're all right?"

She just shrugged.

"It's only because you're so alike," *I said, standing up.* "That's why you both – "

"So alike? Who?" *She half turned to me.*

"You and Daddy. You're both – "

She heaved herself up in the bed and two things shocked me. The first was the huge, and I mean huge, bruise on her face – in the light, it looked black – and the second was the anger in her eyes. "Don't you dare say I'm like him. Don't you dare!"

Her voice had risen and I put my finger to my lips.

"Oh, goody-two shoes Pamela wants me to be quiet, does she?" *Maggie glared at me.* "Well, I won't. I won't suit you or him or anyone else. See what he did to me?" *She pointed at her face.* "See? Do you know how he did it?"

"You were late home." I began to back out of the room. If Daddy heard her, we'd all be in trouble.

"He hit me with the lamp, across the face."

"It was your own fault. You know not to annoy him."

Maggie seemed to slump. "I really believe you believe that, Pam."

"Of course I believe it. You were told to be in by one and you weren't. It's called accepting the consequences, Maggie."

"The way you did when you only got five A's in the Leaving and not seven like he wanted."

"Exactly." Despite the sneer in her voice, I think she was beginning to understand. "Daddy loves you. He worries about you. About us." I smiled at her. "I'll sneak into the kitchen and get some ice for your face. Hang on there."

She nodded and lay back down, but just before I left, she said, "But I'm still not like him, Pam."

I said nothing.

"And he doesn't love us. That's not love."

I didn't bother arguing with her.

"And if it is, then I'm never getting married."

"Sure who'd have you?"

She grinned a bit at that. I smiled too. "I'll just go get that ice."

I was glad things had reverted to normal.

Chapter Twenty-nine

Things were slowly improving on the home front. Very slowly because that's the way things change when my mother is involved. But she did manage to ask about my hospital visit. And even tried to look impressed when I told her about seeing the baby twisting and turning around on the screen.

"Haven't things changed?" she said in a high squeaky voice. "In my day there was nothing like that." Then as was her way, she changed the subject and asked what I wanted for tea.

My sickness had stopped. Now I was eating again. I only hoped I was going to have triplets because I was getting through enough food to feed a small family for a decade. "Whatever you've got," I said.

"Well," Mam stuck her tongue out the side of her mouth. She does that when she thinks. "There's fish, or a nice piece of chicken, some leftover ham from Sunday, or there's even sausages."

"Fine."

"What's fine?"

"The chicken, ham, sausages. Hold the fish."

I think she thought I was joking because she laughed and only gave me the sausages.

I spent the rest of the night raiding the presses for more grub.

Mam's lukewarm interest was unfortunately not matched by the rest of the world. It was totally incredible. I'd never before realised that a pregnant woman's body and condition are up for discussion by just about everyone.

I suppose in some ways I'd asked for it but it didn't make it any easier. Complete strangers talking to me about *me* is my idea of hell on earth. I mean, they only want to know your business so they can discuss you behind your back.

The first inkling that this was about to happen to me, *me*, 'the-only girl-whose-life-is-covered-by-the-official-secrets-act' – that's John's idea of a *hilarious* joke, by the way – happened on the Monday following the cessation of my sickness.

I should have known it would happen, but another thing about pregnancy is that you get stupid.

The bus that I was heading into work on, stopped. Heads swivelled in my direction. I was, as usual, sitting on my own in a double seat up near the front of the bus. "Oh, it's OK," I said to the driver. "I'm fine this morning." I thought he'd drive on.

Instead he cut the engine and turned to me. He was an auld fella, about fifty, grey-haired and smiley. "Didn't I tell you," he said delightedly, in his thick Dub accent, "didn't I tell ya the auld morning sickness would pass?"

He hadn't, as a matter of fact, but I just gave him a curt smile and a nod.

"Lasts about," he screwed up his face, "three or four months and then it goes. I should know, me daughter had a baby last year."

"Right." Another smile, this time slightly more desperate, with the hidden message of 'get the bus moving for Christ's sake'.

He smiled again and turned on the ignition.

Relief.

An old woman, with an old person's smell, slid in beside me. "So you're expecting," she said. She clutched her handbag and leaned towards me. "I was worried about you. I thought you had a disease or something."

"Nothing terminal anyway," I said, getting a sick pleasure out of wiping the smile from her face. "Just contagious."

Another old person laughed. "That shook you, Maudie." Turning to me, "How far along are you, dear?"

I swallowed. The whole bus was tuned in. Except for the people wearing Walkmans.

"Four months."

"Ohhh," she eyed me up and down. "You look bigger than that, doesn't she, Maudie?"

Maudie agreed and then they got onto a fascinating discussion on bump sizes. I was informed that if I got much bigger it'd put terrible pressure on my bladder.

"You'll have to be stopping the bus to let her wee," Maudie cackled to the driver.

He chortled back.

I sat and fumed in humiliation.

Into work. The bus stopped outside the bistro and I got off. I waited until it pulled away before entering. I mean, I didn't want the whole bus knowing where I worked as well. Though John would have said that they couldn't have cared less. He always thought I was paranoid like that.

John. John. John. I shook my head to get him out of my head. It seemed like everything I did, I kept thinking of what he'd say. It really annoyed me.

It didn't take much to annoy me.

Must be my hormones.

In I went. Patrick was sitting at his usual table, reading his usual paper and eating his usual breakfast. He glanced up at me as I went by. "Glad you didn't go out with me," he grinned. "I'd have been suspect number one."

"Pardon?" I began to take off my coat.

"Of course I only asked you out about a month ago, but still . . ." he winked and laughed.

"But still . . .what?" My voice got frosty. I know he was a customer. I know I was the manager. But I didn't give a shit. "But what, Patrick?"

"You're pregnant, aren't you?" He gave another smile. "Congratulations. You and your boyfriend must be pleased."

Little shit. Little smart . . .

"She's dumped her fella," Lucinda said, suddenly appearing beside us with a pot of tea. "Given him deh high jump." She turned to me, unaware that if I could have I would have torn her scrawny neck from her equally scrawny body. "Haven't ya?"

"Lucinda, I really don't think that's anybody's business but my own. Now, when you've finished pouring Patrick his tea I'll want to see you up in the office."

Shaking from head to foot, with as much dignity as I could, I opened the door to the stairway and made my way to the office.

Louis was there which was unusual. Normally he didn't come in until later – I think he'd finally realised that he got on my nerves and it was best to stay clear.

"Aw, here she is," he beamed his gnomy smile at me. His little pointy nose scrunched up and he asked, "So when will you be wanting to take your leave?"

I jerked to a standstill. "What leave?"

"Your maternity leave." He eyed me up and down. "Very soon, I suppose. Aw, leave me high and dry." He wagged his finger. "That's the kind of thing you're supposed to tell future employers, you know."

"And who told you?"

"A little dicky-bird." He tapped his nose.

"Huh, a pelican, was it?"

"What?"

"A little dicky-bird with a big mouth."

"Ho, ho," Louis slapped his thigh and creased up. "You are the driest of the dry, Margaret. That's a good one."

I didn't smile. In fact, I was beginning to wonder if I was trapped in some nightmare world. Like in the film where everyone knows the guy's business and he's appearing on TV and he hasn't a clue about it. That's the way I felt. "I won't be taking leave for another four months, Louis." I spoke quite low so that his laugh drowned out much of what I said.

"Pardon?" He stopped laughing and anxiously looked at me. "When did you say?"

"You heard me." I gave a polite smile and said, "Now I hope that was just between us. Don't go telling the rest of the staff."

"Oh, no."

He'd worry now. He wouldn't know when he'd be left on his lonesome. Serve him right.

A tap on the door.

"It's Lucinda," I said to Louis. "I'd like to talk to her, in private."

He scurried out of the room. No doubt bolting down to Josie to ask her if she knew when the baby was due.

"Hiya," Lucinda came in. "Guess you're going to gimme an ear-bashing about telling Patrick that you're up the pole."

"What . . . *you* told him? Why?"

"Why not?" She shrugged. "He kept asking about

you. Wanted to know if you really were seeing anyone and stuff. I had to tell him otherwise he would've asked you out."

"And who else have you told?"

She shrugged. "No one. Well, maybe just Romano, but like he knew anyway. He kept saying that you were fat, so I just told him."

This was unbelievable. Like, I knew eventually it would be really obvious but I didn't need this. "Well, in future," I snapped, "just mind your own business. My life is not your business. My boyfriend or lack thereof is not your concern."

"Wha'?"

"Just, just keep your mouth shut."

"Fecking *charming*." Lucinda rolled her eyes, folded her arms. "Can I go now?"

"Yes."

Out she went.

I collapsed into a chair and closed my eyes.

I'd have to stay upstairs for the day now. The thought of people knowing all about me panicked me.

But what was done was done.

I'd have to live with it.

Unfortunately.

Chapter Thirty

Mammy rang this morning wondering if I'd like two visitors. Herself and Geoffrey. It seems that her and Mr Parker have progressed to first names now.

Wonderful.

The last thing I wanted was visitors. Shauna was crying, two teeth were coming through, and Mrs Maguire was busy telling me what I should and shouldn't put on her gums.

"Of course," she sniffed, "she's such a cranky child, I doubt anything would work."

"You'd be cranky too," I said, as pleasantly as I could, "if you had teeth growing." I should have said she'd be crankier, but I hadn't the nerve. Still I'd done my bit to stick up for my child. I'd made a mental vow that when Mrs Maguire came, she could give out about me, Dick and the house, but that was it.

It was a relief just to get out of the room when the phone rang. I heard her flicking on the television as I made my way into the hall.

Anyway, I'm digressing. The upshot of it all was that I didn't want to tell Mammy not to come and visit as it'd hurt her feelings. So I told her I'd be delighted and she said they'd arrive around one and not to go to any trouble to make lunch or anything.

Of course, she didn't really mean that. In between rocking Shauna, feeding David – who'd gone nearly dumb since his grandmother had arrived to stay – and humouring Mrs Maguire, I concocted a salad. The fact that it was cold meant that Mammy and Geoffrey didn't have to arrive exactly on time.

But on the dot of one, they came.

"Being on time is no crime," Geoffrey said as I remarked on how punctual they were.

Mammy giggled and handed me a box of sweets. "Something for the children."

"David, come on and say thanks to Nana Scanlon," I called.

David emerged, head hanging, from the kitchen where he'd been following me about all morning. "Ta ta," he muttered, looking at them from lowered eyes.

"Come and give me a big hug!" Mam held her arms open wide.

David toddled reluctantly up the hall and let himself be cuddled by her.

Geoffrey, meanwhile was having a good look around. He banged with his fist on the wall. "Good walls," he remarked. "Nice house."

"Thanks."

"And how's Shauna," Mammy cooed, holding her arms

out for the baby. I gladly handed her over saying, "Aw, she's cutting a few teeth. She's in agony."

"Oh, the poor lamb, the poor lamb," Mammy spoke in a high childish voice and snuggled the baby into her. "Is there lots of toothy woothies coming? Is there? Is there?"

I was glad that someone felt sorry for my child. I mentally gave the two fingers to the old wagon sitting in state in the dining-room watching Emmerdale.

"Mrs Maguire's inside, Mammy," I said.

"Oh, is she? I must go and say hello." Mammy, Shauna in her arms, scurried in.

I heard them talking soon after. Well, Mammy was doing most of the talking. She was great like that. She was totally oblivious to the fact that Mrs Maguire couldn't stand the sight of her. She just chatted on regardless. Sometimes I felt sorry for Mammy; she tried so hard to be nice to the most horrible people.

It was just Geoffrey and me alone in the kitchen. I busied myself setting the table, letting David put out the knives and forks. Geoffrey sat himself down and seemed to be waiting expectantly for the food to be put in front of him. His face dropped about a mile when he saw it was a salad he was getting.

"I did it in case you didn't arrive on time," I said, wondering why on earth he made me feel that I had to apologise. "It wouldn't spoil."

Geoffrey smiled. "Pamela, when I'm going places, I always arrive on time." He had the rich, fruity voice of the man on the Mr Kipling ad. "Mr Punctuality, Mr Practicality, Mr Rationality, that's me." He patted his belly and smiled.

"David, will you go and tell the others that lunch is ready?"

David shook his head and looked at me.

"Please, honey?"

He didn't even bother to shake his head. He stood in the corner and began to wriggle into it as far as he could.

"Funny little man," Geoffrey said loudly. "Says nothing."

I was sick of my kids being criticised. "He's well able to talk. He's just shy," I said sharply, wanting to brain David for letting me down and hug him at the same time and tell him that it was perfectly all right not to talk.

I went and fetched the two nanas myself. Mammy was chatting when I arrived in and Mrs Maguire had the volume on the television up full blast so that she could hear her soap.

"Lunch," I said. I took Shauna from Mammy and deposited her in the pram. She normally had a snooze around this time. Flicking off the television so that she could have some sleep, I followed the two ladies from the room.

Mr Parker was already eating when we got into the kitchen. "Julia," Mammy said, insisting on calling Mrs Maguire by her first name, though she hated it, "this is Geoffrey, a friend of mine."

"Hello," Mrs Maguire gave a sour smile, sat up straight in her chair and began to polish her knife and fork on her napkin. She does that every mealtime and it really gets on my wick.

"So, " Mammy asked, "how are you enjoying your stay with Pamela and Dick?" She looked around the kitchen. "Haven't they the place lovely?"

"I'm looking forward to getting back to my own flat," Mrs Maguire replied as she began to move all the onions to the side of her plate.

"Oh yes. There's no place like your own place," Mammy said.

"Nice ham," Geoffrey said. "Very tasty."

"Thanks."

"I hear your other daughter has got herself in trouble," Mrs Maguire volunteered.

I wanted to kill her. The bitch.

Mammy flushed bright red. "Well . . . yes. Yes, she has. Unfortunately." She turned to Geoffrey, "You're right. The ham is lovely."

"And that her boyfriend has left her high and dry."

Mammy swallowed hard. "Well . . . no. That's not what she – "

"I'm so glad I've no daughters. Dick was the only child and he's done all right for himself. Of course, I never expected to see him settled so early on, but sure, that's the way. You can't live your children's lives for them."

"No. No, you can't."

"Unfortunately." Mrs Maguire speared a tomato and glared at it.

Mammy smiled uneasily.

"So," Mrs Maguire said after she'd eaten a piece of the tomato, "I suppose you've been in shock? Did you kill her?"

Mammy looked like a cornered rabbit. "Well, no. No, I didn't but, you see she . . ."

"Oh," Mrs Maguire sniffed, "you went all modern and trendy on her, did you? Told her it didn't matter. I don't know, the things people accept nowadays. It's a different world."

"It the kind of thing you have no choice but to accept," I

cut in. Turning to Mammy I asked, "Do you want some dessert?"

Mammy shook her head. I don't think she knew what to say.

"Well, acceptance is one thing, condoning that sort of behaviour is another. I'd have tanned her hide for her."

I wanted to brain the ould bitch. Tell her that her son couldn't wait to have his way with me before we got married. See how that made her feel.

Mr Parker nodded assent. "I agree," he said. Then, shoving his plate away from him and ignoring the hurt look my mother gave him, he said, "I'll have dessert. Pamela. I'm not much of a salad person."

"I've yet to meet anyone who is," Mrs Maguire said, pushing her plate away as well. They smiled at each other.

I wanted to kill them both.

Mammy stared at her plate. I knew she was hurt, but she smiled bravely and said, "Well, we're all entitled to an opinion, aren't we?"

"We are indeed," Mr Parker said. "And," he added, "we're all entitled to a dessert."

The two ladies laughed. My mammy giggled slightly too loud and I was unexpectedly reminded of the way she used to be around Daddy.

But she couldn't feel that way about Mr Parker, could she?

I felt sick as I looked at her beaming face.

Since his mother had arrived, Dick had started making every effort to be home on time for dinner. He had also started a *very bizarre family-man routine, making out that the kids and I were the archetypal Brady bunch.*

I mean we were happy but Dick seemed determined to prove some sort of a point to his mother.

That evening, he strode into the house announcing that he'd sweets hidden on him. David began to cower away, clutching onto my jeans and sucking his thumb. But Dick junior gave a yell and pounced on Dick, hanging from his arm and begging for sweets.

Mrs Maguire looked disdainfully on.

"You've to guess which pocket they're in," Dick said, grinning broadly and winking fondly at me.

Dick junior guessed and Dick made a big deal of putting his hand in the pocket and pulling out a packet of Rolo.

"Cool," Dick junior grabbed them from him and raced off to eat them.

Of course, when dinner was served up ten minutes later, he refused to eat it.

"Eat up," Dick said. Quite calmly, I have to say.

Dick junior made a face. "I hate broccoli."

"All children that don't eat broccoli go to hell," Mrs Maguire pronounced from the top of the table.

I bit my lip and hoped she'd shut up.

"What's hell?" Dick junior asked.

"Somewhere where Holy God burns little children."

Dick looked fascinated and terrified all at the same time.

"Mrs Maguire, that's enough."

"I'm only telling the lad – "

"Well, don't."

"Pamela, don't talk to my mother like that."

"Well, tell her not to go frightening the children then."

Dick's face changed. Only a slight change but it made my heart thump down with such force that I felt sick. No one else would have noticed it, the way the little frown-line appeared just over his eyebrows, but I knew him so well. So I babbled out, "Sorry, Mrs Maguire, it's just that, well, Dick junior has nightmares and I don't think that what you said was – "

She held up her hand, "Oh don't bother, Pamela. I'm just an old shoe. What do I know? I just brought up my own child, that's all."

"Now eat up, you," Dick said sharply to Dick junior.

That was the last bit of conversation at dinner. Oh, except for the bit where Mrs Maguire muttered, "Spoilt. That's what's wrong. Spoilt children are the ones most likely to end up in trouble." Then in case I didn't get her drift, she said it again, "In trouble."

I rang Mammy tonight just to have a chat with her. All that day I couldn't get the idea of her and Mr P out of my head. There was no way she could be serious about him. What about Daddy? And I wanted to see if she was all right after Mrs Maguire's horrible comments.

I waited until both Mrs Maguire and Dick had gone to bed. The phone rang for ages before being picked up.

It was Maggie. She sounded a bit annoyed. "Hello?" she barked out.

"Oh, hi, Maggie, it's Pam. I'm looking for Mammy."

"She's in bed. Sorry, Pam. I thought you were," she paused, "someone else."

"Oh, right."

"John. I thought you were John."

"Oh. Did you tell him?"

"Tell him?"

"About the baby?"

"God. No." She laughed a bit. Then sort of sad-sounding, she said, "No."

I didn't know what to say then. "How are you? Are you sick or anything?"

"Not now. Just tired."

"That's normal."

"Is it?"

The way she asked it, sort of anxious, made me feel sorry for her. It was a long time since I'd felt sorry for Maggie. She wasn't the sort of girl you'd feel like that about. "Yeah," I said gently. Then, sort of hesitating, afraid in case she'd tell me to get lost, I added, "Look, if you've anything you want to ask, just, you know, ask me. I'm here."

She didn't say anything for a bit and I was afraid I'd trodden on her toes. But just as I was about to apologise for saying anything, she said, "That's great, Pam. Thanks. Thanks a lot."

"No problem."

Then she said something really strange. She said, "You're lucky. You really are."

I think she must have been drinking. Not that I'm not lucky, I know I am, but for her to say it. That was drink talking for sure.

I made a jokey comment about being saddled with a mother-in-law from hell and she laughed and we hung up.

But it felt nice.

It was nice to laugh with my sister.

Chapter Thirty-one

Once again, I lived in the golden glow, basked in the sunshine of John's – quite frankly – adoration. I tried not to let myself wonder what he saw in me, because then I'd only go all paranoid and think that he was only after what he thought he could get.

I mean what else was there?

But having someone think that you're great eventually seeps into your pores and, little by little, even I began to believe that I was the wonderful being he was convinced I was. I mean, John laughed at things I said. He thought my stubbornness and grouchiness were cute. OK, so it could all be a bit irritating when I was trying to make a serious point and he kept falling over himself laughing at my 'psycho' view of humankind. But I returned the favour by sneering unmercifully at him when someone had done the dirt on him at the radio station. "See what I mean," I chortled when Alice defected from his programme to her boyfriend's. "People are unreliable."

"Aw, she's not unreliable, just infatuated," he'd said.

John made excuses for everyone.

But I liked that he was like that, funnily enough. It made the world seem less horrible than I knew it was.

Saturday the fifth of May. Dick was meant to bring me to the pictures. Instead he drove to his apartment block.

"Aren't we going to the pictures?" I asked.

He winked at me, made my heart into slush. "Nope."

"Oh." I gave a nervous giggle.

"We are going to make an x-rated movie ourselves tonight."

I grew cold. Ice cold. He couldn't mean . . . "You don't mean . . ."

"You drive me crazy, Pamela." Dick drove into his parking space and cut the engine. He turned to face me. "And you know how I feel about you. All I want is for us to be together." He leaned in closer and began tracing his finger along the line of my neck. "And I think that after three months it's about time we advanced our relationship."

"But I can't . . . I mean . . . I want to be married and for it all to be nice and romantic and Daddy would kill me if he found out and . . ."

"Your dad's not going to find out though, is he?" He started kissing my neck. His hands stole up my blouse and found their way inside my bra. He made circles on my back with the tips of his fingers.

I shivered and moaned slightly.

"God, Pamela . . ." he sort of groaned as he covered my breasts with his hands.

I couldn't do this. Mammy would die. And Dick'd have no respect for me. "No. No, Dick!" I pushed him off. "We can't . . . I can't. It's not right."

Dick's face darkened. A little frown-line appeared over his eyes. "So, it's not right to kiss a girl I love, is it not?"

A girl he loved? Loved? He'd never said that to me before.

"You love me?" I said the words slowly, relishing the feel of them. I wanted him to say it again.

"Well, I thought I did." Dick sounded annoyed. He pulled away from me. "Just forget it!"

Oh God. What the hell had I done? I'd ruined everything.

"You've ruined everything," he said sulkily. "I thought you'd like it, us coming here. I had it all planned."

"I do like it, Dick. I love coming here. It's just that, well . . ." I stopped. Gulped.

"Yeah?" He looked questioningly at me. Big brown eyes, so hopeful. And hurt.

I hadn't meant to hurt his feelings. Dick was sensitive. If I so much as refused a sandwich that he'd made, he'd take it personally. And this, this was so much bigger. God, in that moment, I hated myself. I had such a knack of ruining things. Of turning people against me. And if I didn't do something I was going to lose him. And I couldn't face things without him. "Well," I said softly, "if you love me, then I suppose it's OK."

"Forget it."

"No, Dick," I put my hand on his arm, "please. I'm sorry."

"Yeah well . . ."

"I'd like to, you know," I fumbled for the words, "make love to you."

"You would?" He regarded me with glittery eyes.

"Yep." I know I wasn't convincing. I mean, I was so green in those days. I'd always wanted to be married, in a white dress, looking really beautiful before I lost my virginity. But still, Dick was there and that was the main thing. Fingers shaking, I touched his face. "I'm sorry about before."

He said nothing, just kissed my fingers, one by one. "And why did you change your mind?" he asked softly.

"Because of you," I whispered. "I love you, Dick."

He said nothing as he pulled me towards him.

John's bedroom was like the Virgin Megastore. No, wipe that. It was nothing like the Virgin Megastore. The Virgin Megastore has records and tapes and CDs. So did John's bedroom. That's where the similarity ended. In the Megastore they're neatly stacked on shelves. In John's bedroom, they were just all over the place. To get to John's bed, you had to wade towards it, being careful not to stand on anything too precious like first editions (whatever they were) and picture vinyls and stuff like that.

John and I spent a good bit of time in his bedroom whenever Rat was in the house. Rat didn't like me. According to John, he did like me only he had a problem showing it. He liked me as much as he liked anybody, John said. Anyhow, Rat was downstairs, in pretty grouchy humour and John and I were in his room and he was showing me the new demo tape that a band called Diesel had sent in to him.

"It's great stuff. Will I play it for you?"

I didn't bother to nod. He was going to play it anyway. This band was John's find of the decade. They were going to make it big and he, John, was going to help them do it.

"There's a great song, just here," John began fast-fowarding the tape.

I gave a smile and studied all the posters on his walls. Posters of bands, posters advertising gigs he'd gone to. John was a guy that had never grown up. As innocent and as enthusiastic as a five-year-old.

"Here it is," John depressed the play button and turned to me, grinning.

It was a slow song, I think it was called 'Blind Kinda Love'. A love song about love. Soppy.

I was about to slag it off when John put his finger to his lips, "Listen."

You set me free/I'm bound to you/You let me fly/So I stay close/Without you baby, I am nothing/With you with me, I'm a hundred times, a hundred times, a hundred times myself/Don't need no help to recognise/Love is blinding me,/opening up my eyes.

John turned the volume down so the music became a tinkling in the background. "Nice, isn't it?"

"Yeah." It was OK, I guess. For a love song. I don't go in for love songs much. I prefer sad melancholy lyrics. Leonard Cohen and I would be best buddies. If I went in for having best buddies, which I didn't.

"It reminds me of you and me." John moved closer to me. He put the palm of his hand on my face and stroked my cheek with his thumb. "With you here," he kissed me softly on the lips, "I feel, happy, you know."

"A hundred times yourself?" I slagged, not able for this intimacy.

"Yeah." He kissed me again. His hand caressed the swell of my breast. His lips moved towards my neck. "Fecking crazy about you."

"Rat's downstairs," I yanked John's hand away and attempted to look worried. I couldn't, just couldn't let him see how much I wanted him to continue.

"What? D'you want me to give him a call?"

"No! You know what I – "

He started to kiss me again.

Despite all the jangling of alarm-bells in my head, I gave in.

I let him love me.

The sex with Dick was good. I mean, I'm no expert, I've only ever slept with Dick, but he kissed me and did all the stuff you read about in magazines. And Dick said nice things about my underwear that made me squirm though I tried to smile and look pleased.

And I tried to respond to his love-making, I really did. I suppose because it was my first time, I was a bit uptight and it hurt me and I bled.

When he'd finished, he lay on me for a while, panting, then he lifted himself up. And he looked down on me and winked.

"That was my first time," I said. I don't know if I was trying to apologise or let him know that he was special to me.

"Obviously," Dick said.

I felt hurt. I mean, really hurt. I can still remember the hurt.

But I smiled. "It'll be better next time."

"Mmm, I like the sound of that."

I laughed and he laughed.

He loved me with an intensity I didn't know he had. He kissed, caressed and touched me. He told me he loved me. I let him take all my clothes off. I let him take all his clothes off. I'd only been ever into quick, meaningless shags before so this was a bit different. It was different because I think John really, really liked me. And I liked him. And when it was over, I lay beside him and didn't feel disgusted with myself or with him. He lay, looking down on me, his chin resting in the palm of his hand.

"One thing, Maggie," he said, "I feel I have to tell you."

"What?"

"I'm not looking for anything too serious or heavy right now, OK?"

He gave a guffaw of laughter as I belted him.

That night, I cried. I don't know why.

I just cried all night.

Chapter Thirty-two

"I hear Maggie's pregnant?"

Mam stopped dead, turned white and clutching me on the arm, whispered frantically, "Ignore her."

I was quite prepared to do just that, only, like I said, Mam had stopped. It was as if her feet were glued to the ground. Mrs Doyle, the neighbour from across the road that was hated violently by everyone in our house, called from across the street once again, "I hear Maggie's expecting?"

"Well, Mrs Doyle, there's nothing wrong with your hearing is there, whatever about the rest of you."

"Maggie!" Mam whispered alarmed. "Don't get into a brawl."

"Oh hello, Maggie, it's you, is it? I thought you were Pamela."

My arse she did. Pamela was about ten sizes smaller than me.

"Still getting up to all sorts of mischief the way you did when you were younger?"

"A bit like yourself, Mrs Doyle, only I admit it."

"Jesus, Maggie!" Mam began to walk, scurrying away towards our house. I began to follow her, trying to make it look as if my mother wasn't running for her life.

"Bye now," Mrs Doyle called. "Nice seeing you."

I wanted to say something smart in reply, but the strange sensation in my stomach was back. I'd first felt it a couple of days ago and thought that it was just, embarrassing to admit, wind. But it mustn't have been. A sort of cold dread spread through me as I realised that maybe it was something to do with the baby. Maybe something was wrong.

"Tell your chap I was asking for him," Mrs Doyle called, sounding as if she was sniggering away.

"What and have him commit suicide?" Thrilled at my wit, I slammed the front door, shutting Mrs D and her nasty comments out. I turned to Mam to ask her what I should do about the baby, only she was glaring at me and she looked – I can't say furious because my mam never looks furious – but she looked pretty damn annoyed.

"It's bad enough the whole street knowing our business without you shouting at the neighbours as well," she said, her hands clenching and unclenching. "Honestly, Maggie, when are you ever going to grow up? It's bad enough you being pregnant but, I don't know, flaunting it about, now that's not on."

Her attack, if it can be called that, stunned me. And sort of sickened me too. "Flaunting it?" I said weakly.

"Yes."

"So?" I quirked my eyebrows. "You'd prefer if I didn't have it?" I knew that would get to her. She was dead against abortion. Her Catholic upbringing and all that.

"Don't be ridiculous. I – "

"So what else can I do? Wear a girdle? Starve myself?"

"No, I – "

"Let Mrs Doyle shout all the abuse she wants at me?"

"Well, sticks and stones . . ." She didn't finish. She just nodded.

Nodded.

"Just . . . you know . . ." she said, "let her get it off her chest. Keep the peace."

Get it off her chest! I couldn't believe it. But, then, I could. This was *my* mother after all.

"And what about me? *I'm* supposed to take it?" It was a stupid question. Of course I was supposed to take it. It was called accepting the consequences. A favourite in our house. It had never gone down too well with me. "Mam, I'm not like you. I don't take crap from people."

I didn't wait for the lecture she'd brainwashed us with when we were kids. Instead I buttoned back up my jacket, picked my bag off the floor and told her I had to go to work.

I slammed the door.

God, it felt good.

I considered walking around the city centre for a while

as I wasn't due in work until lunchtime, but four-point-five-months-pregnant, overweight women find it hard to keep walking for close on three hours. And there's no point in going in for tea anywhere because the tea only insists on coming out the other end.

Sorry to be so, I dunno, off-putting.

So, I went to work. At least there, I could put my feet up, have a freebie lunch, even if it was only chips, and chill out until I was due on.

There were a few customers in. Pretty good for eleven o'clock. Most of them were from the office-block across the road. They'd started coming in when we'd put Romano outside to hand out leaflets about the breakfast. Some girls had asked if he was on the menu and Romano, not having a clue as to what they were on about had nodded and smiled. Hordes of them had come in that particular day and insisted on Romano serving them.

Lucinda had been furious, saying that the way the girls were treating Romano was sexist. Then Josie had said that it was the only time she'd ever seen Lucinda giving out about having no work to do and a bit of a row had broken out. However, the row, instead of putting customers off, had only encouraged them.

Every day, the amount of girls coming in had increased.

On day three of the windfall, I'd bought some scones on the way to work and sold them with a fifty per cent mark-up.

Every scone had gone.

So I'd asked Josie to cook some for us.

"Bake," she'd sniggered. "Not cook."

"Good," I nodded. "We'll look forward to some baked scones."

Her mouth had dropped open, she'd been about to launch a tirade, then (I think) realising that I was a pregnant woman, she'd spat, "I'm only doing enough for the bleeding eleven o'clock crowd."

"Sure."

I mean, it was a compromise of sorts.

Since becoming pregnant, I wasn't able or interested in fighting so much. Yep, I hate to say it, I was turning into one of those placid pregnant women. Only being placid wasn't so bad. Nothing seemed to upset me so much. It was a nice, liberated feeling.

That day, there were about twenty girls and a few fellas in sitting around eating scones or chips and laughing among themselves.

Lucinda was on her break. Louis, for once, taking the initiative and coming up with a good idea had swapped Romano's break with Lucinda's so that Romano could serve all the girls.

OK, so maybe it was a bit sexist, but it worked. The girls drooled over him.

"Oy, Romano," one of the girls called, "can we have another tea over here."

Romano nodded, scurried to the counter where Josie deposited a pot of tea on his tray. Back to the table, nodding and smiling.

I marvelled at the change in the place. I mean, it was

still a bit grubby and run-down looking, but the food was good and the uniforms looked smart. I was just in the process of sitting down, having ordered a coffee from Josie and mentally giving myself a well-deserved pat on the back when all hell broke loose.

"The nerve!" The girl who'd ordered the tea stood up and the rest of her friends gaped, looking quite shocked. A couple of the lads began to snigger. "Who do you think you are, saying that to me?" She began to advance on Romano who, tray in hand, began to back away. "How *dare* you say that to me?"

Oh God!

Bright understanding smile. "Sorry? What's happening here?" I hurried over and looked quizzically at Romano. "Romano?"

He shrugged.

"I gave him a tip," the girl spat. "In fact, I want it back." She held out her hand, "Gimme my money back."

"What happened?"

"I want my money back!"

"He told her to fuck off," another girl said.

"Yes," a bright smile broke out on Romano's face. "Fuck off, bitch."

"Romano!"

Behind me I could hear Josie cackling away.

"There!" The girl pointed a finger at him. "D'you hear that!"

"It'll be Lucinda," Josie called over, still laughing. "She's put him up to it."

What was I saying about placid? Wipe it.

"Romano, did Lucinda tell you to say that?"

"Pardon?"

I wanted to kill them all. Romano for not understanding, Josie for laughing and Lucinda, well, I was going to crucify her. "Give the girl her money back." I turned to the girl, "I'm sorry about that. He doesn't understand English yet. No offence meant."

She crossed her arms. "Well," she said, quite snottily, "offence *taken*."

I felt angry again, but I had to clamp it. She was the customer after all. I had to remember that.

"Look," I said, "have this tea-break on us and come in later for a dinner too."

"All of us?"

Jesus, but she was a hard bargainer. I wanted to tell her to fuck off myself now. I plastered what I hoped was an insincere smile on my face and nodded. "Sure."

"OK so." She didn't even bother to thank me, just picked up her bag and left. The others followed her.

"Wagon," I muttered. I flung a horrible look at Romano and stalked over to Josie, "You tell Lucinda that I want to see her in my office the minute she gets back."

"But sure it was only – "

"The *minute* she gets back."

Josie and Lucinda arrived up twenty minutes later.

"Here we are," Josie said, entering without knocking. She pushed Lucinda in front of her. "Here's Lucinda."

"It was only Lucinda I wanted to see," I eyeballed

Josie sternly. "Unless you had something to do with it too?"

"Well, no, I didn't, but, well . . ."

"But, well – bye, Josie."

"Look," Lucinda spoke up, "it was only a joke."

"A joke? A *joke*?" Standing up, I walked around the desk to face her. She looked sullenly up at me. It was the look that did it. "For the first time ever," my voice shook with annoyance, "this place is making a few quid. We're attracting customers during the day and all you can do is train one of our waiters to tell the customers to fuck off?"

A hint of a smile appeared on her face.

Behind us, Josie stifled a chortle.

"It's not funny!" I whirled on Josie. "These are our *jobs* I'm talking about here. What if those girls go telling everyone about what happened? What if no one comes any more?"

"Of course they'll come," Josie rolled her eyes. "Jesus, they'll all want to be told to fuck off if it means a free lunch and dinner!"

"That is not the point!"

"That girl is a cow," Lucinda said. "She's always ogling Romano."

"That shouldn't – "

"Naw," Josie interrupted me, shaking her head vigorously. "It wasn't that girl he said it to, Lucinda – it was yer wan with the big boobs."

"I'm trying to – "

"The spotty one?"

"Crater face, yeah."

"Gawd," Lucinda looked impressed. "I wouldn't have thought she'd have made a fuss."

"I'm trying to say something here," I snapped. This was unreal. In London, I'd had brilliant control over the staff but here, in this little poxy piece of Dublin, I might as well have been invisible.

"Sorry," Lucinda did a credible attempt at looking contrite, "what are you trying to say?"

"I'm trying to tell you that if you ever, *ever* pull a stunt like that again, you are . . . aaahhhh." I was about to tell her she'd be fired only the sensation in my stomach was back, I sat down on the desk, hand over my belly.

Immediately, the two of them were on top of me, almost suffocating me with their concern.

"What's wrong?" Josie put her arm on my shoulder and led me to the chair. "Sit down, easy now."

I shrugged her off the minute I was sitting, she didn't seem to notice.

"Have you a pain?" she asked.

I didn't want to answer. Then it hit me that if I didn't get help something awful might happen the baby. For the first time it dawned on me that I was solely responsible for what was growing inside me. *Me?* Responsible for someone else. The thought made me shudder.

Josie once again put her hand on my shoulder. "Are you cold? Have you a cramp?"

"No." I made my voice strong, assertive. "It's just, you know, a funny sensation inside me."

"A funny sensation?" Lucinda said from her vantage point at the other side of the desk. "Is it, like, a fluttery sort of sensation."

My throat tightened. I nodded.

"It'll be a footballer so," Lucinda said. "Jaysus, it must've given you some kick to make you double over like that."

"Kick?"

Both women looked at me. "It's moving. Your baby," Lucinda said as if I was a gobshite. "Don't tell me you didn't know what it was."

I gave a tight smile that could have meant anything.

"At least you know it's healthy," Josie nodded. In a soft voice, she said, "You sit and relax there and I'll bring you up a cuppa, right?"

They were only being nice because they were in trouble, I'd bet my life on it.

"And in future, I'll just let Romano be treated as a sex-object," Lucinda said mutinously.

Josie sniggered.

"Tea'd be lovely, Josie," I turned to the computer, ignoring Lucinda's smart-assedness.

If I was honest, I could have hugged the two of them, just for putting my mind at rest. Well, if I was into hugging and all that shit.

What Lucinda had done didn't seem to matter so much.

My baby was safe.

When they left, I put my hand over my stomach and rubbed it gently. The baby moved again, a soft butterfly-wings type of feeling. And for the first time, I talked to it. "Hiya, in there," I whispered. And then I stopped, feeling stupid.

It was true, pregnancy does make you all moronic. Imagine talking to a bump.

Jesus!

Chapter Thirty-three

I went shopping with Shauna and David today. I bought them piles of new clothes. Shauna needs new everything what with the summer coming and, because David is a smaller child than Dick junior, he isn't able to wear Dick's old summer clothes, so he needed stuff too. It's hard work carrying bags and bags of shopping with two children hanging out of you. I did sort of ask Dick's mother if she'd keep an eye on Shauna for me, but she said that she wasn't a baby-sitter, that her days of minding children ended when Dick left home to marry me. She said other stuff too, the usual stuff about women having children that they can't be bothered minding but I'd heard it all before.

I'd heard it after I'd had Dick junior and I wanted to go back to work. Dick and his mother had said that a woman's place was minding her children and I suppose they're right. I was touched that Dick cared so much about his child that he wanted me at home full time. And besides, we didn't need my money as Dick earns loads. So I stayed at home. And I don't mind it, only it's very lonely at times. Isolated.

Still, I have Mammy. She's good to me.

I bought some clothes for myself too. A few pairs of jeans and some summer tops. I got myself some shoes as well. I love shoes, though I can never seem to buy anything that ever looks, you know, 'in'.

Anyway, when I got home, it was just after one.

Unlocking the front door, I let myself in. There was a thumping, bumping sound from upstairs and, automatically, I pushed David back out the door.

"Hello?" I called, standing in the hallway with the door wide open so that I could escape just in case we were being burgled. David, of course, wouldn't stay outside on his own, he toddled in and latched onto my leg. There'd be no escape now. In the background I could hear Shauna yowling in her car-seat.

Mrs Maguire peered out into the hall. "Oh, you're back, are you?" she said. Pointing up the stairs, she said, "Dick junior is home."

"What?" Disorientated, I looked at her, looked at my watch. "But what's he doing home? He doesn't get off until two." Then anxiety hit me. "He's not sick, is he? Was he sick in school? Who brought him home?" Scooping up David, forgetting all about Shauna, I rushed towards the stairs.

"His teacher brought him home at lunchtime," Mrs Maguire said. "She was looking for you." It sounded like an accusation. "First the school rang to see if you were there and when I answered and told them who I was they said they were bringing him home."

"Dick? Dick?" I called beginning to climb the stairs. "Dick, honey, are you OK?"

"The teacher wants you to ring her." Mrs Maguire said. "I wasn't good enough to be told anything. Oh no, I was good enough to be left looking after him but I wasn't good enough to be told why he was dumped on me."

Dick appeared at the top of the stairs. He looked down on us, his hands behind his back and a sulky look on his face. "He wouldn't let me go first in the line," he said.

"What? Who?" In two seconds I was beside him, feeling his forehead in case he was feverish. "Who wouldn't let you go first, honey?"

"Paul O'Toole. He pushed past me. So I hit him."

"Oh," I cuddled him into me. "You shouldn't hit other little boys, Dick." I ruffled his hair. "So why are you home? Were you sick?"

Dick shrugged, losing interest in the conversation. "Can I play with David?" His gorgeous brown eyes looked up at me. I didn't know what I'd do if he was sick. Relief that he seemed to be OK washed over me. Whatever had been wrong was fine now.

"Sure," I gave him a little pat on the bum and pushed him downstairs. "Bring David very carefully with you."

I smiled fondly as I watched him leading his little brother down.

Mrs Maguire flicked a glance up at me before heaving her ample bosom in the direction of the TV room. "You'd better release that cranky daughter of yours from the car before she throws any more tantrums," she snorted.

I was tempted to say that she must take after her

grandmother, but I couldn't. I just couldn't bring myself to say that about my beautiful little girl.

Instead I restrained myself to the silent, behind-the-back two-fingers gesture.

It was dinner time, we were eating dessert and I was in the middle of telling Dick about Dick junior being sent home early from school when the phone rang.

"You'd better get that," Dick said to me. "It's usually for you."

Getting up, I went into the hall, wondering who it could be. Maybe it was Maggie. I'd told her to ring me if she wanted anything and so far she hadn't. I found myself wishing stupidly that she would call me.

"Hello?"

"Mrs Pamela Maguire, please."

A vaguely familiar voice that I couldn't place. "Yes, this is she."

"It's Alister Gibney here, Mrs Maguire. Principal of St Joseph's School. Dick's headmaster?"

Oh God! I remembered something about having to ring the school. "Yes?" I tried to make my voice sound surprised.

"Didn't you get the message to ring the school?"

I was glad we were only talking over the phone. My heart raced, my stomach heaved, my face flamed red as I lied, "What message? Eh, no, no, I didn't get any message."

"Oh, well, it doesn't matter. I'm ringing about Dick. We had to send him home today."

"He's fine now." I began to twist the phone cord in and out through my fingers. I stopped. If Dick saw how knotted

the cord was getting he'd have a fit. "There isn't a bother on him now."

A pause.

"Mrs Maguire, did you ask Dick why he was sent home?" Alister Gibney sounded annoyed, stunned. Sort of strange.

"Well, yes, I . . . I did."

"And what did he tell you?"

My mind began to buzz. Hum. It was like it was telling me not to listen to this man any more. Sometimes when I was a kid it used to do that, when someone was annoying me, usually Maggie. *"Mr Gibney,"* I spoke through all the static in my head, *"is there a problem? Dick seems fine now."*

"Dick was sent home because he pushed another boy into a wall."

I remembered Dick saying something . . . *"Paul something or other, wasn't it?"*

"Paul O'Toole."

"Yes, he said that Paul wouldn't let him go first," I gave a bit of a laugh. *"You know how boys are."*

"Paul had to have twenty stitches to his head."

I hadn't heard right. I couldn't have.

"Dick pushed him and kicked him in the head."

No, there had to be a mistake. Dick would never do that. Look how gentle he was with David.

"No," I said, *"there has to be a mistake."*

"There's no mistake, Mrs Maguire. Miss Ryan, Dick's teacher, has already highlighted Dick's aggressive behaviour to you and she says that there hasn't been any improvement."

I was numb. I couldn't say a word. The sounds of the

kitchen seemed very far away. I could hear Dick junior laughing loudly at something someone had said.

"I'm ringing you from home now. I'd very much like to see you and your husband on Wednesday afternoon if that's possible."

Dick would freak. "Eh, I'm available but my husband . . ."

"It's important that I see both of you."

He didn't sound like a man who was in the humour for compromise. "I'll see what I can do."

"Mrs Maguire, I need to see both of you. For Dick's sake."

"Oh, right."

"And, eh, I think it would be best if Dick stays off school until we sort something out, all right?"

There had to be a mistake.

"I'll meet you both after school hours. Around three?"

"Fine." *I put down the phone. There had to be a mistake.*

I deserved an Oscar for the way I walked back into the kitchen. For the way I lied about my mother ringing me at the most inconvenient times. For the way I laughed along as Dick told another story about his stupid PA.

He was going to fire her tomorrow and he was loving it.

I didn't want to spoil his good humour.

I'd wait for a while before I told him.

I tackled Dick junior as I was putting him to bed. I love looking at my kids in their pyjamas. Dick is currently big into Action Man. He'd a pair of PJs on him which showed Action Man on a mountain bike. Climbing into his bed, he said his prayers and looked eagerly at me for a story. "A Pokémon one," he said, wrapping his arms about his knees.

Is this Love?

"Did you push Paul very hard today, honey?" I asked.

He shrugged. His eyes narrowed. "He pushed me first," he said sullenly.

"And then what happened?" I tried to be gentle, not to sound accusing.

Dick shrugged. "Nothing. He fell and I hit him with my foot."

"Was he sore?"

"Maybe." He dropped his head. "I don't like him. We all hate him."

"The headmaster wants to see me and Daddy on Wednesday."

I could see the way Dick froze. Slowly he looked up at me. "Daddy?" he whispered.

I nodded.

"Don't tell Daddy."

"I have to." I made my voice stern. Then seeing how worried he was, I added, "But he'll understand that you didn't mean it."

Dick relaxed. "OK." Bright-eyed again, he surveyed the books on his shelf. "Read that one," he pointed to a Pokémon book. "That's my favourite."

I hated myself for the false reassurance I'd just given.

I hated myself full stop.

Chapter Thirty-four

I thought I was being clever this time. I'd brought a book to the hospital to read whilst I was waiting – Roddy Doyle's *The Snapper*. I'd heard of the title, knew Roddy Doyle had won a prize for writing and so, searching in Eason's that morning, before work, I'd seen the book and purchased it on the spot. I'm not a bookshop browser at the best of times and when I do buy, I tend to buy huge tomes that represent good value for money. But I never finish them. So when I saw this book, I thought it looked just the job, medium-sized print and just long enough.

It looked . . . finishable.

Josie and Lucinda had creased up laughing when they'd seen it. They'd both started doing really exaggerated Dub accents, gawking hard at me and saying, "Yer wha'?" and then laughing all over again.

Of course, I hadn't got the joke until I'd opened the first page of the book and now I wanted to belt them both over the head with it.

Had they no respect?

I was their manager for Christ's sake!

How dare they take the piss out of me!

I bristled and fumed as I read the first couple of chapters. I mean, of all the books in all the world why did I have to walk in and choose this one? A comedy about a teenage Dublin girl who finds herself pregnant by an ould fella –

"Good book, eh?"

I looked up. "Great," I agreed, blushing and smiling weakly.

"And how are you?" the same person asked. "How's your baby? Things going all right?"

"Sorry?"

"You know, after the three sections you had on your other three children? How's your husband coping?" The woman looked at me expectantly. "Is he up the wall? I know mine would be. Oh, he'd insist on coming here with me and quizzing all the doctors." This bizarre person gave a chuckle, "That's just the way he is."

"Really." I turned back to my book before she could talk any more. *Who was this woman?*

"I understand if you're a bit down over things," she went on. "I mean, I'd be down too."

This time I said nothing. People were looking and wondering, like me, what this woman was on about.

Or maybe just what this woman was on.

"At least you found your way to the clinic no problem this week," she said.

The penny dropped.

Naw.

Naw, it couldn't be.

I couldn't be *that* unfortunate.

Yep.

Yep, it was.

I *was* that unfortunate.

It was the person I'd asked directions from my first time here. The one I'd told my made-up hard luck story to.

Fuck.

That's all I could think.

And it wasn't just from reading the book either. It was the only word that could adequately convey my despair.

Well, holy shit and fuck.

And, how the hell do I get out of this one?

And then . . . "Have you had *three* sections?" A timid skinny girl with an enormous bump asked beside me. Blushing and stammering badly, she said, "I wasn't listening in. I just, well . . . I couldn't help overhearing and well, my baby's breech and they said that they might have to do a section and well . . . I was wondering . . . you know . . ." her voice quivered, "what it's like? I mean, they say babies aren't as happy later on if they're sectioned." She looked at me and barely whispering she breathed, "Is it true?"

I was the focus of everybody's attention. The three-times-sectioned woman. Star turn of the day. I gulped, pulled myself together, "It's a piece of piss," I lied confidently.

"Oh." The timid woman looked a bit shocked at my chosen expression.

"And my kids are as happy as if they'd exited down the birth canal."

"Great, thanks." The timid woman, sorry to keep calling her that, but that's what she was, you know, she put her hand on my arm, yeuch, and thanked me.

I didn't feel a bit guilty. I mean, I'd cheered her up and made her happy at the fact that she was going to be cut open.

Now that's some achievement, isn't it?

"Any problems?" the doctor asked. He was a different guy to the one I'd seen before.

So I told him about the fluttering. Just in case Josie and Lucinda had been wrong. But, no, give them credit, they were spot on.

"It's the foetus moving," the doctor explained with a smile.

"Good." I nodded.

He folded up my chart and handed it back to me. "See you in," he consulted a little book, "four weeks' time."

"Fine. Great."

I was just out the door when I remembered all the stuff I'd meant to ask.

But I couldn't go back in.

I'd write it all down and save it for the next time.

Mam had something to say.

She was hovering around the door when I let myself in. I hadn't gone back to work, just come straight home from the hospital. Louis had told me that he could handle things at the bistro and though I very much doubted it, I didn't very much give a shit either.

"Hello, Maggie," Mam said, all bright smiles. "How'd your visit go?"

Suspicion set in. Mam to talk about my visit with a smile on her face was not normal. In fact, it was downright creepy. "It went fine. The baby's fine."

"Well, I'm so glad." Pause. "A letter came for you today."

"Oh yeah?" I turned to the hall table, to search for it. She had it standing upright being held in place by the telephone.

"From London. Maybe from John."

I felt sorry at the pathetic hope in her voice. "Well, Mam, if it is from him," I said briskly, picking the letter up, "it's not what you think."

She gave a gay laugh. "Sure, I'm not thinking anything at all."

"Good." I began to rip open the envelope, "'cause I know for a fact he isn't going to beg me to go back to him. And even if he was I'd tell him to fuck off."

"Oh stop talking like that. You're no better than a street girl." She was annoyed now. Her hopes dashed. "Well, I don't know. I can't understand it. He seemed a perfectly nice chap when I met him and he *is* going to be a daddy. I mean, you haven't a hope with Louis now. Not with a – "

I paused in the act of unfolding John's letter, "What?"

Mam reddened. "Just a thought I had. You and Louis."

"The guy that owns the bistro?"

"Well, how many other Frenchmen do you know?"

I'd told her and told her that Louis wasn't French but she preferred to believe in her own little fantasy. "None," I answered.

"Exactly. And anyway, as I was saying, he's not going to be interested in you now. No man wants another man's child. No man should be *expected* to want another man's child. And you'll be left on your own, an old maid with a baby, and all the time you could have that wonderful man in London."

I had to bite my lip to keep from saying anything. I don't think she meant any harm, but I don't think she ever considered anyone's feelings either. To her any man was wonderful. And now that I was pregnant, John had taken on the mantle of Redeemer and Saviour and The Chosen One. In fact, any man would do. She didn't care. Jack the Ripper could propose marriage and my mam would rush out to choose her hat.

"Any man is better than none."

That was it. "I *am* seeing someone as a matter of fact."

"Oh." Her face lit up. "And?"

"He's an ex-con. Sort of crippled, but his other leg is only missing a foot. And, oh, yeah, he can't talk English. In fact, he can't really talk at all." I paused, "Brain-damaged, I think is what they said in the hospital."

"And where did you meet him?"

Point proven. I muttered a 'Jesus' and stomped

upstairs, still holding John's letter in my hand, only now it was crumpled.

"Have you told John yet?"

I slammed the bedroom door and sat down on the edge of the bed. The baby moved inside me and I did the hand on the tummy thing. It was almost like an automatic response. I mean, I was still terrified but at the same time I was beginning to have funny feelings towards the baby. *Maternal* feelings. Not overwhelming love or anything, just a responsibility for looking after it so that it was born healthy.

I wasn't thinking beyond that.

That was far too scary for me.

After the baby had quietened down I opened John's letter. I was determined to remain calm so that the baby wouldn't sense my upset. I'd read somewhere that babies in the womb can sense things about the outside and I didn't want my baby absorbing all my hate feelings and angry feelings. I mean, if it did, maybe it could turn out to be the Antichrist or something.

With my luck anything was possible.

"Keep calm," I muttered like a mantra to myself as I simultaneously read John's letter. Oh, it was a typical John piece of wise-cracking crap and despite myself I got angry. In fact I got so angry that I tore the letter into little pieces and stamped on them. Afterwards I didn't feel a whole lot better.

D'you want to know what he wrote?

Mags – I hated the way he called me that – *I'm shaking so much I can hardly write this. I mean, that solicitor's letter you sent me was the business! Legal fees, court battles, bloody hell I'm in bits here. Anyhow, it's a terrible pity that such a prestigious firm don't seem to have a phone or a fax or even e-mail. And what's more, they're not listed in directory enquiries.*

I'd get out of dealing with them asap. They're a shower of crooks! This letter is a warning. Burn it just in case they come after me for rumbling their dodgy game.

Anyway, just to let you know I've decided not to ring you any more – the bill is costing me a fortune and I don't want to waste my nice four-and-a-half-grand windfall paying to talk to you. Hope you're well and the job is going OK.

I've lost mine. The electrician one. Got laid off. Anyhow I'm glad. There was too much buzz in it for me. Cue to laugh.

Gimme a ring sometime. Love and kisses to all your family. I'd send you some too only you don't want them any more, do you?

All the best from the fair dealer of secondhand wheelers, John.

And that was it.

Bastard.

There was no way I was ever going to contact him again.

Well, not unless I could get a reputable firm of solicitors to write to him. On the cheap.

Some hope.

Chapter Thirty-five

"Aw, Mr and Mrs Maguire," Alister Gibney ushered us into his office, "welcome."

"Dick and Margaret, please," Dick said, shaking the headmaster's hand. "Let's not get bogged down in formalities."

"Indeed." Alister Gibney indicated two chairs and we sat down. He seated himself behind his desk. Then, lacing his fingers together, he peered keenly at us. "I'm sorry to meet you both under such circumstances."

Dick nodded gravely. "How is the little lad – Paul?"

"He's improving. He'll survive."

Dick took my hand in his. "We were up the wall worried, weren't we, Pamela?"

My hand was cold, Dick's hand was warm. All I could do was nod. If I said anything I'd vomit.

"My wife was up crying all night, Mr Gibney – "

"Alister."

"Alister." Dick gave a brief smile. "She was up all night.

And as for Dick junior, I don't think he realised the harm he'd done." He shook his head. *"He watches cartoons and plays video games and, you know, he thought that Paul would just bounce back up again."* He shrugged, *"It's probably all our fault. We're to blame."*

"Oh no," Alister Gibney rushed in to reassure Dick, *"it can't just be down to that. I'm wondering if maybe Dick is hyperactive or something? Anything like that?"*

Dick looked at me. *"No, I don't think so. Pammy?"*

I shook my head. Dick gave a slight squeeze on my hand. *"No,"* I managed, *"he's not."*

"Mmm." Alister Gibney stared at us. *"He's been very aggressive since he started here last September, bullying other boys, shoving, that sort of thing."* He lowered his voice, said carefully, *"Is there a problem at home, maybe? Sometimes we find that –* "

"What sort of problem?" Dick asked. *"I mean, we both love him, he's not short of toys to play with."* He shook his head, baffled, *"I don't know."*

"Is he a bully at home?"

"Sometimes he picks on his little brother," Dick said. *"But Pam would know more about it than I do."* He turned to me.

My eyes watered. I couldn't go along with that. Dick actually was quite protective of David. There was no way I could shoot the little kind things he did down in front of the two men. *"I, I think he likes David."*

"But he's rough with him, isn't he?" Dick pressed.

I shrugged.

"My wife's upset," Dick said.

"It must be upsetting for the two of you," Alister Gibney

said. He sighed. "I hate to tell you this but your boy is on his last chance here. Any more behavioural problems and we either get him assessed by sending him to a child psychologist or he has to leave." He shrugged. "I think maybe you should bring him somewhere – something must be causing his behaviour."

"We'll certainly look into it," Dick nodded. "But I've had a word with Dick and he's promised to say sorry to the boy in question and not to fight any more."

Alister Gibney stood up. "All right, we'll give it one last go." He came around the desk and we stood up. He shook both our hands and said, "You can send Dick back tomorrow."

Dick rolled his eyes, "Afraid not. Wouldn't you know, he's caught the chickenpox and I don't think he'll be back for a week at least."

Alister Gibney laughed. "Give him my best."

"Will do."

And we were out.

Dick caught hold of my arm and squeezed it really hard all the way to the car. "Fucking asshole," he muttered angrily. "Who does he think he is, asking if everything is OK in our house?"

"He's only doing his job," I had to run to keep up with him. "I think – "

"I don't give a monkey's what you think," Dick released me and unlocked the car. "Who the hell do you think you are, keeping the fact that Dick was in trouble hidden from me? What sort of a marriage do you think my mother thinks we have now – huh?"

Is this Love?

He slapped me across the face.

Not hard or anything. Just an annoyed slap.

I deserved it. Letting him down in front of his mother.

And I deserved it for lying to Dick junior.

Dick hadn't understood. He'd gone ballistic. Dick junior was lying in bed at home with a black eye and bruised legs. He'd a small cut over his eyebrow too. When I'd gone in to him that morning, he'd turned away from me and faced the wall. He wasn't crying, which I was glad of but still, his silence was awful. I'd gone to him and rubbed my hand up and down his arm but he'd flinched and pushed me away.

Imagine not knowing what to say to your own child.

I only wish Dick had hit me harder.

Chapter Thirty-six

Painfully slowly, the way things work with me, bits and pieces of my life began to take up residence in John's house. First it was my toothbrush. Then it was my deodorant, underwear, CDs, tapes, shower gels, body lotions and eventually I left a spare bag over in his house for weekends.

I didn't think about it.

I refused to think about what it meant.

Then John asked me to move in permanently with him.

Daddy was diagnosed with cancer. In his liver. There was no hope. Mammy broke the news to me and Maggie. I remember so well. We were in the kitchen and it was spring. She told us that she'd some news. Her face was red and blotchy and her hands shook. She sat down at the table and said, "Girls, your father is very sick – "

Maggie muttered something and we both looked at her.

"Nothing," she shrugged, smiling sweetly.

But it had been. I'd heard her. She'd said, "Well, we know that already."

Sometimes Maggie can be frightening. It's like she doesn't feel anything for other people. I'd only ever seen her cry once and that was when she'd got herself in trouble for being late. But other than that, she just sails her way in and out of trouble and doesn't care a lot about what happens to anyone.

Anyway, Mammy starts again. "Your daddy is very sick. It's can-, can-," she couldn't bring herself to say the word. Instead she said, "It's the big 'C'."

"What? Atlantic or Pacific?" Maggie said then.

Somehow, Mammy didn't seem to realise Maggie was being a bitch. "No, Maggie," she said, gulping hard, "he has cancer." And then she exploded into tears. Weeping and sniffing.

I got up and hugged her close.

Maggie got up and left the kitchen. I heard her in her room playing some record or other.

I felt more sorry for Mammy and me then I did for Daddy. Wasn't that weird?

It was like my cosy little existence was being threatened.

Move in with John?

I looked around his bare living-room and tried to turn the whole thing into a joke. "Sorry. Nope. I'm not into minimalist decor." Kissing him, I grinned, "Sorry, no go."

"Daw!" John rolled his eyes. "I'm not talking about you moving in *here*." He caught my hands in his. "I *meant* let's get our own place. Just you and me. What d'you think?"

"No." I tried to sound nice about it, instead of horrified. "No, I don't think so."

"Why not?"

"Well . . ." Desperately I searched for reasons "First off, what about Rat? He needs you."

That sounded good. I sounded *concerned* about Rat.

"I'll still be around for him. Any anyhow, I've been thinking – "

"And secondly," I interrupted, "this is your house. You can't just give it up."

"I can. All I have to do is . . ." he grinned, "not live here."

"Ha." I laughed weakly. "Good one."

"I mean it."

Oh God. I shifted uncomfortably on the sofa. I hated the way all this was making me feel. Confused. Angry. Terrified. Sort of all churning about together inside me. I wanted to run, to get as far away from this conversation as possible. I gave him a light dig, "Why d'you want to start getting all serious? Aren't things fine the way they are?"

"Yeah, but . . ."

"Good." I hoped the subject was closed. I couldn't bring myself to look at him.

"Things are great the way they are," John said, "but I thought you wanted some commitment."

"Me?" I almost laughed out loud.

"Yeah. You." John sounded annoyed. "At the beginning you do a runner because you're afraid we'll split and now, when I try and show you how I feel about you, you turn me down."

"I didn't turn you down. I just don't want to move in with you."

"But, Jesus," John always said 'Jesus' when he got ruffled, "you're practically living here already! You stay every weekend except when Rat's here. All I'm suggesting is a more permanent thing."

Permanent. Yeuch. "And all I'm saying is that it's not practical. Rat needs you . . ."

"Fuck Rat. I can manage him." He paused, said slowly, "I need *you*."

The words hung on the air.

"So come on? What about it?" He nudged me. "We'll have a laugh. And it'll just be as if we're sort of . . . housemates."

Mmm. "Like, we're just *sharing* a house? As in *friends?*"

"Yep. Like Chandler and Monica."

I ignored that. "And we're not bound together or anything?"

"Jesus, stop. You're turning me on. Bound together. Sounds dead nice."

I giggled. He could always make me do that. But he wasn't going to make me agree by being funny. "I mean it, John – I don't want to be, you know, all dead serious about things."

He looked confused. As confused as I felt. "Mags," he said slowly, "you've a spare toothbrush in the bathroom, you share my bed, you eat breakfast with me, you hang your knickers on my radiators, you nick my jumpers and I never ever see them again. That's serious stuff, you know."

I glowered. "Well, if you've a problem with me taking your clothes you should have said so."

"Naw, that's not what – "

"And *excuse me* for putting my underwear on display. D'you want me to hide it?"

"No way. It's dead kinky."

Despite myself I smiled.

"I love you. I want to be with you." He put his arm around my shoulder and pulled me near. "It's not like we'll get married or anything. You can leave me any time."

I liked that bit. "Mmmm."

"Housemates then?"

I wanted things to be really clear. "Well, if you're going to be my housemate, I'd expect you to do housework and stuff."

He grinned. "I'll iron. I'll even iron towels and socks."

"And will you wash my car?"

"Yep. When I wash my car, I'll wash yours."

"You never wash your car."

"Well, I'll start." He held up his hand. "Scout's honour."

It all sounded OK. But I wasn't going to be a right sap. I shrugged, said nonchalantly, "Well, I *might* move in. Maybe. As long as it's not a major big deal. And I'll still want to keep the flat with Ali."

He gawked at me. "How'll you afford that?"

"I'll move in here. There's no rent on this place and you'll still be able to mind Rat."

He didn't look too happy, but I was. I mean, if I lived in John's house, with Rat there, well, it wasn't exactly moving in with *him*, was it?

"I'll move in here," I said. "Take it or leave it."

He smiled slightly, tweaked my hair. Said nothing.

So I moved in.

Ali told me she'd miss me. I said I wasn't exactly going. As in *going*.

She said a 'yeah' as if she didn't believe me.

I handed her the next month's rent.

She told me I was bonkers.

Only I knew I wasn't.

It was important to keep all options open.

And that's the way things worked for years and years and years.

Until I discovered I was preggers . . .

The day we found out Daddy was sick was the saddest and happiest night of my life. Obviously Daddy being sick was terrible; Mammy cried for hours wondering how she'd cope all on her own. I told her that she wouldn't be on her own, that she'd have me and Maggie. But that wasn't the same, she said.

There'd be no man around.

Everyone needed a man.

"Yeah, they're good for putting the bins out and eating leftovers from plates," Maggie said casually.

Mammy and I looked at her horrified. What was her problem?

"And when you need a lamp flung across a room, call in a man."

309

"Maggie!" Mammy gasped. "Stop! I don't know what's wrong with you! Lamps, bins? What are you talking about?

"Men."

Mammy started crying again and I glared hard at Maggie. She looked slightly ashamed, muttered a 'sorry' and went back up to her room.

It took ages to calm Mammy down. She still wasn't the best when Dick called over later on.

And that's when my night got happy again.

I told Dick I couldn't go out what with Mammy being so upset about Dad being sick and in hospital and all. He was a bit sulky about it at first. Dick hates when plans are changed at the last minute but in the end he agreed to sit in with me and watch telly.

"Well, once it's just the two of us," he whispered as he nibbled my ear.

"It will be," I whispered back. I trembled at his hands on my hips, his breath over my face.

It was a great evening. Mammy took a sleeping tablet and went to bed, Maggie went out drinking with some boy she'd met at a party and Dick and I cuddled up on the sofa. It was like having our own little place.

In the middle of a film we were watching – I can't remember what it was called, anyhow, it's not important – he said something really weird. He had his arm around me and pulling me near him, he said softly, "You're great, Pammy. You make me feel good. Important."

"You are important, Dick." I snuggled further into him. "Well, important to me anyhow."

"And I'm important at work. I earn good money."

"Yeah."

"I do, Pam."

"I know, Dick."

He kissed my cheek and asked hesitantly, "Why do you like me, Pam?"

"Why do I like you?" I laughed a bit and faced him. "What a weird question!"

It was the wrong thing to do. He glowered at me and removed his arm from my shoulder. "Forget it!"

"Oh Dick, don't be like that!" Dick hates being laughed at, not that I was laughing at him, but he's hypersensitive.

"Don't be like what?" He jumped up and began pulling on his jacket. His face was red and sour.

"Oh, Dick," I stood up and put my hand on his arm. He shoved me away from him. I lost my balance, staggered back and hit my head off a table. The pain of it.

Immediately he was beside me. The concern in his eyes, the way he helped me up, the kiss to the sore part of my head. The, "Oh Pam, I'm sorry, I didn't mean it. Oh, I'm sorry. I love you. I'd never . . ."

I put my finger to his lips and shushed him.

And we kissed and made love on the floor.

And afterwards he asked me to marry him.

And I said 'yes'.

The happiest and saddest night of my life.

Chapter Thirty-seven

Profits were up. Not in the millions bracket but certainly up a thousand quid or so. Louis was practically on the ground kissing my feet. Not that he had to bend down or anything, my feet were practically at his lip level.

"So you proved good," he chortled. "After everything."

"After everything?"

He waved his hand and blushed a bit. "You know, everything. Don't mind me. I'm just babbling. This is mighty. A profit. An actual profit."

"I was thinking, Louis, of what you should do with this profit."

Another laugh. His laughs really got on my nerves. And even though I was seven months pregnant, all the placid hormones in the world wouldn't have made me relax at the way he snorted at the end of each chuckle. "I hate when you've ideas," he said, wagging a finger. "It always means spending money."

I ignored him. "We should invest in getting the bistro done up. Buy new equipment, that sort of thing. We should prioritise our needs."

"Prioritise our needs? Oh, now, now."

"Louis," I strove for control, tried not to sound patronising, "whenever a business makes a profit, it's always advisable to pour it back into the company."

"And that's what I'm going to do," Louis said. "I'm bringing all the staff out for a party tonight. We're closing early and heading off for a meal, drinks, whatever."

He beamed at me. I don't think he was looking for approval which was just as well as he would have been wasting his time. "You can't do that!" I spat. "That's just a waste." I was stunned. Louis didn't seem like the kind of man to throw away cash on other people. I mean, his heart broke every time an uneaten sausage went in the bin. And here he was talking parties. The moron.

"Oh but I can," he grinned. "I own this place. And besides, it's not a waste."

"Oh yeah, and how do you make that one out?" I had to sit down, the baby had decided to get in on the act and was kicking and punching like mad.

"Because," he drew himself up proudly, "if I show the staff a good time, they'll think kindly of me – "

"You're not their friend, Louis. You're their employer."

"And," he continued, ignoring me, "they'll work harder, be happier because they think I appreciate them. They won't be so keen to ask for pay rises as it's harder to bargain with someone who's been nice to you." He stopped. "There now."

He made sense. "Where did you think that up?" I asked, sort of annoyed I hadn't thought of it.

He smirked. "I'm doing a business night class and the guy who runs it is very good. That's what he told me to do with the money."

"Oh," I said, standing up, hoping to intimidate him, "so if he told you to flush our money down the toilet you would too, I suppose?"

"Well," he nodded, "I'd certainly think about it."

"And what about the restaurant? Are you going to have parties every time you make money?"

"Not at all," he said. "Whatever's left this time and the next quarter's profits, we'll spend doing up the place."

"Fine." I left the office fuming. The little shit, doing a business course. Huh, he was probably doing it so that when I had the baby I wouldn't be able to come back. Well, feck him. He'd see how hard it was to run things when I left.

"Listen," he shouted after me, "tell the others we close at five, OK?"

I didn't answer.

Louis had booked a fairly fancy place in Bagott Street for nine. Of course, I was the first to arrive. I hated being first. Here I was, a big fat pregnant person that just looked awful in whatever I threw on, arriving first in a restaurant. I was convinced all the staff and customers thought that I was like that guy in the *Monthy Python* video who eats and pukes and explodes. Oh, they were probably all thinking, look at her, she looks like she enjoys her food.

And they'd be right.

Huh, Louis' profits would be gone on just my dinner alone.

Josie was next. Great, another fat person. She arrived in, dressed in a huge orange dress, white high-heeled shoes and a slash of red lipstick on her lips that looked as if she'd cut herself. "Hello," she boomed at me from over the other side of the restaurant. "Fancy place this. Hope the dinners aren't really poxily small." She patted her belly, "I enjoy me grub." She gave the waiter a dig as he pulled out her chair for her, "Remember that now, won't you, young fella?"

"Sure." He nodded and grinned as she sat herself down.

Lucinda arrived soon after. Leather skirt up to her armpits, belly-top, high black boots. The waiter couldn't run after her fast enough. She did her model walk, sashaying down through the restaurant, looking at no one.

"Hi yez," she sat in beside me and began to yank her skirt down, "fancy fucking joint, what?"

"It is." I picked up a menu and hid behind it.

"Romano here yet?"

"No," Josie said. "He was going spare as he'd nothing to wear."

"I think Louis was lending him something," Lucinda said.

"No!" Me.

"Fuck. Off." Josie.

"I know," Lucinda said glumly. "I'd say he'd need to stitch two pairs of trousers back to back to even go near Romano's hips." She sighed, "He's got a fine pair of hips on him."

Josie winked broadly. "I'd say now, just a wild guess, that Romano's hips aren't the only fine things you like about him."

"Arse, face, legs, shoulders, hips." Lucinda listed them off on her fingers. "That fella is sex just waiting to happen."

"You *fancy* Romano?" I suppose I should have guessed. I mean when you thought about it, it was obvious.

"Does she *fancy* him?" Josie gave a snort and people looked. "Does she *fancy* him?" Josie snorted again, this time rolling her eyes in what I suppose was meant to represent orgasmic delight. "She'd lick his jocks she fancies him so much."

For the first time in months, someone had achieved the impossible. My appetite disappeared.

"Aw yeah," Lucinda nodded vigorously, "he's a beaut. Says nothing, keeps smiling and does what he's told. My kinda man, you know."

Josie clapped her hands and chuckled.

I smiled, said without thinking, "Mmm, I like those kinda guys too."

"Yeah?" Lucinda glared at me. "Romano's too young for you. He's only twenty-six."

"I didn't mean – "

"So was your guy, the guy you ditched, not like that then?" Josie asked, leaning toward me, her eyes bright with nosiness.

"He was fine," I snapped. I poured myself a glass of water. She kept staring at me, looking for more information. I shrugged, "His big problem was that he wasn't deaf and dumb. I would've liked him better that way."

The two women laughed.

"Yeah, like me da," Lucinda giggled. "His big problem was that he had a mouth at all. And such a bleedin' *big* mouth. All the better for drinking with, I guess."

I didn't find it funny but she and Josie sniggered.

"One time," Lucinda said, leaning towards me, "my ma watered down all the whiskey in the house, thinking it'd keep him sober. And she was in *bits* in case he'd notice." She giggled slightly. "And he didn't!" She rolled her eyes. "He still got drunk and slapped us around the place. Or like, he *convinced* himself he was drunk."

More laugher from her and Josie.

"Men are such eejits!"

I felt sick as I looked at the two of them. How could they laugh at that? "Your da hit you?"

"Yep. All the time." Lucinda's smile faltered. "I guess you don't think that's funny – huh?"

I shook my head. I couldn't even answer her. It was about as funny as being pregnant.

"Yeah, well," Lucinda shrugged, "I don't either

really but you know, I have me own place now and I have Leonardo and if me da hadn't been such a total bastard, I mightn't have all that, you know what I'm saying?"

I gawked at her.

The girl was mental.

Mental with a 'really seriously off the head' in front of it.

"And wasn't Louis very good to you?" Josie said. "Like, when you ran away from home, didn't Louis find you a place to stay and all."

"He did."

"Our Louis is a scabby fucker but he has his moments."

"He does." Lucinda nodded. "And sure even to Romano he was dead good."

"Romano?"

"Yeah," Lucinda nodded. "Sure he gave Romano a job when no one else would touch him."

"Did he?"

"Yeah, Romano's from some place in Europe, I dunno, some place where all the fellas look like him. Must be a great place. Anyhow, there was a war there."

"Bosnia," I supplied.

"Yeah, yeah." Lucinda looked impressed. "You're dead clever. Anyhow, poor sucker, his whole family were wiped out. His parents, his sisters even his little baby sister. What age did he say she was, Jos?"

Josie shrugged. "I dunno. His English is crap. A few months maybe?"

"Yeah, anyhow, she was only a few months old and she died."

"That's awful." My hand snuck to my belly.

"Yeah," Lucinda nodded. "It was. Anyhow, he came over here, camps in the doorway of the bistro and Louis sees him one morning and offers him a job and finds him a gaff to stay in. Now wasn't that dead nice?"

"Yeah." I suppose it was but Jesus, no wonder the bistro was heading down the tubes, a runaway and a homeless refugee working in the place!

Louis was thick.

"Louis is not the worst, you know," Josie said. "I mean, he's crap at running the place and he's full of shit and he's an ugly fucker but underneath all that he's basically . . ." she frowned. "What would you say, Lucinda? He's basically what?"

"Basic. Just a basic person."

"Yeah, he's basic."

"Who's basic?" Louis, with Romano in tow, appeared suddenly at the table. "Go on, who's basic?"

"Aw just some dickhead we know," Josie answered. She moved up on the seat. "Here, Romano, sit here, beside me and Lucinda."

"Yeah," Lucinda patted her seat and batted her eyes at Romano, "sit here."

I felt sorry for her. She hadn't a hope. There was no way any guy'd take on a girl with a kid.

"Come on," Lucinda said again.

Romano grinned and, moving slowly in a pair of tight short trousers, he gingerly sat down.

"I had to lend him some gear," Louis said. "It's a bit tight on him. He's not as slim as me."

"Not as fucking *weedy*," Josie spat.

Louis reddened. "Uncalled for there now, Josie."

I gazed at the four around the table. It was amazing how one short conversation can change your whole view of people.

Lucinda was *mental*, Louis was *definitely* full of shit if he employed people that weren't fit to even work in a restaurant, and as for Josie, she gossiped about everyone and knew everybody's business.

From now on, I vowed, I'd have to play my cards even closer to my chest.

Chapter Thirty-eight

I know it was a guilt thing.

I know all that.

But I had to do it.

I mean, it's awful when your child won't talk to you. I'd tried and tried to get Dick junior interested in things but every time I opened my mouth he turned away. And what's so heartbreaking is he's normally so bubbly. But now, it's like he's inside himself somewhere and I can't reach him.

Dick says he's only punishing us and not to worry. "And if he keeps treating you like that, I'll belt something out of him," he snapped.

And I know Dick's only trying to help, but I don't think hitting Dick junior will work.

It's weird. Most of my memories of being young are pretty hazy but I remember once when Maggie had got herself into some terrible trouble at home – she'd told Mammy something in confidence about school and Mammy, as she should have, had told Daddy and Daddy walloped Maggie until Maggie got sick.

Maggie hadn't talked to Mammy or Daddy for weeks. But in the end she had.

And maybe Dick junior would too.

Only I couldn't wait that long.

He'd been silent for two weeks. Two whole weeks. And even though his teacher said he seemed much better in school I had a terrible feeling that it wasn't going to last. So, the second Saturday of silence, when Mrs Maguire had taken herself off to visit a friend, I dumped David and Shauna on Mammy and drove myself and Dick junior into town.

He sat in the car in silence for most of the trip. And just as we turned into the multistorey car park, he asked sulkily, "Why are you bringing me here?"

"I thought it would be nice, me and my big boy going to the pictures together. How about it?"

He looked warily at me. "Why?"

That threw me. I gulped. "Because I'm sorry, Dick," I said. "I'm sorry for what Daddy did to you. He only did it because he was angry."

"I only hit Paul because I was angry."

"Yes, well, Daddy loves you. He doesn't want you getting into trouble in school. He did it because he cares." I took the risk of tousling his hair. He didn't pull away. "Now don't tell me you love Paul?"

"No way!"

We both laughed a bit.

"So how about it – a film and then McDonald's?"

"Yeah! Cool!"

He was back. My little boy was back.

I held him to me and kissed his head. He squirmed a bit and pushed me off. "Yeuc-hy!"

We got back to Mammy's around four. Dick junior was proudly carrying his happy meal toy and he couldn't wait to show it to David. "I'll even let him have a go of it, Mammy," he said. "Not Shauna though 'cause she's too small."

"Good boy." The relief of hearing him chatter was overwhelming. I'd been badly frightened, I knew that now. In future I resolved not to let Dick hit the kids quite so much.

I pulled up outside Mammy's, undid the childlock and Dick junior bounced out. He ran slap-bang into some fella.

"Dick," I chided gently, "will you watch where you're going?"

"Sorry," Dick junior, sounding sulky, traipsed away from the man and up the path to Mammy's.

"Sorry about that," I turned to the man. "He's a bit hyper."

"No problem," the man said.

He was quite handsome in a cute kind of way. There was something familiar about him . . .

"It's Pamela – yeah?"

I had been just about to run after Dick junior to stop him hammering on Mammy's door in case Shauna was asleep inside when the guy said my name. "That's right," I looked closer at him. "And you . . ."

He smiled ruefully, coloured slightly, "John. Maggie's John?"

"John!" Of course it was John. "Sorry, I should have known. I'm a bit scatty today and . . ."

"Naw, it's fine. Is she in, d'you know?" He nodded towards the house.

"I don't actually know, I've been in town all day. Mammy's in though — you can wait in the house for Maggie." I wondered if they were back together.

We started walking up the drive. "She just left me, you know," he said out of the blue.

"Did she?" I didn't want to make out I knew anything.

"Yeah." I think he sensed that I didn't want to get involved. He turned from me and focused instead on Dick junior. "You're going to knock that door down if you keep hammering on it like that!"

"Don't care!"

"Dick! Don't be so rude!"

John just grinned. Quietly, from the side of his mouth he whispered, "Ouch! Ouch! Leave me alone! Aaaagghhh!"

Dick paused. Hit the door again.

"Ouch!"

Sparkling eyes turned on John. "That's just you!"

"What's just me?"

"All them ouches and noises!"

"Can you hear noises?" John asked me.

"Nope."

"You can!" Dick shrieked. He hit the door again.

"Ouch! Stop it!"

"It's you!"

John looked credibly confused. "Is your son mad, Pamela? Is he?"

Dick junior almost got sick laughing. "No. No, I'm not!" He made a dive for John. "You're mad!"

I'd never seen Dick laugh as hard in ages. It made me feel warm inside.

The door opened and Mammy appeared. "Honestly, who's that banging on the door? You frightened the life out of the baby!" She was about to say something else when she noticed John. She paled, then flushed, then blabbered, "John? John, is it?"

The smile slid from his face. "Yes, Mrs Scanlon. I've, eh, come to see Maggie."

"Come to talk some sense into her, have you?"

"If I can."

Mammy moved aside and I slid in past her. She motioned for John to come in. "Well, Maggie's not in just at the moment. She's due back in an hour or so. You can wait if you like."

John nodded and stood in the hall. He was nervous. His hands were shoved into his jeans and his shoulders were hunched up around his ears.

"Come into the kitchen," Mammy said. She turned to me, "Shauna's on the floor inside. She's just after waking." She looked pointedly at Dick junior who ignored her. "I've her bottle out here. Bring her out and feed her. I'll make us all a cuppa."

David emerged from the room and proceeded to latch onto my leg. I made slow progress as I scooped a smiling Shauna from the floor and attempted to negotiate my way to the kitchen. "David," I said patiently, "Dick has got a cool new toy he's dying to show it to you."

David looked up at me.

"Show him, Dick."

Dick held out his toy and David made a grab for it.

I escaped to the kitchen.

John and Mammy were sitting in front of large cups of coffee. John looked uncomfortable and Mammy looked as if she was dying to ask loads of questions but hadn't the nerve. Mammy never asks questions really. She always let Maggie and me have our privacy.

"So, John," I asked, as Mammy handed me Shauna's bottle, "did you fly in this morning?"

John nodded. "Yep. I got a cancellation." He took a gulp of coffee. "How is Mags?"

Mammy and I looked at each other.

"Fine," I said.

"She's – fine," Mammy said.

"She's not expecting me," John went on. He gave a bit of a grin. "I sort of thought I'd surprise her."

I didn't know who was going to be more surprised. Maggie when she saw John or John when he saw Maggie. I mean, the poor divil didn't even know she was pregnant. At least I didn't think he did.

"She'll be surprised all right," Mammy muttered dryly.

The three of us stared at each other. It was very uncomfortable.

Dick eased the tension by bounding in the door and pointing at John. "See this guy, David," he chortled. "He's really funny!" He pulled at John's sleeve. "Hey, mister, can you play football? We have a ball out in Nana's garden."

"I'm not mister," John said. "My name is David. David Beckham."

Dick stopped dead.

I giggled.

David's eyes grew wide.

"David Beckham!" Dick said. "No way!"

"Yes way. Come on and I'll show you." He looked at Mammy.

She nodded. "Out you go."

The three left.

Mammy breathed a sigh of relief. "Oh Pamela, I'm not able for all this. Maggie will have a fit. But I mean, she has to see sense – that's the only man that will take her on. Oh, I don't know what I'm going to do when she arrives home."

"We'll sit in the front room and I'll keep you company until he leaves, all right? Or you can come over to my house?"

"Oh, maybe I'll go to your house." Mammy stood up and began to pace the room. "Ooh, I really think that might be best."

"OK so."

"Oh, but then, Gregory is coming over. He hates me not being here when he arrives."

I shrugged. "Well, Mammy, it's up to you."

"Maybe I'll ring him . . ." she paused, dithered. "Or maybe I won't. He hates me ringing him when he's not expecting me to ring him."

"Sure, maybe you'll be back by the time he comes?"

"Mmm." She gave a deep sigh. "Maybe I will. I'll try to be, that's what I'll do."

Her mind made up, she resumed pacing. Pacing and muttering.

Funnily enough, I wasn't too concerned at all.

I looked out the window, at Dick junior running around after John. Dick was calling out to John, trying to pull him down and at the same time he was laughing. David was standing looking at the two of them, his thumb stuck in his mouth. But he was smiling and sort of jumping up and down a bit in excitement. And I knew why I wasn't concerned. Maggie would take John back. The guy was one in a million, even I could see that. I laughed gently as Dick junior rugby-tackled John to the ground. The two rolled about as John pretended to be injured.

Dick never played with the kids like that.

The thought snuck up on me and hit me with such force that I gasped.

"What's wrong?" Mammy asked alarmed.

"Nothing." I shook my head. Of course Dick never played with the kids. He was too busy to do it. Too busy earning money and making a nice home for us.

"They're having a good time," Mammy joined me at the window. "He's good with kids, isn't he."

I nodded, not trusting myself to speak.

Knackered, that's what I was when I got home. Shagged. Totally out of my brain with tiredness. It's coffee-and-bed pampering time, I told myself sternly (joke!) as I unlocked the front door.

"It's me!" I called out just so that Mam wouldn't think it was Gigantic Geoffrey and run out of the kitchen with a gooey smile on her face. Honestly, the way she runs after him is *so* pathetic. But that's my mother, she insists that men are just put on this earth to be adored and worshipped.

Nobody answered me, which was weird. Normally Mam would acknowledge my existence at least and Pam's car was in the driveway so I had expected a bit of noise. But there was nothing.

Maybe they were out the back. I decided to head into the kitchen and make myself the coffee.

The two were sitting at the table. "Oh well," I snorted, feeling a bit put out, "thanks for the warm welcome, guys."

Mammy giggled, a bit nervously, I thought, and Pam rose slightly. "Eh, Maggie, I think – "

She was cut off by the back door banging open as a dirty ragged Dick junior entered. For once the child didn't have a sulky face. In fact he was grinning. "That David Beckham guy is mad," he giggled.

A fella entered, pulling David along.

The guy stopped dead.

David squirmed out of his grasp.

Dead silence in the kitchen.

"Maggie," the guy said.

And I know I keep calling him 'the guy' but honestly, I don't think I could believe what I was seeing. What the hell was John doing in our kitchen? And what had he been doing, playing with my nephews? Who did he think he was?

"What – " I stopped. Blinked. Yep, he was still there. "What are you doing here?"

John didn't answer. Now, instead of looking at me,

he was gawking, transfixed, at my belly. Talk about the height of rudeness.

"Well," Mammy said, in her light, frivolous 'nothing's-the-matter-here-children' tone, "Pamela and I will get out of your way."

And I snapped.

"Did you call him?" I snarled at her. "Did you?"

Mam was scared of me. I think she's always been a bit like that. Anyhow, she began to back away. Clutching onto Pam, she shook her head violently.

"I came myself," John spoke slowly. "It only involved hopping on a plane, Mags."

"Don't call me Mags!"

"Bye," Pam said.

I think she went about gathering up her things, but I can't be sure. All I could see in those few moments was John. And the way he was looking at me. Horror-struck, confused, hurt – you name it, it was on his face.

The slam of the front door as they left broke the silence.

"You're pregnant," he spoke flatly. He sat down at the table and looked at me hopelessly. "Why didn't you tell me?"

I shrugged.

"Well?" His voice had risen.

"Don't shout at me."

"I will shout at you, Maggie. I will." He glared at me, but I don't think his heart was in it. "It's bad enough you run out on me, on *us*, but Jesus, what sort of a relationship have we got when you don't even tell me you're pregnant?"

"We have no relationship, John. That's why I left."

"Bull. Shit."

"Don't shout." I was standing up but I desperately wanted to sit down. The weight of the baby was pushing into my bladder.

"I will shout." Now he stood up. Came towards me. "I loved you, you stupid cow. What? Didn't you think I'd want a baby? Is that it?"

He looked hopeful and I hated him for it.

"No, that's not it. I just didn't want you. I didn't want you in our lives." I put my hand on my belly. I forced myself to say the words that I knew would kill him, but I had to do it. "I never loved you, I thought I did but when this happened, I knew I couldn't be with you forever."

There was a long, long silence.

He gulped down hard.

When he raised his eyes to mine, I saw that I'd done it. Beaten him. The thrill of victory was replaced with flatness. Dullness.

"Oh. Right." He bowed his head again. He gulped. "It is mine, isn't it?"

The nerve! The bloody nerve! "No, it's Rat's." Then knowing John and the fact that he swallowed just about everything, I spat, "Of course it's yours, you thick gobshite. What the hell do you think I am?"

"Naw, naw, Mags, that's not what – it's just with you running away and all, I was wondering – "

"I ran away because I don't love you. I told you that." He flinched at my words. I hated to see him do that. "Sorry," I added.

"You could have told me," he said. But he didn't sound angry. Just really sad. I hated him and I hated me.

He dug his hand into his pocket. Pulled out a folded-up bit of paper. "Here," he put it on the table. "If I couldn't convince you to come back, I said I'd let you have this. I was only joking around." He patted the paper as he put it down. He stared at it a long time.

I stared at him a long time.

Then, shoving his hands into his jeans, he turned back to me. He'd managed to get a sort of grin onto his face. But it didn't make it into his eyes. "Bye, Maggie."

"Bye, John."

"You know where I am if . . ." he voice trailed off. "Well, whatever."

I didn't answer.

Then nodding at my belly, he asked softly, "Can I ever see it? The baby?"

I hated him for asking. I hated him for the gentle way he asked. I shrugged, "Suppose. I'll contact you."

"Thanks." He brushed by me as he left.

The door closed and I sat down. The dullness gave way to an ache. Such a deep ache.

To try and stop it hurting so much I picked up the paper he'd left for me.

Only it wasn't just a piece of paper. It was a cheque.

For four and a half grand.

For the first time since I left John I cried.

I didn't cry for too long. What'd be the point of that? It'd probably only upset the baby and make it into a manic depressive or something awful. When I'd had my stupid blubber over John, I made myself tea – scrambled eggs, beans, waffles and four slices of toast. After that I had a big bar of chocolate that I found in the fridge and then I found a few biscuits. Being pregnant makes you hungry, so just in case I had the munchies when I was watching the telly, I brought a six pack of crisps inside with me.

And a glass of Coke.

I was eating my second packet of Salt and Vinegar when the doorbell rang. Getting up off the sofa was like trying to raise the Titanic.

Anyhow, waddling and shuffling, I made it to the door.

The bell rang again.

It was Mr P.

There was some consolation in my life. No matter how big I got, I'd never match him. He looked like a circus tent in his blue trousers and stripy shirt. "Is your mother there, Pamela?" he asked.

"I'm Maggie, and no she's not."

He looked a bit put out. Insulted. Then he smiled. "Listen, Maggie," he stressed my name. "This isn't funny. I told her I'd be here to pick her up at seven and," he tapped his watch, "seven it is."

I shrugged. "Well, she's not here. She's gone out with Pamela somewhere. I don't know when she'll be back."

"So I'll wait, will I?" He made to come in.

There was no way I wanted him in. He'd probably expect me to cook for him and talk to him and I really wasn't in the mood for that. "No, I'll tell her you called." I know it was rude, but I closed the door on his face. Then I slouched back into the telly and turned the volume up really loud in case he rang.

At least I'd have an excuse not to hear him.

And he did ring. He was very persistent actually. He must have rung the bell for twenty solid minutes. He rang it from the break in *Fair City* to its end.

After a while I heard his car starting up and glancing quickly out the window I saw him drive at speed up the road.

God, it felt really good to annoy someone.

I opened my fourth packet of crisps.

Mam and Pamela arrived back around nine. I don't know why they left it so late – how long did they think it took to tell someone to get out of your life? In they came, all nervy and anxious. Mam sat down opposite me and smiled.

I gave her a smile back.

The telly was blaring out the signature tune for the news.

Pamela stood beside Mammy's chair. "So, Maggie," she shouted over the roar of the telly, "how'd it go?"

I shrugged, fixed my gaze on the screen. "As things go, it went well."

"Ooooh," I could hear the joy in Mammy's sigh. She clasped her hands together, leaned forward in her chair and said, "That is wonderful! Really wonderful!"

"Yep," I lowered the telly, just so that she'd hear what I had to say and just, I suppose, so that I could see her shattered face. "I told him to go and he went. Brilliant!"

It took a few seconds for it to register with her. "What? You mean – "

"I mean John is gone and I'm still here. Now, aren't you glad?"

Her smile wobbled frantically. "Well, oh yes, well, of course I'm glad you're here but Maggie, John, well, I mean John . . ." Her voice trailed off.

"John's not here?" I supplied helpfully.

"Yes." She nodded. "And he's such a lovely young man. And he came all the way over to see you. Pamela and I were just saying to each other how much he must love you."

"Mam," I said mock-patiently, "fifty minutes on a plane does not constitute undying love. The guy hopped on a plane, probably got a cancellation and arrived on your doorstep. I mean, hello?"

"Yes, well," she was looking a little annoyed at my flip tone, "that's all very well to make a laugh of the poor fellow. But, Maggie, you've got to think of your baby. What is that child going to do for a father? Every child needs a father."

I despised her for those words. I did. I stiffened, was about to say something horrible but held back. There was no point. Instead I smiled and laughed. "Yep, I guess so. I mean it'd be biologically impossible to exist without a father."

I'd confused her. She looked as if she was about to agree and then realised that she could be agreeing to anything. No such luck with Pam though. She really got on her high horse.

"Maggie," she said sharply, "it's no joke. You know very well what Mammy means. She just thinks that it's in your and the baby's best interests to keep the contact with John. What if you have a boy? He'll need his dad. Even a girl needs a dad."

It was one thing Mam saying it, but Pam. *Pam.*

"I didn't need a dad." My hands dug into the remote control. "In fact, I'd have been a lot better off without one."

"Maggie!" That was Mam. The only thing that ever managed to disturb her serene view of life was criticism of the Pater. "I won't have you talking like that about your daddy."

"So sue me," I gave a bit of a laugh.

"I won't have you saying those things."

"What things?" I opened my eyes, nice and wide. "The truth? The things I used to always say? Like . . ." I pretended to search my mind, "like the fact that he beat me and Pam senseless whenever we got stuff wrong in school? Or the fact – "

"That is all in the past," Pam said loudly. "He just had his way of doing things."

"Oh, he did all right," I nodded. Maybe it was losing John or being pregnant or maybe it was just the way I absolutely hated my existence, but I lashed out, "I mean, he was so disappointed when you only got five A's in the Leaving, wasn't he, Pam?" She whitened. "So disappointed that he broke your arm. And only for me pulling him off you he would probably have been up for murder and – "

"Don't be ridiculous, Maggie," Mam cut me short. "You always made a big drama out of everything!"

"Yeah," I lifted myself out of the chair. "And you never did. As far as you were concerned everything was hunky-dory, wasn't it?"

"He was a good man," her voice was breaking.

"I mean, you highered up the volume of the telly any time trouble broke out, didn't you? Ooops," I made my voice high, "Daddy's in a bad mood tonight, maybe I should higher up the television so that the neighbours won't hear the screaming."

"Stop it!"

"And the only time he was ever in good form was whenever he was out screwing the neighbours!"

"Maggie, stop!" Pamela shouted. "Stop it!"

But I couldn't. It was like I was purging myself. Things I'd never said before poured out of me. "Mrs Doyle and him were at it like rabbits and everyone knew."

"They were not!" Mammy sobbed. "They were not!" She turned to Pam. "Make her stop, Pamela!"

"There's no proof of that, Maggie," Pam said, trying

to sound all reasonable and failing. "Let's just stop."

"No." I shook my head vigorously. My head swam. "No, no, I won't. He was a horrible dad and I don't see why you two just can't say it."

"Because he wasn't," Pam said. And like, the way she said it was scary, as if she believed it.

And the way she said it dried me up. I gawked at her.

"He loved us a lot, Maggie. I mean, if he hadn't he'd never have hit us. His emotions were more intense where we were concerned."

"No! No, you don't hit people when you love them. That's all wrong."

"It's not. It's right."

"So, like, if Dick hit you or the kids, you'd let him?"

Pam went white. She blinked rapidly. I think it was because I'd struck home. Of course she'd never let anyone hit her precious kids. "Look, Maggie," she said, again in her reasonable voice, as if I was a moron. "I don't know why we're all getting so upset. Why are we even talking about Daddy? All this has nothing to do with John. I mean, that's what we *were* discussing before you started dragging Daddy into it."

And suddenly it hit me. Why I'd come home, why I felt I had to come home when I could have gone anywhere. All this had *everything* to do with John. Everything. And I had to ask her. Just to see. "Pam, don't you *remember* how awful he was? Or like, is it just me? And if it is, what's wrong with me?"

Pam shook her head. Mammy started on about

exactly what was wrong with me. I'd turned down a grand fella, that's what was wrong with me. I'd never known when I was well off.

I picked up the crisps and left the room.

I cried tonight.

All night.

I haven't cried all night since Dad hit me with the lamp. That night, the one when I'd been hit, I'd known I didn't really have a dad and now, now I knew I didn't really have a mother or a sister.

I was on my own.

And I was scared.

For the first time in years I had a nightmare.

I woke up screaming.

Shauna and Dick woke up with the noise.

Dick told me to take Shauna and calm her down and only come back to bed when we could sleep without disturbing him.

I took Shauna downstairs and rocked her in my arms and when she was quiet I kissed her head and let my tears wet her hair.

Chapter Thirty-nine

"Thanks for telling me Geoffrey called," Mam sniped the minute I came down for breakfast next day.

"Geoffrey called," I said flatly.

"He said you refused to let him in."

"Oh, by the way, I refused to let him in."

"Don't – be – so – so . . ." she stopped. Shaking her head, she threw a cup into the sink. It splashed into the basin and water dripped out onto the floor.

I crossed to the kettle and flicked it on.

Mam threw another cup into the sink. Her shoulders started to shake.

I stood uneasily by the kettle and watched her. I knew what she wanted me to do. I'd done it in the past, well, Pam had mostly done it in the past – I was never one for touchy-feely type of things. Mam wanted me to cuddle her, to tell her I was sorry for what I'd said. That I hadn't meant it.

I couldn't do it. I didn't want to do it.

My nails dug into my palms. Sweat broke out on my forehead.

Mam's shoulders continued to shake as she cried.

I couldn't do it. Say the words she wanted me to. Sullenly I stared at her.

She sniffed and shook and sobbed.

Jerkily I walked towards her. I patted her awkwardly on the shoulder. I couldn't get the words out.

"You, you said some awful things last night," she sobbed. She wiped her eyes with a sudsy fist. "Your poor father."

"Look, Mam – "

"But you didn't mean them, did you? You couldn't have meant it. Your daddy was a good man. When I met him, he used to buy me flowers, chocolates. He was a gent. He had a quick temper, I know that, but, Maggie," more sobs, "the things you said."

I was losing myself. Drowning. "Sorry, Mam."

"And he was a good man. Don't you know he loved you?"

I nodded. Hated myself. Hated her even more.

But I loved her too.

I mightn't have needed a dad but I think somewhere, some part of me knew that no matter what, everyone needs a mam.

Dick's mother was driving me mad. How had he ever thought she was wonderful? I remember, before I'd met her, thinking that she must have been a saint the way Dick went on about her. But she wasn't.

Or if she was, she was the Saint of All Bitches.

It was all her fault what happened at dinner.

"Any post?" Dick asked, riffling through the bits and pieces of junk mail that had come in that morning. I never threw out junk mail any more. Dick said you never know what you could find if you just took the time to read them. Of course, he never did, but he liked to think he did. Anyhow, he rummaged through the post.

"Nothing," I said as casually as I could. It was great that I didn't have to look at him, I'm a hopeless liar. I busied myself putting Shauna into her high chair. She's as strong. She's able to sit in a high chair already.

"That child," Mrs Maguire nodded disdainfully at her, "is the spit of that little alien in the film, what's his name, the one that wants to go home."

Tears pricked the back of my eyes. But I couldn't let her see them. Even Dick, still looking through the post, stiffened at the comment.

Shauna gave her nana a gummy smile.

Mrs Maguire sniffed and turned to glare at the dinner I'd given her. "What is this?"

I didn't answer. I put Dick's dinner on the table. He nodded his thanks and sat down. "Listen, Pam," he said, "I'm expecting my bank statement tomorrow. If it comes, gimme a ring in work. They never send the bloody things out on time."

"Yes, OK, I will."

"A letter came today," Mrs Maguire said, "and Pamela opened it and brought it upstairs."

I dropped Dick junior's plate. His dinner went all over the floor. "Oh, sorry, Dick junior. Mammy'll get you – "

"What letter is this?" Dick asked slowly, as he watched me scooping up the remains of Dick junior's dinner.

"Oh, nothing," my voice shook. "Nothing. Just a letter from a girl I used to work with."

"Really?" His voice was measured. "So, what's the big secret?" He put his foot on a piece of dinner I was about to pick up. I raised my eyes to his.

"It's no big secret."

My words fell into black silence.

Even the kids stopped eating.

David, sensitive to atmospheres, began to whimper.

"So get it for me. I mean, why did you bring it upstairs?"

"Just to read it. I threw it out then."

"So go look for it."

I attempted a laugh. "Oh, Dick, come on. It's only a letter."

"And you know our rule." He ground the piece of dinner further into the floor with his shoe. "We have no secrets."

"The way it should be," Mrs Maguire spoke up.

I stood up. I don't know how I managed it because blind panic made me want to fall down and never get up. I was caught. I was stupid and I'd been caught.

"Of course I've no secrets, Dick," I babbled, "but it's just, well, I was going to show it to you, only after your dinner."

"How considerate." He eyed me speculatively. "But I don't mind. Run along and get it."

"Her dinner will go cold," Dick junior spoke up.

"Shut up, you!"

Dick junior glared at his father. I was terrified he'd say something and get himself in real trouble. So, I said, "Well,

I'll get the letter now. It's just upstairs." To give myself time to think up something, I put my dinner back in the oven. Trying to walk confidently, I left the kitchen.

The hum of conversation between Dick and his mother resumed as I mounted the stairs.

Oh God. Oh God. What was I going to do? Dick was going to go mental. He'd flip big-time. And of course, it was all my own stupid fault. I was such a disaster. I couldn't even cry I was so terrified. All sorts of ideas flitted into my head. I mean, I even thought of taking tablets and killing myself just to get out of having to produce the stupid letter.

"Pamela," Dick shouted from the kitchen, "I'm waiting."

I knew that sing-song tone. Sweat damped my armpits. Could I write a letter and say it was from my friend? Would I have time? I began to scrabble frantically for some stationery and a pen when I heard him pounding up the stairs.

He burst into the bedroom door and glared at me. "Well?"

I wanted to die. The sensation overwhelmed me. I wanted to die with fear. Then, out of the corner of my eye, I saw Dick junior peeping around the door. His eyes were wide and his face was chalk white. I knew I couldn't die. What sort of a mother would I be to him then? I had to show him that everything was perfectly normal. "I'm just looking for it, Dick," I said as brightly as I could. "I can't quite remember . . ."

"Well, you'd better remember," Dick said sharply. "It must be something if you weren't going to show it to me."

"I was going to show it to you – "

"Just find it, Pamela."

There was no turning back. I opened my make-up bag and unfolded the letter. "Here."

I watched as he opened it. It's a funny thing, sometimes you can be so scared that you don't feel anything. That's the way I was. It was like I was outside my body watching the whole scene.

Dick looked at the letter. He looked again. His eyes narrowed and his nose reddened. The little frown-line appeared over his eyebrows. "Eight hundred quid," he breathed. "Eight hundred quid." His voice was soft. Quiet.

"I didn't think it was – "

"How the fuck did you manage to run up eight hundred quid on the credit card?" His words spat themselves at me. "How did you do it? One hundred, that's all I told you you could have." He came towards me, brandishing the letter. "How the fuck did you manage it, you silly cow?"

I backed up towards the wardrobe. I clutched the rim of it with my fingers. Dick's face was inches from mine. "Clothes for the kids," I babbled. "Stuff for me – "

He hit me across the face. My world grew bright and dazzling as stars and fireworks popped inside my head.

From the brightness somewhere, I heard Dick junior run into the room. "Leave Mammy alone! Leave her!"

Dick put his arm out and Dick junior flew across the room like a rag-doll.

"Dick, stop," I said. "I can expl – "

He hit me again.

I don't know how long it lasted. I don't know really what happened. I remember Mrs Maguire saying, "Huh, you can't even control your wife."

I remember her looking at the two of us as if we were the scum of the earth.

That made Dick hit me again.

It was the last thing before the world went black.

To top off a surreal and totally depressing day, Rat rang. Like John, he rang as I was sitting down to eat.

Mam thought it was Geoffrey and she almost danced out the kitchen door in her eagerness to answer the phone. And when it wasn't, her good humour disappeared. "It's for you," she said stomping back into the kitchen. "And don't be too long. It's reverse charge."

And she started into a moan about how it was all very well for *some people* to be getting calls while *other people* didn't know if they were ever going to get a call again. How *some people*, the one getting the calls, were so rude to *other people's callers* and now it looked as if the *other people* were not going to get calls. Blah! Blah! Blah! I closed the door on her as I left. I'd had enough martyrdom from her that day to get me into heaven.

I picked up the telephone. "Hello?"

"Is that Maggie?"

"Yeah. Who's this?"

"It's Declan."

"Declan?"

"Rat."

"Oh, right." Momentarily speechless, I gazed at the receiver. "Well . . . eh . . . what?" Then suddenly, fear squeezing my insides out, I babbled, "Is John OK?"

"Well, he used to be," Rat said and his voice didn't sound too friendly, (not that he ever had anyway), "but he's a right bloody mess now."

"Sorry?"

"So you should be. He says you've left him."

I almost laughed. Did Rat *actually* think he had a chance of getting me back with John by making a crummy phone call? Huh, John had probably put him up to it. I felt a bit sorry for John. He was really making a fool out of himself.

"He says you've left him," Rat repeated.

"Mmm."

"Does that mean yes?" Rat spat.

"Yep." They should have worked the script better. Rat was not exactly endearing me to him.

"And did you tell him it was because of me?"

"Get a grip. Of course it wasn't because of you. I left John because the whole thing was over!" So Rat was ringing because he felt guilty. Nice touch.

"And that's what I told him!" Rat sounded triumphant. "I fucking told him that. I told him things end all the time. I told him that you left him because you left *him* not me. You know? And now you have to tell him that too."

"Sorry?"

Rat's words tumbled over each other. "Ever since you walked he's been nagging me to go clear. Jesus, the big fucker always nagged me and I always ignored him but he's gone mad now. He's thrown me out. I only did a line or so when he went off yesterday. Now he's dumped me out and I've nothing. And it's all your fault. I think he thinks if I change you'll come back to him."

"What?" Totally thrown, I couldn't even think straight.

"You have to tell him, see," Rat said intensely. "You have to explain that even if I change you are not coming back. You are leaving him. You don't care what I do. See? You have to tell him so he'll leave me alone."

"Sorry?"

"You have to explain, see?" Rat was getting desperate. "You have to make him understand. It's all your fault – "

All my fault? Explain to John? What sort of a low-life was this bastard? I really wished he had been ringing on John's behalf, I think I could have stomached it better. But Rat didn't care about John, about me, about anyone. A smouldering anger began to build. How dare he? How dare he expect me to right his world for him when he hadn't said two civil words ever to me? "Rat," I said sharply, "where did you get this number?"

Halted mid-sentence, he got confused.

"This number," I barked. "Where did you get it?"

"From your fat friend, the one who keeps calling into John and telling him you're coming back."

"Ali?"

"I dunno. I told her I was going to try to talk sense into you, she wished me luck and gave me the number." Rat sniggered a bit. "Oh, I got it out of her no bother, the fat cow. She keeps – "

"Well, Rat, what I suggest is you tear up my number and you never ring it again – got that?"

"Haven't you been fucking listening to a word I've

said?" Rat barked. "John hates me, see? He likes to blame me for everything."

"No." I bit my lip, tried to keep my calm. "John, John doesn't do stuff like that. He's . . . he's good . . ." My voice shook. I had a pain in my chest.

"That's shit. Shit. He hates me. He thinks I'm an addict. I just dabble. You have to talk to him. To explain about how you – "

"No!"

"Jesus!"

The way he said 'Jesus' sounded like John. Suddenly my anger vanished. Tiredness almost knocked me over. "Bye, Rat," I muttered, feeling sorry for him. "Take care."

"No!" Rat virtually screamed into the receiver. "You don't understand. He's got you brainwashed too, hasn't he? Like the way he has with everyone else? I'm not a fucking addict. And John knows it but that bastard hates me ever since I crashed the car. He hates me only he won't say it out. But I know he does. And as for you, you stupid bitch, all you have to do is – "

"Rat, I'm going."

"Don't you fucking hang up on me, bitch. I'll get – "

I put the phone down. This wasn't my problem.

I wanted to vomit.

Poor John, the thought came before I could stop it, poor John having to put up with him.

Still, as my mother was fond of saying, you've made your bed . . .

Dick had made up the bed. When I woke up, I was propped up on pillows with a clean nightdress on. Dick was sitting on the bed, staring anxiously down at me. A basin of water with a face cloth was on the bedside table.

It was hard to open my eyes. The left one seemed to be really swollen.

"Take it easy," Dick whispered. "It's a bit bruised." He dipped the face cloth into the water and gently washed around the eye. It stung and I winced.

"Sorry," he muttered, still cleaning it.

I let him wash my face, I stayed very still while he dabbed ointment on my lips. When he seemed satisfied that I was cleaned up as best as possible, he studied me. He dropped his eyes and I saw him gulp hard. "I'm really sorry, Pammy," he choked out. "But, I got such a shock when I saw the bill. I guess I flipped."

His hair fell across his forehead; his face was pale with worry about me.

I wondered how the hell I'd spent so much. I never had before. Stupid, stupid me.

"Pam, you know I love you. You know I do, don't you?"

I nodded.

He moved closer to me on the bed. "But you know, you broke two rules. First, you told me we didn't get any letters and next you spend eight hundred quid."

"I know." I nodded miserably.

His palm caressed my cheek. "And we have to have order, don't we?"

"Yes."

"Otherwise it all falls apart. Us. Our family. We have to have order."

"I know. I know, Dick."

"And it's not as if I ask that much of you is it, Pamela?"

"No." And he didn't. All Dick wanted was a nice house, a hot dinner and a good wife to come home to. That was it.

"No," he agreed. He put his arms very gently around me. He kissed my hair and nuzzled my neck. "I love you, Pammy. More than anything. You know that, don't you?"

I nodded. I loved him too.

"And I love you too, Mammy," Dick junior said from somewhere.

I remembered something about him falling against the wall. I pulled free of Dick to glance across where Dick junior stood in the doorway. There was a bruise on his face but nothing major. I looked up at Dick and he nodded.

"Come here, honey." I patted the bed and Dick junior bounded across the room and jumped up beside me.

"I've told him not to interfere when we're arguing," Dick said, but he was smiling. "That way he doesn't make Daddy angry."

Dick junior snuggled into me.

"D'you want a cup of tea?" Dick stood up.

"That'd be great."

He gave me another smile before leaving.

"Sorry, Mammy," Dick junior whispered. "I didn't mean to make Daddy angry."

"You didn't. It was all Mammy's fault. She did a silly thing."

He cuddled me. "I won't let Daddy kill you," he whispered solemnly. "I won't let him."

"Daddy wouldn't do that," I said, shocked. "He loves me, Dick junior."

"Mmm," Dick junior didn't look convinced.

"He does, honey."

"OK." Then, "And guess what?" Before I could guess, he giggled, "Nana Maguire is going home. She says she doesn't like being here any more."

"Oh God!" Dick would go mad if she left. I made to get out of the bed. I had to stop her.

"And here's the – " Dick stopped. "Where are you going, Pamela?"

He always called me Pamela when he was annoyed.

"Just, just to stop your mother from leaving. I – "

"She's going," he said flatly. "She won't change her mind." He carried the tea across to the table. "Don't worry about it. You can apologise when you're feeling better." He rubbed my hair. "Don't worry about the house, I'll take care of it. You rest now."

He nodded to Dick junior who scurried out of the room.

"And when you're better," Dick whispered, his eyes dancing, "I'll bring you out and we'll have a great night. We'll do dinner and take in a show – what d'you think?"

"Lovely."

"Drink up your tea before it gets cold."

"I will."

I watched as he left the room. I ignored the pain in my eye. Instead I focused on what I could do to show how sorry I was.

Maybe I could bring some of the clothes I'd bought back to the shop? I hadn't worn half of them.

I had to do something.

It was no less than he deserved.

Chapter Forty

I'd fully intended going to my new niece's christening. But three things happened that stopped me.

The first occurred about a fortnight before the christening.

John and me were sitting in his car listening to some tapes. It was a ritual we did once a week. John played tapes that had been sent in to him by various bands and I, as an ignorant punter, had to give my opinion. It helped him have a nice balance between good music and pulp music, he said.

John, hate to say it, was a music snob.

Anyway, the ritual over, John slotted in a tape of Diesel. The song 'Blind Kinda Love' began to play.

"Remember that?" he whispered.

"Uh – huh." My heart started to hammer the way it always did when John started to go all sexy on me. It was the song he'd played just before we'd made love for the first time.

"Good." He took my hand. He kissed my fingers one by one. He looked into my eyes and I squirmed. "I'm nuts about you, Mags."

"Naw, you're just nuts."

He gave a small grin and dropped the bombshell. "Marry me."

The sides of the car began to close in. Marrying him had never, ever been an option. "Get lost!" I managed a passable scoff. "How could I marry someone who listens to meaningful music!"

"Naw, Mags, look, this isn't a joke. I mean it. Marry me."

I pretended not to hear that. I fiddled with the tape and talked crap.

He eventually got the message.

But it set me worrying.

It made me wary of being too nice to him.

I began to spend a lot of time with Louise.

Dick didn't always hit me. Not that he did much. I mean the night we got engaged, that wasn't a real hit, that was just an accident.

The first real hit he'd given me had been a few months into our marriage and, looking back on it, I know I deserved it.

I discovered I was pregnant. I was so thrilled. I remember coming in from work and shoving loads of lovely M&S food into the microwave. By the time Dick got in, I had soft candles burning and a gorgeous Indian meal on the table. He came in, pulled off his tie and kissed me really hard.

I told him to sit down.

He sat.

I told him I'd a present for him.

He grinned and closed his eyes. I pinned a badge saying "I'm going to be a Daddy" on his shirt.

"Open up," I giggled.

He looked down and read the badge.

There was a silence. I wasn't expecting a silence. When he looked at me his face was white. He got up and left the kitchen without a word.

I remember being confused.

I didn't go upstairs after him, I just stayed in the kitchen wondering what I'd done wrong.

Over the next few weeks, Dick hardly spoke. He wouldn't touch me in bed and in the end I asked him what was wrong.

"I don't want a baby," he said. "Not now."

"It's a bit late for that," I remember smiling. I patted my tummy. "It's on the way."

For some reason it infuriated him. He pulled my hand away from my stomach and squeezed it. "Don't laugh at me," he spat. "Don't you dare. You think you can pull one over on me by getting pregnant, don't you?"

"No. No, Dick."

He pushed me away from him and I fell. I crashed into the table.

He dragged me up and I felt a punch.

Right in my . . . well, I lost the baby.

But it was an accident. I mean, he didn't want me to lose the baby. He cried a lot afterwards. He said he'd never forgive himself.

But it was my fault. I mean, I should have discussed getting pregnant with him first and if I had done he would have been prepared. It's a terrible shock for a man to discover they're going to become a father, Dick said. It's hard to adjust sometimes.

Anyhow, that was the first time he hit me.

But I understand it now. I mean, you have to have order in a house or else things get out of control.

The second thing and the third thing sort of happened together. Firstly, I began to suspect that I was pregnant. Like I said before, charting my cycle is like charting a trip to outer space. But one night, two days before the christening, I was sleeping over with Ali. I did that on a regular basis just to show John I was still a free single woman. I was stretched out on the sofa munching my way through a giant bar of chocolate and Ali was nibbling daintily on a packet of Rolo.

"What's up?" I asked. "Are you on a diet or something?"

Ali shook her head. "Period cramps. 'Urts like 'ell. Still, maybe if I 'ad them a bit more often I'd be thinner – yeah?"

And it hit me. I hadn't had a period in ages.

My hair prickled, my scalp crawled and I went cold all over.

Something inside me told me I was preggers. It was like I knew.

I wanted to puke.

But I figured that it was all in my head and I didn't bother finding out one way or the other.

Instead I rang Pamela and told her I couldn't come to the christening. I mean the last thing I needed to see was a baby – right? And Pam got all huffy and Mam got all huffy and even John said that I could have given them all a bit more notice.

I told him to fuck off. He told me to grow up. I stomped into work the next day, fought with one of the customers, bawled a waitress out of it and got fired.

I didn't tell John I'd been fired. I left the house for work every morning and wandered around town until my shift was over. There was no way I wanted John to find out how awful I'd been to the waitress. He'd know for sure what a cow I was then.

And because I'd lost my job and was now fighting with the only three people, bar Ali, in the whole world that I talked to, I decided that life really couldn't get any worse. Despite the fact my boobs had swollen and my waist had thickened, I knew God, if He existed, wouldn't throw any more shit my way.

So I did a pregnancy test.

And God dumped cartloads of crap on my head.

I was pregnant.

And the terror of knowing that John was going to be in my life permanently freaked me out.

Panicky thoughts went through my head. Maybe I could have an abortion and no one need ever know? God, I was tempted until I remembered how upset Pam was when she'd lost a baby at fourteen weeks. She's said that the foetus had been the shape of a baby and everything. Even though it wasn't formed, she said, you could still see it was a person.

So I didn't get the abortion.

Instead, I left John. It was the best thing to do. I could dump John, get him out of my life. I didn't have to tell him about losing my job. I wouldn't have to tell him about the baby.

And I wouldn't have to keep fending him off when he wanted to know stuff about me that I didn't want to tell him.

Plus, I could go home and tell Mam that I'd left John and as a result I was out of a job. And then, I figured, when I'd got golden girl Pam rubbed up the right way, I'd tell the two of them about the baby.

And that was it.

Brilliant.

Before Dick Junior was conceived, we'd decided to have a baby. I think Dick only agreed to please me, to make it up to me.

When he was born, Dick wouldn't come into the labour ward. He didn't like slime, he said. And his mother said that there were things that men were not supposed to see. I was so happy to be having a little baby that I didn't care. I was dying for the three of us to be a family.

I remember when they placed Dick junior into my arms. I kissed the top of his head and whispered to him all about the wonderful life he was going to have.

Dick came in at that moment. He stood watching me from the door. I held the baby out to him and he didn't make any move to take it.

Is this Love?

"You've a little son, Dick," I smiled.

"The nurse told me," he said sullenly. His dark eyes glared at the two of us. "I wanted a girl."

The baby whimpered in my arms.

When we got home he hit me because it wasn't a girl.

So I'd tried to have another baby, to give him his girl.

David arrived.

Things got worse.

And when I had Shauna – he'd wanted a boy.

But at that stage, I loved him more than ever. Poor Dick was so vulnerable. So insecure. I realised that he was just jealous.

Afraid that he'd lose me to the kids.

I told him he'd never lose me.

That I loved him more than I loved myself.

I just got hit then when I did stupid things. Like maybe . . . I dunno, make something he hated for dinner or have the kids messy when he came in. Things like that. As Dick says, if I'm at home all day the least I can do is do things right.

He only lashes out at me to make me into a better person.

It's because he loves me, you see. It's because his mother never really loved him and he won't admit it. He wants to hang on to my love.

I understand him so well.

Plus, he loves his kids.

He wants the best for them.

And so do I.

I love my kids.

Chapter Forty-one

What is the most embarrassing thing that can happen to a woman? I mean, really think now. Then when you've got it, multiply it by about a thousand. That's how I felt when my waters burst on the 46C bus.

At first, of course, I wasn't aware of what was happening. I was thirty-seven weeks gone, big and mountainous, barely able to walk but still heading into work every day because I wanted to make sure that things would be still in place by the time I got back from my maternity leave. Louis found my concern hilarious. "A control freak," he kept chuckling. "Can't believe we'll survive without her!"

"Aw, yeah, we'll survive," Lucinda assured me. "You should take it easy. You look ready to pop any minute."

A customer came in.

"Yeah, what's it to be?" Lucinda asked. Turning to Josie, she said, in what was meant to be a whisper, "I can't feckin' stand this arsehole."

The 'arsehole' looked up.

Josie and her laughed.

Romanio chuckled along too about ten seconds later.

Louis disappeared.

Shower of morons.

I was determined to give them a crash course in customer relations before I left. So there I was on the bus mentally plotting out what I'd say to them to improve their attitude, when I felt it. A sort of trickle.

Oh God, I thought. This is what happens when you don't do your pelvic-floor exercises. I had visions of myself not able to laugh or sneeze without wetting myself. So I decided better late than never and I began to do the holding and squeezing routine. The exercises were useless. I sat there, trickling away, frozen with fear, in the front of the bus, beside the old woman with the old woman smell who was busy telling me about her grandson. I prayed that people would think it was her that had wet herself. She looked old enough. I moved up nearer her, just to position myself.

"Please God, you'll have a boy," she whispered. "Girls are nice but you know, a boy is a boy."

I nodded, smiled, hoped she wouldn't get off before I'd finished.

And then all hell broke lose. And I mean hell. I literally splashed all over the place. At first, through the sheer horror and embarrassment, I thought my kidneys had erupted. I thought I was going to need a transplant. And then the old woman screamed, "Oh God, your waters. Your waters. They've broken!"

Thank you very much. Thank you, Mrs. A part of me withered up and died.

"What's that?" the driver asked.

"This girl's waters have broken," someone else shouted. "She needs to go to the hospital."

Everyone was looking at me. I tried to smile. I stood up, my trousers dripped. Sorry about this, but that's the way it happened. "Eh, listen, I'd better go and maybe see if I can get a taxi."

The old woman yanked me down. "You can't go out like that," she hissed. "Look at you. Wait here."

The driver pulled in to a stop. "I'll radio the depot and see if they'll send a taxi to the bus."

"Oh, no, no, honestly." Once again I made to stand up. I had to get off. Everybody was looking. One small boy opposite was sniggering away wondering how a big person could wet themselves so much. "But there's loads," he kept saying. "Look, Mammy!"

The driver gave me a sympathetic smile. He was young and trying to be manly about the whole thing. "Just sit there," he said to me. "I'll get you a taxi."

I wanted to clean the floor up. I had to do something. But I knew if I got down they'd need a crane to get me back up so I sat, feeling mortified and miserable as the old woman patted my hand told me all about her own labours.

"Is there anyone you'd like to ring?" a young fella asked holding out his mobile phone to me. "Your fella or anyone."

Everyone looked.

I supposed I should ring my mother. But I couldn't, not in front of the whole bus. "Eh, no, no thanks."

"Oh you should ring someone," the old woman advised. "Your pains could start any minute and I'll tell you from experience they'll be no prancing along hospital corridors making calls then."

"Really?" I gulped.

"No." The mother of the sniggering boy shook her head. "That's not true. I was in labour so long I could have rung up the entire population of America."

That comment was about as comforting as manic depression. I took the phone from the young man and dialled.

"Hello?" My mother had her simpering voice on. I realised she thought it was the elusive Mr P.

"Mam, it's me."

"Oh, you." A sniff. "What do you want?"

"I've, eh, well, my waters burst."

"What!" She began to hyperventilate. "When? Now? In work?"

"No, on the bus."

"Oh my God, Maggie. You have to get off the bus. What will people think? Oh my God! Oh my God!"

"They're ringing a taxi for me," I said. "I'm going into the hospital. Will you pack a few things and bring them in for me?"

"On the bus," she breathed. "Oh God!" Then, "Listen, I'll pack a case for you and bring it into the hospital. Just, just get off the bus as quick as you can. Don't tell them your name."

I hung up.

"Thanks," I gave the mobile back.

The old woman continued to pat my hand and tell me that I'd be fine. Other women began to tell me of their birth experiences. One of them had given birth in a chipper. "So you think this is bad," she giggled. "I had my baby on the floor and after I'd gone they cleaned the place up and apparently started serving chips again."

I managed a laugh as others about groaned.

The taxi came ten minutes later. The driver insisted on escorting me down the bus and out onto the road. As I climbed down the steps, some people on the bus started shouting out 'good luck' and other stuff.

It made me feel, I dunno, sort of warm.

I tried not to think about the mess I'd made or who'd have to clean it up.

They were the sort of things my mother would surely worry about and I didn't want to be like her.

The pains started about an hour later. Very mild cramp-like pains. At first I didn't notice them, I mean they weren't bad. I was in bed, propped up on pillows and Mam was sitting on the edge, eating some chocolates she'd bought for me and making me swear over and over that I hadn't revealed my true identity on the bus. "It's the sort of thing they print in papers," she warned, "and you know, it's bad enough the neighbours knowing you're expecting without the whole country getting in on the act."

I wished she'd go. It was funny how she could make me feel alone by being there.

"I rang Pam," she said then. "I told her you'd gone into the hospital. She said she might call in later, maybe dinner-time."

"How's her eye?" I asked. Pam had called up last Sunday for the first time in about two weeks. Her eye had been swollen and she had a nasty cut on her lip. She'd been playing ball with Dick junior and he'd kicked the ball at her face.

"She said it's getting better," Mam said. She shook her head. "And Dick is so good to her. For the first week or so after it happened he took a few days off and looked after the house. He did everything, Pam said. He made dinners, he got the kids organised in the morning. Of course, Pam said David won't let Dick near him. He insisted on Pam dressing him. She has the child ruined."

I said nothing. I knew what was coming.

"I mean if anything happened you, who'd look after the little one?" Mam nodded at my belly. "No woman can do everything on her own and you'll not find a man willing to take on another man's child."

I was hoping she'd say that. "Romano in the restaurant is seeing Lucinda. She has a kid by another man."

Mam sniffed, unimpressed. "Oh, he's probably just after," she lowered her voice, "after what he can get. That's all."

It was a comment I would have made. The horror of

it hit me. *I would have said that.* And worse, I would have believed it. But I knew it wasn't true. Not in Lucinda's case. Romano did actually like her.

So maybe there were good guys out there.

Maybe.

"That's not true," I snapped. "Not all men are like that."

Mam, sensing an argument, lifted herself from the bed and gave a gay laugh. "I'd better go," she said lightly. "I'll drop in later. You'll probably still be here."

I watched her scurry out of the ward.

Two hours later the pains had grown slightly worse. There was a tightening around my stomach, a sort of squeezing sensation. It was like having period cramps. "What exactly does labour feel like?" I eventually asked a girl on my left. I'd been doing my best not to talk to the other occupants on the ward, I wasn't into swapping amusing stories about my pregnancy or about my 'man' or about anything else really.

The girl in the bed looked at me, puzzled. "I dunno. It's my first, but I thought you knew." She frowned at me, still puzzled looking. "It *is* your fourth, isn't it?"

"What?"

"Well, the girl across the way told me you'd three sections."

Was this lie going to follow me about for the rest of my life? Just how gullible were people anyhow? What woman in her right mind would head for a fourth child after having three sections? "Not me." I gave what I hoped was a disbelieving laugh. "She must have confused me with someone else."

"Oh," the girl said. "Well, maybe she did."

That was the end of *that* conversation. There was no way I was chatting to anyone now and there was no way I was calling a nurse. I didn't want them sniggering at my ignorance. I got out of bed, pulled my curtains around me and opened up a magazine. *How To Improve Your Man Without Him Knowing* was the title of the main article. I wondered about a lobotomy? Hypnotism? Brainwashing techniques? Nope. Apparently all you had to do was feed him low-fat food. It made him lose weight and he'd enjoy the tasty recipes that the magazine had kindly provided. Wow!

I was going to cut that out for Mam.

Sneering away to myself at the eejits that actually believed the crap that I was reading, I didn't hear Pam pull back the curtain.

"Hi," she said in her quiet voice. "How's things?"

I jumped.

"I didn't mean to startle you," Pam dumped some more magazines on the bed. "So what's the story?" She gave me a tentative smile.

There was something in her face, in her eyes that made me feel sort of tender towards her. OK, so she could be a judgmental cow sometimes and OK, we didn't exactly 'click' any more, but she was my sister and I did love her, I think. I gave a sort of smile back. "Nothing really." I hesitated. "I'm just getting a sort of pain every now and again."

"Like what sort of pain?" Her eyes widened. "An achy sort of pain?"

"Mmm."

"And your tummy? Does it go sort of hard?"

I was about to nod when the pain came again. "Ooooh." It hurt a *lot* more this time. I felt Pam's hand on my belly and then she was buzzing the nurse.

"Don't," I attempted to flap her hand away. I wasn't going to look a fool in front of anyone.

"Stop!" Pam snapped. She buzzed again. "You're in labour. They'll have to check you out."

Her words hit me like a shot of whiskey. I jerked, shuddered and felt sort of sick.

A nurse bustled into the cubicle.

"She's in labour," Pam said, sounding very authoritative.

Another pain hit. Jesus, they were getting bad. I closed my eyes and groaned.

"Breathe," Pam ordered. "In. Out. In. Out."

The nurse shoved Pam out and began examining me. I mean, isn't it the last thing you want, someone sticking their hand you-know-where when you're convulsed with agony?

More buzzing. More bustling.

"Take her to the labour ward. She's six centimetres."

I was lifted into a wheelchair. Pushed out of the ward. And suddenly I felt scared. So terrified. And it wasn't the pain. And it wasn't that I didn't know what was going to happen. It was just the fact that my life was going to change. I was going to be a mother. *Me*. Me.

Nausea rose and I thought I was going to pass out.

Another pain hit.

I wanted John.

I wanted him there with me, holding my hand, telling me I was going to be OK.

They were pushing me very fast along the corridor.

I was vaguely aware of Pam running behind.

"Pam," I called, "will you . . .?"

Her answer was a clasp of my hand.

Don't ask me what happened after that. It all went very fast which I suppose is good. I mean, I wasn't in pain for hours and hours on end like some people.

I had the epidural, but near the end when the pushing starts, that had worn off. And stupid me, I'd actually thought that once the pushing started, the pain would end.

The pain got bloody worse.

Sorry now to all you who haven't had kids but that's the way it is.

"Push," the midwife said.

I pushed.

"No, down," she said. "You're pushing into your face."

Another pain.

"Push," the midwife said.

I pushed.

"No! Down! You're pushing into your face."

I'll push me foot into your face, you ould cow, I thought bitterly.

Pam's hand clasping mine tightened. "Push like you're trying to shite," she whispered.

I started to giggle. It's hard to giggle when you're in pain but Pam saying the word 'shite' was akin to the Pope streaking thorough St Peter's Square.

Another pain.

"Push!" the midwife said.

I screwed up my face and pushed.

"I can see its head," someone said.

More pain.

I pushed again.

"Oh, oh Mags, I can see its head too," Pam's voice rose excitedly. "Oh, oh Mags!" Her grip tightened. Tears sparked her eyes.

Jesus!

Someone wiped my face.

More agony. I got ready to push.

"No, no," the midwife called anxiously. "Just pant. We have to get the shoulders out."

This was unreal, I thought in my fuzz of pain. They wanted me to pant just when I'd got the hang of pushing. I couldn't do this any more. "I can't do this anaaaahhhh!"

"Pant," Pam said. She rubbed her hand over my face. "You're doing great, Mags, really great." She gave a smile. "It'll be over in a few minutes."

"OK," the midwife said, "next pain, give an almighty push and you're there."

I was going to be a mother in a few minutes.

The next pain and I'd have a baby.

I more than anything didn't want to push.

I felt the pain rising. My belly tightened. I closed my eyes. Pam gripped my hand. "AAAGGHHH!"

And suddenly there was nothing. Just a lot of splashy, squashy sounds. A cry. Pam half-laughing, half-crying.

I was afraid to open my eyes.

"D'you want to see your baby," one of the nurses asked happily.

"No!" I shook my head. "No. No, I'm scared."

Why the hell had I said that?

Something was placed in my arms.

I didn't want to look.

"Mags," Pam said softly, "don't you want to see your baby?"

They'd all think I was weird if I didn't look. But what if the baby hated me? What if . . .

"Mags?" Pam asked and there was a hint of unease in her voice.

Slowly, cautiously I opened one eye. A purple, squirming bundle lay across my arms.

"Isn't she beautiful?" Pam whispered. "Oh, Mags, she's perfect."

Perfect? The child was purple! "But, she's all purple!" I reached out and a tiny hand clasped my finger. Something shifted inside me. I looked at her closer. "I have a little girl?"

"Yeah." Pam smiled at me. "A baby girl."

"Don't worry about her colour," one of the nurses said, lifting her away. "She'll pink up in a minute or so.

Now, we'll just weigh her and dress her and you can have her back. You need to get to know her."

Pam smiled ridiculously at me. There were tears running down her face.

She was a right eejit.

I made myself smile back at her.

I didn't know what I should feel.

I was numb really.

The baby was ten pounds eleven ounces. She had brown hair, tiny hands and feet and according to the nurse was quite long.

I tried to feel proud at that. I smiled as if I was delighted to hear it.

After I'd been freshened up and stitched up, they wheeled me and baby back to the ward.

"Any names picked?" Pam asked.

I shook my head. I was still a bit shell-shocked over the whole thing.

"I love this bit," Pam confided to me. "I love holding my baby and being wheeled along the corridor."

I just loved the idea of crawling into bed.

"And now you can take the time to examine all her bits and pieces," Pam said. She rubbed the top of the baby's head gently. "She's beautiful, Mags. Wait till Mammy sees her."

I smiled automatically again.

I looked down on the tiny bundle and willed myself to feel something. I wanted a feeling of mad love to rush over me but it didn't. I willed myself to feel happy, but I couldn't. It was like I was in some grey numb world.

The baby stirred in my arms. She opened blue eyes and focused them on me. I stared back at her.

This is your daughter, Maggie, I told myself. This is your baby daughter.

Nothing.

As the nurse helped me into bed I handed the baby to Pam.

I wanted to curl up and sleep.

I never wanted to waken.

Chapter Forty-two

Mammy and me and the three kids visited Maggie tonight. I had hoped Dick would mind the kids for me but he couldn't. He was working late and he couldn't get away.

I think I annoyed him a bit when I asked what time he'd be home.

"Pamela," he said, "I took a week off to mind you when you hurt your eye, I have a lot of catching up to do."

I hung up the phone. I wanted to have the nerve to say to him that it was his fault that I hurt my eye but I chickened out. Well, if I'm honest, saying it wasn't an option. Lately though, I don't know what's come over me, I'm thinking all sorts of angry thoughts about Dick. It's only in the past couple of days, ever since Maggie had her baby in fact. I feel so disloyal thinking bad things about Dick. He works so hard and gives us a lovely home and everything.

I think it's just that I'm sort of annoyed he was never at the birth of our kids. He said he'd rather see them clean than covered with slime.

It hadn't hurt at the time but now, thinking about it and seeing Maggie's baby being born, it did hurt. I don't know why.

Anyhow, like I said, me, Mammy and the kids went in to see Maggie.

Mammy hated going to see Maggie and the baby. It wasn't that she didn't like the baby, she loved the baby, she rocked it and cooed at it and everything – it was the fact that Maggie had no male visitors in to see her.

"They'll all know she's been let down," Mammy said.

"Who'll know?"

"The ward, everyone."

"Well, bring Mr P in. They might think it's his."

Mammy gasped, a little shocked. "Pamela!"

"Well, the poor baby can't help it, can she?" I snapped. Tears pricked my eyes. I don't know what was happening to me. "It's only a poor little baby; it needs all the love it can get from us." I glared at Mammy. "Are you going to let it down?"

"All I'm saying – "

David started to whimper in the back seat.

"Is your mammy scaring you?" Mammy asked him. "She's shouting at your poor nana, isn't she?"

David buried his head in his hands and started to rock back and forward.

Dick junior started chanting 'vegetable' at him and poking him with his finger.

"Dick junior, stop it!" I shouted.

David started to cry, Mammy shook her head and I wanted to scream.

To Mammy's immense relief there were two male visitors

with a big woman at Maggie's bedside. One of them was a scrawny-looking fella with a loud voice who was hidden behind a huge bunch of flowers that he carried. The other was a young lad, foreign, with dark eyes and a devastating smile.

"I need a vase for these," the scrawny man was saying.

"Ask a nurse you gobshite," a big brawny woman hissed. "D'you think a fucking vase is just going to appear because you want it to appear?"

The scrawny man tittered a bit and, turning, banged into Mammy. "Ooops, sorry," he said. "Just looking for a vase."

"It's all right," Mammy said brightly. "No harm done."

She looked eagerly at Maggie awaiting an introduction. "Louis," Maggie said. "And this is Romano and Josie."

"Hello," Romano smiled. "Hello. Pleased to meet you. Very pleased."

Josie just nodded.

Mammy smiled approvingly at Romano. "Do you work with Maggie?" she asked.

"Sorry?"

"Do you work with Maggie?"

"I work wid . . . sorry?"

Mammy raised her voice. "I asked do you work – "

"He's foreign, Mam. He's not deaf," Maggie said laconically.

Josie chortled. Mammy flushed.

She turned her attention to the baby. "And how's my little mite?" she simpered.

Maggie handed the baby to her. "She's good," she said. "She slept well last night. Almost four hours."

Maggie seemed brighter today. The past couple of days it

was as if she was in a trance or something but she seemed to have perked up.

Louis arrived back with his vase. He was staggering under the size of the thing. He banged it down onto Maggie's bedside locker. "No stingy bunch of blooms that," he said, sounding proud. "We know how to look after our best manager!"

Mammy positively melted with excitement. "Oh, she's a great girl ," she giggled. "A great worker."

"Next time bring in some chocolates," Maggie snapped. "I know where you got those flowers, you scabby fecker. You took them off the tables in work, didn't you?"

Josie guffawed as Louis reddened.

Mammy shot Maggie a furious look and Maggie smirked back at her. I envied Maggie in that instant. I don't know why. It wasn't as if she had anything.

Dick junior began rifling in Maggie's drawer. "Dick junior," I said, "come away from there!"

Dick junior shot me the same smirky look Maggie had just given Mammy. "I want some sweets," he pouted.

"Me too," David piped up.

"He talked!" Mammy exclaimed, making David huddle into me.

"Is it sweets ya want, luv?" the big woman asked. I'd forgotten her name. She held out her hands. "Come on with me and we'll see what's going in the shop."

Dick junior, eager as ever, hurtled around the bed and grabbed the woman's hand. "My name is Dick," he said, all sweetness and light. He pulled David over, "And this is my brother David. He's two."

377

"Hello, Dick and David," the woman said. She looked at me. "Is it OK if I . . ."

"Oh, yes, sure. Go ahead."

The three left, Dick junior keeping up a rapid conversation as David clung onto his hand for dear life. I smiled fondly. Dick junior was so gentle really.

"So, Maggie," Mammy plonked herself on Maggie's bed. "How's things? How are you feeling?"

"OK."

Mammy tickled the baby under her chin. "Any names picked yet?"

"Nope."

"You could call her Frances after your Dad," Mammy offered.

"I could call her Shitface after Dad but I don't want to," Maggie spat.

I wanted to die with shame. Mammy surprisingly just laughed and flapped her hand. "Postnatal blues," she said. "Makes you narky and weepy. You'll be fine."

"Oh, oh," Louis nudged Romano, "we'd better go. Women's things!"

"Not at all," Mammy beamed, "don't go on our account."

Louis shook his head. "Lucinda – she works in the restaurant – she's in charge at the moment." He snorted and tapped his nose. "Not a good idea really but the rest of us wanted to come and see Maggie."

"How nice of you," Mammy simpered.

"More like yez wanted to skive off early," Maggie muttered.

Mammy inhaled sharply.

Louis started chortling. "She's as hard as nails, this

378

young one." He tousled Maggie's hair. *"Normally I'm afraid of her but it's hard to be intimidated by a girl in a teddy-bear nightdress."*

Mammy laughed and clapped her hands. I managed a grin and Maggie glowered.

"Best be off," Louis smiled at us and pranced out of the room.

"Isn't he lovely?" Mammy asked. "And that other fellow with him, isn't he nice?"

"Spoken for, Mammy," Maggie said. "He's seeing a girl with a baby by another man."

That comment screwed the conversation up for the whole night.

We left early. Mammy pretended that she was meeting Mr Parker. She kissed the so-far-nameless baby goodbye and nodded to Maggie.

"Thanks for coming," Maggie said, looking a bit more contrite. I saw her gulp slightly, "Thanks."

"Bye now," Mammy said again.

I picked up Shauna, who was being very good and who hadn't cried for her eight o'clock bottle at all. Dick and David, who'd been quiet since the woman had bought them armloads of sweets, jumped up when they saw me leaving. "Well, Maggie, see you when you get out," I said. I didn't know what else to say – I was afraid she'd take my head off, she seemed to be in that kind of mood.

"You will," she said. I don't know if I imagined it, but her eyes glistened. I wanted to put my arms around her but I didn't dare.

Very quietly, she said, "And Pam?"

"Yes?"

"Thanks for being at the birth, I know you mightn't have wanted to come and . . ."

"Not wanted to go?" I said incredulously. "It was great, Maggie. I wouldn't have missed it for the world. I was glad to go."

"You were?"

"Uh-huh."

I wasn't imagining it. Her eyes were glistening. I gently put Shauna down on the bed. I reached out and touched Maggie's hair. "You'll be fine, you know," I said, giving her a bit of a cuddle. "You have me and Mammy and you have the baby."

"Yeah." Her voice sounded small. She pulled away.

Maggie was never a feely type of person.

"It's just the blues," I explained. "You'll be fine."

She nodded but didn't look at me. I felt slightly hurt. I busied myself picking up Shauna again. "Come on, prettiness," I cooed. "Let's get you home."

Trying to smile at Maggie, I rushed out into the corridor.

Today was the last day in the hospital. I'd learned how to bathe and change the baby. I'd learned how to make up her bottles and how often to feed her. I seemed to have learned everything about her except how I should feel. I was almost glad when I got depressed yesterday. It meant that at least some part of my numb brain was working. I kept looking at the baby and wanting to cry. I wanted to cry at the way she looked at me, at the way she depended on me. I wanted to cry when the other girls in the ward seemed to know each other so well and I was left floundering.

But I never cried. So I snapped at people instead. I was horrible to Louis when he came in to see me. He didn't notice though. He never does. Him and John are a bit the same like that. And I was awful to Mam and Pam. And Pam wrapped her arms around me before she left and I wanted more than anything just to sob my heart out, but I couldn't. I'd never get over the shame. And all the other girls in the ward would wonder if I was disturbed or anything. Pam didn't seem to mind though. She just picked up Shauna and said goodbye.

I spent the whole morning in the ward just in bed. I wasn't interested in going to exercise classes to get my stomach flat or any of that crap. My stomach had never been flat anyhow. I spent the day in bed, lying on my side, gazing at the baby in her cot.

I still didn't know what to call her.

Her eyes were closed and she lay flat on her back with her hands on either side of her head. Her little fists were curled tightly. She was a long baby. Much longer than the others in the ward. She was the heaviest too. I grinned ruefully. She obviously took after me on that one.

"Well, at least you're smilin'!"

Lucinda's voice broke the early-morning silence.

I hauled myself up on my elbow and managed another smile for her. "Hiya."

"I couldn't smile for about a *month* after havin'

Leonardo," she said loudly as she approached my bed. Her platform heels clomped across the floor. Yanking down her handkerchief skirt she sat on the chair beside the bed. "Give us a look," she whispered.

She peered in at the baby. "Aw, she's gorgeous."

"Mmm."

"So how are you?" she asked. "A bit stunned or what?"

I gawked at her. How did she know I was stunned?

"I – *fecking – couldn't* get over the birth of Leonardo for ages," she confided loudly, rolling her eyes. "Deh *shock* of it. In labour for twenty-four hours I was. And de fact that he wasn't planned made it worse, yeh know?" Without waiting for me to answer, she swept on, "All I kept doin' was looking at him and thinking that I was in someone else's life." She shook her head. "You like that?"

I shrugged. "A bit," I admitted reluctantly.

"I bet you are," Lucinda nodded as if it was the most natural thing in the world to feel you were in another person's life. "It took me ages to get used to the idea. Mind you, one of me mates had a baby there last month and she feels the same. She says she just can't feel like a mother." She gave a chortle. "I think she thought she was goin' ta come out of the labour ward in an apron and hairnet, you know?"

I managed a weak smile. "Did she?"

"Yeah. And I had to explain to her that the whole thing sort of creeps up on ya, ya know?" She looked at me as if she expected me to say something. When I didn't, she went on, "I mean, for me, the time I copped on to the fact that I was a mother was when Leonardo got sick. Imagine the poor kid had to get sick before it hit me. He was about . . ." she screwed up her face, "about a year or somethin' and he was in hospital and I kept thinking to meself what the fuck I'd do if he died, you know. And I knew then that I wouldn't know what to do with meself. I wouldn't have a clue how to fill in all the time." She sighed dramatically and sniggered, "I'd – turned – into – a – mammy."

I gave an obligatory smile.

"Mad, what?" She gave a bit of a laugh and began to rummage about with a plastic bag she'd brought in. "Here," she shoved a green-wrapped parcel at me, "here's a present for you. It's from all of us. We didn't have time to get anything yesterday."

"Oh, you shouldn't . . ."

"You're our boss. Of course we have to. I chose it," she added proudly.

It was a BodyShop basket of soaps and shower gels. A big basket. "Louis said to get the best one in the shop," she said. A bit of a giggle. "He thinks if he spends money on you that you'll definitely come back after your maternity leave."

I gazed at the basket. They'd bought something for *me*. "Thanks," I sniffed. "It's lovely."

"Yeah, it's nice to get stuff for yourself," Lucinda said. "The baby gets *everything*. I remember with Leonardo he got loads of stuff and I got fuck all. Fuck All."

I nodded, not able to speak. I'd hated myself for feeling like that and here was Lucinda -

Her chatter broke into my thoughts. "So, now if I buy something, I always get it for the mother, you know?"

"Yeah. Thanks. It's great." I put the basket on my locker.

"So," Lucinda asked, rubbing the baby's head with her finger, "what's it like for you? Are you one of those real mammy people who love your baby from the start?" She looked curiously at me.

I wanted to lie. I didn't want to tell her anything. But she'd been so open with me, though to Lucinda that just seemed to be chit-chat. I slowly shook my head. "It's," I took a breath, "it's awful scary."

The minute I'd said it I wanted to pull it back.

"Fucking sure it is," Lucinda nodded agreement. "You're responsible for someone else now. It's shit-making stuff."

Shit-making stuff.

For the first time since the baby was born I really smiled.

Maybe I *would* manage. Lucinda had managed and she'd been younger than me. A few months ago I would have thought 'and stupider than me'. But she wasn't.

Lucinda was very clued-in.

Leonardo was a lucky kid.

I looked at my baby and I made a silent promise. I was going to look after it the best I could. The very best I could.

I suppose that was a love of sorts.

"So," Lucinda asked, bending towards me and looking sympathetic, "have you managed to shit yet? I swear, it'll rip the arse outa you. After Leonardo was born, every time I shat, it was like trying to crap a Stanley knife. You like that?"

I gave a watery smile and didn't answer.

There was being open and there was being open.

Chapter Forty-three

I was upstairs when I heard Shauna begin to cry. "Dick junior," I called, "is Shauna OK?" He yelled up a 'yes' and I went on with my big clear-out.

I'd offered Maggie some of Shauna's old clothes and I was busy balancing on a chair pulling everything out of the top wardrobe in my bedroom. Clothes, Babygros and tiny coats littered the floor. It was nice to be able to help Maggie. She was being a lot more approachable since the baby was born. We chatted, a bit awkwardly, about nappies and puke and food. The sort of boring chit-chat mothers always find fascinating. We had a right laugh on Sunday when Maggie brought down one of the baby's nappies for me to examine. "Is it meant to be that funny green colour, Pam?"

And I opened the nappy and had a good sniff and a bit of a poke. "Looks fine, " I said.

Mr Parker had to leave the room. Well, he had to leave the house. He loathes babies and all the mess they make. "Call me," he snapped to my mother.

Maggie started to laugh and so did I then.

But it wasn't really that funny. Mr Parker thinks that Mammy has been too easy on Maggie over the whole thing and Mammy is miserable worrying. And Maggie told Mammy to cop onto herself and Mammy told Maggie that if she hadn't been such a tramp Mr Parker would be -

Shauna screamed again. "Dick junior," I called anxiously, "is Shauna OK?" I'd left Dick junior in charge — it always ensured that he didn't do anything too bold himself.

"She's OK," he called again. "She's just bold."

"Babies aren't bold," I called indulgently. "She's only small. She can't — "

This time Shauna howled.

I nearly fell off the chair and twisted my foot in my haste to get down to see what was happening. I clenched my fists and half-closed my eyes as I approached the dining-room door. I don't know what I'd do if I ever found one of the kids with something wrong with them.

There was the sound of a smack, more screams and I rushed into the room. "DICK JUNIOR!" I screeched, grabbing him and yanking him away from Shauna.

The baby had huge red streaks across her face. Tears ran down her cheeks. I scooped her up and hugged her to me. I gazed horrified at Dick junior.

David ambled over and stood looking at the three of us.

"What . . ." I could hardly get the words out. Sickness crawled up my belly. "What are you doing?"

Dick junior shrugged. "She grabbed my Lego and I said 'No, no' but she kept grabbing it."

Shauna was shaking and I held her really tight in to me.

A small cut bled over her eye. "And?" I asked. I wanted to sound firm but I couldn't. My voice was as weak as my legs.

"She kept doing it so I hit her."

"You don't hit little babies. You don't hit little girls!" My voice rose as I screamed into my son's face.

He pulled away. He looked as shocked now as I did. "But – " he paused. Bit his lip. Tears welled up in his eyes. "But I love Baby Shauna."

"Well, if you love her you don't hit – " I stopped. Snap! Snap! Snap! went my head. It was like the whole world shifted on its axis. Like I'd suddenly wiped a grimy windscreen. The past, present and future marched into my head. Bang! Bang! Bang! I can see clearly now the rain has gone.

Jesus.

Jesus Christ.

"I love Baby Shauna," Dick junior whispered.

I reached over and pulled him to me. "I know you do, Dick. I know."

And I loved Baby Shauna.

And Dick junior.

And David.

I loved my kids.

I was such a yellow belly. Four weeks into being a mother and I still hadn't told John that he had a daughter. I don't know why I kept putting it off – well, I do actually, I was afraid of what he'd say. I mean there isn't any guidebook, is there, for telling ex-boyfriends what they've fathered?

Anyhow, Mam kept nagging me. "Oh," she kept saying, "you'll want to tell him sooner or later. Huh, the child will be making her Confirmation and you still won't have told him."

"She won't be making her Confirmation," I shot back.

That shut her up. Well, for about sixty seconds.

"Well, that's a fine way to be. Flouting everything you've been taught about right living and decency. Wonderful."

Mam has got a bit more backbone these days. I don't think it's courage, I think she just blames me for the way Mr P is treating her. Honestly, the man is such a prick. He threw a wobbler the other day because the baby was sick. Mam and I were worried about her and Mam didn't get around to making his tea for him.

"An army marches on its stomach," he said nastily, glaring at Mam.

"Well, so could you," I said. "In fact you'll trip over yours it's that big."

I thought they'd laugh. But nope. He asked Mam was she going to let me away with talking to him like that and Mam said no and then she started rustling up some eggs for him.

It made me angry to think that she lets him treat her like that. But then maybe that's what men do. I don't know.

John never went on like that.

John. Bloody John.

I decided that I'd better ring him. The baby, who I'd

called Jane by the way, was asleep. Normally I tried to get some kip when she slept but that morning I decided to bite the bullet and ring John. I rang his work first. I know. I know. I'm awful. I know it's not the done thing to tell someone they've a baby girl when they're probably wiring a dangerous socket or something. Anyhow, it didn't matter. John wasn't working in the place any more. And then I remembered that he'd told me that. So the next thing I decided to do was to ring his house. Another yellow-belly decision. I figured I'd leave a message on his answering machine. I practised my jolly voice and my little speech before I rang. "Hi, John, tried to get hold of you but you're not in work. You have a lovely baby girl. Byee."

I guess if a guy had done that I'd call him an asshole but hey, this was me. I rang. My mouth was dry, my heart was thumping and to my horror someone lifted the phone. I was about to slam it back down again when a voice from the other end, a *female* voice I recognised said, "'Ello."

Enraged, I gazed down the receiver. Well, that was just lovely, I wanted to say. Just bloody lovely. Here I was after giving birth to his child and already, *already*, he'd replaced me with someone else. And not just *anyone* else. Bloody Ali. I mean, what else would she be doing in his house at eleven-thirty on a Thursday morning?

"Ali," I said and my voice dripped frost. "What a surprise."

There was a second's pause before she said, "Maggie? Maggie? Is that you?"

She sounded a bit taken aback as well she should. "Of course it's me," I said. "Or does John have any other women ringing him?" I tried to make it sound like a joke, just to show that I didn't care if the whole population of Britain took up phoning John.

To my gratification, Ali got flustered. "Well, no, 'course not. John don't 'ave any other women calling around. 'E misses you, ya know."

"Obviously," I gave a bit of a snigger.

"So, 'ow's things?" Ali asked, totally missing my sarcasm or else choosing to ignore it. "'Ave you 'ad the baby yet? I must say, Maggie, when John told me, I was a bit 'urt. You could 'ave let me know, you know."

Yeah. Right.

I spat out, "I had the baby a few weeks ago – she came early. I just rang John to tell him he has a baby daughter." Then I added, "That's if he's interested, of course."

"Of course 'e's interested. 'E's mad about you, ya know."

I didn't bother answering. Who did she think she was kidding? No wonder she'd never rung me after I left. She was too busy getting it on with my fella. And the nerve, the *nerve* of John to try and get me to come back to him while all the time he had Ali on the back burner.

"What d'you call 'er?"

"Jane."

"Oh, that's nice. After John's – "

"Yeah." I wish I hadn't now but at the time I thought it was the least I could do to make it up to John.

391

"So, 'ow you feeling?"

"Great."

"Good." Ali paused. "John's not though," she said softly. "'E's 'ad a hard time."

"Well, I'm sure you're managing to help him along." I couldn't help it, my voice took a nosedive into the deep freeze.

"Wot?" She sounded startled. "Is that wot you think? Thanks a lot, Maggie."

I felt a tiny flicker of shame somewhere deep inside. "Yeah, well," I muttered. "What else are you doing in his house so early in the morning?"

"I've been 'ere since last week," she snapped, sounding totally unlike the 'couldn't-get-annoyed-if-you-hummed-incessantly-all-day' Ali that I knew. "And so 'ave lots of other people. It's where you should be, Maggie. Only you did a runner, didn't you?"

"Pardon?" I didn't like her tone. How dare she tell me where I should be.

"'E wasn't going to let you know," she said sharply. "Because of the baby and all, in case it'd upset you. I mean, 'e considers other people, Maggie." The remark was so pointed, she almost stabbed me.

"Going to let me know what?" I tried to say disdainfully. The way she sounded though made me feel uneasy.

"What?" I demanded again.

She snapped out, "Rat's dead. 'E died of an overdose last week. The funeral is tomorrow."

I couldn't speak. The words were like blows.

Eventually I muttered, "Rat?"

"Rat," Ali repeated. Her voice was softer now, as if she felt sorry for snapping at me. "He died last week." Her voice wobbled. "Poor John, Maggie. 'E blames 'imself. He threw Rat out, d'you see. And now 'e's dead."

I'd never been madly fond of Rat but I felt so sick for John. "When is the funeral?" I asked numbly.

"Tomorrow at ten," Ali said. Her voice softened further. "I'm just 'ere ringing up everyone to tell them wot's happening. John's gone to get the coffin and stuff."

"If I came, could I stay with you?" I asked. I marvelled at my nerve.

"Oh, you don't 'ave to come."

"Yeah. Yeah, I do, Ali."

"Well, you'll 'ave to sleep on the sofa," Ali said. "I've a new flatmate since you left."

Another pointed remark.

"Thanks. I'll try and get a flight for the morning."

"OK."

There was another silence. I said then what I should have said nine months ago. "Sorry for leaving you in the lurch, Ali. I just sort of panicked."

"I figured as much." She sounded now as if she was smiling. "That's wot I told John. Maggie panics. She'll come round."

I didn't bother to answer that. Me and John were a totally different matter. I just didn't think I loved John.

"Bye."

"Bye, Maggie," she said, "and give Jane a kiss from me."

I'd just hung up when the doorbell rang. Someone began hammering on the door. Jane began howling upstairs. I was going to kill whoever was calling.

I don't know what came over me. I just remember picking up Shauna, pulling on her coat and ordering Dick junior and David to get their coats from the closet.

"Where are we going?" Dick junior trailed behind me as I grabbed bits and pieces for Shauna and began stuffing them into her baby bag.

"We're going to visit Nana Scanlon," I muttered. I glared at him. "Will you get your coat, Dick, for God's sake!"

He jumped at the sharp tone and with a mutinous look on his face he stomped off to get his coat.

I know I didn't think one thought as I began to bundle clothes into a small bag for David and Dick junior. I didn't want to let myself think. It was all a feverish packing. Ushering the two boys out to the car, I shoved them inside, belted Shauna into her car seat and revved up the car engine.

I don't remember the drive to Mammy's at all. All I remember is pulling up outside the house and hammering and ringing on the door.

Maggie answered and she looked as white as a sheet and then when she saw it was just me, she got angry. "Well, thanks for waking the baby, Pam," she snapped.

"Is Mammy in?"

"No, she's gone out with Flubber Man."

"Well, can you ask her if it's OK if the children stay with her for a while? Maybe for tonight?"

"Why don't you hang on and ask her yourself?"

I didn't bother to answer. I ran down the driveway and into the car. I ignored David as he began toddling down the path after me.

As I drove away, I saw Maggie catching David by the hand and the two of them staring after me as I left.

Well, that was bloody marvellous. Pam only dumped her three kids on me. I had two babies to mind the whole afternoon. I didn't bother looking out for David and Dick. Basically they could have demolished the house and I wouldn't have cared. I put Shauna in her bouncer, rocked Jane on my knee and began ringing the tour operators looking for a flight to London for the next day.

I drove home. I drove home and made myself a cup of tea. A really strong cup of tea. For the first time in years – decades – my mind was totally calm. Totally focused. I knew, probably for the first time in my life what I had to do. And how I had to do it.

Dick wasn't due back until the following evening. He was away down the country on business. I only hoped the delay wouldn't make me lose my nerve.

I added some vodka from the press into my tea.

There was no harm in getting drunk.

After all, I was on my own. I could do what I wanted.

Tina Reilly

After downing the tea, I put on my mucky wellies and stomped all over the living-room carpet.

I jumped on the sofa.

And then I laughed.

Really really laughed.

Chapter Forty-four

Seven o'clock the next morning, I sat on the plane, having shelled out a small fortune for a first-class flight to London. It was the only one that would have me there in reasonable time. As the plane took off, I closed my eyes and tried to have a sleep. I was like a zombie these days. Jane was a full-time job and she still wasn't sleeping a full night, though apparently, at four weeks sleeping from twelve to six in the morning was considered great.

"Huh," Mam had said, "the poor child's afraid to wake up. That's why she's so good."

Honestly, Mam was becoming a real pain. Still, I couldn't give out too much. She was minding Jane for me. And she'd Pam's three kids.

When she and Mr P had arrived home the night before, Mr P had been horrified to see David belting some saucepans with a wooden spoon while Dick junior sang at the top of his voice into the saltcellar. He couldn't have chosen a nicer song either. It was the one about us all being mammals and doing it like they do on the Discovery Channel.

"What are *they* doing here?" Mr P demanded. He said 'they' as if Dick and David were the scum of the earth.

"Pam wants you to mind them for her, Mam," I said, ignoring him and smiling sweetly at Mam. "And, eh, I've to go to London tomorrow so I wonder if you'll mind Jane for me?"

I didn't tell her that it was to a funeral I was going. I was hoping she'd make her own assumptions. And she did. Her chest swelled, her face went red with pleasure and I thought the beaming smile she gave me would wither me up. *"Of course. Of course,"* she said.

"Good," I smiled. "John's brother has died. I guess I should make an appearance at the funeral." I walked out of the kitchen holding Jane. I wanted to escape before Mam changed her mind. I mean, even Mam couldn't honestly think that John and I would get back together at his brother's funeral. Even she couldn't be that stupid.

I jumped as Mr P bellowed at Dick junior and David, "Will you shut up with that filthy song! You'll rot in hell, both of you."

As I reached the kitchen door, I could hear David begin to whimper.

Dick junior sang on unabashed.

Good man, Dick, I wanted to say.

"Is he going to stop or will I make him stop?" Mr P demanded.

My blood began to boil at his tone. Who the hell did he think he was?

"Oh, it's just high spirits, Geoffrey," Mam chirped. "Just ignore him."

"SHUT UP!" Mr P bellowed at Dick junior, ignoring Mam instead.

"You're not my daddy," Dick junior said. "You can't shout at me."

"Oh, can't I?" Mr P seemed to be squaring up to Dick junior.

"Dick, love, just stop the singing for a little while," Mammy said. "I'll give you a nice bar if you do."

"OK." Dick threw the saltcellar onto the floor and marched over to Mam. "Can David have one too?"

"Yes." Mammy ruffled his hair.

"Bribery," Mr P scoffed. "No respect at all."

"And you sit down and I'll get you a nice fry," Mammy gave him an encouraging smile.

"Well, I hope you've got the Denny pudding, I don't like that other one you buy. Too much fat in it."

"Bribery, Mr P?" I couldn't resist it.

The back of his neck reddened and he said nothing. I got away while the going was good.

Things were quiet until tea-time. Mam made us all a fry minus the Denny pudding – which she'd forgotten to buy – and Mr P had been highly offended. He stomped out after a bit of shouting and pouting. The slam of the door as he exited made David cower under the table, sobbing.

The child is weird.

Dick junior had just continued eating and talking as if nothing had happened. Both Jane and Shauna woke up and Mam, blaming herself for being so stupid, had dissolved into tears.

And me. Jesus. I felt totally helpless. I hadn't felt like that in years. I sat frozen for a second or two before grabbing Jane and bringing her upstairs.

I heard Mam in the kitchen, still weeping, trying to make David stop crying. I heard Dick junior telling Mam that David hated fights but that *he* didn't. He didn't care and he always minded David when fights started.

"Well, mind him now then!" Mam snapped before going out into the hall.

I heard her pick up the phone and start dialling.

I think she dialled Pam to see if she'd come and collect her kids. But Pam mustn't have been home. After a while Mam came up to me. I shoved Jane into her basket and pretended to be asleep. There was no way I was minding Pam's kids while my mother made a fool of herself haring out after Mr P.

Don't get me wrong, I would've minded them for any other reason but Mam had done all the chasing to appease our dad and it had all been for no good.

She was better off without him.

"Maggie," Mam whispered loudly, "are you awake?"

I gave a sort of snore in reply.

"Well for some," she sniffed as she left.

When I was sure she'd gone, I lifted myself up on my elbow and looked in at Jane.

She was sleeping on her back, little lashes brushing her cheeks. She gave a small smile in her sleep.

My heart gave a funny kind of flip.

I reached out and touched her baby-soft face. "You'll never have to worry about me being like Nana," I promised her. "Never ever ever."

"Will all passengers please fasten their seat belts as we are now approaching Heathrow airport."

The voice jolted me awake. I rubbed my tired eyes and blearily clipped my seat belt closed. I wondered if Jane had woken for her feed yet. I hoped Mam would hear her. Maybe I should give a ring when I landed just to check that – Jesus. I shook my head.

What the hell was happening to me?

It was a bumpy landing and not exactly being a great flyer at the best of times, I wondered vaguely what would happen to Jane if I was to die.

John would take her I suppose.

I didn't know if I'd like that.

I wondered if I should make a will.

The slam of the plane as its wheels hit the tarmac almost made me think it was too late. "Jesus!" I yelped.

The man sitting beside me threw me a condescending smile. "Don't fly much, do you?" he asked.

"Not in planes like this I don't," I grumped back at him.

God, I hated men.

Of course, after snapping at him, I then had to endure ten minutes of avoiding his eyes as the plane taxied to a halt. Then I had to get my overnight bag down from the overhead locker without once looking at him. And then, I stood up far too early and didn't want to lose face by sitting down again, so I stood like a moron as I waited for the plane doors to be opened. Once opened of course I had the advantage. I was first out and because I had my bag with me I didn't have to queue up like all the other suckers and wait for my bags to arrive at the conveyer belt. I hate those things. The way everyone waits at the wrong one just because other people happen to be standing at it. Then spotting your bag on the belt and being afraid that someone else is going to run off with it.

Instead I got out of the airport and found the taxi rank and hailed a taxi. An hour later I was standing outside Ali's flat.

It hadn't changed. More paint had peeled from the outside walls. The buzzer had A and R on it now instead of A and M. Looking at it, I knew things had changed so far that nothing could ever reverse it. It's a weird feeling, knowing that someone else is in your old space.

Buzzzz.

"Yo!"

A male voice?

A *male* voice?

Ali had a *male* lodger.

"Eh, hi. I'm looking for Ali?"

"Not here."

"Oh. Well, I'm Maggie. She said I could – "

The buzzer went to let me in.

I tramped up the stairs, each step I took hammering it into me that everything had changed. It seemed like a million years ago that I'd been in this place. Now I had a baby and I didn't live here any more. I tried to push the feeling out of me but it sort of hovered over me like a mist.

The door was open and I let myself in. "Hi," I poked my head cautiously around.

"Morning." A guy I vaguely recognised was sprawled across the sofa. He was tall and lean and wore black jeans and a T-shirt. He eyed me up and down. "Robert," he said, eyes encouraging.

Then I remembered. He was a mate of John's. Some guy he worked with on the radio show. I'd never been into meeting John's friends before as I knew they'd hate me. But, I guess, it didn't matter any more. "Hi, Robert," I said. I injected some cheerfulness into my voice. "Are you living here now?" I dumped my bag on the ground so that I wouldn't have to look at him. He probably knew all about me and he probably thought I was a right cow.

"Yep." Robert pulled himself up from the sofa and, picking my bag up, carried it to my old room. "You're staying in here tonight," he said, depositing my bag on the bed. "Can't have a new mother sleeping on a sofa."

"Oh, no, I couldn't . . ."

"Tea? Coffee? Beer?" He strode out of the room. "I think we got time before the funeral starts."

"OK." I blinked back tears. Hormones are awful

bloody things. "I'll have a coffee. I'll be out in a sec." I glanced at myself in the mirror. Plump tired face framed by messy hair. I hastily wiped my sleeve over my eyes and, locating a hairbrush in my bag, pulled it furiously through my hair. The pain made me wince but it blanked the sadness.

I followed Robert back out into the kitchen.

He'd put two cups on the table and was standing beside the kettle waiting for it to boil. "Good flight?" he asked.

"Great," I responded.

Silence.

"We'll go to the church in about half an hour. Ali went ahead to get some flowers organised."

"Oh. Right."

More silence.

"Thanks for letting me have your room."

He poured some water into my mug. "It's OK." He handed me the coffee jar. I spooned some into my cup.

There was so much I wanted to ask him. About Rat. About John. But I couldn't. I wasn't a part of it any more. And anyhow, I hardly knew the guy. Imagine one of John's best mates and I hardly knew him. What did that say about me?

After loads more small talk and even more silences, Robert drained his cup and said that we'd better leave. "You ready?"

I nodded. My heart was thumping. I dreaded seeing John. I think I hated the idea of him being upset.

To my surprise and my horror, Robert grabbed my

hand. Just as quickly he let it go. "It's good you could come," he muttered. "John will appreciate it."

I shoved my hand into my jacket. "Yeah . . .well . . ."

"Let's go." He pushed open the door.

I felt sick.

I felt sick. I don't know if it was the slight hangover or the fact that what had woken me was the sound of a key in the lock.

"Pamela!" Dick's voice, sounding irritated, came from downstairs.

I sat up in bed. I was still fully dressed, my wellies on the floor beside me.

"PAMELA!"

His voice made me jump. A huge lump formed like magic in my throat. What had I done? Jesus what had I done?

"CHRIST!" Dick's voice came from downstairs. I knew what he'd seen. The sofa, all mucky. David's toys scattered across the floor. The remains of supper lying on a plate beside the fireplace.

The house the way it should be with three kids.

I pulled the duvet up to my chin and sweat broke out on my face. A cold clammy sweat. I was going to be sick.

Dick stomped up the stairs. "Pamela? Are you there?" He came to a halt at the door of the bedroom. His narrowed eyes took me in. "What the hell are you doing? What's happened downstairs?"

My mind searched for an explanation. Frantically. I opened my mouth to speak and nothing came out.

"Well?" He slowly came towards the bed. "Well?"

I stared at him hopelessly. Dumbstruck. What was I at?

"Were you out last night?" he demanded.

I shook my head. I wondered which part of me he'd hit first.

"LIAR!" He yelled into my face. "I rang and no one answered. Were you with someone?"

"No." It was like a croak the way it came out. "No, Dick, honestly!" He always liked me to be in when he rang. He never told me when he was going to ring but if I wasn't in he always thought I was with some other fella. He was dreadfully insecure.

"So where were you?" He glared at me.

"Nowhere."

He caught my arm and twisted. "Right." He sounded as if he didn't believe me. "And why is the house such a mess? What happened to the sofa?"

His eyes burned into mine. "Please, Dick. Let me – "

"And where are the kids?"

The kids. The mention of the kids made it change. The whole picture shifted, just the way it had yesterday. I don't know if Dick saw something in my eyes but his grip slackened for just the tiniest fraction of a second before he tightened it again. "Well?" he demanded.

"The kids are in my mother's," I said. My voice was firmer. My mind crystal clear. It wasn't meant to be like this. I had it all planned out last night. Calmly tell him we want him out. That's what I'd said to myself in the mirror before conking out on the bed.

"In your mother's?" His voice had the teasing, mocking tone he adopted when I'd just made some awful blunder.

"Yes."

More arm-twisting. He knelt on the bed and hissed into

my ear. *"Didn't I tell you not to let them spend too much time over there? Didn't I?"*

I nodded. My mouth dry.

"And you let them spend the night? What? Did you think you'd get away with it? Have them all collected before I came home?"

Oh God! Oh God! I gulped. Closed my eyes. *"They're staying there."*

"What?"

If he hadn't been hurting me so much, I might have laughed at the shock in his voice. *"They're staying there until you move out,"* I said.

"What?"

"I'm leaving you, Dick." The words were free. It was as if my heart crushed and swelled all at the one time.

"Leaving me? You're leaving me!"

I opened my eyes. Nodded.

Waiting . . .

And he started to laugh.

I wished he'd hit me black and blue. I wished he'd killed me. But he laughed. He let me go and he threw back his head and laughed.

I stared, stunned, at him. The hurt of it. The pain.

"You are not going anywhere," Dick shook his head and reached out to take my chin in his hands. He squeezed it a little tightly and said, *"Go collect the kids."*

He'd laughed.

"Go on," he said, sounding amused.

Dazed, I stood up. I crossed to the mirror to get my car keys.

"You can clean up when you get back."

"Fine."

I was downstairs and about to open the front door when I saw it lying against the radiator in the hall. It looked so tiny against the radiator. Shauna's baby-shoe. She must have lost it in the rush out the door yesterday. Absently I picked it up. God, but it was so small. And she was so small.

And Dick junior had hit her.

I crushed the shoe into my hand as I remembered her tear-streaked face. I clenched the shoe so hard my nails dug into my palms. I closed my eyes and my heart started hammering so hard that I thought it was going to burst out of my ribcage.

"Will you get a move on?"

Eyes snapping open I stared at Dick where he stood at the top of the stairs. The leer on his face, the sneer in his eyes.

I was outside me as I said, very slowly, very clearly, "Don't you talk like that to me – I'm your wife."

"Yeah, right."

The indifference.

"And," I continued, the blood rushing into every part of my body so that suddenly I felt alive and dizzy and breathless, "I am leaving you. I am. And you better get out of this house." I felt as if I poured cold water over myself. The shock, the reality. My hand clenched and unclenched, totally crushing Shauna's shoe. "I can't take it any more, Dick. And the kids can't take it." I turned to leave.

"Oh for God's sake!" He was down the stairs before I got the door open. He caught me by the hair and snapped, "You're not going anywhere. If you try to leave, I'll kill you."

"I am," I gasped. "And – " I yelped as he pulled my hair.

My resolve buckled. And then, I don't know how it happened, some ancient sense of self-preservation kicked in. And anger too, I suppose. And the desire to have that alive feeling with me all the time. "You lay a hand on me and I'll ring up your work and tell them all exactly what you're like and I'll tell all the neighbours too."

"You wouldn't dare!"

I thought of Dick junior and David and Shauna. I'd made a promise when they were born. I'd told them that they'd love me. That they'd be happy. "Try me," *I said half-hysterically.*

He let me go.

Hardly daring to believe it, I opened the door once again. I waited for the blow, the kick, the dig, but nothing happened. I paused, hand on the door. I was free to go. Free to go. And I found I couldn't. I don't know why, but I turned back.

Dick was staring at me. I don't know what was in his eyes. "Don't leave me, Pam," *he said.*

I was glued to the ground.

"You don't understand me. I love you so much, that's why – "

"No, Dick," *I said.* "That's not why." *The admission made me sick.*

"It is," *he said reaching for me. His brown eyes looked bewildered. I wanted to hug him.* "I do love you."

"No." *Tears hopped into my eyes from nowhere.* "No, Dick. You hit me. You hit the kids."

"Because I love you." *Tears were in his eyes too. I really think he believed it. I really do.*

I'd believed it for years or I'd made myself believe it. "Well," *I stopped,* "it's not, it's not what I want any more."

A tear dripped onto my nose, hung there and plopped onto the ground.

Dick reached for me and I flinched.

I hated the hurt look in his eyes as he withdrew his hand.

"I won't hit you any more."

"You've said that for years, Dick, and you always do."

"This time I won't."

I shook my head. The anger was going. Desperately I tried to hold onto it. But I couldn't. I felt so sad, not just for me but for both of us. Somewhere along the way both of us had been damaged. Him by his mother probably and me . . .well, I bit my lip, more tears fell. "Bye." I rushed out of the house and slammed the door.

Starting up the car, the hugeness of what I'd done dawned on me. I didn't feel free or happy. All I felt was terror. It was like a bird being caged for so long and then suddenly being given the sky to play in.

Suddenly its cage seems the safest place in the world.

Chapter Forty-five

We arrived at the church just before eleven. Robert walked before me up the aisle. "John's up at the top," he whispered. "D'you want to go up to him?"

"No!" The word came out too loud and people turned disapprovingly towards us. "Afterwards, I'll see him," I whispered.

Robert nodded and, leading the way, he slid into a seat halfway up the church. Whispered 'hiya's' were exchanged and then a hand was pressed into mine. "'Ow are you?"

"Ali," I turned to her and I couldn't help it, I gawped. She looked better than I'd ever seen her look before. Her hair gleamed and her skin glowed. She wore a lovely black trouser suit. "Hiya," I stammered. "You look well."

She gave a cackle. "If it was a wedding, I'd be delighted with that compliment. But 'ere . . ." she let her voice trail off.

I smiled back, not that I wanted to.

"So," Ali clambered over Robert to sit beside me. "Tell me, 'ow's the baby?"

"She's fine."

"And you?" Her eyes searched my face.

I didn't need her concern. "Great." I ignored her look of doubt and turned away.

"John's up there if you want – "

"I'll see him afterwards."

"Oh. OK."

The funeral began. It was the most horrible funeral I was ever at. I don't think anyone cried and I don't think anyone came because of Rat. They all came because of John.

What a waste of a life.

Outside, John stood accepting handshakes and condolences from everyone. I slipped out a side door and watched him. He looked lost in his black suit, standing slightly apart from the rest of his relatives. His hair needed a cut and his face was pale. But John being John, he managed to grin and be nice to everyone. That annoyed me. I don't know why, but it did.

After five minutes or so, I couldn't see him any more. He was swallowed up by a circle of his friends and of course, I hadn't the nerve to intrude in among them. They'd all start whispering about me and saying things about what a bitch I was.

After a few more minutes people began to cross to their cars, some heading to work, some more going to

the crematorium. I couldn't face it. I couldn't face John.
I wouldn't know what to say to console him.

Anyway, he had his friends. He needed me like a
hole in the head.

*I fully intended going straight around to Mammy's and
explaining everything to her but I was crying so hard I found
that I wasn't able to see properly through the windscreen. I
pulled into a lay-by, switched off the engine and cried.*

*I don't know how long I stayed there, but it wasn't long
enough. There just seemed to be so much grief inside me
that I could have stayed there for days and never stopped.
And it wasn't just for me and Dick; it was for everything.
It was for my life, my time; it was for the me I knew was
slipping away; it was for my kids. It was for so many
hundreds of things that had never made me cry before. But
it was the only time I knew I'd be able to cry. Three kids
don't need a weepy mother. They need someone to look after
them, to mind them.*

Finally I was going to be a proper mother.

Only it hurt.

I went back to the flat, let myself in with the key Robert
had given me, and immediately found solace in some
crisps that I found in Ali's press. I sat down with a glass
of Coke, the six-pack of crisps, the remote control and
my mobile. I took off my shoes and sat with my feet on
the sofa, the way I used to when I lived in the flat. As I
dialled home, I looked around. The place looked tidier
than when I lived in it and there were even some fresh

flowers in a vase on the table. Robert was obviously having a good effect on his surroundings.

The phone was picked up at the other end.

"Pam?" Mam said, sounding anxious. "Is that you?"

"No, it me. Hiya, Mam."

"Oh, Maggie, hello." Mam sounded flustered. "I can't contact Pam at all. I rang this morning and there was no answer. I don't know what she's thinking of. She didn't pack any clothes for David and there's no formula milk for Shauna or anything. And then I rang again and Dick answered and he just hung up when he heard my voice. I don't know – "

"Is Jane, OK?" I asked, cutting her short. Mam could never cope with little domestic dramas.

"She's fine," Mam said. "A bit whingy but fine. But Pam – "

"What do you mean a bit whingy?"

"Whingy! You know crying and stuff. I'm talking about – "

"Well, she likes to be rocked to sleep in the morning," I said. This was me talking. *Me*. I could hardly believe it myself.

"Rocking!" Mam shrieked. "When would I have time for rocking? I've Shauna starving, well, I gave her some of Jane's milk and David asking when his mammy is coming back and Dick junior tormenting the cat. I ask you, when would I have time for rocking?"

She *was* in a bad mood. "Sorry," I apologised.

"I'd better go," she muttered and the line went dead.

I stuck the phone back in my coat pocket and morosely opened a packet of crisps.

It suddenly felt lonely being all on my own in the flat. Funnily enough I missed Jane or maybe I missed the routine of feeding her and changing her in the morning. And the way she depended on me for things, that was nice. And I even missed work. I missed the bitchiness of Josie and the laziness of Lucinda and the thickness of Louis and the stupid grin on Romano's face. I suppose being here among people who weren't my friends made me realise that I did have a life of sorts now and I did have people that I even liked a bit. I suddenly couldn't wait to go home. I swore to myself that I'd try and be a lot nicer, well, a bit nicer anyhow, to everybody.

"What the fuck d'you you fink you're playing at!" Ali burst through the door.

I jumped up, spilling Coke down the front of my black jumper. "What?"

"You!" She stood in front of me, eyes blazing.

I'd never seen Ali angry before.

"You didn't even come to the crematorium! Christ, you're even more selfish than I thought!"

My vow to be nice vanished. "Pardon?" I said, my voice dripping ice.

"Don't try and make me feel scared," Ali said, trying to make it sound as if she wasn't scared. "You always did that when I lived with you. Well, it won't work now!"

I shrugged. Who did she think she was?

"You didn't even bother to shake hands with John, did ya?"

"He had all his friends there!" I said it in such a way that the subject was closed.

"He didn't 'ave you though, did 'e? I mean, why'd you come if you don't want to see 'im? Wot's the point of that?"

"I thought I could face it and well . . ." I shrugged. "I couldn't."

"Couldn't face shaking hands with him?" Ali sounded disbelieving. Adopting a caustic tone, she simpered, "Aww, poor Maggie can't face it! Poor Maggie can't face shaking 'ands with her ex-fella at his brother's funeral."

"Shut up."

"No, I won't. You make me sick, Maggie. You do!"

"Shut up!"

"You don't deserve 'im. You really don't."

"So tell me something I *don't* know!"

Ali stopped her tirade. I turned from her and busied myself wiping down my clothes.

There was an awkward silence.

"I told 'im you were tired," Ali said then. "I told 'im you'd call to the house before you left."

"Did you?" I glared at her. "Well, what if I don't? What if I don't want to?"

She shrugged. "I'll just tell 'im some more 'orrible lies that he won't believe."

"You don't have to lie for me."

"No. I have to lie for him."

416

Smart bitch. "Since when are you so pally with him anyhow?"

"Since you walked out on both of us. I mean, I thought you were my friend and he thought you were his, I dunno, his future, I guess."

"Yeah, well, I'm sorry about all that."

"So that makes it OK, does it?"

"Well, what else can I do?"

"Go to see John for a start."

We were glaring at each other. She was really angry with me. I didn't answer. I didn't know what to say. Instead, I spat out, "I don't know why I came."

"You came because you're not a selfish bitch." Her voice softened slightly. "Look, Maggie, I've known ya for years, yeah? I dunno wot the story is between you and John. All I know is that 'e's a dead nice guy who thinks the sun lives up your backside."

I managed a bit of a smile.

"I'd kill for a guy like that. In my whole life I never 'ad a guy like that. All I ever got was the dregs. The plonkers. I'd get 'urt by some fuck who wouldn't know me from 'is mother in the morning. If it was me, I wouldn't let 'im go."

"Ali – "

"You're so lucky."

Yeah. Right.

Her voice softened some more. "Just talk to 'im. Tell 'im you're sorry about Rat. Tell 'im about the baby. That's all he wants."

I guess the spilling of the heart routine was to soften

me up. I hated the fact that it had. I shrugged agreement. Then I added, "I'm not that lucky, you know."

She rolled her eyes. "You've a guy who's mad about ya, a new baby, a mother who takes you in, a new job. Yeah, you've a bum life, Maggie."

I glowered at her, angry again. She didn't know the half of it. "You don't know the half of it."

"Mmm," Ali nodded. Her eyes narrowed, "I'd swap ya." She sounded a bit pissed-off. "I got no fella, a weight problem, no mates, oy, hang on," she frowned, seemed to be thinking and finally shook her head, "naw, that person wasn't a mate, she upped and left and didn't say a word."

Bitch.

"So," she continued, "no mates, a crummy job, parents who couldn't give a fuck about whether I live or die and, oh yeah, a string of one-night stands and a long-term fella that ran off with me best mate." She quirked her eyebrows. "Wanna swap?"

"I didn't – "

"Know? Yeah, well, it don't matter no more." She looked a bit embarrassed now. Changing the subject abruptly, she asked, "So, you coming to see John or wot?"

"What? Now?"

"Yep."

"Maybe tomorrow."

"Maggie!"

"Why do today what you can put off till tomorrow?"

I said. I gathered my bits and pieces from the sofa. "Tomorrow," I said firmly.

This time the subject really was closed.

I arrived at Mammy's around four. My eyes still looked a bit red but so what? Mammy would be bound to know I was crying. I mean, your marriage doesn't break up every day, does it? I was still in the clothes I wore yesterday and I reeked. The smell of sweat mingled with the odour of alcohol. I parked the car outside the house and steadied myself before getting out. I'd only locked the car door when Mammy came tearing down the drive.

"Pamela," she said, "what is going on? I've been trying to contact you all night and all this morning. Where have you been?"

"Is it Shauna?" I gasped. I couldn't take much more. "Is she OK? Is it one of the boys?"

"No!" Mammy flapped her arm. "It's you. You haven't packed for those mites at all. Anyway, I suppose it doesn't matter now – you'll be taking them home, I suppose."

She began to walk back to the house.

"Well, actually, Mammy," I said, "I won't be taking them home."

She did an about turn and almost knocked me over. "What do you mean you won't be taking them home?" she asked. "Sure where else would you be going?" She gave a bit of a giggle and a bit of a flap of her hand. "Unless you're thinking of moving them in with me."

"I am," I gave a bit of a giggle too. A really unsure giggle. "I've left Dick."

419

Her eyes widened. Then they narrowed. Then she giggled again. "Oh, for God's sake! Left Dick!" Another flap of her hand before she turned and again began walking toward the house. "Left Dick!"

"I have." My eyes filled again. "It's for the kids' sake, Mammy."

"Will you go on out of that? Honestly, what are you thinking of? The kids' sake! Sure, they love their daddy. All children do. Left Dick." She closed the door behind me as I stepped into the hall and before I could say any more she called, "Dick junior! David! Mammy's here!"

Two bodies hurled themselves from the television room and into the hall. David latched onto me while Dick junior threw himself at me, nearly knocking me over. "Hi, guys," I ruffled their hair.

Mammy watched us for a second, before saying, "Your mammy's come to take you home now, boys."

David buried himself further into my leg. Dick junior pounded upstairs to grab his bag. "It's all packed, Mammy."

I stared at Mammy. She wouldn't meet my eye. "There's an excited boy now, ready to go home," she said cheerfully.

I wondered how Maggie had done it. I wondered what she'd say if she was here. "Well, he'll be a disappointed boy when he realises he'd not going home, won't he?" I said evenly.

"All right!" Mammy gave a tolerant smile. "What happened? A little tiff, was it?"

I started to cry again. I couldn't help it. She looked so understanding. David looked up at me fearfully and I tried to get myself under control. "A big tiff, actually," I said. I wiped my nose in my sleeve.

"Oh, oh now . . ." Mammy smiled uneasily.

Before she could say any more, Dick junior came down with an enormous bag of gear. "I put all David's in as well," he said proudly.

"Not going," David said. *"Not going."*

"We are," Dick pulled at David. *"Sure, Mammy's here."*

"No." David pulled away.

"Dick, honey, we might be staying in Nana's for a little while longer, OK?" I strove to keep my voice steady.

Mammy clicked her tongue. "That's not the way things get sorted out," she whispered, sounding slightly panicky. *"Look at your sister . . ."*

"But why aren't we going home?" Dick asked. *"What about Daddy? He'll be on his own."*

"See?" Mammy said triumphantly. *"See?"*

Oh, I saw all right. "That's the way kids are," I said. *"No matter what, they still love their parents."* Fresh tears threatening, I pulled Dick and David in my wake. *"Let's go tell Shauna that she's going to have a little holiday,"* I said.

"Some holiday," Mammy sniffed. *"I don't know – a perfectly good house in Clontarf and now all they want to do is to come on top of me and squash into one room. And all over a tiff! I don't know!"* She laughed slightly. *"I do not know!"*

But I did.

At long bloody last.

Chapter Forty-six

Robert dropped me off outside John's the next day. "See ya later," he called as he beeped the horn.

Robert was a nice guy, I decided. I felt almost sorry that I hadn't bothered getting to know him when I lived in London – at least it would have been one friend of John's I could have got on with. John had never minded me blanking his friends. He'd just kiss me and tell me to give it time and that it would all be fine in the end.

Sucker.

Things had never been worse.

I'd almost done a runner only for Ali insisting that Robert give me a lift over. "You know what buses are like," she'd said to Robert, "and a taxi'd cost a fortune."

I'd fumed as they'd discussed me as if I was a parcel or something.

Still, now I was here and part of me was glad. At least John would know I bothered to show at the funeral. He wouldn't think I was a complete bitch.

I rang the doorbell and while I waited for an answer, I ran my hands through my hair.

There was no answer.

I rang again.

From deep inside the house, I heard footsteps. The door opened and a face peered out. A girl.

I almost got sick.

"Hiya," she ventured. "Eh, what do you want?"

I took a deep breath, trying to ignore all the jealous feelings that rushed up me. I shouldn't feel like that. I was the one who'd dumped *him*. "Is John in?" I barked.

I think the girl was a bit taken aback at my tone. She flinched and then, looking slightly uneasy, she asked, "Who wants to know?"

Who wants to know? I ask you!

"Maggie."

She gawped. "Maggie? Eh, *that* Maggie?"

"Is there more than one?" I asked in my best bitch's voice.

She reddened. Holding the door open, she stammered, "Come in, come on. John's in the kitchen. I, eh, stayed with him last night, to keep him company."

"How nice of you," I smiled.

She was a bit thrown. I think the horrible voice combined with the smile confused her. This girl was not the sharpest knife in the drawer, that was for sure.

"John," she called, leading the way, "you have a visitor."

"I don't want to see . . ." John's voice trailed off when he saw me.

"Hiya, John."

There was a silence, except for the radio in the background.

"I'll, eh, I'll just make myself scarce," the girl said. She picked up a jacket from a chair. "Maybe I'll go out."

"Yeah, thanks, Alice," John flashed her a small smile.

She smiled back.

Neither of us spoke until the door slammed.

"Do you – "

"I'm sorry – "

"You first," I mumbled.

"D'you want a cuppa?"

Tea was the last thing I wanted. The main thing was a flight out of the country followed very closely by oblivion in a vat of whiskey. "Sure. Thanks."

He turned to put on the kettle. "What were you going to say?" he asked.

"Just, that, you know, I'm sorry about Rat." I slid into a chair.

He stiffened. "Yeah. Thanks."

More silence as we waited for the kettle to boil. I noted that the kitchen had been done up. Someone had painted the walls bright blue and some blue and green curtains hung in the windows. "I like your kitchen," I ventured.

"Ta." He handed me a cup of tea and sat down opposite me. He looked rough. His hair was uncombed and stuck up from his head, stubble covered his face, and his eyes, normally so bright, were red and dull.

I fiddled about with my cup, staring into the tea. "I, eh, did go to the funeral yesterday," I said then. "It's just, you know, you had – "

"All my friends around and you didn't feel right coming over?"

"Something like that."

"It's OK."

He made it sound as if it *was* OK. For some stupid reason I felt like crying. John never expected me to be different to what I was. "So how are you?" I asked then.

"Fine." His voice sounded too bright. Too forced. I think he knew it because he flushed. "Well, I'm coping," he amended.

"That's all you can do," I said and immediately regretted it. How crap! How trite!

"Yep." He looked away from me, began to rub his finger up and down the table. "I wasn't going to let you know," he muttered. "What with, you know, the baby and . . . and everything."

An awkward pause before I said, "The baby arrived early."

"Yeah. Yeah. Ali told me." He gave me a brief smile. "And she's fine? You're both fine?"

This was bizarre. "Yeah, we both are."

"Good."

I didn't know if it was the right time, but I said hesitantly, "I have a picture of her with me, if you'd like . . ."

Hurt flashed over his face. "Yeah. I'd love to. Great."

I was glad of the opportunity to turn away from

him. Rummaging about in my bag, I found the picture. It was a large one, a portrait that I'd got taken in the hospital. Well, my mother had had it done for me. I hadn't cared less. "Here," I passed the photo towards him.

Almost reverently he picked it up. My heart twisted at the tender way he gazed at it. He didn't say anything for a few seconds. Eventually, he murmured, "She's lovely."

"She was over ten pounds," I smiled. "A monster, like her mother."

John grinned, and he suddenly looked like my John again. "What'd you call her?"

"I thought Jane was nice."

"Jane." He said the name slowly. "Like my – "

"*After* your mother," I clarified.

I saw him swallow hard. "That was nice."

"Well, if your mother's name had been Florence or Bertha she wouldn't have had a chance."

John smiled again and then his eyes grew shiny.

My heart plummeted. Oh God, I begged, don't let him cry. I couldn't bear it.

He looked up at the ceiling as if he could see something interesting up there and I looked quickly away as a tear slipped down his face.

I pretended to zip up my bag. "You can keep the picture," I babbled, still unable to look at him.

He didn't answer. Slowly I turned to him. He'd stood up and was standing with his back to me, staring out the window.

"John," I gulped, wanting to leg it out of there, "are you all right?"

He nodded, still said nothing.

"I can go if you want?" I offered. "I didn't mean to – "

"It's just," he stopped. Gulped. Started again. "Aw, Maggie, I dunno . . . looking at her . . . you know . . . well, I'm on my own now. Mum and Dad dead and now this. Now Rat's gone."

The lonely voice didn't sound like John. I didn't know what to do. I got up from the chair and stood behind him. "You've got Jane."

"Not really."

"You have. I promise you that."

He bowed his head. "Thanks." His shoulders shook. Then softly he said, "I did my best for him after they died. I really did, Maggie."

It took me a minute to refocus. He meant Rat.

"I know." I reached out and rubbed his back. His shirt was the same one he had on yesterday.

"I just didn't want to face it that he'd a problem. I couldn't let him go, you know. He was my brother."

I said nothing, not because it was the right thing to do, just because I hadn't a clue what to say. Pam should have been here; she was good at this stuff.

"I bailed him out again and again and again," John went on, his voice shaking, "and then, I dunno, I flipped. Everything was falling apart on me. You not wanting me any more, losing my job, no matter what I did it was turning out crap, you know?"

I still said nothing.

"So I said," again he gazed at the ceiling, blinked rapidly, "I said to myself that I was going to do one thing right. Just one fucking thing. I was going to get Rat sorted. And I tried. I *did*. I even threw him out, told him I wasn't helping him any more. And look what's happened. He's dead now."

"Oh John." I pulled him around and tried to hug him. "Don't. It's not your fault. You were good to Rat. You loved him."

"Naw." John pulled away from me and wiped his eyes hastily. "I hated him sometimes. I hated him for crashing the car. I hated him for a long time. And he knew it."

"You didn't hate him. You were probably just angry at him."

"Naw. Naw. I hated him."

I couldn't imagine John hating anyone but I didn't say it.

It had just felt good to touch him.

I'd missed that.

"I don't know what you're like," Mammy said. "I just don't know. What am I supposed to make of all this?"

I shrugged. I was past caring what she was going to make of anything. All yesterday and this morning she'd been making light of the whole thing. She valiantly kept ignoring my tears, telling me that everyone had their ups and downs, making me feel guilty for leaving. I'd expected some sympathy, some understanding. Instead I'd been presented with a wall of small talk.

"I can't handle this all on my own." Mammy stood up, "I'm going to ring Maggie. I'm going to tell her to come home. This has got to be sorted out."

I laughed to myself at Mammy looking for Maggie to sort out anything. Maggie had never sorted out a thing in her life.

"Maggie will tell you it's no joke rearing a child on your own," Mammy went on. "She's up every night with that baby and no one to help her."

I'd been up on my own with Shauna night after night too, I realised with a pang.

"And where's Maggie now?" I couldn't help it. Mammy didn't care a bit about me and what I was going through, I thought dully. All she cared about was that I rush back to Dick as quickly as possible. She didn't want the details; they were my own business, she had said. "I don't see Maggie anywhere here now," I reiterated.

"That's 'cause she's gone to John's brother's funeral," Mammy smiled. "Gone to see John. Gone to see sense."

I felt my anger build as I watched her pick up the phone and begin flicking through her address book.

"Aw, here's her mobile. I'm going to tell her to come back quickly."

Her hand shaking, she began to dial.

Everything changed in that moment.

I had something to say to Maggie too.

The ringing of my mobile shattered the moment.

John moved away from me while I began frantically to tear my bag apart looking for the stupid thing. "I'd better answer. I told Mam to ring if she'd any problems with the baby." Then I remembered that the phone was in my coat pocket. I pulled it out and switched it on. "Hello?"

John went out of the kitchen.

"Oh, Maggie, thank God!" Mam sounded really upset.

"What's, what's happened?" My heart went cold. I knew now what Lucinda meant about turning into a mother. It'd been only four weeks and I was out-performing even my own miserable expectations. "Is Jane OK?"

"Jane is fine," Mam snapped. "It's Pam!"

"Pam?" Another stomach lurch. "What's wrong?" I could barely get the words out. It was then that I knew how John must be feeling.

"*She's* what's wrong," Mam said. "She's only gone and left Dick!"

From car crashes to mortuary slabs my mind focused on what Mam had just said. "Pam has left Dick?" I couldn't believe it. "No way!"

"Yes." A deep shaky breath. "And she's staying with me. And she won't go home. And I can't cope with it, Maggie. I mean, my two daughters with no men and children coming out their ears. I mean, what can I do? What *did* I do? I need you here. You have to come home."

I ignored all the last part. Mam would just have to cope. I mean, she was our mother after all. Anyway there was no way I'd be able to get a flight now. A few hours wasn't going to make any difference. "Why did she leave him?" I asked.

"Oh, I don't know," Mam flapped. "Something and nothing, I suppose." A pause. I heard her talking to someone. Then, "Hang on Maggie, Pamela herself wants a word." Then whispering, so Pam couldn't hear, I guess, she added, "Will you ever talk some sense into her!"

I almost laughed at that. Me? Talk sense into Pam. Pam was sense personified.

"Maggie?"

"Hiya, Pam." I guessed I'd better say something. "So, Mam tells me you've left Dick."

"I have." Pam raised her voice – for Mam's benefit I guess. "And I'm not going back."

She sounded different. Not at all the meek Pam I knew. Maybe she was just angry over something. I didn't know what to say.

"I hear you're wondering why I left him?"

"Oh, well no, not exactly – "

"I left him because you were right, Maggie," she said then, quietly.

"Pardon? Right about what?" Jesus, I hoped she wasn't going to lay blame at my door. Mam'd never talk to me again.

"Right about everything," Pam continued. Boy, she did sound angry. "You were right about Dad, right about love, right about the crap we had to put up with." She gulped. "You were right."

Time stopped.

"He, he ruined us, Maggie. He twisted us all up inside until we didn't know what anything was. And

I'm sorry it's now I'm saying it. I only just understand now. And that's why I've left Dick. He's the same."

Mammy grabbed the phone from me. "How dare you!" she yelled. "How dare you!" Slamming the phone into its cradle, she faced me. "How could you say that!"

Behind me the kids went silent. Even Shauna stopped babbling.

"It's true, Mammy," I whispered.

She hit me across the face.

The phone went dead but I hardly heard it. All I heard were the echoes of Pam's words telling me I was right. I'd been right all along. Telling me that love wasn't hitting and violence. It was tender and happy and soft. Telling me what I'd never dared to believe all along.

The world shifted. Someone wiped my foggy glasses.

I could see clearly.

"Maggie," John appeared at the kitchen door, looking concerned. He was over to me in two strides. His hand cupped my chin. "You're white," he said, sounding shocked. "What's happened? What's happened?"

Being with John had been different from what I'd always known.

So bloody scarily different.

Warm and funny and tender.

"Maggie?" John asked again. "Are you all right?"

It was too late.

It was the wrong time.

I pushed him away from me. "I'm fine. Grand." Then, "It's not the baby. She's fine," I said, knowing that that's what he thought it was.

"So what is it?"

How did I tell him what it was? "Nothing." I got myself together. "I'm fine. I just, you know, I have to go now." Hastily, I picked up my bag. "I'd better go now. I've to pack, you know, the flight and all." My voice was coming out all disjointed. I hardly knew what I was saying.

"But you've had a shock – "

"No. No. It's fine." I had to get away from him. I had to before I made a fool of myself.

"You sure you're OK?"

"Yeah. Yeah." I buttoned up my jacket all wrong, hoisted my bag on my shoulder and then I heard it. A faint tinkling on the radio. But I knew the song. *You set me free/I'm bound to you/You let me fly/So I stay close/Without you, baby, I am nothing/With you with me, I'm a hundred times, a hundred times, a hundred times myself/Don't need no help to recognise/Love is blinding me/opening up my eyes.*

The tune petered out, the DJ's voice stomped all over the remaining lyrics. "And that folks was 'Diesel' a new band on the edge of the big one. We'll be hearing a lot more from them, and now . . ."

I couldn't move. I couldn't meet John's eyes. And it wasn't the fact that it was 'our' song, it was the fact that for the first time the lyrics actually meant something to me. I understood them. All the other times I'd laughed away at it, but now I knew. I knew that was what love was. Giving someone freedom. Letting them be. And if you gave someone that, they didn't need to run. And that's what John had given me only I hadn't known it.

The empty space inside me began to ache.

I had to get out.

I had to say something about the song though. It'd be weird if I didn't.

"So they," I couldn't think of the band's name, "they made the big time, did they?" I nodded to the radio, my voice as light as I could get it.

"Eh, yeah," John said. He looked uncomfortable. "That's why I had the radio on in the first place. Alice and I knew they'd be playing the single today. It's a nationwide station."

"Good for Diesel."

"Yeah."

"You were right about them."

"Yep."

More silence. My awkwardness intensified. "Anyway, I'd, eh better go."

He held the door open for me. I walked out of the house and out of his life.

I'd had it with being slapped. I'd had it. I put my hand to my face and glared at Mammy. She took a step or two back, first staring at me and then staring at her hand.

"You never do that again, Mammy!"

"I will." Mammy took a deep breath. "If you slander you father again – I will!"

I gulped. "The truth hurts, Mammy."

"And so do lies."

"I wasn't lying, Mammy, and you know that. I was telling the truth."

"I'm not listening to this. I'm just not listening." She put her hands up to her ears the way Dick junior did when I gave out to him. "If you say one more word against your father, you can leave. I mean it, one more word."

"Do you know why I left Dick, Mammy? Do you?"

Her answer was a slam of the kitchen door.

Both Shauna and Jane began to cry.

"Mammy, Baby Shauna's crying!"

Lucky Baby Shauna, I wanted to say.

I walked down John's street and right past the bus stop. I didn't feel like jumping on a bus and anyhow, I had loads of time before the flight. All I wanted was to be on my own.

My head was like a washing machine, everything tumbling around inside it. I didn't know how I felt at all. And I was afraid to find out. I was afraid I'd cry, or realise that I'd fucked up. I was afraid that I'd have to take action and sort things out.

And I thought I had things sorted out.

Well, as sorted out as a fucked-up mind like mine can get things.

OK, I was a single mother, but I had a job and I was happy.

I was sorted.

Sorted.

Only why did I feel so empty all the time? Or did everyone feel empty all the time?

Head hammering, I turned into a little park that's just at the top of John's road. I sat down beside the ornamental lake and tried to concentrate on some kid flying a kite. The father had got it up in the air and he handed the toggle to his little boy. "Nice and steady now," he said. "Keep her steady."

I smiled as the little lad began to yank at the cord in excitement.

Then the kite began a nose-dive to earth. I winced. It was going to break. His dad would go mad.

But he didn't. He set the kite going again and once again handed the toggle to the little boy.

He probably didn't hit him because I'm here, I thought. And then I shook my head. No, he probably didn't hit him because . . . well, because . . . he's a nice man.

There *were* nice men out there.

Romano was nice. He'd never hit anyone.

Even Louis wouldn't hit someone. Well, anyone that hires his kind of staff deserves to be hit themselves, I thought wryly.

And John . . . I shook my head.

John was history.

It was all so confusing. I pulled a tissue out of my pocket and rubbed my eyes. How did you know? How did you know if you were loved? How did you know if you were picking the right guy?

All my life I'd been told that my dad loved me. Even

though he hit me and berated me and made a joke out of me, he loved me. He loved me because it was all done for my own good. And for a long time I believed it. I believed it until I went to a birthday party and Melissa, the birthday girl, had spilled her drink on the carpet. I'd stared horrified at the stain as it slowly spread. Her mother had come in and calmly began to wash it out. I'd bent down to help. "It's not nice to get hit on your birthday," I'd confided to the girl's mother. "Maybe if we get it out, you won't tell Mr Byrne."

Mrs Byrne had looked at me and flapped her hand. "Will you go and enjoy yourself. It's only a bit of orange."

I'd been like a cat on a hot tin roof wanting to go home. I couldn't bear to see Melissa getting hit in front of all of us. And when her dad had come in and hoisted her onto his shoulder shouting, "And how's the big seven-year-old," I'd been convinced that he was just putting on a show.

But it made me think.

And I studied people.

And I came to the conclusion that not everyone got hit.

By the time I was twelve, I'd hated and loved my dad in equal measure. And when I said I hated him Mam and Pam had made me think I was wrong. Our daddy loved us more than other people's daddies. He wanted us to succeed. He wanted us to do him proud. He never wanted us to leave him. He bound us tight.

So tight that Pam got married just as soon as she

found someone and me, well, I never wanted that. I needed freedom.

I knew what I wanted. All I needed was a bit of a shag now and again, no strings. And that's what I'd had until John.

And he wasn't like Dad.

And he wasn't scared off by my caustic comments.

He was gentle and kind and funny.

And though I thought I loved him, I couldn't be sure. I mean, John didn't lose the cool, didn't flip when I burnt our dinner and no matter how far over the edge I drove him, he'd never hit me. Did that mean he didn't love me?

Or did it mean he did?

Oh God.

The young fella had crashed the kite for the millionth time. His dad walked over and picked it up. "It's broken now," he said, examining it and sounding faintly amused. "I think it's given up."

I wondered if he'd clobber his boy now. The kite was banjaxed.

I clenched my hands together and prayed that he would.

No, no, I prayed that he wouldn't.

The little boy began to cry.

So he *was* going to get hit.

Disappointment filled me up.

"I'll fix it tonight," the dad said hastily. He put his arm around his son's shoulder. "It'll be all right by tomorrow. Come on. Stop it." He threw an anguished look in my direction and rolled his eyes.

I smiled back.

"And will it fly again?" the boy asked, wiping his eyes.

"If it's not too scared," the father joked, laughing over at me. He ruffled his son's hair and I watched them both leave.

I stayed there for a long time.

So long that I missed my flight.

But I would have had to miss it anyway.

I knew what I had to do.

Chapter Forty-seven

The following morning was even worse than the previous night. Maggie had failed to come home.

"Oh, typical Maggie," Mammy sniffed. "She's probably abandoned that child now. That's what happens when there's no man around. It makes you go like that." She studied my three kids. "They'll probably end up as those latch-key kids you read about in the papers. No one to mind then during the day, the oldest child bringing up the youngest." She gave a big sniff. "Poor Shauna."

I clenched my hands and said nothing.

"And I was thinking about your," Mam dropped her voice and winced, "situation," voice up again, "last night."

"Yes?" I tried to sound polite about it.

"Now, Pamela," Mammy said firmly, "I don't want you to think badly of me now or anything."

I suppose that meant I was going to think badly of her.

I raised my eyes to hers. "What?"

"Well, I was thinking last night about all this, this

business. And well," she licked her lips, "I mean, I was thinking of, you know, what people would say. And they will say things, you know."

"And?" Absently I passed David a piece of toast.

"And, well, I mean, I'd have my two daughters living with me. I mean, now, come on! People will wonder what's going on at all!"

"So?"

"Well, I mean, what are we going to tell them?"

I was beginning to think really badly of her. "Well, Mammy, I don't know about you, but I'm going to tell them the truth."

"The truth!" She looked shocked. "You can't do that." She blessed herself. "Ohmigod, you can't do that. A nice little story about Dick being away and you not wanting to be in the house on your own, is what I thought."

"Is Daddy away?" Dick junior asked. I swear, my son has ears like a bat.

"No, Dick," I said slowly, "He's just not going to be living with us for a while. Maybe for a long while."

"Oh, for God's sake!" Mammy hissed.

"Why?" To my surprise, Dick junior's eyes filled up. "Does he not love us any more? Is it 'cause I slapped Shauna?"

"Oooh," Mammy said, feigning horror, "you slapped your little sister! Oooh, that's not what nice little boys do."

I wanted to strangle her. "Dick, I'll explain it to you later," I said. "It's nothing to do with you slapping Shauna. Now mind David for me. I have to have a little chat with Nana."

Still looking worried, he took David's hand and told him they were going in to see the WWF wrestling.

"I'll give you a chokeslam," he told him. "Wait till you see how it's done. It's class."

"It's no wonder he hit Shauna," Mammy tut-tutted, "watching that rubbish on the telly." She stood up and began to clear off the table.

"Mammy," I said firmly, "let's just get one thing straight. If people ask what my situation is, I'll tell them. I'm not ashamed of it."

Mammy rolled her eyes. "Look, Pamela, it's temporary, this thing between you and Dick. Mark my words. And sure, why bother telling people what's happening when you'll go back to him in the end."

It was like slamming my head off a brick wall. "Mammy, I'm not – "

The phone rang and Mammy, abandoning the dishes, ran out to answer it. She came back in seconds later, beaming. "That was Maggie," she said, "and she said she missed her flight last night and she's sorry she didn't ring last night but that she'll try and see if she can get home today." Mammy winked. "I don't believe it for a minute – she was with John. I know it."

I shook my head. From believing that Maggie abandoned her kid to getting it on with her ex, my mother didn't live in the real world at all.

Maybe she was better off.

I let the subject of me drop for the moment. When the time came to put her straight, I would.

"Maggie," John looked astonished as he opened the door. "I thought – "

"Yeah, I missed my flight yesterday."

He held the door open wider to let me in. To my relief, there was no Alice in sight. "Well, come in," John said. "I have the kettle on." He walked before me into the kitchen. He looked better today, more together. He had a nice pair of brown levis on and a brown and cream striped polo shirt. He was barefoot. "So, what brings you here again?"

I opened my mouth to answer, all my carefully prepared responses at the ready. Ali had told me to be honest with him. I mean, I hadn't even told her what I was doing, where I was going and, yet, as I was on my way out the door that morning, she said, "Now, Maggie, I'm telling ya. It ain't no good if yer not 'onest wiv 'im."

"With who?" I grumped, feeling highly sensitive.

"Aw, fuck orf!" She waved her hand at me and rolled her eyes.

So I'd slammed the door.

"Well?" John asked interrupting my thoughts.

I gulped. "Oh, just, you know, in the neighbourhood."

"At nine in the morning?"

"Yes." It came out cranky and defensive.

"Oh. OK." He turned to fill the cups with water.

All John seemed to do these days was make me tea and I wouldn't mind but I hated the bloody stuff.

"So you were in the neighbourhood and decided to call, is that it?"

"Yeah."

He didn't say anything more, just continued making the tea, dunking a tea bag into both cups and carrying the cups to the table. "There you are."

"Thanks."

"So how come you missed your flight?"

I gave a tight smile and took a sip of the tea. It burnt my mouth. "I, eh, decided to do some thinking and then, well, I got carried away and then it was all too late."

He looked baffled.

"And, well," I licked my lips, "I have something to say to you."

He put down his cup and stared at me.

It was very disconcerting.

"I have something to say," I repeated, flinching from his gaze.

John nodded. "So you said."

"I have to say," I said, "that I, that I," I found it hard to get the words out, "that I want you back."

The silence was deafening. I don't know what I expected but it wasn't a total blank wall of silence.

"Well?" I said. "What do you think?"

He wasn't smiling. He didn't even look a bit happy about it. "You want me back?" he repeated.

"Yeah." I attempted a smile. "If, well, if you want."

"Just like that, you want me back."

"Well, I don't know. I've thought about it and, well, it seems the right thing." I didn't like the way he was glaring at me. Anyone would think I'd said something awful to him. I squirmed in my seat.

"And why do you want me back?" he asked. "So you can dump me again when it suits you?"

"No." I didn't like this. This wasn't the way it was meant to be. He was supposed to be happy for God's sake. "I want you back because, well, because, well, I miss you."

"Like you'd miss a slave or something?"

"No!" He was twisting everything. "No, not like that at all."

"Well, then, like what?" He came around the table and I cowered away from him. He looked really mad. "Like what, Maggie?"

This was too hard. He was meant to jump at the offer. "Oh, oh, forget it," I stood up. "This isn't working. Obviously you're not interested."

He grabbed my arm and I screamed.

He let it go, shocked.

"Don't you lay a finger on me," I said. "Don't you . . ." I couldn't go on. I pushed him out of the way and ran to the door.

"Maggie, come back!" he yelled after me.

I ran as hard as I could. The feeling of humiliation was making me cry. I wasn't upset. I wasn't. I was just mortified that I wasted my time on such a jerk.

"Maggie!"

He was yelling after me down the street.

"Maggie!"

Oh God, he was getting closer. He must be coming after me. I couldn't face him. It was great that I was in my runners and track bottoms.

445

"Maggie!" Another yell followed by a "JJJEEEEsus!" Then "Fuck!"

I turned around. He was only a few feet behind me and down on the ground. His foot was bleeding.

"Stood on something, have ya, sonny?" an old lady asked.

"Glass," John winced as he pulled a shard from his foot.

"Well, that's what shoes are for," the woman said.

"I hadn't time to put on my shoes, did I?" John grumped as he took some more glass out of his foot.

"Well, sorreee!" the woman said, stalking off.

John made a face at her retreating back and I gave a half-smile. Then, realising I was smiling, I glowered again.

There was a small silence broken only by John saying shit and fuck.

"Are you OK?" I asked snappishly after a bit.

"I think so," he stood up on one foot.

"Well, I'll go so." I turned to leave.

"Aw, Mags, don't be like that. Can't we just talk?"

"I did talk. I told you what I wanted and you didn't seem too happy. That's fine."

He looked hopelessly at me. Blood dripped from his foot onto the path. People passing by stared at us. "I need more than that, Mags," he finally said quietly. "I need to know you. To know why you're changing your mind. That's all."

That's all! That was all! "I told you why," I said. "And you do know me."

He shook his head. "Nope, I don't. I know I love you 'cause of the way you are, and like, I always believed you loved me but then you wouldn't move in with me and you wouldn't marry me and I told myself that it didn't matter, we were happy. But then you left me, Mags, and you were having our baby and you never told me. Can you imagine how I felt?"

I glared at him. He was too good at this.

"So now, Mags, it *does* matter. I need more from you. It's too scary for me otherwise."

Too scary for him.

"Scary?"

"Yeah."

He was scared. He must really love me to be that scared. "And do you love me, John? I mean – really?"

"Mags, I'm fucking standing here with my foot cut open, freezing cold, making a muppet of myself. Yeah, I love you."

"Oh, John, I've been such a bitch – "

"Aw Mags. Come here."

He pulled me to him and my words were lost in his shoulder.

Mr Parker had arrived for dinner. Mammy let him in. "Now, Geoffrey," she said, "sit here, I've kept you your favourite place. Dick junior, get your elbows off the table. Nice boys don't have elbows on the table."

"So how do they eat so?" Dick junior made a big deal of trying to eat while keeping his elbows away from the table. "All the food'll fall out my mouth!"

"No, it won't," Mammy shot me a look that said 'keep him under control or else'.

"Dick junior," I said sternly, "behave."

"I've cooked your favourite, Geoffrey," Mammy said, taking some steak from the oven. In fact it looked like the whole side of a cow, it was so big. "I cooked you steak and roast potatoes with pepper sauce."

"Sounds good, Doreen," Mr Parker patted his belly.

David was cowering against me and I had to push him off into his own seat.

"David," Mammy said, "sit in your own seat, honey. Nana will get you your dinner now."

"He doesn't want to sit on his own, Nana," Dick junior said. "He's afraid of that man, aren't you, David?"

David squashed in beside me even more.

Mammy gave an embarrassed laugh I glared at Dick junior. He was really trying to stir it.

"Oh, now, now," Mammy said, piling the spuds onto Mr Parker's plate, "there's no need to be afraid of Geoffrey, David."

"It's cause he shouts," Dick junior explained helpfully. "David hates shouting."

"I don't shout," Mr Parker snapped.

"You did the other night," Dick junior said. "You didn't like the pudding that Nana made with your sausages."

Mr Parker blushed.

Mammy looked as if she'd like to kill Dick junior.

I wondered if I'd heard right. Surely Mr Parker couldn't have done that. But he must have done because Mammy was chattering on the way she used to when Daddy was alive. Smoothing over all the awkwardness.

Mr Parker gave Dick junior a glare before he began to tuck into his dinner.

Mammy served us all before getting a plate for herself.

"Enjoying that?" she asked us.

"It's lovely, Mammy," I couldn't eat it. All I kept thinking was that she was going to get more involved with Mr Parker and that it would end up in tears.

"So, Pamela," Mr Parker startled me. "When is Dick getting back?"

"Pardon?"

"Your mother tells me that — "

"Oh, a week or two," Mammy said hastily. "More potatoes, Geoffrey?"

"Yes, Doreen." He pushed his potatoes to one side of his plate so that Mammy could fork more on. "So where is he?" Mr Parker asked me then. "Very successful man, your husband, I'm told."

"Yes, he's successful," I said. I glared at Mammy. How dare she?

"Off foreign or what?"

"I don't know actually because I've left him."

Mashed spuds peered at me from his monstrous mouth. "Pardon?"

"I've left him." I cut my steak. "Our marriage is over."

"What does that mean, Mammy?" Dick junior asked. "When your marriage is over?"

"If it's a joke, it's in poor taste," Mr Parker said.

"Peas, Geoffrey?" Mammy jumped up like a scalded rabbit.

"It's not a joke," I replied.

"What did you mean about a him being on holiday, Doreen?" Mr Parker turned to Mammy.

She gulped. "I've some more lovely carrots in the saucepan. Maybe you'd . . ." Her voice trailed off. "Well," she said defensively, "it's not the sort of thing you go shouting from the rooftops, is it?"

"It is not," Mr Parker agreed. "I'll take those carrots, Doreen. It's a sin, is what it is. Flying in the face of God."

"What is shouting from the rooftops, Mammy?" Dick junior was looking from one to the other of us.

"Nothing, honey." I should have kept my mouth shut. I got up to get a glass of water.

"Flying in the face of God," Mr Parker said again.

I could feel his eyes boring into my back. The cheek of him. I took a sup of water before I got up the nerve to ask, "So God approves of wife-bashing, does he?"

"Pamela!" Mammy was about to collapse. "Stop it! There's a time and a place."

"There is," I said. My voice was shaky, "And it's not here and I don't need his opinion."

"It's not mine. It's the church's."

"How dare you pass judgement on me!"

"I'm not. I'm just saying that what you've done is a sin. Marriage is until death do us part."

It was the calm way he said it that infuriated me. As if he was so right. And the way Mammy was looking so respectfully at him.

"Come on, kids," I grabbed Dick junior and David's hand. "Let's go to McDonald's." I had to get away from the two of them.

As I shoved them out the door and put Shauna in her pram, I heard Mammy giggle. "Don't mind her, Geoffrey. She's just going through a bad time."

My mother. She'd sell her soul for a man.

There was nothing else for it, I'd have to contact a solicitor and see about getting money from Dick until we sold the house.

I couldn't stay with Mammy any more.

John poured me a whiskey, topped it up with red and told me to drink it down really quick. "Why?"

"It'll make you drunk. Make it easier for you to talk."

"I don't need to be drunk to talk."

"Well, you don't talk when you're sober."

I stared into the whiskey glass. He had a point. I took a sip and the warmth of it filled my mouth.

"I'll just get a plaster or something for my foot," John hopped out of the room. "Back in a sec."

I did think about running. About just leaving and forgetting the whole thing, but I'd never get John back then. But I wondered if I told him all about me, would he hate me anyway? I wondered if it was worth the risk.

He came back just then, a huge oversized towel wrapped around his foot. Plonking himself down on the sofa a bit away from me, he looked at me encouragingly.

I swirled the whiskey around the glass. I didn't know where to start. Even telling him I loved him was a big deal for me.

"Well?" he said. "Go on, Mags."

"I don't know what to say." I felt stupid all of a sudden.

"Well, I dunno, tell me why you left me."

Why had I left him? I didn't really know. "I was scared, I think," I said eventually.

"Of me?"

I nodded. "Sort of."

"But why? Jesus, we were happy."

"I was afraid that I'd never be able to escape if I had to. I didn't want us to be trapped. Me and the baby."

"Trapped?"

I was hurting him. He hadn't expected this. "Yeah."

"And now?"

"Now I think I know that you won't trap us. That you'll be . . ." I shook my head. I was explaining this all wrong. "At home, I was trapped," I said. "There was no escape. I can't let that happen to me again."

"Who trapped you, Mags?"

I shook my head. This was hard. I knew I was going to cry. It was like some crappy American feel good picture, only I felt shite.

"Mags?"

And out it came. Everything. About Dad. Mam. The way I couldn't, just couldn't let people in. They'd hurt me. The terror of being happy and knowing that it wasn't real. The way I felt so angry all the time. All the time. And even when I was sad, I was angry. And how I lost my job in the restaurant for being mean to a waitress and making her cry. John didn't bat an eyelid at that – I thought he'd hate me. And of how I couldn't let his friends get to know me because I knew I was horrible only I couldn't help it. And of how I was so scared of moving in with him because it was so important to be able to run away if you had to. And of how I wasn't going to let Jane be like me. She was going to be happy. And of how Pam had said that I was right. I was right. After all the years, I was right. And it had felt good. It was good to know that there must be good people out there, somewhere. And then I told him of how, even if there were good people, I probably didn't deserve anything good because I'd laughed the day my dad got buried. And I was horrible because I was glad his parents were dead because they'd hate me. He did flinch at that bit but he took my hand.

And eventually, after I don't know how long, I stuttered to a stop.

It was as if I'd shrunk.

I felt lighter somehow. Not happier, just physically lighter. And that was some job, believe me.

I'd drunk all the whiskey without knowing and John filled me up again.

"Sorry," I sniffed.

"Naw, don't be." He reached over and traced the line of my face with his thumb. "*I'm* sorry. God, Mags, it must have been tough."

"Yeah."

"And how are you now?" he asked. "About your dad?"

"He ruined my life. I still hate him."

John opened his mouth to say something and then stopped.

"What?"

"Nothing. Nothing," he shrugged.

"No, go on."

"You mightn't like it." He waited for me to object and when I didn't he said hesitantly, "I used to think that about Rat. You know, that he'd ruined my life. Like I know it was an accident and everything, but he still killed Mum and Dad and I did hate him, Mags. I did." There was a catch in his voice as he talked. "But then, you know, I started to be happy again. I moved on and I guess the hate didn't seem so important any more."

"So what are you saying? That I haven't moved on?"

"That you haven't let yourself. You have to let go, Mags."

"I can't. I can't. You don't know what he did to us."

"What he's still doing to you."

"No. No. He can't touch me now."

John didn't say anything. Then, unexpectedly, he grinned, "D'you know when I really stopped hating Rat?"

"Is this a funny story?"

"You'll like it." He topped up my whiskey. I think he was trying to get me drunk. "It was one night, I was going mental 'cause Rat was meant to have come home from work and he hadn't. So I had to do my usual search of his haunts. I had a big list I used to carry with me and when I visited one, I'd mark it off. Anyhow, one of them was this dingy nightclub in the East End and in I walked and guess what?"

"What?"

"At the bar in front of me was the most gorgeous pair of legs I'd ever seen. Class A legs, I'm telling ya. And I knew I couldn't leave until I found out who the legs belonged to and guess what?"

"What?"

"They were only owned by the love of my life." He stopped. Kissed his finger and placed it on my lips. "I'd never have met you if it wasn't for Rat and, just think, you'd have never been in the nightclub if you'd been happy at home."

I gave a reluctant smile. "Fuck off! That's not true."

"Cross my heart. And you know, Mags, if you're happy, I mean really happy, you won't hate your dad so much and living will be a lot easier."

Lucinda had said that. Almost the exact same words. How come I was so stupid that I'd never looked at things in that way before?

Maybe because I'd never been happy before.

Tears pricked my eyes. "Thanks, John."

"Didn't I say I was like Jung when I first met you. Didn't I?" He pressed his forehead against mine.

"I love you."

"And I bloody adore you, Maggie Scanlon. Come here and give us a kiss."

And that's what love was too, I realised then.

A knowing.

And accepting.

When we arrived home, Mr Parker had left. Mammy was

sitting in the kitchen reading the evening paper. I shoved Dick junior and David into the front room and went in to see Mammy.

"Your husband rang," she said as I pushed open the door. "He's very upset about all this business."

"Is he? Is he as upset as me?"

"Now, Pamela, I am not getting into a battle with you. I don't like that sort of smartness. I'm only telling you what I heard. That poor man is missing his children and missing his wife. He wants to talk to you."

"I hope you told him I didn't want to talk to him." Even as I said the words, I felt a pain in my heart. I'd loved that man so much.

"It's your business," Mammy muttered. "I'm not getting involved."

"Well, there's a surprise!"

Mammy cringed slightly but said nothing.

"How is it," I said, "that you always take the man's side? You never ever side with me or Maggie? Why is that, Mammy?"

"Oh, Pamela, I haven't time for all this — "

"You've time to read the paper."

"I don't know what's got into you. You never talked to me like this before." She shook her head sadly. "Being a deserted wife must bring out the worst in you."

"I'm not a deserted wife. I'm a battered wife."

"Oh for God's sake," she stood up and folded the paper. "I've told you, it's your own business. At least when Maggie arrived home she didn't go giving me a blow-by-blow account of her and John."

"*She knew better.*"

Mammy ignored me. Pushing past me, she said, "Now, if you'll get out of my way, I want to get some things out of the fridge for the tea."

"*I suppose Mr Parker is coming?*"

"*Yes, though why, I don't know. You were so rude to him today.*"

I bit my lip. And gulped hard. "You care more about him than us, don't you?"

"*I haven't time – "*

"*You care more about what he thinks and the neighbours think than you do about me and the kids, don't you?*"

"*Now you're being ridiculous!*"

"*I'm not! You care more about that fat bastard who only comes when he needs a feed than you do about me.*"

"*I'll not have that sort of language – "*

Dick junior peered around the door. "Mammy, Mammy, are you OK?"

"*Get back inside, Dick!*"

"*A fine way to talk to your children." Mammy began rummaging about in the fridge.*

"*At least I talk to them. It's more than you ever did." I was either going to cry or throw something. "At least I tell them the truth which is more than we ever got."*

Mammy still said nothing. Calmly, as if I hadn't spoken she took out a head of lettuce, some tomatoes and a cucumber from the fridge.

"*I never liked Mr Parker," I said, determined to say something to crack her facade, "and I thought at first it was because he was taking Daddy's place, but it's not that."*

She walked up the kitchen and I followed. Turning on the tap, she began to rinse the lettuce.

"It's the fact that he's exactly the same as Daddy and the fact that you treat him the same way you did Daddy." I bit my lip. "It was scary then and it's worse now."

"Is it now?" she started to rinse the tomatoes. She reached across me and took a knife from the block.

"You licked up to Daddy and fawned all over him and did whatever you were told. Maggie and I never stood a chance. It was always you and him against us."

"Look, Pamela, I'm not getting into all this." She began to chop the tomatoes with a vengeance, but her voice was still calm. "Your husband rang. It's up to you to sort out your own life. Trying to blame me or Mr Parker won't help. Now, do your lot eat cucumber?"

The bland change of subject hurt me more than anything. It was like I had to hurt back. And the thing that hurt my mother most, I realised now, was the truth. I took a deep breath and said, as firmly and as unemotionally as I could, "Dick hits me. He hits the kids. Do you want me to go back to that?"

She rolled her eyes and said nothing.

"He's just like Daddy was."

The knife paused in its cutting.

"Exactly like Daddy was," I went on. "He rings me up to check if I'm at home and if I'm not I have to say where I've been."

"Well, isn't that nice? He wants to talk to you. He cares about you." She resumed cutting again.

She was unbelievable. "He doesn't want to talk to me," I

said. My voice was getting more hysterical as I tried to make myself understood. "He just wants to know where I am."

"Oh now, Pam, you're being paranoid."

"I'm not! I'm not!" I sought for other things he did. "He, he wants everything his way. He tries to keep us under his control. We have to be clean when he gets in, have the dinner ready. He goes mad if his dinner isn't on the table when he gets in from work – "

"Men like their food on time. Mr Parker is like that. Your father was like that. It's the way they are."

She was speaking in a voice she normally reserved for the kids. The voice she'd used on Maggie and me all our lives. The 'explaining' voice.

"Your father," she went on mildly, "used to have a fit if I didn't have the saltcellar exactly centre table. Do you remember?" She gave a soft laugh. "Oh, he was as odd."

"He wasn't odd. He was, he was," I heaved, feeling sick as I said it, "he was a bastard and Maggie was right about him."

A moment's silence. I wondered what she'd do. I braced myself for another slap. Instead, she turned bland eyes on me and said, "Language, Pamela."

She was washing away what I was trying to say. Trying to make me think I was overreacting. She'd done it to Maggie for years. No, I corrected myself, we'd both done it to Maggie for years. Shame filled me but I knew now I could beat her. I gathered myself up. "And if Dick rings again, you can tell him we've moved out. I'm not going back to him – I've kids to think of. They deserve more."

A crack appeared in her calmness. "More?" she scoffed. "More? For God's sake, those kids have everything. They've nice clothes, a nice home, food, warmth." She rolled her eyes, "What more could they want?"

"The more that Maggie and I never had," I shouted into her face. "A father that treats them well and, and more importantly, a mother that looks after them."

That was it. The words that cracked her open. I almost felt guilty as tears pooled in her eyes. "So," she whispered, nodding and swallowing, "I wasn't good enough, was I? I failed the, the mother test."

I was about to say 'no' that of course she hadn't but I didn't. All my life I'd reassured her. Now it was her turn.

"I did my best," she said, the knife quivering in her hands as she stared at the chopping board. "I did my best."

I suppose she had. "Yeah."

"I did," she repeated as if trying to make herself believe it.

I said nothing.

"In those days," she said shakily, still not meeting my eyes, "you couldn't just up and leave your husband. There was nowhere to go and . . . and the shame of it." She bit her lip. "I did think of it, many times. I did, Pamela, but I, I . . ." her voice broke and she began to cry.

I wondered if I should hug her, but I couldn't. She hadn't hugged me.

The crying went on until finally, getting herself under control, she said falteringly, "Anyway, he wasn't the worst, Pamela. And you had food, clothes, everything."

"Not everything," I said quietly.

"Almost everything," Mammy insisted. She dropped the knife and stared blindly at the chopping-board. "And, he did love you both. I know he did. He wanted you to be the best at whatever you did. That's why he got angry." She rubbed her hand over her eyes. "I don't know why you and Maggie just can't see that."

I still said nothing.

"He was troubled," Mammy said. "Very troubled. But that made us all the more important to him. He was terrified that we'd all leave him. He was afraid of being on his own, d'you see?"

I didn't reply. Even after all the years she was still making excuses for him.

"And men shouldn't have to feel that way. And I loved him so much. I didn't ever want him to be on his own. If I'd been a better woman I could have made him happy."

"No, Mammy, that's not true."

"It is." She nodded and more tears fell. I still couldn't put my arms around her. "I thought that if I could be a good wife, make him happy, then we'd all be happy. I mean, if I'd left him, Pamela, what sort of a wife would that make me? I'd be a failure."

She wanted to be a wife more than she wanted to be a mother. That was the difference between us, I realised.

God, it hurt.

"Maybe I," Mammy stopped, hiccuped, "maybe I was wrong." She looked up at me. "Was I wrong, Pamela?"

She'd spent years blocking out how wrong she'd been. I didn't know if it would do her any good now.

I shrugged, said the closest thing to the truth I could, "We can only do what we think is best at the time."

She looked so pathetically grateful. "Yes. Yes. You're right."

"And that's why for me leaving Dick is the best thing."

She reached out and held my hand.

One favour traded for another.

"OK then," she said softly, putting my hand to her cheek. "If it's what you want."

"It's for the best, I think."

"And what I did, that too was for the best." She sniffed, kissed my hand, "And, well, if you're disappointed in me, or if Maggie is, well . . ." her voice trembled before she said, "well, I'm sorry about that."

She'd said sorry.

I wrapped my arms around her. She nestled her head under my chin.

Isn't it funny how, no matter what, you still love your parents?

Totally, unconditionally.

John wrapped me up in his duvet on the sofa. Then he squashed up beside me and kissed me. Soft, slow kisses. He whispered how he loved me. How he'd love me forever. He told me that I was the one for him, that no matter what I wanted he'd get it for me.

I had all I wanted, right there on the sofa.

I was free.

Dick rang again that night. At first he sounded angry. He abused, threatened. I thought of my mother and of how I didn't want to end up like her.

I told Dick that he could say what he wanted, that I was never coming back.

He said he couldn't believe it, that I was unbalanced.

I didn't reply.

He pleaded with me to reconsider. Told me he'd miss me. He'd miss the kids.

I told him I wanted to sell the house and he started to beg. He told me he loved me and that whatever I wanted him to do, he would.

I told him to sell the house.

When I put down the phone I was crying.

Mammy managed to pat me on the back. She even managed to splurt out something about once I was happy that's what mattered.

I wasn't happy.

But then again, I'd never been happy. I'd spent my life trying to make Daddy happy, Mammy happy and Dick happy. But I'd never managed it for myself.

But now, now I was free.

Free to find happiness.

Epilogue

I went on my own. I'd hadn't visited in years, but that day I felt that I had to. There was someone else there already – standing, looking sort of lost and lonely. It was only when I got up close that I recognised Pam.

I was surprised to see her there.

She's not the devoted daughter she once was.

I got a fright when I saw Maggie coming towards me. I hadn't told her that I was visiting Daddy's grave that day. It was his anniversary and I knew Mammy would be up later and I didn't really want to have to listen to her go on and on about him, so I'd come on my own.

"Hiya," I said to Pam.

She nodded to me and turned back to the grave. She's changed a lot. I mean, she's still quiet and gentle and everything, but there's a harder streak in her now. She moved out of Mammy's last week and into a lovely house that she bought with the money from the sale of the one in Clontarf. I don't know what the score is between her and Dick; all I know is that the night I got back she told me that he was like Daddy.

I gave her an awkward hug and told her that she was doing the right thing by leaving him and she hugged me back, really tightly, and said that she knew all that.

And she told me again how sorry she was for everything.

And I told her how sorry I was for landing her in shit all her life.

I think we're friends now.

I stood beside her and we both stared at the gravestone. "He was a bastard, wasn't he," I said conversationally.

Pam giggled.

Honestly, Maggie is the worst one!

Imagine saying it straight out!

I nodded though. "I hate him now," I admitted. "I came up here just to tell him that."

Maggie gave me a gentle shove. Honestly, since she's got back with John, she's a different person. OK, she's still bolshy and sarcastic and all that but sometimes I get the feeling she doesn't it mean it the way she used to. John is the nicest guy. Maggie's so lucky.

"I used to hate him too," Maggie said then. "But now I just couldn't give a fuck about him."

"Jesus, Maggie!" I held my hand over my mouth, afraid to laugh. "Will you stop!"

"I came up here to tell him that*," she grinned.*

At least Pam laughed.

I could never do that.

She hasn't got it in her to hate like me. I'm a pro, unfortunately.

After she's finished her hating, I bet she'll be happy.

Anyway, she was happy when I asked her to install some computer software in the restaurant. Yep, folks, we're entering the twenty-first century in Louis' Bistro. At first Pam hummed and hawed and said she'd been out of it for years but in the end I persuaded her to give it a try.

She's trying to set up on her own, you see. We'll be her first contract. And it's not as if she's out of date or anything, she reads loads of computer magazines all the time.

As regards the bistro, I've told Louis I'm leaving at the end of the year. I've got the restaurant up and running and I'm proud of that. Louis is going to run it. He's completed this course he was doing – a business-type one and I think he'll do well. He's almost a natural.

Well, except for the fact that last week he hired in a new cleaner. I wouldn't say that the woman cleans herself, never mind anything else. We have to fumigate the place when she leaves.

"She's had it hard," Louis said.

I was going to bawl him out of it, but I didn't. Maybe she has had it hard.

At the end of the year, Jane and me are going to live with John in London.

He did offer to come over, but all his mates are over there and let's face it, I've got no mates so I'll have to poach some of his or else make a few of my own.

Louis is giving me a glowing reference and he's told me there'll always be a job for me if I can't cope with the big time.

But I'll cope.

I'll do more than cope.

I've got my first job, installing computers and software in Maggie's restaurant. I'm a bit worried but Maggie said that Louis wouldn't know a computer from a vagina. Isn't she awful? Anyway, I'll give it a go.

I'll miss Maggie and Jane when they leave at the end of the year, but I've got my kids and with them I'll cope with anything.

Even with the fact that Mr Parker is still on the scene. But I guess Mammy's life is her own. I can't live it for her.

And at least now I'm not a kid any more.

"Come on," Maggie said eventually, "let's head. We'd better give Dad some time to cool down."

And I laughed.

I laughed as I left the graveyard.

Only unlike the last time I'd been here, seven years ago, I didn't have to pretend that I wasn't laughing.

Pam and me, we laughed out loud.

THE END